Music and image

Music and image

Domesticity, ideology and socio-cultural formation in eighteenth-century England

RICHARD LEPPERT
Professor of Comparative Studies in Discourse and Society
University of Minnesota

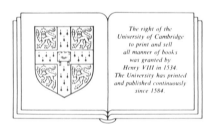

The right of the
University of Cambridge
to print and sell
all manner of books
was granted by
Henry VIII in 1534.
The University has printed
and published continuously
since 1584.

CAMBRIDGE UNIVERSITY PRESS
Cambridge
New York   New Rochelle   Melbourne   Sydney

Published by the Press Syndicate of the University of Cambridge
The Pitt Building, Trumpington Street, Cambridge CB2 1RP
32 East 57th Street, New York, NY 10022, USA
10 Stamford Road, Oakleigh, Melbourne 3166, Australia

First published 1988

Printed in Great Britain at the University Press, Cambridge

British Library cataloguing in publication data
Leppert, Richard
Music and image: domesticity, ideology
and socio-cultural formation in
eighteenth-century England.
1. England. Music. Social aspects,
1700–1800
1. Title
780'.07'0942

Library of Congress cataloguing in publication data
Leppert, Richard D.
Music and image: domesticity, ideology and socio-cultural
formation in eighteenth-century England / Richard Leppert.
    p.   cm.
Bibliography.
Includes index.
ISBN 0–521–36029–3
1. Music and society.   2. Music in the home.   3. Upper classes –
England – History – 18th century.   4. Music – England – 18th century –
History and criticism,   1. Title.
ML3795.L36 1988
780'.07'0942 – dc 19   88–11884   CIP

ISBN 0 521 36029 3

For Adam and Alice

Contents

Illustrations

Acknowledgments

I am grateful to the staffs of several research libraries for their untiring assistance on many aspects of this project, in particular those of the Witt Library, Courtauld Institute of Art, University of London; National Portrait Gallery Archive, London; Interlibrary Loan Services and Special Collections, O. Meredith Wilson Library, University of Minnesota; Henry E. Huntington Library and Art Gallery, San Marino; Beinecke Rare Book and Manuscript Library, Yale University; Yale Center for British Art; Music Division, Library of Congress; Department of Prints and Drawings, British Museum; William Andrews Clark Memorial Library, University of California, Los Angeles; J. Paul Getty Center for the History of Art and the Humanities, Santa Monica; Paul Mellon Centre for Studies in British Art, London; Research Libraries of the New York Public Library; Houghton Library, Harvard University; and the National Museum of Science and Technology, Smithsonian Institution, Washington, D C.

I am deeply indebted to several institutions and foundations for their generous financial support: the John Simon Guggenheim Memorial Foundation, the National Endowment for the Humanities, the American Philosophical Society, the Yale Center for British Art, and the University of Minnesota's Graduate School, College of Liberal Arts and Office of International Programs.

Special thanks are due to the many individuals and institutions, both public and private, for providing reproductions of art works and for granting permission to publish them. I would especially like to acknowledge Sarah Hyde, Witt Library, London; Sarah Wimbush, National Portrait Gallery Archive, London; Anne French and Jacob Simon, The Iveagh Bequest, Kenwood (London); and Beverly Carter, Paul Mellon Collection, Washington, D C. The auction firms of Christie and Sotheby, both London, were extremely generous in supplying photographs, as were the London art dealers Sabin Galleries, Agnew's Galleries, Spink & Son and Leggatt Brothers.

Among the many individuals to whom I owe a debt of gratitude are the late Edward Croft-Murray, Department of Prints and Drawings, British Museum, for his generosity and tirelessness in helping me locate important images; Ellen D'Oench, Davison Art

Center, Wesleyan University, for generously supplying me with hard-to-obtain photographs of paintings by Arthur Devis, and for her advice concerning this artist; Tilman Seebass, Duke University, for his thoughtful suggestions on a portion of the study; Cynthia Adams Hoover and Helen Rice Hollis, both Division of Musical Instruments, Smithsonian Institution, for their kind assistance concerning the development of early keyboard instruments; and Mr. John Thomson, founder of *Early Music*, for his longterm support and advice on the project. On repeated visits to the Yale Center for British Art two individuals among a staff of unusually helpful people must be singled out: Teri Edelstein and Anne-Marie Logan. I express gratitude to my editor at Cambridge University Press, Penny Souster, for her support and professionalism every step of the way, and to my text editor at Cambridge, Gillian Law.

Particular thanks are due to Marlos Rudie and Monika Stumpf, Department of Humanities, University of Minnesota, for their untiring and patient assistance in helping with manuscript preparation, correspondence and endless other assorted labors without which my task would have been much more difficult. I especially value their many years of friendship and encouragement. I am grateful to Jon Bassewitz for his assistance in proofreading.

My wife, Ann, and my children, Adam and Alice, have together helped make this book a great pleasure to think about and to write and also provided for me an ever-present locus, as loving companions, of the personal and familial significance of the topic.

Finally, I wish to thank Mary Finn-Shapiro who for three years was my research associate. She worked tirelessly, accurately and imaginatively, tracing family records, pouring over thousands of pages of letters, diaries, memoirs and works of literature and philosophy. Through her efforts I gained access to countless documents I would not have found on my own. I acknowledge her as a co-worker and as a friend.

Richard Leppert
Minneapolis, August 1987

1 Introduction: music visualized

Music is realized in musical life, but that life conflicts with music.

(T. W. Adorno)[1]

In power that may exist but is not visible in the appearance of the ruler the people do not believe. They must see in order to believe.

(Norbert Elias)[2]

THE IDEA FOR THIS BOOK began some years ago with the intention to write a social history of non-professional domestic music-making among the English upper classes in the eighteenth century, based on a study of period music, written accounts such as diaries, letters, memoirs, newspaper and magazine materials, imaginative literature, philosophical tracts, sermons, etc., and visual representations of musical activity in contemporaneous paintings, drawings and prints. But during the initial years of research two things gradually became apparent; first, that written references to music by contemporaneous practitioners were many but almost invariably non-descriptive and brief (of the sort, "We had some music last night"); second, that the most interesting questions I was formulating – and which I had the greatest difficulty answering even tentatively – developed not from written accounts of musical activity or from music itself but from visual representations of music-making, especially in painted portraits of individuals and families. My concern with images arose from an awareness of internal and external contradictions apparent in these representations vis-à-vis their musical referents. The difficulty developed not simply from what I "saw" in the pictures, but rather from the fact that what I "saw" did not square, or squared only in odd ways, with what I "knew" from primary and secondary accounts of music and musical activity of the time and place. This of course raised additional questions concerning the nature of visual representation and its relation to what might be termed, somewhat simple-mindedly, historical truth. To address these issues I reconsidered the entire project and eventually shifted its focus. I decided to study not only the actual practice of music among the English upper classes, but also the *idea* of music in their lives and, equally important, in their ideologies of self, class and national identity. In other words, I chose to concentrate on the relationship of domestic musical activity, as both practice and idea, to culture, and of culture to society. In fact my concern became less the musical practices themselves than what lay behind them.

Now this marks an important limitation of the project: it is not a social history of music, nor of performance practice, nor of the history of musical instruments; it is least of all a history of music in pictures. Rather it is a history of an ideology of music – yet one

anchored in actual musical practice, which is to say that I do not
view the book specifically (or only) as a contribution to the history
of ideas. I have tried to understand how music, as shaped by
socio-cultural forces, itself contributes to socio-cultural formation.
In other words, I am not interested in demonstrating how music
mirrors anything, but rather in how, in what ways and why music is
an agent. (And it is these issues that ultimately drew me ever closer
to visual representations of musical activity; later I will discuss in
detail why this is so.)

My subject is music's agency in the private domestic lives of
upper-class amateurs.[3] I want to suggest, by means of the book's
chapter arrangement, how I have addressed the topic. But I will
begin by making clear that my concern is less the music itself that
amateurs played, or how they played it, than *why* they played in the
first place and what the playing meant. (The book does not consider
the upper classes in their capacity as patrons or performers of
"public" – or semi-public – music, such as concerts and opera,
except to the extent that these activities illuminate my primary
subject, the relation of music to domesticity and what leads from
it.)

Societies perpetuate themselves by sexual and cultural reproduction: through children. Among the English upper classes cultural
regeneration (my concern) occurred first and often almost exclusively in the home through sanctioned educational processes,
formal and informal, conscious and unconscious. Hence, the study
of music's relation to culture and society must begin with its place
in education. (Education in England was not yet officially or even
unofficially State organized, though obviously the State and home
mutually mediated each other.) Given that education was perceived
as a family responsibility, it is not surprising that the closest and
most self-conscious concerns of education centered around "family"
issues, the dominant among which were gender identity and gender
responsibility – in part, the sexuality of power. These were the
microcosmic parameters within which developed the larger, extra-
family issues of socio-cultural definition and formation: from the
family the nation, so to speak. I will consider music's role in the
larger educational agenda as regards practices both ideal (Chapters
2–3) and real, and look closely at one highly specific activity, the
music lesson (Chapter 4).

Concern with the mutual relations among music, power and
sexuality will ultimately lead to a discussion of the human body
itself and of the body's representation in publicly witnessed physical movement, the dance (Chapter 5). Here my subject is the
problematics of physicality itself, its visual analogy to order and
disorder and the implications of both for class boundaries and social
organization.

The last part of the book (Chapters 6–8) focuses once more on the home and on issues of identity engendered therein for the two sexes, through adulthood, as regards the role of music – first for males separately, then females, then men and women together as spouses and as spouses with children. In the epilogue (Chapter 9) I will address questions of physical space and the ideological differences between the domestic enclosure and the street, of the ways that these spaces demarcated class boundaries – social order and social ordering – and of music's agency in these issues.[4] This will lead to an outline for a future project concerning the agency of elite and popular musics in structuring a culture of separate spheres. In the context of these topics, I need now to explain in detail my understanding of visual representation, the importance of which to my project is especially evident in the last half of the book.

PROBLEMATICS OF VISUAL REPRESENTATION

Reference to music occurs in visual art not because musical sound exists but because musical sound has meaning. As a topos in visual art music itself is silenced, existing only as a "remembrance of things past": all that remains of music in the image is its trace as a socialized activity.[5] The question arising from visual representation is hence one of music's socio-cultural function. This in turn leads directly back from the abstract realm of ideas and their history to a grounding in social practice. But ordinarily only certain kinds of musical activity were represented in visual art, namely, those that constituted recognizable signs of socio-culturally sanctioned modes of behavior and thought (of greater significance than music itself), regarding which it was a pre-eminent function of the image *to attest*. (Thus music's function as a subject in visual representation was not randomly to replicate musical practice per se. This is most obvious from the fact that England's upper classes themselves viewed music as a highly problematic social practice.)

Representation is necessarily and always highly selective. That which is asserted visually was not intended only as the mirror of that which *is*, but as the indicator of that which *is and is to be*. That is, visual representation is the product of an act whose conscious or unconscious purpose was to perpetuate a particular way of life. By definition the image re-presented the past (for time stops in art), but was *about* the future. And once again, when music played its part in representation it did so precisely by providing a visual means of registering the correctness of the "present-past" and hence the correctness of the future that this present–past directed the viewer toward. Thus the image of music, re-presented as a social practice, was always already by definition political, to the extent that the future necessarily must be shaped – in effect *caused*. As such the future was a dimension of social contestation.

My particular interest in visual art lies in equal measure between the adjective (visual) and the noun it modifies (art). What is for me so essential about visual art is that it is first and foremost art (that is, artifice) and, as it were, accidentally visual. The importance of vision to visual art is not the physiological phenomenon of seeing (animals see; they do not make art) but perceiving, which of course is governed by the eyes in conjunction with the brain and indeed with the entire human organism in its perceived relation to external reality.[6] That is, I am interested in the ways that music functioned as a visualized activity, but not in the literal sense of "how it looked." Instead, it is how it was *made to look in art* that draws my attention. This naturally raises the question of "original intention"; yet recovering that intention, were it ever possible, is not my goal. For what the artist (consciously) thought he or she was representing, even if that could be known, in no sense circumscribes what the image "contains" or means, either to its original (and ideal) audience or to the historian, nor for that matter does "original intention" define what to the historian may be most significant. For the most part I will skirt the question of intention, though I am hardly contemptuous of it, and concentrate on something much more interesting, something not necessarily the result of conscious thought in making images, namely, conventions of pictorial representation.

Conventions, pictorial or otherwise, are "simply" the way people do things at a certain moment in time and place. But they are never "innocent" or accidental. They are inevitably the product of efforts to naturalize, hence deproblematize, the hegemony of certain modes of action or behavior – even when, as in art or etiquette, such actions or behaviors may otherwise be quite arbitrary. (In fact the more a behavior is arbitrary, the greater is the necessity to deproblematize it.) And the greater the extent to which conventions have *been* naturalized, the more they are explicit responses to certain social demands and certain definitions of culture.[7] Conventions are operative principles of order, just as order itself is always the expression of power. In a social context conventions are the rendered-unconscious expressions of ideology (and, indeed, a visual condensation of social praxis).

The visual representation of people at music is in turn governed by these same conventions, thus exposing the representation of music itself as always already and necessarily ideological. In other words, the representation in visual art of music as a socialized activity is specifically informative of a group's or society's perceptions of music's cultural locus and its ideological use value, conscious or unconscious, for it is unreasonable to assume that music would be represented in such a way as to appear patently false or out of accord with perceived reality as *defined* by those who constituted the image's ideal audience. These were of course the very individuals whose dominant social position largely determined their significant-if-partial control over the construction of ideology. This is the ultimate "truth" behind the often "false" appearance of music in art. (It is obvious that images were made in accordance with the wishes of the ideologically converted; as such images provided self-justification for such individuals' positions, the significance of which should not be underestimated. Yet beyond this quite narrow function, all such images simultaneously implied an audience of the unconverted, even though – ironically – these people ordinarily did not have ready access to the images themselves.) My concern with visual representation is essentially equal to my interest in music precisely because I understand these two contemporaneous phenomena as socio-culturally complementary and, of course, literally linked, the one "preserving" a trace of the other. "The picture is not a pre-existing concept in susceptible form; it is, however, just as much a product of the permanent intellectual activity of the mind."[8]

I have not made any conscious selection of images by reason of aesthetic valuation per se, for my concern is neither with questions of connoisseurship nor of masterworks. Nevertheless, technical competence will from time to time surface in the discussion with respect to particular artists, but only when the larger issues I have identified play against technique. Thus an artist of meager accomplishments who nevertheless understood pictorial conventions sometimes attempted more than he or she could render. This technical "failing" can inadvertently be profoundly revealing – self-problematizing as it were – by "removing" the protective "naturalized" covering otherwise achieved by flawless technical mastery, thereby exposing the ideological pressure to which pictorial conventions were self-disguising responses.

Art reveals; it also hides. As Pevsner pointed out, the English portrait "keeps long silences, and when it speaks, speaks in a low voice . . . Or, to put it differently, the English portrait conceals more than it reveals, and what it reveals it reveals with studied understatement."[9] Art creates a self-enclosed world unique to itself. But it invites its viewer to recognize that world either as his or her own, or as what that world ought to look like. (This is especially the case in genres like portraiture.) Visual art reveals in the precise degree to which it attempts to hide; art's conventions are the means by which something is both "said" and left "unsaid." By naturalizing modes of representation, conventions stabilize *certain* behaviors, *certain* ways of looking at the world, etc. Through their selectivity they are fundamentally ways of telling lies, or, better, highly partial truths. They are never objective, but always *interested*. Now I do not mean by this that paintings never tell the truth. Indeed, paintings always tell both truth and untruth simultaneously.[10] But what is usually the more important for the historian to determine is not what truth the image seems to assert, but what it wants us to forget by making the assertion. In other words, visual art is about memory, or the construction of memory. And the control and construction of memory itself possesses, once again, an obvious political dimension. History, as Walter Benjamin pointed out, belongs to the victors.[11]

Whatever portraits included, they left even more out. By this I do not refer to the numbers of objects represented or omitted; my point is rather that the pictures portrayed a world where everything *has been* set straight, made right. The world of the portrait is Eden; the world of the portrait is, again, a lie. But, like all lies, it contains the truth by its very attempt to hide the truth: the portrait inadvertently may "confess" by drawing our attention to its "present absences," thereby providing us access to that which we are not meant to see. Portraiture admits antagonism only to the extent that antagonism is conquered, leaving in its place a symbolic surface as smooth as the paint surface itself. Indeed, the necessity to create the "smooth surface" is occasionally, if always indirectly, revealed in remarks by painters themselves, but typically *not* by those who by portraiture prospered and climbed to the very social and financial status of their sitters (Reynolds of course being the supreme example of such good fortune). Thus James Northcote, only modestly successful, wrote bitterly in his sitters' book of his own class position and underemployment – in spite of his claim to having learned the "language" of portraiture. He attacked (but most privately) his patrons in singular and explicit political discourse that inherently recognized the problematic of the portrait enterprise itself:

The neglect of the Art of painting is such in this country that the poor Artists may by long labour and application in giving up their health and lives in Learning a language the which when accomplished they will not find an Auditor. I cannot with patience see those wretches dancing at a ball on the spoils of a nation who ought to dance from a Gibet in a North East wind or see those carcasses drest out in finery that ought to be droping bone after bone from chains.[12]

The specificity of art must be respected, in the sense that each art form "behaves" according to its own particular formal history. Art is not mere illustration standing ready, innocently, for the historian's eyes. To write about art one must know its own history, and understand the various means – educational, technical, economic, etc. – by which it was made and its making mediated. But in saying this I do not intend to romanticize or mystify the relationship of any art form (visual or otherwise) to the other histories outside it, of which each is always also a part. One must know the external histories within which art operated and to which it explicitly responded and in turn helped shape. In this respect it must be kept in mind not only that art and society are inseparably intertwined, but also that for the most part the arts essentially are from the start on the side of power (as is inherent to portraiture),[13] or are made so in the later histories of their reception: the works of Beethoven and Goya now mean very differently at Carnegie Hall and the Prado, respectively, than when they were first heard and seen.[14] The ways in which art serves power will constitute a prime concern of my study.

The images that I will discuss in greatest detail are single and group portraits, the latter being the so-called conversation pieces. Among all the privileged classes of Europeans the English were easily the most addicted to portrait representations of themselves, a fact that has many times been pointed out, in our own time and in theirs alike.[15] (In the eighteenth century itself some writers complained sarcastically about the English sitters' vanity in this regard,[16] others about the negative impact of portraiture on other genres considered by artists to be of higher artistic caste, especially history painting.) The portrait flourished not only because it was a means by which to preserve the image of those one loved – including oneself – but for its immediate and long-term value as propaganda[17] (something easily recognized in official State portraits – Rigaud's of Louis XIV or Holbein's of Henry VIII). As such it was an extraordinarily important business, over which large sums were spent and, for some artists, veritable fortunes amassed.[18] In other words, portraits were always more than monuments to personal vanity, their function considerably less passive than mere commemoration permitted. Portraits served as primary tools for managing social position, in some measure because of their singularity. The painted image had an impact far greater in the eighteenth century than is probably the case with analogous images today, precisely because the portrait existed in a culture where images were automatically and necessarily received in the context of their own uniqueness. They were not mechanically or electronically reproduced; they existed in only one place in time. Only certain people could have them; only designated people could see them. (In the one reproductive medium that enjoyed considerable status in the eighteenth century, mezzotint, great technical skill was required to achieve beautiful results, and the numbers of prints that could be made from a plate before it began to deteriorate was quite small, thus severely restricting even the print's potential audience.)

Among portrait types, the conversation piece is especially valuable to my subject, given its focus on family representations. This genre, popular in England from roughly the beginning of the second quarter until the end of the eighteenth century, shows its sitters full length, but on small canvases (usually not more than two feet by three feet), in intimate settings, and involved in some "usually non-utilitarian activity." Narrative content of some sort is common.[19] (It might be thought that the small size of these compositions, combined with the numerous sitters represented, reflected a genre appropriate essentially to the middle classes of English society on the grounds of simple financial economy, but this is actually not the case. Conversation pieces were also popular with the aristocracy,[20] which is to say that these images represent the full range of social groups with which I am concerned.) Conversation pieces were valued by the upper orders of English society for one or two primary reasons. In the first instance, the genre's convention of informal representation was itself deeply symbolic of Englishness itself; informality in visual representation was virtually a patriotic gesture (the direct and specific opposite to its French courtly counterpart). The "naturalization," through pictorial convention, of informality was also a sign of both privilege and confidence. Thus there is nothing "on guard" about the sitters in conversation pieces: people sit rather than stand, or if they stand they do so with the weight resting on one leg. They are at ease (or at least the men are at ease; I will have cause to consider this later). Second, and closely related to the first, "this class of picture was only concerned with those who led their lives freely in surroundings of luxury and ease."[21] The presence of sitters' own surroundings (estates or interiors – whether actual or accurately rendered hardly matters) were painted in loving, sometimes quite tactile detail, rather in the spirit of the seventeenth-century Dutch still lifes whose fundamental raison d'être was the celebration of commodity wealth. What was painted was *theirs*, and by means of what was theirs they were able to assert what they were and what they held dear. Indeed, as the century wore on portrait convention itself changed to accommodate an increasing sense of self-importance that sitters wished to convey.[22] The questions to which these observations require constant return are the relation of the musical image to power, and to the definition of an ideological structure that simultaneously explains and hides power (naturalizes it in culture) and justifies on that account certain modes of social praxis.

SOCIETY AND ECONOMY

It remains to make a few remarks about the social classes and the economic realities in England during this period, and to indicate more precisely the groups with which I shall be concerned. But I shall begin with the caveat that precision is difficult to achieve on any of these topics. Eighteenth-century writers gave considerably varied accounts of the divisions between (and even definition of) social classes, and modern historians are unable to provide more than quite general accounts of economic circumstance for the various groups. The one apparent constant is that economic stability never lasted long, major economic shifts often coming annually or at least every two or three years. The economy seesawed between periods of high and low employment, stable prices and inflation, relative prosperity and depression, though not all areas of the country were similarly affected at once.[23] Daniel Defoe ranked England's social classes as seven:

1. The great, who live profusely
2. The rich, who live plentifully
3. The middle sort, who live well
4. The working trades, who labour hard, but feel no want
5. The country people, farmers, etc. who fare indifferently
6. The poor, who fare hard
7. The miserable, that really pinch and suffer want.[24]

Among these groups, in 1700, "nearly eighty per cent lived in the countryside, and almost ninety per cent were employed in agriculture or in the processing of agricultural products."[25] (As late as 1801, apart from London with a population of about one million, only five cities had populations over 50,000: Manchester [with 84,000, the largest], Liverpool, Birmingham, Bristol and Leeds; only eight towns had populations between 20,000 and 50,000; only thirty had populations between 10,000 and 20,000.)[26]

The numbers of people at the top of the social spectrum, remained constant from the late seventeenth century until the 1780s; there were less than 200 members of the nobility (by contrast, contemporaneous Spain claimed over half a million). Very few were impoverished, as was the case with some European aristocracy; most were in fact very rich. (As many as a hundred non-noble families possessed estates, hence wealth, of a size comparable to those of English aristocrats – 10,000 acres or more.) A few of the nobility had fabulous fortunes – the Duke of Newcastle in 1715 realized £32,000 from his lands in thirteen counties. In 1800 twenty peers held estates in excess of 100,000 acres each. By comparison, in 1800 the gentry (baronets at the top, followed by knights, esquires and gentlemen) numbered about 15,000; their annual income around 1790 ranged from as much as £2,000 to as little as £400 (by 1815 up to as much as £4,000 and £600, respectively).[27]

Near the century's end the great landowners held between twenty and twenty-five per cent of the land, the gentry about fifty per cent, yeoman freeholders fifteen per cent, the church and crown ten per cent together.[28] The nobility and gentry thus controlled most of the country's wealth. In numbers they represented a tiny minority – some few tens of thousands among a population that grew from 5.29 million in 1700 to 9.16 million at the start of the nineteenth century.[29] The lower classes made up the vast majority of the citizenry. The middle orders – the families of professionals, tradesmen, shopkeepers (of which there were about 170,000 by late in the century), manufacturers and the like – by the close of the period numbered upwards of half a million, many more than at the century's beginning. Those at the top had very substantial incomes, those at the bottom (like shopkeepers) often little; near the end of the seventeenth century the range extended from as little as £45 to as much as £5,000 per year.[30]

In rural society, beneath landlords came the yeomanry (freeholders, copyholders and leaseholders – thus both farmer-owners, some with only a few acres, others with thousands, and tenant farmers) making from very little a year to as much as £1,200. Below them came agricultural workers, hired either by the year or only for a specific job or by the day. Some received food as well as a wage. Their daily earnings averaged about 16d.–17d. near the end of the century. To make ends meets the entire family normally worked if able.[31] Toward the century's end between forty and fifty per cent of the population constituted wage earners, among which servants numbered between 600,000 and 700,000.[32]

In the towns and cities wage earners continually struggled to make ends meet; there was seldom much margin between "a tolerable existence and destitution" – income went for the essentials of food, clothing, shelter and fuel.[33] A London male wage earner, working a 300–day year, typically brought in £25 in 1700, £30 by 1750, a figure that remained constant until 1790.[34] In 1688 it was estimated that a family with three children required £40 a year to survive without poor relief[35] (poor laborers might make only £10 for a year's work; over half the families in the country lived at subsistence levels or worse) – at a time when the greatest lords had incomes of £5,000, £10,000, and even more.

Among all these groups it is the middle and upper orders with which I shall be concerned; that is, with the families of simple gentlemen and above – individuals whose income was sufficient to allow some leisure and formal education, who developed as well some preference for performing art music, loosely construed.

2 *Music, socio-politics, ideologies of male sexuality and power*

NUMEROUS EIGHTEENTH-CENTURY written accounts complained of the arrogance and meager talents of male upper-class amateur musicians. Often the most frustrated expressions of this viewpoint came from professional musicians, who typically supplemented their incomes by giving music lessons to amateurs and by playing alongside them in the musical ensembles organized for amateurs' private concerts – the professionals' role therein known as "stiffening." English composer and essayist William Jackson twice framed the issue succinctly: "How many a concert is spoiled by gentlemen whose taste is to supply their deficiency of practice and knowledge?";[1] and, in direct reference to the musical skills of his friend, painter Thomas Gainsborough: "How often do presumptive amateurs spoil the success of a concert by contributing their efforts under the mistaken conviction that they are adding to the enjoyment of the affair, whereas in reality they are only giving offence to the unfortunate composer of the music?"[2]

An anonymous drawing of an amateur–professional orchestra rehearsing (Fig. 1) echoes Jackson's critique by representing the disarray caused by an ensemble more interested in social intercourse than in making music. The unknown artist delineates the amateur–professional bifurcation – hence the antagonist – protagonist duality – by giving amateurs hats to wear and by keeping the professionals hatless. It is a scene of every man for himself, containing no hint that the group will or even can come to play together: some men practice their parts, some tune, some talk, some gawk. At the far right a professional in an exaggerated operatic gesture tears at his hair as if in frustration. Discord defeats harmony.

Robert Bremmer in his *Thoughts on the Performance of Concert Music* (1777) complained

that when gentlemen are performing in concert, should they, instead of considering themselves as relative parts of one great whole, assume each of them the discretional power of applying tremolos, shakes, beats, appoggiaturas, together with some of them slurring, while others are articulating, the same notes; or, in other words, carrying all their different solo-playing powers into an orchestra performance; a concert thus rebellious cannot be productive of any noble effect.[3]

Amateurs were occasionally confronted with the problems Bremmer identified, as in an April 1791 notice addressed to the gentlemen of Edinburgh's Musical Society asking them "to attend the Forte and Piano passages & to play their parts plain as Marked in the Musick without any Flourishes. In accompanying the Songs the Ripienos ar allways too strong for the Voice. They are therefore desired to play Piano when the Voice comes in."[4] These criticisms, involving dynamics and balance between instruments and voices, suggest problems of a very basic order – the injunction to avoid flourishes probably indicating a lack of ability to execute them either together or well.

The avid and talented amateur Roger North, writing at the turn of the eighteenth century, alluded to the difficulties experienced by gentlemen musicians, explaining that the frustrations of some London amateurs led them to give up music altogether:

1 Anonymous (eighteenth century), *An Orchestra Rehearsing*, pen and black ink, brown wash on buff paper, 27 × 40.5 cm.; New Haven, CT, Yale Center for British Art, Paul Mellon Collection

It is most certein the gentlemen are not oblig'd to aime at that [same] perfection, as masters who are to earne their support by pleasing not themselves, for it is their day labour, but others. And therefore audiences are not so well [for gentlemen] when their owne enterteinement is the buissness, because they indulge their owne defects, and are not distasted or discouraged by stopp, errors, and faults, which an audience would laugh att. But it is so unhappy that gentlemen, seeing and observing the performances of masters, are very desirous to doe the same; and finding the difficulty and the paines that is requisite to acquire it, are discouraged in the whole matter, and lay it aside; which is cheifly to be ascribed to this

towne which is the bane of all industry, because many other pleasures stand with open armes to receive them.[5]

Indeed, the wretched playing of amateur musicians was a standing joke so widely appreciated as to produce a virtual sub-genre of visual satire, evident in widely available, mass-produced prints (Figs. 2–3) as well as drawings (Fig. 4). The same theme was often repeated in popular literature and on the stage. Thus the hero of James Bramston's satirical poem *The Man of Taste* happily proclaimed the musical sensibilities of a buffoon:

Musick has charms to sooth a savage beast,
And therefore proper at a Sheriff's feast.
My soul has oft a secret pleasure found,
In the harmonious Bagpipe's lofty sound.
Bagpipes for men, *German-flutes* for boys,
I'm *English* born, and love a grumbling noise.[6]

Bramston's musician complements an assessment offered in the seventeenth century by Obadiah Walker who remarked on music: "I advise not . . . To thrumb a *Guitar* to 2 or 3 *Italian* Ballad tunes, may be agreeable for once, but often practised is ridiculous. besides [*sic*] I do not remember to have seen any *Gentleman*, tho very diligent and curious abroad, to qualify himself with that skill, but when he came to any maturity, he wholly rejected it."[7]

The basic John Bull Englishman's dual lack of interest and ability in music, though often satirized in contemporaneous fiction, was nevertheless generally sympathized with. In a letter addressed to Mr. Town, in London's weekly *The Connoisseur* from 1756, Aaron Humpkin (read musical bumpkin) railed at length about his wife's passion for music, convinced she was stark mad and blaming music for his domestic turmoil:

But what makes this rage after catgut more irksome and intolerable to me is, that I have not myself the least idea of what they call Taste, and it almost drives me mad to be pestered with it. I am a plain man, and have not the least spice of a *connoisseur* in my composition; yet nothing will satisfy my wife, unless I appear as fond of such nonsense as herself.[8]

In fact the real purpose of this fictional epistle is simultaneously to attack both his wife and foreign, especially Italian, music and musicians – the woman making a fool of herself over the trappings of a foreign culture and, worse, foreigners.[9] But most interesting is that Humpkin is able to set himself up as a sympathetic, long-suffering character in part by bragging that he is musically ignorant, except that "I have also a strong rough voice, which will enable me to roar out *Bumper* 'Squire Jones, *Roast Beef*, or some other old *English* ballad, whenever she begins to trill forth her melodious airs in *Italian*."[10] Humpkin could be conflated with Bramston's hero; both are first cousins to Squire Western in Fielding's *Tom Jones*

2 James Gillray (1757–1815), *Playing in Parts*, hand-colored engraving, 22 × 28.6 cm.; New Haven, CT, Yale Center for British Art, Paul Mellon Collection

3 James Gillray (1757–1815), *A Little Music or the Delights of Harmony*, hand-colored engraving, 22 × 28.6 cm.; New Haven, CT, Yale Center for British Art, Paul Mellon Collection

(cf. Fig. 3, the man at the extreme left), though Fielding genuinely mocks his character. It was the Squire's

Custom every Afternoon, as soon as he was drunk, to hear his Daughter play on the Harpsichord: For he was a great Lover of Music, and perhaps, had he lived in Town, might have passed for a Connoisseur; for he always excepted against the finest Compositions of Mr. *Handel*. He never relished any Music but what was light and airy; and indeed his most favourite Tunes, were *Old Sir* Simon *the King,* St. George *he was for* England, *Bobbing* Joan, and some others.[11]

There were those who eschewed music, and there were those who took to it, but poorly, like the fictional Sir Symphony, "a fanatico per la musica," and his equally talented friends, created by Thomas Southerne in his comedy *The Maid's Last Prayer* (1693). Symphony plays the "base" viol and a Cremona violin (for which he paid £50). According to Southerne's stage direction, Symphony beats time and continues to talk throughout a chamber music performance with his friends:

Come, pray let's begin – O Gad! there's a flat Note! There's Art! How surprizingly the Key changes! O law! there's a double relish! I swear, Sir, you have the sweetest little Finger in England! ha! that stroak's new; I tremble every inch of me: Now ladies look to your Hearts – Softly, Gentlemen – remember the Eccho – Captain, you play the wrong Tune – O law! my Teeth! my Teeth! for God's sake, Captain, mind your Cittern – Now the Fuga, bases! agen, agen! Lord! Mr. Humdrum, you come in three barrs too soon. Come, now the Song.[12]

In notably similar terms John Berkenhout, writing at the end of the eighteenth century, described a Mr. Roebuck who lived in York-

4 Isaac Cruikshank (1764–1810), *A Concert of Vocal and Instrumental Music, or the Rising Generation of Orpheus*, pen and ink and monochrome gray wash, 16.5 × 21.3 cm.; San Marino, CA, Henry E. Huntington Library and Art Gallery

shire, "a gentleman of fortune and a *gentleman*-fidler: by a *gentleman*-fidler, I mean a scraper; for such, gentlemen fidlers generally are. 'Damn it,' he would say, 'those rascally composers invented these Cliffs on purpose to puzzle gentlemen.'"[13]

In satires of all kinds it is especially males who bear the brunt of critical attention. On the rarest of occasions the exceptional man appears, whose singularity only proves the rule. Thomas Twining, friend to Charles Burney, described such a find in a Mr. Tindal, recently settled in the neighborhood. Yet even here Twining's accolades for Tindal's musicianship are severely circumscribed:

He plays the fiddle well, the harpsichord well, the violoncello well. Now, sir, when I say, "well," I can't be supposed to mean the wellness that one should predicate of a professor who makes those instruments his study; but that he plays in a very ungentlemanlike manner, exactly in tune and time, with taste, accent, and meaning, and the true sense of what he plays; and, upon the violoncello, he has execution sufficient to play Boccherini's quintettos at least what may be called very decently.[14]

COURTESY AND CONDUCT

These various accounts, some actual, others fictional, all typical of a much larger body of primary sources, point to the existence of a problematic and ambivalent relationship between upper-class men and music. The question is why is this so? And it is an important question, for these were the men who shaped English society and English culture. They were at once patrons and practitioners of all that they determined worthy of their attention or concern. As regards music and society they had a dominant hand in molding both. The clearest answers to the question raised are to be found in class and sex attitudes, the best guides to an understanding of which are English courtesy and conduct books. I will devote the remainder of the chapter to this kind of source material.

Courtesy books classify and explicate a wide range of social behavior within contexts of class ideals and gender responsibilities.[15] Some are written in the form of parental advice, often in the guise of a father to a son or a mother to a daughter, sometimes father to daughter, rarely mother to son. Others, less intimate, are addressed more generally and simply to a "nobleman" or "noblewoman." Here I will speak only about males. Courtesy and conduct books tell a young man how a proper gentleman behaves and what sorts of knowledge befit his station, what are a gentleman's virtues and intellectual acquirements, and what constitutes good breeding. Assessments are made about what in life is essential, what optional and what to be avoided. Some are philosophical in both tone and content; some bear strong relation to the sermon; others are little more than collections of maxims. English courtesy books are sometimes original, indigenous productions. Others are translations of Continental – especially Italian and French – sources (though I have concentrated on original English works); classical borrowings are evident, and extensive scriptural citation – as boilerplate – is common.

From Tudor times to the early seventeenth century, a spirit of Renaissance humanism prevailed in this literature with regard to music. Indeed, Castiglione's *Courtier*, whose positive statements on the role of music in the life of a gentleman are well known, was translated into English by Thomas Hoby as early as 1561 (the book first appeared in Italy in 1528) and was reprinted in London as late as 1724. Following in the footsteps of Castiglione, Henry Peacham in his *The Compleat Gentleman* from 1622 accused any man who does not love music of "brutish stupidity."[16] But Peacham's was one of the last English courtesy books so openly admiring of music. By the middle of the seventeenth century and throughout the eighteenth, the point of view changed dramatically. For the most part music's place in the education of a gentleman degenerated at best to that of a polite and essentially optional accomplishment.

The prevailing attitude in the eighteenth century can be summed up in the words of John Locke in his famous and influential essay, *Some Thoughts Concerning Education*, first published in 1693, by 1801 in a tenth edition:

[Music] wastes so much of a young Man's time, to gain but a moderate Skill in it, and engages often in such odd Company, that many think it much better spared: And I have, amongst Men of Parts and Business, so seldom heard any one commended, or esteemed for having an Excellency in Musick, that amongst all those things that ever came into the List of Accomplishments, I think I may give it the last place.[17]

Negative attitudes toward the musical education of the upper-class young were no doubt strengthened by those writers who claimed, long before the eighteenth century in some cases, that music provided an affront to morality. Some seventeenth-century Puritans maintained this position, but their voices were not the first to be heard on the subject. For example, Philip Stubbes, the English pamphleteer born about 1555, published in *The Anatomie of Abuses* (1583) a virulent attack on the manners, customs and amusements of the period; music comes high on his list, though there is little original in his diatribe. He was mostly inclined to quote the ancients to make his case:

I Say of Musicke as Plato, Aristotle, Galen, and many others have said of it; that it is very il for yung heds, for a certeine kind of nice, smoothe sweetnes in alluring the auditorie to nicenes, effeminancie, pusillanimitie, & lothsomnes of life, so as it may not improperly be compared to a sweet electuarie of honie, or rather to honie it-self; for as honie and such like sweet things, received into the stomack, dooth delight at the first, but afterward they make the stomack so quasie, nice and weake, that it is not able to admit meat of hard digesture: So sweet Musick at the first delighteth the eares, but afterward corrupteth and depraveth the minde . . .

But being used in publique assemblies and private conventicles, as directories to filthie dauncing, thorow the sweet harmonie & smoothe melodie therof, it estraungeth the mind, stireth up filthie lust, womannisheth the minde, ravisheth the hart, enflameth concupisence, and bringeth in uncleannes.[18]

The bond cemented by Stubbes between music and effeminacy indeed formed a recurring trope in courtesy literature, usually coupled with moralistic statements and fears for the decline of religion. John Brown wrote in the mid eighteenth century that the polite arts, unless rendered subordinate to the "higher Views of *Religion, Morals,* and *civil Policy*" degenerate taste and character alike, "drawing down the Mind from higher Pursuits, no less than Effeminancy itself: Perhaps, thus circumstanced, [even the truest taste] may even by styled a *Species of Effeminancy.*[19] Solomon Eccles, prior to his conversion to Quakerism c. 1660, had been one of the finest and most successful music teachers in London, in his younger days earning upwards of £200 per annum as an instructor on the virginals and viols. Once a Quaker he abandoned music, supporting himself in later life by selling shoes (though in his will he called himself a chandler). Religious fanaticism is evident in both his writing and behavior. Eccles described the rigors of his beliefs:

I sitting alone, with my mind turned in, the Voice of the Lord said, *Go thy way, and buy those Instruments again thou lately soldest, and carry them and the rest thou hast in thy house to* Tower Hill, *and burn them there, as a Testimony against that Calling.* So I obeyed the Lord, . . . and burnt them there . . . and I had great peace.

He then described how bystanders put the fire out, leaving him no alternative but to smash the instruments with his feet, which he did "with much indignation, though my Father, and Grandfather, and Great-grandfather were Musitians."[20]

Eccles represents an extreme view, to be sure. He is unusual in that he condemned music with insider knowledge as a former practicing professional. The length of discussion he devoted to the topic is equally atypical. In courtesy and conduct literature, by contrast, few writers gave much space to music. If it was to be condemned outright, as on moral grounds, the statements tended to be short, often telescoping music with other forms of abuse. Thus an anonymous tract from 1699, written in the form of letters from a London gentleman to his friend in the country, urged the latter for his own good not to come to town. A letter on education – on what might be learned of good breeding in London – stated: "Indeed, if you have a Mind to learn to Fiddle and to Dance, and shew little *Apish-tricks,* or to be exact in the Rules of playing the

Fool, or the *Pedant*, here you may be equipt." And in the next sentence the letter recommended London as the perfect place to become proficient in the "arts" of whoring, drunkenness, debauchery and profaneness.[21] Certainly some of the fear expressed depended on the relationship between music and the occasions in public places for its presentation (these notably included the public house and the playhouse). This was more forthrightly stated by writer David Hartley: "It is evident, that most Kinds of Music, Painting, and Poetry, have close Connexions with Vice, particularly with the Vices of Intemperance and Lewdness; that they represent them in gay, pleasing Colours, or, at least, take off from the Abhorance due to them; that they cannot be enjoyed without *evil Communications*."[22] The association that consistently troubled these writers was that of music with lust.[23]

Jeremy Collier's account of music in his conduct book began with a brief historical sketch from ancient times and made a strong case for a music "rightly order'd" which exalts the mind, calms the passions and affords pleasure (he had in mind a simple devotional music). Yet he feared music of all kinds because of the alterations it effected on the listener; he hinted of its anarchic powers. Music "Raises, and Falls, and Counterchanges the Passions at an unaccountable Rate. It Charms and Transports, Ruffles and Becalms, and Governs with an almost arbitrary Authority. There is scarcely any Constitution so heavy, or any Reason so well fortified, as to be absolutely proof against it." In the end Collier lumped secular and devotional music together and implied that it might be best to do without both:

Yet to have our Passions lye at the Mercy of a little Minstrelsy; to be Fiddled out of our Reason and Sobriety; to have our Courage depend upon a *Drum*, or our Devotions on an *Organ*, is a Sign we are not so great as we might be. If we were proof against the charming of Sounds; or could we have the Satisfaction without the Danger; or raise our Minds to what pitch we pleas'd by the Strength of *Thinking*, it would be a nobler Instance of Power and Perfection. But such an Independency is not to be expected in this World, therefore we must manage wisely and be contented.[24]

Closely related to traditional and conservative views of music and morality were those of class and occupation. To preserve the visible image of the gentleman no activity was proper that might mirror in any way the activities of the laboring classes. Music caused special problems here, even in a culture that had a long-standing tradition of gentleman–amateur performers (the fabled English consort players), especially with the advent of the eighteenth century. Music and musicians alike were caught in the hopeless bind of a changing economic and social order, one where Whigs challenged Tory hegemony, where trade challenged agriculture for capital domination, but where at the same time the outer trappings of class status remained in most obvious ways fully intact – old and new wealth alike continued to mark status by means of country houses, landed estates, collections of paintings, fine furniture and music. Among these, music, as a status marker, was different: its realization required a physical act to be repeated over and over again (unlike, say, a painting which once realized remained ever present). Music needed someone to play it. In an increasingly self-conscious separation between labor and leisure, by means of which the eighteenth century provided a major dividing line in Western history, music qua work was very much on the minds of writers trying to hold up the standards of what defined the true gentleman. (This is to say that courtesy and conduct literature was fundamentally conservative, essentially a literature of reaction that by and large stood in opposition to the changing economic order. Ironically, of course, the newly wealthy were generally every bit as eager to play by the same rules of decorum and self-presentation that courtesy and conduct literature described, however much the underlying and unspoken governing ideologies were intended to curb these very challengers.)

In eighteenth-century English high society, music increasingly functioned as entertainment which a (passive) audience paid for and which was increasingly performed by foreign, especially Italian, professionals, who came to England – in what was viewed by the natives as an invasion – seeking their fortune from public performances and (ironically) as music teachers to the wealthy who simultaneously commonly derided them. At this historical juncture chauvinism entered the equation I am describing, sometimes of a particularly virulent sort. Beyond the centuries-old antipathy of the English for the French (so ubiquitous that the word "French" was sometimes generically used to denote any foreigner), with regard to music and the preponderance of Italian musicians the issue was complicated by anti-Catholicism to which many writers contributed. Moreover, patriotism was inserted into the debate. The Italians came to London in the opening years of the eighteenth century in large measure because of the establishment of Italian opera at the Haymarket Theatre, the chief proponents of which were Whig noblemen. Tory writers, forming the musico-political opposition, argued the glories of native English singers and music alike and decried the Italian invaders (the Tory's special rage was directed toward the *castrati* whose physical alteration served as prima facie evidence of both Italian and Catholic barbarism). This issue was in turn further complicated by the jealousies of the legitimate-stage acting companies whose livelihood was threatened by the immense popular success of the Italian opera in London.[25]

Writing late in the century, when these antagonisms were still proliferating, essayist Vicesimus Knox remarked that "a peer may be pleased with music, without associating with fidlers; he may be

delighted in theatres, without making players his bosom friends."
He continued with a hyperbolic story of a lord who

fills his noble mansion in the summer with opera singers, Italian dancers,
comic actors, musicians, firework makers, who dine, and sup, and sleep
for months under his roof; while his door never opens up to the clergy in
his neighbourhood, to any of the professions, to capital artists, to men of
letters and science, or to the poor. Thus he forfeits his popularity, loses
much pleasant conversation, and renders, as far as his influence extends,
the whole Peerage contemptible.[26]

Knox insisted that the obligations of the nobleman were too serious
to allow him traffic with performers or – by implication – for him to
become a performer himself. Knox's argument delineated
boundaries:

He must possess but little MIND, who can acquiesce in the society of
persons, who, whatever dexterity or agility they boast, . . . are usually
unprepared by education and company to become the familiar confidential
associates of hereditary Law-givers, high-born and high-bred Peers of the
realm. There are public places for all amusements, and they are there
conducted with the greatest skill: he who is not contented with attending
these, but chuses to *domesticate* the performers, evinces that he has no
resources in himself; that letters, science, politics, have no charms for him;
and that he is unworthy the distinctions which the laws of his country
allow *him*, SOLELY because his forefather earned them.
    You will never be reduced to the wretched necessity of keeping buf-
foons in your house, if you preserve a relish for rational conversation with
persons of sense and character; . . . and, above all, if you give your
attention to state affairs – the public happiness – the proper province of a
real Nobleman.[27]

James Puckle, writing much earlier than Knox, succinctly foreshadowed the latter's views as well as those of Locke cited previously:
"Musick takes up much time to acquire to any considerable perfection . . . It's used chiefly to please others, who may receive the same
gust from a mercenary; consequently, is scarce worth a gentleman's
time, which might be much better employ'd in the Mathematicks,
or what else would qualify him for the service of his country."[28]
    Courtesy books often expressed fear that the attentions deman-
ded by music would tear a young man away from greater responsibilities falling to his class and gender. Among the most ardent
spokesmen for this position was Philip Dormer Stanhope, Lord
Chesterfield, whose letters to his natural-born son of the same
name were published in 1749. Though Chesterfield's aim to turn
this child of inferior blood into a gentleman ultimately failed, the
published letters of advice became famous and were often quoted.
On the subject of music Chesterfield minced no words. Writing
from London to the boy who was then in Venice on the Grand
Tour, he cautioned him – in a statement brimming with chauvinism – that

As you are now in a musical country, where singing, fiddling, and piping, are not only the common topics of conversation, but almost the principal objects of attention, I cannot help cautioning you against giving in to those (I will call them illiberal) pleasures (though music is commonly reckoned one of the liberal arts) to the degree that most of your countrymen do, when they travel in Italy. If you love music, hear it; go to operas, concerts, and pay fiddlers to play for you; but I insist upon your neither piping nor fiddling yourself. It puts a gentleman in a very frivolous, contemptible light; brings him into a great deal of bad company; and takes up a great deal of time, which might be much better employed. Few things would mortify me more, than to see you bearing a part in a concert, with a fiddle under your chin, or a pipe in your mouth.[29]

Twenty-two years later, in February 1773, the aged Chesterfield wrote to his godson, again named Philip (born in 1755), also in Italy on the Tour and asking for music. In the interim of a quarter century Chesterfield's views had not mellowed:

The music you sent for will get to you as soon as possible, but it is because you say it is for a lady, for you know that when we parted you promised me never to turn piper or fiddler. I do not know by what strange luck music has got the name of one of the liberal arts. I don't see what can entitle it to that distinction, and for my part, I declare that I would rather be reckoned the best barber than the best fiddler in England. Nothing degrades a gentleman more than performing upon any instrument whatever. It brings him into ill company and makes him proud of his shame.[30]

Prescriptions of one sort or another against music never represented the attitudes of all upper-class English society. Throughout the seventeenth and eighteenth centuries there were writers who defended the art as worthy of a gentleman's attention. But what many of this minority group had in mind had less to do with the practice or performance of music by amateurs and more with the development of a theoretical knowledge thereof. These writers favored what was typically termed the "science of music," eighteenth-century nomenclature for music's medieval membership in the four mathematical subjects of the liberal arts' quadrivium.[31] Here music's curricular status could be maintained, and at the same time its rank as a fine art could be denigrated or ignored. Well into the nineteenth century Thomas Worgan, in allowing for the study of what he termed "Intellectual Music," still repeated the condemnations that were so common in the eighteenth century:

A fiddle, flute, or any other musical instrument, placed in the hands of an adult, is tantamount to a whistle or a penny trumpet; and the genius of a musical composition is a dead letter to him who takes up music merely as an accomplishment. Such effeminate trifling is a disgrace to those who ought to give the lead to that sex [that is, women] from whom they commonly take it. I do not mean to say that music is not a proper accomplishment for a gentleman; tout au contraire; but I contend that, in men, it ought to be an elegant superstructure, founded on the basis of intellect.[32]

About 1778 an anonymous writer, probably a clergyman active around Bath, produced a pamphlet called *Euterpe; or, Remarks on the Use and Abuse of Music, as a Part of Modern Education* in which he complained that young gentlemen seldom became agreeable performers, urging them instead to spend their time more profitably in the theoretical study of music. He made explicit a perceived relation of music to mathematics, on account of which value accrued to the art:

Music is a *science* established on the most sublime parts of mathematical truths; its *theory* founded on the doctrine of *Proportion*; on the most *wonderful*, though the most *simple* and *few Principles*; the knowledge of which, fills the enquiring mind with the most transcendant pleasure, and admiration of the wisdom of the Creator, who "*hath filled all things with good.*"

The author recommended several treatises, ancient and modern, and concluded his argument with an appeal to social class. The study of the science of music, he said, "is the pursuit worthy of a Gentleman's attention; and this the knowledge which alone distinguishes the *Musician* from the *Fidler*, and the *Architect* from the *Bricklayer*." He saw in music's theoretical principles what he called – in characteristic Enlightenment terms – the "one invariable *Rule* and *Ordinance*" by which beauty is defined. And though he allowed for the study of applied music in the education of the gentleman, he justified music in the degree to which it may "promote that *complacency* of mind which the *virtuous* only know," in regard to which he acknowledged the corruption of music and its current social role as a "*vain* amusement," thus hinting of irreligion.[33]

There were writers who judged secular music practice proper to gentlemanly accomplishment. The Rev. William Darrell was typical, his views expressed in a highly successful conduct book first published in 1704, by 1732 in its tenth edition. Dancing and music, he said, "embellish Quality, and give a pretty turn to Breeding; they furnish a Man with all the little Ingredients, necessary for a *quaint Address*, and usher him into Company with Advantage." But to this Darrell added a richly metaphoric qualifier that significantly undercut his initially stated remarks. He drew a distinction between the work of the mind, proper to a gentleman, and physical labor, proper only to those beneath him. The practice of music is a physical exercise as he presented it, and as such it was suspect on both gender and class lines. Darrell's qualifier is entirely in keeping with others that recurred in almost every tract otherwise partially supportive of music:

But don't over-rate these Talents, nor place 'em among the first Rate Qualifications of a Gentleman; for in reality they only fit you up for a modish Address and a female Entertainment. Let a Man rather trim up his Mind, than this Body: Those Embellishments are more *noble* and *rich* that lie in the Brain, than those that sink into the Feet, or *perch* on the Finger's End.[34]

Indeed, even as enthusiastic a spokesman for music as Henry Peacham in the seventeenth century felt obliged to assign music only a modest role in the life of a gentleman:

I might run into an infinite sea of the praise and use of so excellent an art, but I only show it you with the finger because I desire not that any noble or gentleman should (save at his private recreation and leasurable hours) proove a master in the same, or neglect his more weighty imployments: though I avouch it a skill worthy the knowledge and exercise of the greatest prince.[35]

Jean Gailhard in 1678 virtually repeated Peacham's opinions of fifty years earlier, in the midst of considering physical exercises recommended to gentlemen ("Vaulting, Trailing the Pike, spreading Colors, handling the Halbard, or the two handed Sword") – all military activities, hence of noteworthy virility:

Also it will not be amiss to learn to play upon one Instrument or other, of Musick; as the Lute, Gittar, Violin, or other he hath a mind to; because *when he is alone in his Chamber,* he may use it sometimes for a diversion. Some also give themselves to vocal Musick, and learn to sing, which is a fine quality, specially when they have a good voice; for Art can perfect that good disposition of nature; and though they have no very good voice, 'tis well to learn the Rules; for sometimes a man in his retirement *singeth to please himself, and not others*: and though he would not sing at all, yet 'tis a satisfaction to know when others sing well, or when they do not, and *to be able to judge* of it. [The italics are mine.][36]

Four points are noteworthy about his remarks, the first three of which reiterate preceding discussion: first, that music is a diversion from greater responsibilities; second, that in some way music helps discipline the mind through the practitioners' learning principles upon which order depends; third, that by knowing music one can judge it, repeating the Boethian position that it is better "to know" than "to do," again, an argument built on the foundation of class awareness; and fourth, that music is an activity the gentleman carries out in private quarters.

It is this last point that provides entry into the underlying ideology regarding the practice of music by men. Music was to be tolerated, if only because the young took to it so readily – but, unfortunately, even passionately. Hence, its practice had to be controlled, properly channeled. It was an activity always under suspicion. At root most writers of conduct literature agreed that music, broadly understood, was essentially ungentlemanly; music was improper for a man because it was unmanly. Weighed against Gailhard's list of physical exercises the roots of music's "unmanliness" become clearer: the *visual* semiotic of men performing music is one where power has no play; indeed, it is the direct opposite of power, for the result of the physical exercise (on the instrument) is simply sound, a product that in its ethereality cannot be properly measured, and, worse, one that immediately disappears. There is in music no economy of prestige equivalent to the physicality of, say, military exercise, whose product is not only the body of one's enemy but his property as well. The musical gentleman by his interests and actions semiotically deconstructed – hence potentially threatened – the definition of gender upon which both the society and the culture ultimately depended. It is this, I believe, which justified the phenomenal attention devoted to the control of music in English society at the beginning of the modern era. (The ways in which this was played out with regard to music and women were different, of course, but fully complementary to the thesis I am proposing, as I will show in later chapters.) In this respect, it is noteworthy that discussions of music in courtesy and conduct books, when occurring at all, often followed discourses on the gentlemanly pursuits of fencing, hunting and fishing, activities metaphorically or literally involving the taking of life, all considered more important and appropriate to the sex and class. Music by contrast was an activity almost shameful in character, hence best practiced in private and out of public view. To do otherwise was to violate an acknowledged taboo – the Earl of Mornington (d. 1781), father of the Duke of Wellington, gained distinction "as the first member of the British aristocracy who dared to walk through the London streets openly and unashamedly carrying a violin case."[37]

Some writers found justification for musical practice on only the most imaginative of grounds. Thomas Bisse, for example, published a sermon in 1726 in which he claimed that music was ordained by God the principal entertainment in human life, building his argument on the Panglossian idea that "the two principal organs or faculties in the make of man [by which he meant hands and ears], seem chiefly framed for the performance, and for the reception and conveyance of musick to us."[38] He spoke with the conviction that God made hands so that the fingers could pluck strings. Approaching the connection between the hands and music from the opposite direction, Richard Mulcaster (1530–1611) much earlier claimed that practicing an instrument while young brought to it the advantage of exercising the small joints and making them nimbler.[39] In the eighteenth century, the non-musical Dr. Johnson summed up for the defense as well as anyone when he described music as "the only sensual pleasure without vice,"[40] a view to which many of his contemporaries by no means subscribed.

A few conduct books described modes of ideal behavior for the nation's entire population, and hence arranged discussion around the differences of social class. This is the case in a well-known conduct book written by an apothecary named James Nelson. Here the classes were defined as five (though Nelson indicated that infinite subdivision was possible): (1) the nobility, (2) the gentry, (3) the genteel trades ("all those particularly which require large

Capitals"), (4) the common trades and (5) the peasantry.[41] The level of education and details of curriculum were to be adjusted to the social responsibilities and economic circumstances of each group ("'Tis a fine thing to be a Scholar! True, it is so: but surely it is a sad thing to be a learned Beggar; and worse yet to be a learned Blockhead: an unlearned Cobler is a Prince to either of these").[42]

As one would expect, no expense was to be spared on the education of the nobility's children and on the eldest sons – heirs – of the gentry; this included music as an ornamental accomplishment.[43] However, male children from the third, mercantile, class caused Nelson difficulty. He advised that they be educated like the gentry, so long as parents had the means to afford it, but with an emphasis on practical subjects directly supportive of future employment. Nelson recognized the rising status of this pivotal group, the incipient middle class, but with uncertainty and ambivalence – like many others of his time, he was profoundly ill at ease with the pressures of social rising: "Nothing is more frequent than for Men in different Stations to ruin themselves by rashly aspiring; and he who has Reputation and Credit in one Sphere, is perhaps undone if he moves beyond it."[44] The social position of this third class demanded some of the trappings of their betters but which ones was unclear. Nevertheless, Nelson emphasized the relative unimportance of this group by failing, for the first time, to distinguish separately between the education proper to males and females: from here downward *lumpen* characteristics become increasingly evident – by contrast it would have been unthinkable not to draw sharp distinctions between the sexes among the upper classes, where power was vested and from which women were excluded, hence making differentiation essential. (In Nelson's scheme the musical education of children from the fourth class, the common trades, was allowed for those who pursued it as a profession, otherwise only for leisure: "Care must be taken that they may stop here."[45] When he came to the peasantry, the fifth class, music disappeared altogether, boys being left with reading, writing and at least basic arithmetic.)[46]

To be sure, courtesy and conduct books dealt with the ideal gentleman rather than the real one. Yet it was within this philosophical and social framework that male amateur musicians from the upper classes practiced their art: the encouragement was scant, the suspicions many; on the one extreme music was derided, at the opposite extreme it was at best excused and tolerated. That these attitudes affected even the most devoted of musicians is evident in their defensiveness when speaking of music. Samuel Pepys, who was little less than obsessed with music-making, as his diary makes abundantly clear, nevertheless felt uneasy about his passion. He wrote (for instance) on 17 February 1662 of that day's renewed music-making after a long hiatus: "at last broke up and I to my office a little while, being fearful of being too much taken with musique, for fear of returning to my old dotage thereupon, and so neglect my business as I used to."[47]

A few decades later the equally devoted amateur Roger North, an avid writer on the subject, felt obliged to describe the self-imposed limitations on his pleasure: "But I never made musick a minion to hinder buissness; it was a diversion, which I ever left for profit, and layd it downe, and resum'd it, as time inlarg'd or straitned with me." Nevertheless, his self-control was not wholly the result of his own act of will, as he confessed: "It may be I might have run too much into the sottish resignation that some shew to this slight enterteinement, musick, if my brother, with whome I used to converse and very much revered his authority, had not sometimes given me a gentle check for hunting of musick, as he called it; which made me a litle ashamed of owning too much of it."[48] It is now time to consider how the writers of courtesy and conduct literature regarded, by sharp contrast, music in the lives of upper-class females.

3 *Music, sexism and female domesticity*

MARY GRANVILLE – the famous Mrs. Delaney, friend of Handel – wrote in the 1730s to her cousin Mrs. Pendarves that she knew of no accomplishment for a lady so great as music, "for it tunes the mind."[1] Most courtesy and conduct writers of the period, like Mrs. Delaney, favored the musical education of girls, though like her they were often imprecise about the supposed benefits expected to accrue from it. Erasmus Darwin explained the typical activities for girls – music, embroidery, drawing, dancing, etc. – as having "the purpose of relieving each other; and of producing by such means an uninterrupted cheerfulness of mind; which is the principal charm, that fits us for society, and the great source of earthly happiness."[2] Darwin's concern, masked by a convoluted explanation, was that well-born girls had a lot of time on their hands which it was the duty of parents to occupy, especially during adolescence – that is, prior to marriage. Writer after writer drove the point home; for example, John Essex, writing in 1722: music "is certainly a very great Accomplishment to the LADIES; it refines the Taste, polishes the Mind; and is an Entertainment, without other Views, that preserves them from the Rust of Idleness, that most pernicious Enemy to Virtue";[3] and Henry Home, Lord Kames, writing in 1781: "In this country, it is common to teach girls the harpsichord, which shows a pretty hand and a nimble finger, without ever thinking whether they have a genius for music, or even an ear. It serves indeed to fill a gap in time, which some parents are at a loss how otherwise to employ."[4]

The phenomenological dimension of time was of the greatest importance in English society, particularly to man. Time was an experiential parameter, the control over which helped determine both one's power and one's prestige. As such the control of time was ideologically defined, along class lines, to be sure, but also by gender difference. Both sexes lived in identical time frames, but each experienced time differently: one sex controlled it; the other sex was controlled by it.

Time for the male was a developmental parameter lived socially. For women, time was non-developmental and lived familially. (Jane Austen, ever sensitive to such matters, in *Persuasion* [1814] ironically described the gender difference: "the Mr Musgroves had their own game to guard, and to destroy; their own horses, dogs, and newspapers to engage them; and the females were fully occupied in all the other common subjects of house-keeping, neighbours, dress, dancing, and music."[5]) Activities viewed as non-developmental and expressive of stationary time, such as music, were peripheral to men's lives and fundamentally improper for them to engage in. But for females such activities were considered *by men* appropriate and important, as delineators both of gender difference and of gender hierarchy. Music helped produce an ideologically correct species of woman; in the eyes of men music accordingly contributed to social stability by keeping women in the place that men had assigned them. These are the issues that I will develop in this chapter.

MUSIC, "VIRTUE" AND CONFINEMENT

One disadvantage of educating a girl was its expense, and expressions of resentment about the costs of daughters' education occurred throughout the period, whereas similar expressions regarding boys' education were rare. Nevertheless, upper-class parents typically opted for their daughters' musical education, often without regard to apparent native ability or interest, and despite warnings of potential financial waste in such instances as voiced by writers of courtesy and conduct tracts ("It is a manifest absurdity to impose on children a task, which they can neither perform with pleasure to themselves, nor credit to their Teachers. It is a waste of time, and useless expenditure of money."[6]) Overriding questions of ability or interest, the culture demanded music as an appropriate mark of both femininity itself and female class status. As such music was routinely viewed by parents as an asset to their daughters' future matrimonial stock. It was an investment aimed at preserving family honor, for a father thus risked neither the social shame nor the economic burden of producing an old maid. If a girl were to be properly married the typical father assumed that she had to be like her mother, and to assure that, she had to be kept away from anything that might suggest alternative behavioral models. To this end music played a central and conservative part, and it was that fact which eventually won out over other considerations like financial cost or reservations regarding talent:

Music is not only a harmless amusement; but, if properly directed, capable of being eminently beneficial to [our] fair Countrywomen. In many instances, it may be the means of preventing that vacuity of mind, which is too frequently the parent of libertinism; of precluding the intrusion of idle and dangerous imaginations; and, more particularly among the Daughters of ease and opulence, by occupying a considerable portion of time, may prove an antidote to the poison insidiously administered by the innumerable licentious Novels, which are hourly sapping the foundations of every moral and religious principle.[7]

It cannot however be said that music was universally judged fit for women as an antidote to more harmful activities. There were a number of concerned moralists in eighteenth-century England who took strong exception to this position. The Marchioness de Lambert, for example, warned of the "fatal Consequences of Passions" caused by music and listed it prominently among the "Retinue of Sensual Pleasure" for women to avoid.[8] Essentially her view reiterated that of Philip Stubbes (1583) who claimed: "if you would have your daughter whoorish, bawdie, and uncleane, and a filthie speaker, and such like, bring her up in musick and dauncing, and, my life for youres, you have wun the goale."[9]

With respect to the relation of music to sensuality most concern was actually focused on song texts. William Darrell in his popular conduct book addressed to men called secular vocal music of the day "lewd to Scandal, and irreligious to Excess; here you have Lewdness in *Folio*, crowded in a *Couplet*, and an *Iliad* of Mischief in a *Nut-shell*." For men it was bad:

But if it be performed by a Woman, it's then Poison thrice boiled, mortal and sudden: It attacks not Vertue by Siege and Approaches, but like Gun-powder blows it up in a Moment; it's down-right Provocation; for tho' she seems to vent the Poet's Thoughts, she warbles out her own, and covers her Amours under the fabulous Names of *Cloris* and *Sylvia*. A Woman that courts in Musick, sollicits in good earnest.[10]

As antidote to the problem the Rev. John Bennett recommended that young women study sacred vocal music exclusively,[11] whereas Vicesimus Knox suggested that music masters provide substitute texts "of similar metre, and of established reputation, . . . with great advantage, to the tune, to the morals, to the taste," adding that young ladies could demonstrate their own poetic talents by writing substitute texts themselves.[12]

These tracts were less concerned with what they literally claimed, namely, the protection of female virtue, than with a fear of female sexuality and an abiding interest in controlling it. Indeed, the potential sensuality of women seems to have been understood by men in specifically developmental terms: once released it would grow without bounds, converting women into monsters dangerous less to themselves than to men (the literature says virtually nothing about the negative influence such women might have on, say, young girls with whom they might come into contact). It must be admitted, however, that the connection between song texts and female morality was rather old hat by the eighteenth century. It was not a new issue but an old one hanging on. In general the containment of female sexuality – the de-sensualization of upper-class women – had already been accomplished by the establishment of an ideology of domesticity and by the social structures designed to institutionalize it. Men had in effect "won" but they nevertheless remain vigilant. Precisely how this "victory" was accomplished, and the role music played in it, are the important questions.

Females, young and old alike, lived out their lives within the metaphorical or literal confines of domestic walls. They spent their time learning and then practicing the so-called "accomplishments": politeness, dress, drawing, needlework, music and the like.[13] Women, charged with two essential tasks – marrying and producing children – were otherwise ornaments to men. Beyond that the greatest challenge faced by females of the leisured classes was how to be leisured, to which contemporaneous fashion plates, perhaps more than any other type of image, consistently (and necessarily) attest (Fig. 5). The role of the fashion plate, after all, was utterly regressive – not because it illustrated the forthcoming season's clothes but because it produced a particular image of the ideal

5 Robert Dighton (c. 1752–1814), *Fashion Plate for Autumn*, one of a set of four illustrations of the seasons, watercolor, 34 × 26 cm.; Minneapolis, MN, The Minneapolis Institute of Arts, The Minnich Collection

woman who would want to wear them. Since female fashion itself at once mirrored and reproduced the fully domesticated female, every aspect of its visual representation within an imagined setting had to produce only appropriate and highly specific resemblances to male-perceived ideals of femininity. (By no accident were fashion-plate designers men.) In particular, fashion plates visually reinforced women's ornamental function by representing them in lavish dress (as one would expect from a fashion print) but for no apparent purpose. Women were typically represented alone (isolated) with their music, and bored, as evinced by utterly blank countenances – though, to be sure, boredom itself was a sign of social status. Women's duty was to wait, and waiting dominates fashion plates.

A similar stifling atmosphere pervades a 1780s illustration called "Morning Employments" (Fig. 6) where the most essential accomplishments are displayed,[14] together with attributes of motherhood (a child clinging to his mother's knee – not by accident the ideal offspring is male) and fidelity (the dog, four-legged surrogate for the husband/father out and about his worldly responsibilities). Ironically, the scene is fundamentally asocial; the women seem self-absorbed and isolated. The same is true of a portrait of a

6 Peltro William Tomkins (1760– 1840), *Morning Employments*, monochrome print; London, Victoria and Albert Museum. By courtesy of the Board of Trustees

stern-faced Lady Jane Mathew observing her daughters at needle-work and drawing (Fig. 7). All four sitters are serious, humorless. One looks down at her sewing; another to the far right, perhaps at the objects she draws. No eyes meet those of the viewer – the standing woman looking outward actually stares off into space. But what is most striking in this portrait of four women spaced closely together is that they do not interact. Their demeanor echoes the confinement of their status, the imprisonment of their accomplishments, their life of ceaseless deferring. It is significant that the space they are *placed in* is not theirs; it is less a domestic space than a ceremonial one in which the domestic furniture seems out of place and oddly squeezed in, in spite of the obvious vastness of the room. The space is male-defined, down to the classical bust or relief on the

7 British School (eighteenth century; previously attributed to John Dowman), *Lady Jane Mathew and her Daughters* (c. 1790), oil on canvas 90.5 × 90.8 cm.; New Haven, CT, Yale Center for British Art, Paul Mellon Collection

back wall, and quite out of character with the delicacy of the female activities.

This contrasts sharply with the situation of men (Fig. 8), in this case a group of gay blades in Rome on the Tour, the male version of finishing school for the upper classes, often for parents lamentably expensive. Their chief "accomplishment" is freedom. They pose as if the whole world is theirs. They carry their swords – signifiers of rank, responsibility, authority and virility – with ease. They possess an excess of swagger and pretension, though mediated comically by the short, skinny boy at the center who seems too slight for his mannish costume and tricorne. Rome and its history are merely a backdrop, a setting conducive to the full enjoyment of a rite of passage into adulthood. The Colosseum and the Arch of Constantine establish the relevant geography for the youths' experience. More important, the ruins accentuate the parameter of time. The architecture is rigid, in a sense dead, partly decomposed, partly buried. It is out of time, the distant past. By contrast the sitters are fluid, young, alive and fashionable. The contrast is perfect and complete: theirs is the vital, flourishing present, that which matters. Rome is at their feet, picturesque and charming, to be sat upon or leaned against and occasionally gestured toward, but nothing more (certainly not studied; their gestures toward the ruins are entirely vague). Least of all is Rome held in awe, à la Winckelmann

8 British School (eighteenth century), *English Connoisseurs in Rome* (c. 1720–63), oil on canvas, 94.6 × 134.6 cm.; New Haven, CT, Yale Center for British Art, Paul Mellon Collection

or Goethe, though, to be sure, the sitters are posed with sufficient attention to the monuments to satisfy the minimal requirements of the typical parent seeing the image when it was shipped home. Fundamentally, Rome is simply being "done" by a tour group mostly interested in its own collective social life abroad ("herding together," to use Lady Mary Wortley Montagu's complaint).[15] These men are part of an historical continuum, a development in time from a glorious but distant past to a self-conscious present; these are the new Caesars, conversing in front of monuments to military triumphs and gladiatorial combats, as if they constituted a kind of general staff. By contrast the Mathew women, except for their fashionable dresses and hats, are literally out of time. They are a collective embodiment of the "permanent" woman (hence the architectural enclosure and classical bust), immobilized, marking stasis. Unlike the men, whose poses emphasize dynamism and movement, the women appear as though they have always been sitting in this room and always will be.

COURTESY, SEXUALITY, MISOGYNY

The ideologies that inform these representations predated the eighteenth century and survived well beyond it. Yet during this period competing and mediating ideologies also found an audience; the ideological underpinnings of male–female relations were examined, challenged, defended and condemned with great vigor. Those whose established positions were threatened commonly mounted a virulent defense. Fundamentally, the debate centered on the definition of sexual hierarchy, within which the "natural" inferiority of the female was established on the grounds that women were "that thought-abhoring Sex"[16] (men reasoned, hence acted; women felt, hence reacted). As the average male writer of conduct tracts saw it, women's dissatisfaction with the gender hierarchy encouraged them to aspire to be like men. Virtually all such writers, and there were many of them, agreed that no woman could succeed in the effort, but could cause great harm in trying ("Amphibious Things indeed! Whose impotent Eagerness to be like *Man* serves only to shew, that they are but mere mechanic Rote-repeaters of *his* Words and unsuccessful Mimics of *his* sense").[17]

George Savile, Marquis of Halifax, like many "father–authors" addressing their "daughters," devoted considerable attention to justifying sexual inequality via the assertion that it was part of the natural order. Men were the "Law-givers, [having] the larger share of *Reason* bestow'd upon them; by which means [the female sex] is the better prepar'd for the *Compliance* that is necessary for the better performance of those *Duties* which seem to be most properly assign'd to it." Women naturally and properly being the weaker sex, "maketh it reasonable to subject [them] to the *Masculine Dominion*."[18]

Since female inferiority was commonly posited on grounds of intellectual inadequacy, women's education was automatically a subject of intense male concern. A fine line had to be walked. A girl could not be kept ignorant; her class standing demanded otherwise. But too much of learning, or access to the wrong subjects, would bring even worse results. Jonathan Swift's views on this were mainstream, at least during the early decades of the century:

> When she once begins to think she knows more than others of her sex, she will begin to despise her husband, and grow fond of every coxcomb who pretends to any knowledge of books; that she will learn scholastic words; make herself ridiculous by pronouncing them wrong, and applying them absurdly in all companies; that, in the meantime, her household affairs, and the care of her children, will be wholly laid aside.[19]

Among writers who defined females as naturally inferior, Lord Chesterfield, in another of his published letters of advice to his natural son, not only summed up the prevailing attitude but also captured precisely the tone in which it was ordinarily expressed:

> Women, then, are only children of a larger growth; they have an entertaining tattle, and sometimes wit; but for solid reasoning, good sense, I never knew in my life one that had it, or who reasoned or acted consequentially for four-and-twenty hours together . . . A man of sense only trifles with them, plays with them, humors and flatters them, as he does with a sprightly forward child; but he neither consults them about, nor trusts them with serious matters; though he often makes them believe that he does both; which is the thing in the world that they are proud of; for they love mightily to be dabbling in business (which by the way they always spoil).[20]

Yet Chesterfield's seemingly extreme views were actually moderate by comparison with a large number of more rabid misogynists writing throughout the period who endlessly cited authorities, ancient to modern, secular and sacred, sometimes via heavily annotated dissertations,[21] but more typically in rhyming couplets ("Woman! the fatal Authress of our Fall: / Woman! the sure destroyer of us all"[22]), maxims or short question–answer exchanges, all of which repeatedly professed women's inferiority, in what can only be understood as an effort to convince themselves of the opposite of what they feared (that women were men's equal):

> "*Q. How is it that women go so unwillingly to bed, and rise the next day so lusty?* A. From the perfection they receive from the man, in that they then know they are women indeed . . .*Q. what's an excellent receipt to keep a woman honest?* A. For her to be always cross-leg'd . . . Q. *Why have women thicker bloods then men?* A. By reason of the coldness of their nature which doth thicken and congeal their blood.[23]

Over and over again, sometimes filling entire books, male writers sustained these attacks. Almost all such texts were of the pocket variety designed to be carried on one's person. They could be consulted anywhere. Men in casual company with one another might open the book and share a misogynistic line or two, of which a single collection might contain several hundred. Ironically, man-the-reasoner, in perpetuating the ideology of female inferiority, gave preference to jokes rather than sustained arguments in an effort more to assert a position than to prove it. And it is noteworthy that women's sexuality was the *idée fixe* in most of these diatribes.

The surface refusal to take women seriously, evident in comic verse and question–answer vulgarity, nevertheless belied deep anxiety about women (evident in the passage from Swift as well), one obvious contributing factor to which was that men – however much they loathed women – were still expected to marry them (obviously I do not mean to imply that all men shared these views). Indeed, the most misogynistic of writers seldom advised men against marriage, though they used every opportunity to attack the institution: "Marriage is a Lottery, nay, the greatest Hazard imaginable; an *East-India* Voyage is not half so perilous . . ." (followed by a catalogue of wifely faults to plague husbands).[24]

The role of women in marriage was narrowly circumscribed by most writers, who commonly insisted that women should be closely monitored for their attention to sanctioned responsibilities. These prescriptions were not necessarily followed to the letter, but they constituted an ideal that husbands were urged to promote. In sum:

It is the chief duty of a woman, to make a good wife. To please her husband, to be a good oeconomist, and to educate their children, are capital duties, each of which requires much training . . .

Women, destined by nature to be obedient, ought to be disciplined early to bear wrongs, without murmuring. This is a hard lesson; and yet it is necessary even for their own sake: sullenness or peevishness may alienate the husband; but tend not to sooth his roughness, nor to moderate his impetuosity. Heaven made women insinuating, but not in order to be cross: it made them feeble, not in order to be imperious: it gave them a sweet voice, not in order to scold: it did not give them beauty, in order to disfigure it by anger.[25]

Lord Kames summarized the male role in relation to the female with a simple statement: "A man indeed bears rule over his wife's person and conduct: his will is law."[26] Finally, Robert Burton, preceding Lord Kames by 160 years, stated the issue simply: "Vertuous women should keepe house."[27]

MUSIC AS DANGEROUS NECESSITY

Authors of courtesy and conduct books stressed the importance of music as a domestic accomplishment, but no writer showed so clearly that the expectation transferred to social practice as Jane Austen, the accuracy of whose views on social reality is well established. Thus in *Mansfield Park* her heroine Fanny, coming to Mansfield Park from lower middle-class parents in Portsmouth, is confronted by her female cousins of distinctly higher social rank. They are appalled that Fanny "says she does not want to learn either music or drawing," to which one replies: "To be sure, my dear, that is very stupid indeed, and shows a great want of genius and emulation." Later in the novel Mary Crawford, herself devoted to music (she had her harp transported to Mansfield Park from London), is engaged in a conversation with the unmusical Fanny concerning the Misses Owen, the exchange tinged with Austen's characteristic irony:

> "How many Miss Owens are there?"
> "Three grown up."
> "Are they musical?"
> "I do not at all know. I never heard."
> "That is the first question, you know," said Miss Crawford, trying to appear gay and unconcerned, "which every woman who plays herself is sure to ask about another. But it is very foolish to ask questions about any young ladies – about any three sisters just grown up; for one knows, without being told, exactly what they are – all very accomplished and pleasing, and *one* very pretty. There is a beauty in every family. – It is a regular thing. Two play on the piano-forte, and one on the harp – and all sing – or would sing if they were taught – or sing all the better for not being taught – or something like it."[28]

There is no question that musical skills were valued as one of the domestic talents a man sought in a wife. As Jonas Hanway obliquely expressed it: "It seems to be no unlucky circumstance to the man to whose lot the most accomplished young lady-musician may fall, if she has also been taught the *science of housewifery*, especially if her husband should be of a *true English taste*."[29] In what I have suggested thus far, the benefit of educating a girl in music essentially accrued to her parents and future husband. The advantages to the girl herself, in many writers' views, apart from capturing a man, were considerably less certain. In part I assume this resulted from the fact that the pleasure music might afford a child seems seldom to have been a justification for the musical education of daughters. Music instead met the other agendas I have been discussing. Nevertheless, a question arose over what a female was to do with music once she learned it, especially once she reached adulthood. And about the only thing the average writer arrived at once again centered on the

relation of music to the parameter of time, specifically phenomenological or experiential time. The Rev. John Bennett defined music's
benefit as increasing happiness, inspiring tranquility and harmoniz-
ing the mind and spirits, during those *"ruffled* or *lonely* hours,
which, in almost every situation, will be your lot."[30] That is,
music's pleasure accrued from its compensatory potential as a balm
to isolation.

The boredom of housewifery for the upper-class woman was
tacitly acknowledged by both male and female writers. Yet when it
came to music, that seemingly innocent devourer of time, not only
was its performance to be in private company, among family and
friends, but the woman was further cautioned that she treat it
"Carelessly like a Diversion, and not with Study and Solemnity, as
if it was a Business, or yourself overmuch Affected with it."[31]
Ironically – and impossibly – the very performance of music was to
be accomplished with the utmost metaphorical and literal passivity.
This is echoed by Erasmus Darwin, among many others, who
recommended that a woman literally restrict the development of
her talents, in effect so as not to compete with her husband in the
public eye:

It is perhaps more desirable, that young ladies should play, sing, and
dance, only so well as to amuse themselves and their friends, than to
practice those arts in so eminent a degree as to astonish the public; because
a great apparent attention to trivial accomplishments is liable to give
suspicion, that more valuable acquisitions have been neglected. And, as
they consist in an exhibition of the person; they are liable to be attended
with vanity, and to extinguish the blush of youthful timidity; which is in
young ladies the most powerful of their exterior charms.[32]

The Rev. William Darrell expressed concern that musical education
specifically encouraged females to act beyond the bounds of the
modesty and deference expected of their sex, further evident in the
sharpness of his discourse that grates with sarcasm:

And now Miss leaves the Nursery to ply at the Dancing-School, and to
finger the Guitarr, or the Virginals; and when she has master'd a *Minuet*,
and an Air *Alamode*; when she can practice a Brace of Grimaces, and wave
the Fan, Good God! how Mamma Titters; she is now fledg'd for the
World, and sets out for Company . . .
   In the mean time, Age comes upon her, Passions get a Head, Temptations follow without Number, Desires without Bridle, and Vanity without Check . . . She has been set up by the Mother for a little Goddess, and
the Family adores her like a Household Divinity.[33]

Darrell thus anticipated with dread the adult who would develop
from such seed. A woman who became an accomplished performer
signaled a variety of changes in her relationship to her husband and

9 Thomas
Gainsborough (1727–
88), *Ann Ford (later
Mrs. Philip
Thicknesse)* (c. 1760),
oil on canvas, 197.2
× 134.9 cm.;
Cincinnati, OH,
Cincinnati Art
Museum. Bequest of
Mary M. Emery

to her place in society. She became *visually* prominent, especially if she performed outside the drawing room, particularly if she gave a public recital, thus upstaging her husband and, implicitly, suggesting to her husband's friends that she was out of control, leading a life of her own not defined by domestic regulations and responsibilities. A well-bred woman who took music so seriously constituted a threat to social boundaries. Accordingly most courtesy and conduct literature charged women to view music as a trivial pursuit, like virtually everything else they did apart from bearing and raising children.

The trivialization of women's activities, to men and women alike, was an essential component in maintaining the status quo to gender hierarchy. Now, clearly, it can be argued that music nevertheless created a compensatory space for women condemned to live within these contradictory parameters, yet it was a compensation whose negative dialectics were constantly reasserted. That is, whilst a woman needed music in order for her to reflect well on her husband, she had to restrain any acknowledgment of musical devotion and also hide – or limit the development of – her talents, almost as if they were family secrets (outside the circle of friends for whom she would perform at parties).

Ann Ford (Fig. 9), third wife to Philip Thicknesse, was a case in point. She was an accomplished musician who sang, and played the English guitar, the viola da gamba and the musical glasses; for the last she wrote a tutor book. But she was allowed by her father to give concerts solely at home. When she was twenty-three he had her arrested and confined to prevent her from performing in public. She later made a second and ultimately successful attempt to give a concert, but not before being arrested again. Her career ended, as one might expect, when she left London in 1762 with her friends the Thicknesses.[34]

Gainsborough's portrait interests me particularly because it was painted at the time of Ann's dispute with her father (the painting was probably commissioned by him or, less likely, by Philip Thicknesse whom she married in 1762 after the death of his previous wife). The artist set Ann Ford in a non-specific space which can nevertheless be described as "portrait-convention domestic," judging from the carpet and the table she leans on. Only the elaborate drapery at the back and the viola da gamba hanging on the wall seem explicitly theatrical. Ann herself is painted as a figura serpentinata, a form more or less echoed by the shapes of the musical instruments.[35]

Taken independently, a figura serpentinata suggests motion or action, hence is complementary to freedom. Yet I take this portrait to signal social limitations bordering on oppression, whether of her as an individual or of her gender in general. The serpentine line Gainsborough employed in this and other portraits of seated

women is gender specific; the formal aesthetic is not devoid of meaning. The curvilinear form, like all artistic form, is deeply informed by history. It is not simply the unproblematic, "natural," timeless and autonomous expression of female beauty or anatomy. The serpentine line is also, dialectically, reflective of age-old suspicions about womanly cunning and, as a corollary, of female sexual voluptuousness conventionally at once desired and condemned by men.

In this portrait the (liberating) motion inherent in the serpentine form is fully contained, thereby creating a tension: Ann Ford has at least visually been "tamed." She sits with legs crossed, from which position only rest can be assumed. More important, she has been silenced as a musician, in spite of the fact that she is surrounded by musical instruments. Her viola da gamba now hangs on the wall – in a position that virtually reduces it to an icon of taste and status. Moreover, in the eighteenth century the viola da gamba was normally played in duet (at the least) with a keyboard instrument. Thus the absence of such an instrument to complete an ensemble strengthens the sense of her containment. Moreover, Ann's pose precluded her playing the English guitar in her lap. One hand gingerly touches her head, the other lightly fingers the instrument's back strap. The very delicacy of her touch (Gainsborough is remarkably adept at showing this) has a poignancy that is unnatural, strengthening our awareness of her pose. Beyond that, music books atop the table are closed and the single sheets of music half covered. There is no concert here, not even in private. The instruments, as much as Ann herself, are merely visual ornaments to her family's position.

The English guitar she holds was a solo instrument used almost exclusively in the home and played virtually always only by women. Its very presence, and the functional precedence it takes here over the viola da gamba, define the gender role appropriate to her as a daughter and a future wife. Ann Ford's musical talent, in other words, is not simply visually proclaimed, it is also specifically controlled. External control is also manifested by the turn of her head: she looks away from the viewer toward nothing we can share. By not meeting our eyes she herself is more easily looked at, hence objectified into a family icon, not accidentally by means of the implicit sexuality of her serpentine pose, her crossed leg emphasizing the line of her thigh.[36]

There were a few writers, even in the early decades of the century, who openly condemned the restrictive position of women in marriage ("The Estate of Wives is more disadvantageous than *Slavery* itself . . . Wives may be made Prisoners for Life at the Discretion of their *Domestick Governors*").[37] And even before the end of the seventeenth century some complained that a woman whose knowledge was limited to "meer good Housewifry" (the skills of the home economist) was pointlessly disadvantaged.[38] Daniel Defoe, in his account for an academy of women, condemned the hypocrisy of reproaching women's "folly and impertinence," yet denying them equal education, and encouraging them instead to spend their youth learning "to stich and sew or make baubles."[39] But when it came to musical education there was disagreement as to whether it was a mere "accomplishment" or something more. For example, Theophilus Dorrington placed music together with philosophy and history as important female subjects, but based his view on the necessity of keeping women's minds on morally decent topics.[40] (His view thus preserved dominant conservative ideology: he saw the prime function of the curriculum as moral surveillance.)

Almost a century later Mary Wollstonecraft, the century's best-known – and much attacked – feminist, pointed out that girls learning only "something of music" did not learn enough to "render it an employment of the mind." She argued that once a girl could play a few tunes, she imagined herself an artist for the rest of her life, whereas in fact her knowledge rose little above the level of banality and as such contributed nothing to her intellectual development. Wollstonecraft, understanding perfectly the politics of education in English society, granted music and the other accomplishments a place, so long as acquiring them did not prevent the learning of subjects that might help women achieve intellectual equality with men.[41]

Writer Hannah More also recognized that women's study of music implicitly served the interests of men by preventing women access to the kinds of knowledge, hence power, that men possessed. In her *Strictures on the Modern System of Female Education* she indicated, via a footnote, having received "from a person of great eminence" a calculation of the hours of practice one young lady devoted to her music. Hannah More repeated the calculation as a generalizable supposition, and accompanied it with the ironic claim that the individual on whom it was based was "now married to a man who *dislikes music*!" The passage is significant in that it is an instance where a woman identified clearly the problematic of time, and the relationship between time and power in women's lives.

Suppose your pupil to begin at six years of age and to continue at the average of four hours a-day *only*, Sunday excepted, and thirteen days allowed for travelling annually, till she is eighteen, the state stands thus; 300 days multiplied by four, the number of hours amount to 1200; that number multiplied by twelve, which is the number of years, amounts to 14,400 hours![42]

Ironically, some writers voiced the complaint that women who studied music while they were young, either to delight their parents or to help themselves acquire a husband, gave it up when they reached adulthood or when they married, a view held in England as early as the late sixteenth century.[43] No writer better expressed this phenomenon than Jane Austen in *Sense and Sensibility* (1811):

In the evening, as Marianne was discovered to be musical, she was invited to play. The instrument was unlocked [a wry hint at what is to follow], every body prepared to be charmed, and Marianne, who sang very well, at their request went through the chief of the songs which Lady Middleton had brought into the family on her marriage, and which perhaps had lain ever since in the same position on the pianoforté, for her ladyship had celebrated that event by giving up music, although by her mother's account she had played extremely well, and by her own was very fond of it.

Marianne's performance was highly applauded. Sir John was loud in his admiration at the end of every song, and as loud in his conversation with the others while every song lasted. Lady Middleton frequently called him to order, wondered how any one's attention could be diverted from music for a moment, and asked Marianne to sing a particular song which Marianne had just finished.[44]

Austen returned to this subject in *Emma*, in a conversation between the young musical devotee Emma Woodhouse and the awful, even detestable, Mrs. Elton, who makes unbelievable protestations of being "passionately fond" of music:

[Mrs. Elton to Emma:] "I hope we shall have many sweet little concerts together. I think, Miss Woodhouse, you and I must establish a musical club, and have regular weekly meetings at your house, or ours. Will it not be a good plan? If *we* exert ourselves, I think we shall not be long in want of allies. Something of that nature would be particularly desirable for *me*, as an inducement to keep me in practice; for married women, you know – there is a sad story against them, in general. They are but too apt to give up music." . . .

"When I look round among my acquaintance, I tremble. Selina has entirely given up music – never touches the instrument – though she played sweetly. And the same may be said of Mrs Jeffereys – Clara Partridge, that was – and of the two Milmans, now Mrs Bird and Mrs James Cooper; and of more than I can enumerate. Upon my word it is enough to put one in a fright. I used to be quite angry with Selina; but really I begin now to comprehend that a married woman has many things to call her attention. I believe I was half an hour this morning shut up with my housekeeper."[45]

The situations these authors variously describe is perhaps best summarized by a character from a 1762 London comedy given at the Theatre Royal: "I dare say this passion for music is but one of the irregular appetites of virginity: You hardly ever knew a lady so devoted to her harpsichord, but she suffered it to go out of tune after matrimony."[46]

Some explanations for a married woman's abandonment of music are obvious. Women had houses to manage and children to raise. But this does not go far enough, for among the leisured classes day-to-day household tasks and parenting were largely the responsibilities of servants. Upper-class women, again, always had time on their hands. Clearly, some gave up music once they were free of parental instruction simply because they had no musical interests. In other instances women's music-making irritated their unmusical husbands, as in the story of Mr. Humpkin and his wife printed in *The Connoisseur* which was quoted in the previous chapter. Jane Austen implied that music was left by married women for the more exciting whirl of ever more trivial activities. I think there is another explanation as well, namely, that in some instances women rebelled against music in the recognition that its function in their lives was the re-enactment of their oppression. Indeed, this is hinted at by both Wollstonecraft and More. (I will return to this matter later; music in matrimony will be the subject of Chapter 8.)

MUSIC AND CLASS

In the late sixteenth century Richard Mulcaster addressed the question, "*how much* a woman ought to learne," His answer: "so much as shall be needefull."[47] But, as with men, in practical terms the answer varied according to one's social class. The question became more pressing in the late eighteenth century when a greater degree of upward mobility was possible, so that the lower orders aped the middle classes, the middle classes the upper. Writers expressing concern, in some cases outrage, at the evidence of social mobility typically directed their attacks against women. They often had music on their minds. As Jonas Hanway had it, music "is most to be esteemed in *women*, and in women of fortune and polite education; for others can hardly find time to apply to it."[48]

James Nelson's five-part division of the social classes, looked at earlier with regard to men, was likewise applied to women and the proper education for them among each group. In the first class, the nobility, a girl's education must distinguish her from the crowd. She was to have "Reading, Writing, Working [probably meaning embroidery], Dancing, *French, Italian* and Music . . . and that not superficially."[49] For Nelson's second class, the gentry, a girl's education depended on whether she was an only child, hence an heiress, or whether she had a brother. In the first instance she should be educated much like the nobility, but in the case of the second, "where a Brother sweeps away the Estate," her education need not be either so "brilliant" or expensive. Nelson waffled on this issue, variously recommending music ("but not to Perfection") and suggesting its avoidance (his lightly veiled preference):

But supposing that either to gratify herself of her Friends she engages deeply in the Study of Music; Parents are here often cajoled out of their

Money, and their Senses too, by their Daughter's fancied Excellence: and the same Man that is lavish in his Praise to the fond Father's Face, will perhaps in the very next Company swear the Girl squeaks like a Pig.[50]

(As remarked in the previous chapter, with the third, fourth and fifth classes, those of the genteel trades, the common trades and the peasantry, Nelson simply lumped the sexes together.)

Priscilla Wakefield in a courtesy book addressed solely to women divided society into four classes: (1) the nobility and all those who rival them in power, either on account of high office or wealth, (2) those who by their own means "procure a respectable subsistence approaching to opulence," (3) those who live above want but without the "means of splendid or luxurious gratification" and (4) the laboring poor. The rank of women in this hierarchy was determined by birth or marriage. Music was appropriate to the first two classes. Among women of the first class music constituted one of the "lighter studies," one of the "sources of the most refined entertainment."[51] And for both groups, musical composition, oddly enough, was cited as an appropriate field of endeavor for female professionals![52] The story changed with respect to the less fortunate. Wakefield lamented that tradesmen and mechanics, fond of educating their daughters for gentility, spent more money than they could afford. These young women, said Wakefield,

should not only be prohibited from learning the ornamental arts, such as music, dancing, drawing, foreign languages, and costly works of taste, . . . but they should never be placed at a school where those arts are taught; for it is a natural propensity of the human mind, to prefer that which is beautiful and pleasant, to those things which though useful are unadorned. Respectable schools, not aiming at gentility, as it is usually termed, should therefore be established for the express purpose of educating young women of this class, where they might acquire whatever knowledge is conducive to render them useful in their station, without having their simplicity corrupted by an intercourse with those, who have a reasonable title to the indulgences of affluence, and the acquisition of liberal accomplishments.[53]

By the end of the eighteenth century acquirement of the ornamental accomplishments among the lower middle orders was no longer highly controversial, Wakefield aside, though it was still commonly objected to. Nevertheless, the ambitious middle-class male parent seeking these acquirements for his daughters (or the daughters seeking them in spite of their fathers) consistently made fools of themselves as stock figures in visual caricature, literature and on the stage.[54] Arthur Young, writing in the *Annals of Agriculture*, noted his considerable annoyance at finding a pianoforte in a farmer's parlor: "I always wish [it] was burnt."[55] Allaston Burgh in 1814 sarcastically noted that "the Daughters of Mechanics, even in humble stations, would fancy themselves extremely ill–treated, were they debarred the Indulgence of a piano-forte."[56] Finally, a distinctly ill-spirited, anonymous statement published in *Gentle-man's Magazine* in 1801 reflected clearly the underlying class consciousness affecting these attitudes: "Instead of dishing butter, feeding poultry, or curing bacon, the avocations of these young ladies at home are, studying dress, attitudes, novels, French and musick, whilst the fine ladies their mothers sit lounging in parlours adorned with the fiddle faddle fancy work of their daughters."[57] However impotent these sarcasms they each exhibit reaction to a changing social order. But what is more interesting is that blame for the loss of tradition (the good old days) is specifically – and ironically – laid at the feet of females, more accurately – and ridiculously – at the feet of girls (and their doting parents). It is the rising-yet-inferior class and the unempowered gender that is at fault.

The farmer's daughter seeking the accomplishments appropriate to her social betters was meanly satirized by the always trenchant James Gillray (Fig. 10) in a print from 1809. The older generation of women gossip cattily behind a fan, having already examined the needlework signed "B[etty] Giles" atop the table. Farmer Giles and his wife feel satisfaction and give encouragement as daughter Betty, upon her return from boarding school, demonstrates her talents on the square piano in a performance of the "Bluebells of Scotland," hardly high art but apparently all she can handle – and clearly more than her younger sister is able to sing.

Betty's needlework is no better. A framed sampler on the back

10 James Gillray (1757–1815), *Farmer Giles & his Wife Shewing Off their Daughter Betty to their Neighbours, on her Return from School* (1809), engraving, 32.5 × 47.5 cm.; New Haven, CT, Yale Center for British Art, Paul Mellon Collection

wall, signed by the young girl at age sixteen, includes an alphabet in upper and lower case, numbers from one to twelve, a proverb ("Evil communications Corrupt good Manners") and a pair of birds flanking entwined hearts, an incongruous mix! Betty's drawing is a good deal worse; her rendition of the family estate, titled "Cheese-Farm"(!), shows elementary problems with perspective: in the foreground a woman milks a cow, beside which stands a gigantic rooster; a two-storey-tall horse looms above the cottage roof in the background.[58]

Similar to Gillray's print is one from the following year called "A Naturel Genius" (Fig. 11). In this instance a lumpish (thus class-marked) farmer's (or some such) wife and daughter, in equally preposterous costumes (ill-fitting – note the daughter's gloves – and overstated), are being shown around a boarding school by its headmistress. She holds in her hand a card on which can be read "Terms of B[on] Ton^s School." In the corner there is a square piano with music, and on a chair next to it a needlework picture of Charlotte weeping at the tomb of Werther (Goethe), the image being pointed to and identified by the school mistress. To this the mother responds, "A very pretty piece I pertest! my Dater has a Genii for Drawing! Penelope my dear! you shall work Charlotte at the Tub of *Water*," to which Penelope responds, "La Mother! I shall like that! you know Mounseer Gumboge says: I *make Water* as natural as Life."[59]

11 British School, *A Naturel Genius* (1810), engraving, 22 × 32.5 cm.; London, British Museum. By courtesy of the Trustees

The Edgeworths in 1801 identified an underlying ideological concern with females of the lower classes learning the accomplishments, namely, that by being made common these distinctions lost caste among those who previously had been privileged with their sole possession:

Stop at any good inn on the London roads, and you will probably find that the landlady's daughter can shew you some of her own framed drawings, can play a tune upon her spinnet, or support a dialogue in French of a reasonable length, in the customary questions and answers . . . Accomplishments have lost much of that value which they acquired from opinion, since they have become common . . . In a wealthy mercantile nation there is nothing which can be bought for money, that will long continue to be an envied distinction.[60]

In a dialogue called *The Levellers* from early in the century two young women trade notes on their education in a manner foreshadowing the concerns more typical toward the period's close:

You know my father was a tradesman, and lived very well by his traffick; and, I being beautiful, he thought nature had already given me part of my portion, and therefore he would add a liberal education, that I might be a compleat gentlewoman. Away he sent me to the boarding-school; there I learned to dance and sing, to play on the bass-viol, virginals, spinnet, and guitar . . . My father died, and left me accomplished, as you find me, with three-hundred pounds portion; and, with all this, I am not able to buy an husband. A man, that has an estate answerable to my breeding, wants a portion answerable to his estate; an honest tradesman, that wants a portion of three-hundred pounds, has more occasion of a wife that understands cookery and housewifery, than one that understands dancing, and singing, and making of sweet-meats . . . I conclude, our parents are great causes of this evil, in educating their children beyond their estates.[61]

The point of this story is deadly serious, for it metaphorically predicts the destruction of family and social order alike. Yet as regards the responsibility of women for social dissolution there is here a difference between the classes. The functions assigned upper-class women were designed to preserve their passivity. With women of the lower classes, by contrast, functions assigned were organized around activity – the special activity, labor, necessary for the prosperity of their superiors. Young farmers' daughters learning the piano were, in effect, staging a strike. Music for them was a passive activity by comparison with their traditional daily labors, but it was politically active and even assertive in its challenge to dominant ideology, if on their part unconsciously so.

In these two chapters I have cited numerous texts written across a considerable span of time – from the late sixteenth century into the second decade of the nineteenth – whose genres incorporate a wide gamut: courtesy and conduct literature, educational tracts, novels and stage plays. Yet whatever the differences in time and type of discourse, there is consistent import among them vis-à-vis the relation between the social roles assigned men and women and the function of music in their lives. The underlying subject of these diversions is the relationship of men to women defined by the ideological linchpin of male domination. For all practical purposes, in the common regard of men for women in eighteenth-century English upper-class society, there survived an ancient ideology, given life in social structures, identifying women as part of men's property. The details of how these attitudes were reproduced in musical education are the subjects of the next chapter.

UPPER-CLASS BOYS, especially aristocrats, were generally educated privately at home until early adolescence, after which they commonly attended university, matriculating as early as age fourteen or fifteen, though as the century wore on the age for admission to the university tended to increase. After university boys usually took the Grand Tour.[1] In families of distinction the eldest son's education was the most seriously attended, and was sometimes carried out solely within the confines of the home under a private tutor, residing with the family, who was responsible for the entire curriculum. For the well-to-do living in London, however, individual non-resident private teachers were often engaged for single subjects, music and dancing among them.[2] Boys' curriculum, broad but shallow, included languages (at least French), arithmetic, geometry, algebra, geography, historical chronology, history in general (ancient and modern, domestic and foreign), rhetoric, a bit of Latin and sometimes Greek, perhaps logic, ethics, metaphysics, a little natural science, theology and law, and a variety of physical exercises. Drawing and dancing preceded music in bringing up the rear as polite accomplishments.[3]

Upper-class girls were educated more haphazardly, usually at home under the guidance of the mother or a governess, otherwise at boarding school. Either way, the goals were not lofty. Given that upper-class females had few opportunities outside the home, little was to be gained in spending money to educate them beyond the requisite skills of housewifery.[4] Resident governesses were almost invariably paid only a few pounds a year plus room and board, and were commonly secured by the placing of advertisements stressing qualities tangential to education, respectability before anything else:

WANTED to be A companion and a Go-ness to a Young Lady, a middle aged single lady, a native of England, and a protestant, of unexceptionable morals and character, attested by persons of undoubted credit and veracity; she must have had a virtuous and useful, as well as polite and ornamental education; must be a mistress of the French tongue, and of her needle; if she is conversant in music, and drawing, still the more agreeable.[5]

In 1710 one candidate for a position in the household of Lady Thunderton announced her capacities as, "I can sow white and colourd seam; dress head suits, play on the Treble and Gambo, Viol, Virginelles and Manicords, which I can do, but on no other."[6] When it came to music few of these women could have possessed more than rudimentary skills.

Throughout most of the century, and particularly after 1750, the London and country newspapers carried advertisements for boarding schools accommodating one or the other of the sexes; handbills and trade cards also announced these institutions. The quality of education provided varied enormously; those seeking upper-class boys offered a full curriculum, as indicated above. Those for upper-class girls gave much less, ordinarily some French or Italian, sometimes a bit of geography, and especially domestic skills and "ornamental accomplishments." Thus an advertisement for a country school for girls, whose faculty consisted of a single "gentlewoman from London," claimed to offer the following:

Waxworks of all sorts, as one's picture to the life. Figures in shadow glasses, fruits upon trees, or in dishes, all manor of confections, fish, flesh, fowl or anything that can be made in wax. Philigrim work of any sort, whether hollow or flat. Japanese work upon timber or glass. Painting upon glass. Sashes for windows upon sarsnet, or transparent paper, straw work of any sort, as, houses, birds or beasts. Shell work in sconces, rocks or flowers, twill work, gum work, transparent work, puff work, paper work. Platework on timber, glass or brass. Tortoise shell work. Mould work, boxes and baskets. Silver landskips, gimpwork, Buglework. A sort of work in imitation of Japan very cheap. Embroidering, stitching and quilting Truepoint or tapelace. Cutting glass. Washing gazes or Flanders point and lace. Pastry of all sorts with the finest cuts and shapes that's now used in London. Boning fowls without cutting the back. Butter work. Preserving, conserving, and candying. Pickling and colouring. All sorts of English wines. Writing and arithmetic. Music, and the great art of dancing, which is a good carriage and several other things too tedious to mention.[7]

Music was in the curriculum of most girls' boarding schools, and even fairly common to boys' schools, though in almost all instances it was offered as an optional add-on available for an extra fee. There is little evidence to suggest that the musical standards were high in boarding schools; and to my knowledge not a single institution in the eighteenth century could be favorably compared with the best seventeenth-century schools such as Mrs. Perwich's for upper-class girls at Hackney, established in 1643 and in operation for seventeen years (employing sixteen non-resident music masters for instruction in singing and on harpsichord, lute, organ, violin and other stringed instruments; the school also maintained an orchestra led by Susannah, the daughter of Mrs. Perwich),[8] or Josias Priest's renowned girls' school in Chelsea, for whose students Purcell wrote

Dido and Aeneas in 1689.[9] Indeed, the most common surviving
written references to music education in the eighteenth century
represent complaints about and satires of music masters. Playwright Thomas Shadwell was already poking fun at the subject in
the late seventeenth century. In *The Scowrers* (1690) one of Shadwell's female characters belittles "for Musick an old hoarse singing
man riding ten miles from his Cathedral to Quaver out the Glories
of our Birth and State, or it may be a Scotch Song more hideous and
barbarous than an Irish Cronan"; to which her companion responds: "And another Music-master from the next Town to teach
one to twinkle out *Lilly burlero* upon an old pair of Virginals, that
sound worse than a Tinkers kettle that he cries his work upon."[10]
(Very little information survives about instructional methods in
music at boys' schools, but for girls' ample information is available.
Girls were often instructed in groups which explains why music
fees at boarding schools cost a fraction of the rates typically charged
for private instruction. In group lessons the master spent only a few
minutes with each girl, while the others sat idly by waiting their
turn.)[11]

Methods of appointing teachers point up the inadequacy of much
musical instruction at boarding schools, though the situation in the
country may be presumed worse than in the city where there was
more competition of students.[12] Sir George Smart, the conductor,
organist and composer, as a young man of twenty-two in 1798, was
recommended to teach music at the school of a Mrs. Cameron
in London and auditioned before a Mr. Twiss, said to be a
"tremendous critic." Smart related:

The first question put to me was: "Can you play at sight?" I boldly
answered "Yes." He then placed before me a very difficult sonata, and put
his ear close to the pianoforte. I saw at once that the sonata was too much
for me, but I dashed at it and rattled over the right and wrong notes. Mr.
Twiss expressed his perfect satisfaction and reported . . . that I must be a
very capable teacher.[13]

Boarding school education was satirized in a drawing by Edward
Francis Burney, "An Elegant Establishment for Young Ladies"
(Fig. 12). In this instance, however, the inadequacy of the pedagogy,
musical or other, is less the subject than the utter triviality of the
curriculum itself and the coquettes it produced (the image was of
course the master for a print and was undoubtedly directed toward
parents as a warning; it is nonetheless profoundly anti-feminist in
the degree to which the students, and not their teachers, are emphasized, thus making the girls willing participants in their own degradation). In the upper left in a back room the school's governess is
seated at her desk working on accounts – the lower portion of the
cabinet stands open, key ring dangling from the lock, revealing a
strong-box inside, along with some tied money bags. A painting on

the wall above her shows a waterfowl looking into her nest where only empty shells remain, her brood swimming off in the stream behind her: the schoolmistress's students are soon to set out into the world.

The school's curriculum covers a broad set of accomplishments, each taught by specialist masters. Thus the young lady suspended by the neck at the picture's center works on her deportment, aided by the weight of dumbells and assisted by a professional hangman. Similarly, a Guardsman at the left, well rehearsed in handling military recruits, teaches a young lady to keep her back straight; a less fortunate girl at the lower left is attached to a chair specially made to hold her neck in place and force her shoulders back; two other girls are secured in iron neck-and-head braces. Two dancing masters attend, both center stage. One, a Turk, teaches his student to hold a tambourine; the other, undoubtedly French, foppishly posed, has pinned on his back a drawing of a costumed and dancing dog. Elsewhere in the room young ladies are instructed in painting, sculpture and drama. A musical performance takes place on the extreme right, with a singer and accompanist executing a "Gaping and Sneesing Duet," the text of which reads "snuffs good for our noses." At the far left two students examine a doll sent from France wearing the latest Continental fashions. On the bookcase next to them the library of liberal studies includes volumes entitled *Court Guide, Court Calendar, Rules of Coming Out, Rules of Etiquette* (a very

12 Edward Francis Burney (1760–1848), *An Elegant Establishment for Young Ladies,* watercolor, pen and ink, 72.4 × 49.2 cm.; London, Victoria and Albert Museum. By courtesy of the Board of Trustees

thick tome) and *Magazine of Fashions*. Just visible through the window is a school sign advertising "Man Traps are Set in These Premises"; at the window a young lady elopes. (The school is located on the road to Gretna Green, the notorious Scottish village on the English border where elopements were legalized in marriage.) Through the window there is a view across the street to a seminary for young gentlemen aged three to eight years – the numbers have been changed to read thirty to eighty, suggesting that the boys will never grow up. Their scholarly pursuits are on a par with the young ladies': flying kites, blowing bubbles, pouring water, or worse, on each other's heads and climbing the roof.

Burney's watercolor drawing, in comically encapsulating the prevailing criticisms of boarding school education, not only touched on its shallowness, pretentiousness and expense, but also on the opportunities it provided for the moral corruption of pupils. As to the last of these, to which I shall return when discussing music lessons, parental fears were sufficiently general for the print market to respond to the subject (Fig. 13, whose verse caption reads):

See, with what Warmth the am'rous Dotard grins,
Admires, instructs, and in Instructing sins!
Nature's too prompt to kindle up Desire,

13 John Faber, Jr. (c. 1684–1756), after Philippe Mercier, *A School of Girls*, mezzotint, 27.5 × 32.6 cm.; New Haven, CT, Yale Center for British Art, Paul Mellon Fund

Without the Masters Touch to stir the Fire.
Parents, beware what Guides for Youth you chuse,
Least where They should admonish, They abuse.
Girls thus, indeed, may sooner learn What's What;
But some Instruction's better lost than got.

MUSIC TEACHERS AND SOCIAL BORDERS

Apart from the governesses and generalist tutors attached to some households, most music teachers in eighteenth-century England taught only music, and those active in London tended to specialize in one or two instruments. (Harpsichord teachers commonly taught thorough bass; others claimed to instruct in "composition," generally meaning rudiments of music, in addition to teaching an instrument.) Outside London demand was apparently insufficient for music masters to survive with pedagogical skills on a single instrument; such individuals in common course advertised competency on several ("Walter Claggett, Musician and Dancing-master, . . . Waits on Ladies and Gentlemen at their Lodgings, To instruct them in DANCING, And the Use of the following Instruments, viz. The Violin, Violoncello, Guitar, German-Flute. Likewise Tunes Harpsichords and Spinetts.")[14] Especially in London teachers also commonly played professionally in the various theater orchestras; others were church musicians.[15] Many were English, but the most sought after were Italian immigrants who came to London in large numbers during the later seventeenth century and throughout the eighteenth. They found ready employment as instructors to the children of the rich, but as aliens, Catholics and musicians, they were at the same time victims of continuous ridicule and condescension. As with Italian opera singers who had made such a mark in London from the early years of the eighteenth century, Italian music teachers were viewed with suspicion as so much foreign rabble. So ubiquitous were these individuals in London society that they were regularly satirized in print and on the stage – it is indeed difficult to find a comedy of manners wherein a music master is represented as English-born. Whether on the stage or in printed dialogues Italian music masters were invariably mocked by their own speech, always given in grotesquely broken English ("Shon, pring te tesk, te moosic pook, / Sholter your muskit, master Shacky; / Alderman for your rossin look, / Fy, vat dam laze tog, dat lackey!")[16] English musicians for their part regularly expressed concern over the competition brought by what they viewed as a foreign invasion. Thus John Playford lamented that every mother in London was "ambitious to have her Daughters Taught by Mounsieur La *Novo Kickshawibus* on the *Gittar*."[17]

Indeed, the social position of music masters was not enviable. Not only were they publicly satirized, they were also made to suffer indignities at the hands of their employers and sometimes even from their students. The German musician John Sigismond Cousser (1660–1727), in London from Christmas 1704 to May 1707, probably supporting himself as a teacher, kept a pocket-sized commonplace book that among other things included a list entitled "Was ein virtuose, so in London kommt, zu observiren sol." It is a compendium of advice, thirty-three items in all, provided him by fellow German Jakob Greber who had been in London giving recitals in 1703–4, including several suggestions on how to behave before the English:

13. Be proud but greet everyone politely, for the English like to be flattered.
14. Dress yourself particularly well, for the lords like to see that . . .
16. Don't let them make a controversy of you. They are masters at this.
17. Prepare yourself with music to fit their taste – no pathos certainly, and short, short recitatives . . .
19. Devote yourself to the English language, and sing an English aria from time to time. That pleases them very much.
20. Praise the deceased Purcell to the skies and say there has never been the like of him . . .
30. The usual honorarium for performing at the home of a nobleman is ten guineas. If afterwards you are invited to dinner and are expected to eat with the steward, make it clear that you would rather leave, then you will be seated at the nobleman's table. NB: This is true for all such engagements . . .
32. If after the meal one is invited to remain when they [the noblemen] begin to drink, one sometimes accepts but sometimes leaves, which pleases them, for although one mixes freely with them, one is not on equal terms. It is better if one joins the wives and drinks tea or coffee with them.[18]

Greber's advice was to be at once proud, which helped establish one's status as an exotic (items 13–14), yet deferential (16). To be successful one played the music the English liked (17), played on their chauvinism (19–20) and at the same time acknowledged one's own fundamental inferiority (30, 32). The reward for all this, as Greber carefully emphasized, was financial gain (a third of the items impinge on economics). As R. Campbell put it in his *London Tradesman*, "in this Country especially, those who practice [music] for Bread are in but small Repute."[19] Charles Burney's career as a music master at a boarding school in Bloomsbury was apparently considered sufficiently injurious to the dignity of his memory that Fanny Burney "did her best to delete every reference to it in her father's 'Memoirs' and other papers."[20]

Yet whatever their ambivalencies, the English received music masters into their homes, and paid them sufficiently that many

foreign teachers were willing to put up with often degrading attitudes toward them in exchange for regular employment. Hannah
More at the close of the eighteenth century complained, hyperbolically, about their ubiquitous presence among the female children of
London parents:

The science of music, which used to be communicated in so competent
degree to a young lady by one able instructor, is now distributed among a
whole band. She now requires, not a master, but an orchestra. And my
country readers would accuse me of exaggeration were I to hazard
enumerating the variety of musical teachers who attend in the same
family; the daughters of which are summoned, by at least as many instruments as the subjects of Nebuchadnezzar, to worship the idol which
fashion has set up. They would be incredulous were I to produce real
instances, in which the delighted mother has been heard to declare, that the
visits of masters of every art, and the different masters for various gradations of the same art, followed each other in such close and rapid succes-
sion during the whole London residence, that her girls had not a moment's
interval to look into a book.[21]

Little was written about the choice of a proper music master for
boys, but for girls a great deal was said, most of it revolving around
the question of respectability. Erasmus Darwin for example
advised that teachers (the vast majority of whom were male)

be chosen . . . as are not only well qualified to sing and play, or to dance
themselves; but also who can teach with good temper and genteel behaviour: they should recollect, that vulgar manners, with the sharp gestures of anger, and its disagreeable tones of voice, are unpardonable in
those, who profess to teach graceful motion, and melodious expression;
and may affect the taste and temper of their pupils, so as to be more
injurious to their education; than any thing, which they are able to teach
them, can counterbalance.[22]

Darwin's tract appeared in 1797, by which time a considerable
relaxation in class relations had occurred as compared with the
beginning of the century. Nevertheless, the text preserves a concern for class distancing and class definition. The music master,
who by standard practice came to the house to give his lesson, was
something of a servant to the family, but he was also an entre-
preneur, at once a tradesman and professional, and also literally an
interloper. His class standing was thus considerably blurred, which
in a society of highly articulated class differentiation constituted a
social threat by its very inexactness. The music master performed in
a way very different from laborers or producers in the normal sense
of the terms. There was prestige attached to his occupation; his
labors did not involve sweat or dirt; the "product" he produced
(skills at music) ultimately was intangible (musical sound). Ironically, in all these ways the music master gave the *appearance* of being
a gentleman. He dressed like one and behaved liked one, at least in
front of his employer (all hyperbolic claims to the contrary not-

withstanding); most important, by the nature of his work he gave the appearance of *being* rather than of *doing*, accordingly sharing in the advantageous side of the equation by which class ranks were established. These were men who might also earn substantial livings, who could come and go as they pleased (though obviously not from their standpoint since they needed employment) and – very important – who had momentary power over a member of the family. (This was very different from the positions of resident governesses and tutors to children of the nobility who resided with the family as part of the extended household. They were classed among servants and thus had little privilege and no status, though they might gain the affection of the children under their care.)

Darwin assumed that the master's behavior would be coarse relative to that of the family, hence the master must adapt himself to his new station and learn how properly to serve his betters. His manners, gestures and voice must all be reformed into something they apparently were naturally not. By such reformation and deference social order was implicitly reconfirmed; this was essential precisely because the music master was perceived as threatening to that order. However, the danger he presented was not limited to his ambiguous class standing. There was an abiding fear of his effect on the character development of his female student. Here was engaged a problem internal to the family, namely, the concern that a daughter might be wrongly constituted by an outside influence and thus either reflect badly on her father, injuring his prestige, or take on those characteristics of the music master that could be reckoned as challenges to the father's authority within the family. To be sure, such a challenge would not ordinarily take the form of an outright revolt; indeed, that behavior could easily be contained. Instead, what was most threatening was a girl child (far worse than a boy) who through whatever means failed to learn the limitations that gender placed on her actions. Hence, those around her, by whom the daughter was molded, must reinforce only female behavioral characteristics. The ideologically perfect music master therefore needed to adapt female character traits as defined by the culture. Repeating Darwin, he had to be of "good temper" and gentility, lack vulgarity, exercise no physical constraint (no "sharp gestures of anger") and exhibit softness of voice. The ideal music master, in other words, should be a male-gender version of girls' mothers, not substitute fathers. Music teachers were thus put in an extraordinarily difficult situation which produced, simultaneously, considerable suspicion, contempt and loathing, all of which was heightened by the fact that music masters were nevertheless universally recognized as sexual creatures, with implications accruing thereto as regards fatherly authority, inter-class relationships and the like. (This will be discussed later.)

Music masters, always eager to attract new students, promised

quick results and ease of effort, their advertising consistently making these claims ("Music. THE Guittar, Harpsichord, and Singing taught in a most easy and elegant manner, by an eminent master
of undoubted character and abilities, who engages to teach any
person unacquainted with music to play ten tunes the first month,
and in three months to be so far accomplished on the [English]
guittar as to be able to play any common piece of music at sight").[23]
And once employment was secured, common wisdom suggested
that music teachers would shamelessly flatter the least talented
pupil to keep the lessons going.

> On terms agreed, Miss C.D.E.
> Is introduc'd to Mr. B.
> *Miss* eyes her future *Master* well,
> While he, *Lavater-like*, will tell
> How much in *Musick* she'll *excell.*
> Whether or not, he's sure to flatter
> *Miss* and her *Parents* on the matter;
> . . .
>
> Just so our *Master*, Mr. B
> Pedantick talk'd of '*tweedle dee*
> And *tweedle dum*' to C.D.E.
> Assur'd her parents, his tuition
> Would make her soon a good Musician.[24]

But for upper-class parents undeserved flattery was not easily
defended against. On the one hand, there was social use value
attached to a daughter's taking up music; an unaccomplished girl
was a poor marriage prospect. This awareness encouraged parents
to accept flattery about their children uncritically. On the other
hand, to accept flattery at face value ran the danger of making one a
fool at the expense of a social inferior, a fact that might henceforth
be *socially* demonstrated every time the daughter was asked – as
they invariably were – to play at family-sponsored house parties.
The inherent tension between the emotional encouragement for
and the social dangers of flattery leads in several directions.

In particular there was the question of the music master's competence. How could an unmusical father judge whether he was get-
ting his money's worth? His wife might help decide, if she were
ever consulted, but then she typically gave up music once she
married. The parents might themselves be concert or opera goers,
but that did not necessarily provide them with a means to judge
pedagogical skills – and for the most part the father would have
little interest in such intricacies of his daughter's education. Refer-
rals were of course of immense importance, though they could not
always be trusted, given that the advice might have come from
someone equally unmusical or uninterested. Accordingly, it is not
surprising that warnings about the dangers of flattery were endlessly repeated in courtesy and conduct books (that is, in a specifically
conservative literature whose primary function was the preserva-

tion of every conceivable socio-cultural status quo), precisely because flattery was so difficult to deal with:

> You will readily allow, that for a young person who has no turn for the
> study I am speaking of, to be condemned both to mortify herself, and to
> punish her acquaintance, by murdering every lesson put into her hands, is
> a very aukward [sic] situation, however much her master may, for the sake
> of his craft, flatter her or her friends; assuring them, perhaps with an air of
> great solemnity, that he never had a better scholar in his whole life.[25]

Not surprisingly, lack of talent was often recognized immediately by those outside the family circle. In 1743 Horace Walpole
complained in a letter written to his friend in Florence, Sir Horace
Mann, that his sister, Lady Mary, had just been visited by a young
Norfolk heiress who after less than three hours in the house, and
visiting for the very first time,

> notified her talent for singing, and invited herself upstairs to Lady Mary's
> harpsichord; where with a voice like thunder, and with as little harmony,
> she sung to nine or ten people for an hour . . . We told her, she had a very
> strong voice – 'Lord, Sir, my master says 'tis nothing to what it was.' – My
> dear child, she brags abominably; if it had been a thousandth degree
> louder, you must have heard it to Florence.[26]

As one author put it, the girl lacking proficiency was nevertheless
trotted out "into *public company*, and exhibits her performance, to
the *well-bred* admiration and *astonishment* of the *ignorant many*; but to
the silent *Pity* of the *judicious few*."[27] What portended was a double
bind for the girl's father. She had to have music; her social station
and marriage prospects demanded it. Yet to let the girl perform in
semi-public could lead to ridicule. And even if she were talented,
public performances raised an equally serious danger of encouraging her independence and lack of deference.

MUSIC LESSONS, SEXUALITY AND SOCIO–FAMILIAL STASIS

For the upper classes the music lesson itself provided an initial
contact with music experienced actively through performing, as
opposed to passively through listening. As a class-based educational
activity, the music lesson constituted a specific point of focus for
parental decisions about the shaping of children in regard to dominant social ideologies. (Whatever the ambivalencies about music
masters or about music itself the lesson was recognized as having
disciplinary value, especially for boys, for whom discipline per se
was almost universally judged an educational sine qua non.)[28]
Because the vast majority of pupils were young females and the
teachers almost always adult males, the music lesson in particular
provided a focus for concerns involving sexuality and its role in
defining social order, to the extent that the social order itself was
built on domestic foundations and highly individuated gender

roles. The music lesson was a means of reproducing the status quo, but it was at the same time recognized as undependable in that regard: its use value could be undercut by the sexual advances of an employee; the violation of a daughter was in such instances the violation as well of class hierarchy, hence doubly threatening. "I wish the singing master may not get one of my Lady Busby's daughters, which you know is a commonly don [*sic*]."[29]

If parents were otherwise unwary of music masters, countless moral tracts, educational guides, novels, verses, stage plays and images were present to warn them, either via deadly serious tales of woe or by high comedy wherein fathers were portrayed as unwitting fools. In nearly all instances the young females were portrayed as weak both physically and morally.[30] Their latent sensuality had to be controlled by others, since they were incapable of attending to it themselves.

One of the more interesting sources on this subject is a transplanted Italian, Joseph Baretti, who in his *An Account of the Manners and Customs of Italy* (1769) described a woman's playing the harpsichord as an auto-erotic experience. His discourse, ripe with sexual imagery, thereby not only represented women as natural seductresses, but at the same time titillated his English male readers with a forbidden, hence desired, image:

Let your imagination represent to you an Italian lady young and beautiful, with all that warmth of constitution peculiar to her country, arrayed in the thinnest silk favourable to the sultry season, sitting at her harpsichord, her fingers in busy search of the most delicate quavers, and languishing to *Mi sento morir* of one of our most feeling composers! Where is the judicious parent who would wish to see his child in so dangerous a situation?[31]

Baretti somewhat ironically admitted that propriety might be maintained in teaching music to English women, in that the English climate might guard them against the warmth of passions innate to Italians, thus cleverly formulating an unfavorable assessment of the erotic economy of England (Baretti's book represented a defense of Italian culture against a spirited attack published a year earlier by Samuel Sharp).[32] At the same time, however, he confessed that Italian music masters typically acquired a "general character of immorality" ("Such is the voluptuous and wicked turn of mind that music gives in Italy to the generality of its professors, the singers especially, that it has brought them into universal disrepute"), and these were of course the very musicians emigrating in large numbers to England. (Baretti hence recommended that girls be taught by "musical women.")[33] Roger North's solution to the problem, writing at the end of the seventeenth century, was to hire older male teachers, those married and with families, who would also have had more teaching experience: "I might add other reasons, such as seducing yong people and betraying them to ruin, which they are too apt to doe; but of that I suppose parents are apt enough to take thought, for if not, their children, being fortunes especially daughters, are in much danger from such gamesters."[34]

John Bicknell, a lawyer and miscellaneous writer, in 1775 published a satire on Burney's musical travel books under the pseudonym Joel Collier. The book was sufficiently successful to be issued in five editions up to 1785, and a final, much altered sixth edition 1818 (which concerns me here). Joel Collier's odyssey took him to Birmingham where he was introduced to a gentleman whose daughter was said to be in need of a music master, a skill Collier professed. He reported that the old man was "of a very severe and suspicious aspect." Collier, trying for the job, claimed "a new and very expeditious mode of teaching to play . . . by which I would undertake to give any young lady of tolerable parts, a *shake* in two lessons, and a *swell* in three." Upon hearing this the old man had Collier thrown out of his house and roughed up by the servants. Collier later learned that the gentleman's daughter, "a very rich and beautiful heiress," had just eloped with her music teacher.[35] The sexuality of the "shake" and biological import of the "swell" is of course the focus of the story, all the more because Collier ironically professed not to understand why his speech had enraged the father.

In a play called *Tunbridge Walks* a man from the country, a Mr. Woodcock, has a daughter whose education concerned him, though he feared her becoming a Town Lady, according to which circumstance

First she's sent to a Dancing School, where she's led about the Room by a Smooth-fac'd Fellow, Squeez'd by the Hand, and debauch'd before she comes into her Teens: I'le be Sworn Dancing Masters, Singing Masters, and such followers o' the Women, make greater Havock among Maidenheads in *London*, than the *Germans* did among the fine Fiddles at the Battle of *Cremona*.[36]

What these and many other accounts of music lessons share is an ideology that renders control of female behavior the responsibility of men, but which is built on the conjunction of two opposing types of males. First are fathers who by their position and status as head of family are responsible contributors to social stability, and whose status must at every step be confirmed by their family's behavior. Second are music masters, by comparison déclassé and viewed as predators. The predacity is sexual, directed against what was viewed in the society as the weakest, least worthy link in the social-familial chain, daughters.

Two satirical drawings of music lessons by Thomas Rowlandson (Figs. 14–15) base their comedy on the sexual play between master and pupil, and on the ignorance or too-late discovery thereof by the male parents, in addition to Rowlandson's typical comedy based

14 Thomas Rowlandson (1756/7–1827), *The Comforts of Bath: The Music Master*, watercolor, pen and ink, 12.1 × 18.8 cm.; New Haven, CT, Yale Center for British Art, Paul Mellon Collection

15 Thomas Rowlandson (1756/ 7–1827), *Reflections, or the Music Lesson*, watercolor, pen and ink, 10.4 × 15.6 cm.; New Haven, CT, Yale Center for British Art, Paul Mellon Collection

on opposing body types (slim handsome lover, fat grotesque father).[37] The images are compositionally similar. In both an elegantly attired young woman sits at a square piano, willingly responding to her teacher's advances while her father (possibly her husband, though it hardly matters) snoozes, or just awakens, before the fireplace in ironic allusion to the archetypal family seat, the locus of privatized domestic bliss. In the first image the daughter wears feathers in her hair, a bird poached. The father is twice mocked: by his sexually assertive daughter (itself a double breach, one of gender rules, the other of the deference expected of her toward her father's wishes) and by a male who is his social inferior.

There are a few images that partly counterbalance Rowlandson's cynicism, such as a drawing by George Romney of a mother and daughter reading from a music book beside a keyboard instrument (Fig. 16), essentially an uncomplicated picture of mutual love and devotion in which music functions as a visual binder for sharing – though Romney's handling of the image is sufficiently classical and, simultaneously, religious in flavor as to dehistoricize it. Its sitters

16 George Romney (1734–1802), *The Music Lesson*, pen and brown ink, 20.3 × 17.8 cm. Photo © Christie's

hardly appear English. Moreover, no outsider to the family partici-
pates. More unusual is a painting of a father instructing his daughter
on the harpsichord (Fig. 17). It is the rarest of representations in its
expression of a father's warm and open love of his daughter,
poignantly evident in his gaze directed solely on her. The girl's
hand position, unusually exacting and correct, confirms that both
teacher and student know something about the harpsichord. Therein lies the explanation for the scene. Mr. Collins, the father, is not
an upper-class gentleman, but almost certainly a professional musician earning his living from music. His bourgeois values permitted
a portrait representation that for a "true" gentleman would have
severely violated portrait – hence social – convention (the male
head-of-household in effect deferring to his daughter by means of
his gaze; ordinarily of course his eyes would meet ours and the
daughter's be averted).

17 John Francis
Rigaud (1742–1810),
*Mr. Collins Teaching
his Daughter to Play
the Harpsichord*
(1789), oil on canvas,
91.4 × 71.1 cm.;
Swettenham Heath,
near Congleton,
Cheshire
(Clonterbrook
House), Collection
G. D. Lockett

ADULT MUSIC EDUCATION AND SELF–TUTORING MANUALS

Music education was not entirely confined to children and adolescents. There are accounts of adults, both men and women, taking up music or continuing its study. The best-known example is of course Samuel Pepys whose 1660s diary makes frequent mention of his formal studies on several instruments as well as voice, and of his wife's unsuccessful efforts as well. (She took up music only in order to please him; by Pepy's account she had a bad ear. Both were brought to ill humour over her lack of progress, and in a last-ditch attempt to achieve something, Pepys finally arranged to pay his wife's singing teacher 10s. – a considerable sum – for every new song she actually managed to learn.)[38] The aristocrat and devoted amateur Fulke Greville summoned the young Charles Burney for harpsichord lessons and supposedly was so pleased with Burney's skills that he paid £300 to Thomas Arne, to whom Burney had been apprenticed, to buy him off and hence let Burney take the job. (It was through Greville that Burney, aged twenty, received his entry into polite society.)[39]

Private musical instruction from a music teacher was often supplemented by the use of published lessons or tutor books that were widely available throughout the eighteenth century for the instruments most commonly played by upper-class amateurs of both sexes. (Tutor books were already marketed in the last quarter of the sixteenth century, and their numbers increased significantly during the seventeenth.) Their popularity is evident in some cases by the numbers of editions required to satisfy a growing audience; John Playford's *A Breefe Introduction to the Skill of Music*, for example, first published in 1654, ran through fourteen editions by 1700 and nineteen more up to 1730 with appropriate revisions along the way.[40]

Tutor books reveal important information about the tastes, state and practice of music among the upper classes, precisely because it was this group of people for whom they were written; moreover, many were written expressly for adult beginners, rather than children.[41] Tutor books met a number of needs for both producers and buyers, most of which ironically had little to do with music itself. Potential financial gain was naturally a strong impetus for both authors and publishers. Music teachers wrote tutors not only to augment their income from direct sales, but also in the hope of attracting new students from the books' readership. That publishers recognized tutor books' financial potential is evident not only in the large numbers of tutors printed throughout the century, but also from the enormous amount of pirating, or at least free borrowing, from one book to another. (On the other hand, the market was so saturated that prices remained modest throughout the century, usually not more than 2s., though harpsichord tutors cost as much as a guinea by about 1750.)

Most tutors were pitched as manuals for self-instruction, either directly or by implication, though in fact hardly anyone could have accomplished much from these books if they began without some grounding in music; even then little progress could be gained without the assistance of a music master. Nevertheless, from the adult buyer's point of view tutors typically promised exactly what was demanded. This included, first and foremost, easy and fast results for dabblers. Tutors thus responded to the demands of cultural fashion: a man or woman could become *à la mode* in little time and with a minimum of effort or money spent.

However, I believe that these stated or implied promises appealed somewhat differently with respect to the two genders. For men self-instruction avoided dependence, as an adult, on a socially inferior music master, and also offered an opportunity to try out an instrument, which if it proved impossible or not to one's liking could be dropped without the embarrassment of a semi-public failure in supervised instruction.[42] For women the issue may have been economic. That is, fathers or husbands may have encouraged self-instruction via tutor books as a means of saving money that they did not want to spend on private lessons for their children or spouses.

Tutor books whose titles included phrases like "Compleat Instructions," "New and Easie Method" or "Plain and Easie Directions" all promised more than they could deliver, though some advertised ease on the covers but in their contents urged that a music master be hired as well. Even Francesco Geminiani, in the preface to his famous *The Art of Playing on the Violin* (1751), falsely advised his readers: "I have added twelve Pieces in different Stiles for a Violin and Violoncello with a thorough Bass for the Harpsichord. I have not given any Directions for the performing them; because I think the Learner will not need any, the foregoing Rules and Examples being sufficient to qualify him to perform any Musick whatsoever."

More than one hundred keyboard instruction books appeared during the century, far more than for any other instrument. (Most were for harpsichord, but about 1770 title pages began to list the piano as well, and by about 1790 began listing the piano first; by about 1795 the harpsichord is commonly dropped from the title altogether.) The earliest keyboard tutors of the century, those by the famous publisher-seller John Walsh, were in fact essentially collections of short dances with some added instructions. Walsh published these texts in a continually updated series featuring new music, thus responding more to public demand for fresh pieces than for instruction per se. In fact, Walsh's tutors in both content and form were mirrored by the majority of such books published throughout the eighteenth century. For example, John Nares' *Il Principio. Or A Regular Introduction to Playing on the Harpsichord or*

Organ (London, 1760?) consisted of only two pages of text followed by thirty-five of music, the whole constituting eight lessons each comprised of one complete piece. Nares claimed that the tutor would "conduct the Scholar step by step from the first Essays of playing to the Execution of difficult Music" – yet his instructions were rudimentary: "a Speck or Dot after any Note makes it half as long again."

The "average" tutor (among roughly 350 published in England during the century) had about twelve pages of text, interspersed with musical examples. The author assumed no knowledge of music on the part of his reader. In fact the entire texted portion often provided instruction only on the basics of notation, fingering, clefs, flats, sharps, natural signs, note values, time signatures, the major and minor keys and basic ornaments. This was followed by the "lessons," typically repetitive, and short dance pieces that from first to last demanded very little of the performer: uncomplicated rhythms, simple key signatures, usually not more than three flats or sharps, narrow compasses and the like.[43] The average tutor book provided only the barest of details even as to how to read music. And missing from nearly all of them is what was most urgently required if real music were to be made: an understanding of what lay beneath notation, namely meaning, and its mutually dependent coefficient, expression. What the vast majority of tutor books imparted was a kind of musically dead positivism: how to count, where to place your fingers.

The pattern I have outlined by the examples of keyboard tutors follows through for every other instrument amateurs played. And the exceptions are few.[44] A case in point was the first surviving tutor in any language devoted solely to the violin, *Nolens Volens or You Shall Learn to Play on the Violin Whether You Will or No* (London, 1695). In one form or another, through later editions with the same title (an eighth *Nolens Volens* appeared in 1716) and paraphrases, the book remained in print to the very end of the eighteenth century.[45] The fact that a 1695 instruction book, one requiring only elementary technique at that, could survive through the entire period is undoubtedly indicative of the minor level of accomplishment among amateurs. *Nolens Volens* and almost all of its successors were books for beginners. As with tutors for other instruments, the music provided consisted mostly of dance tunes and popular airs, continually updated in new editions, mostly for solo violin with or without accompaniment.[46]

The musical education of the English upper classes marked the starting point for music's participation in the on-going reproduction of society. As I have suggested, educational practices operated within the parameters established by dominant ideologies, themselves given expression in courtesy and conduct literature. In subsequent chapters I shall discuss the ways in which the socio–cultural formations molded through educational practices were played out in the musical lives of adults. But first I want to consider another closely related aspect of upper-class education, for children and adults alike, the dance, in order to move from perceptions of music viewed as an abstract, intangible form of expression, to perceptions of music's more direct impact on the physical body, and the relation between the body itself and social order.

Music and the body: dance, power, submission

EIGHTEENTH-CENTURY courtesy and conduct writers addressed
dancing in the same breath as music. And while many opposed the
study of music at least by men, most clearly favored dancing for
both sexes of the well-born. Briefly, men and women were encouraged to pursue dancing for two primary reasons – both simply
stated, the second ideologically packed. First, as vigorous exercise
it was considered beneficial to health; second, it promoted the
development of good body carriage. With respect to the latter I will
argue that dancing promoted a certain *sight*, both on (and more
important) off the dance floor, a visual affirmation of social position, accomplished by means of the way one stood and moved.
But, as I will show, the subject of dance and its practice by men and
women alike was viewed with confusion, contradiction and
ambivalence throughout the century, for reasons that touch on
central perceptions of cultural, social and gender identity, and even
politics. And in regard to all of these, dancing's intimate relation to
music mediated the way in which both forms of expression operated within the society among this social group. My purpose ultimately is to define an ideology of social dancing, relying primarily
on dancing's visual presentation of the body – or more specifically,
of its presentation of one body in relation to others.

In 1722 John Essex suggested that the knowledge of few if any of
the arts and sciences were so necessary or advantageous as dancing,
especially under the tutelage of a good dance-master, both as a
diversion and as an essential exercise. In these remarks, in which
dance instruction is recommended to begin as soon as children (of
the well-born) "can well Walk," Essex acknowledged the art as a
means of correcting or minimizing the *appearance* of birth "defects," literal or metaphorical, misfortunes that were not confined
to the less fortunate classes but which nevertheless were highly
articulated *signs* of lower-class standing. In this way Essex perhaps
inadvertently encapsulated the essential function of dance as the
presentation – and ritualization – of status through grace of body,
accomplished by careful attention to a rule or the imposition of a
particular order. Essex understood that dance was culture, not

nature, ideally to be "naturalized" in children at the tenderest age for the purpose of visually representing social position and thereby helping preserve a status quo. His remarks in other words constitute the (partly hidden) essence of my topic:

> I reckon those who are crooked or ill shap'd, Splay-footed, Baker-kneed, or of an aukward Gate, ought to be the first Persons who should learn to Dance; not because they are aukward only, but because it is high time to correct the Misinformation of Parts, and acquire such a Habit of Body from Dancing, and the Master's Rules of Position, as shall cure, or at least make their Defects less visible. Children should be taught to Dance as soon as they are capable of learning, that is as soon as they can well Walk; the Advantage whereof is this, that it strengthens the Fibres, confirms the Tone of the Parts, and fashions the whole Body to a graceful and becoming Carriage: So much therefore of Dancing as belongs to the Behaviour, and handsome Deportment of the Body, is not only useful, but absolutely necessary.[1]

PHYSICALITY, SEXUALITY AND IDENTITY

John Playford's *The English Dancing Master: or, Plaine and Easie Rules for the Dancing of Country Dances*, first published in 1651 (in print well into the eighteenth century; an eighteenth edition appeared in 1728), was easily the best-known dance collection of its time. As such its short opening address to the reader is significant given its defensive tone:

> The Art of Dancing called by the Ancient Greeks *Orchestice*, and *Orchestis*, is a commendable and rare Quality fit for yong Gentlemen, if opportunely and civilly used. And *Plato*, that Famous Philosopher thought it meet, that yong Ingenious Children be taught to dance. It is a quality that has been formerly honoured in the Courts of Princes, when performed by the most Noble *Heroes* of the Times![2]

(He continued the paragraph by mentioning the health benefits of dance and its aid in teaching gentlemen proper carriage.) Playford published his little book only two years into the Commonwealth and its official recognition of Puritanism, the position of which against public music and dance is well known, though both activities continued of course under prohibitions that were never made absolute. Yet Playford's sensitivity to the ambivalent position of dance in English society carried through the next century and a half, long after the short-lived Commonwealth, and his defense was in many ways characteristic of those that followed him. He cited the authority of the ancients – placing the appropriate words in italics to rivet the eye: he mentioned Greek names for the dance (therefore the Greeks danced) and named the philosopher who approved of it. He asserted the appropriateness of dancing as an upper-class activity ("fit for yong Gentlemen"), one manly in aspect ("*Heroes*"). Playford acknowledged dancing as recreation, yet the pleasures it provided were as such devalued: dancing's worth, as defined by a man presumably keen on profiting from the sales of his dance collection, was not dancing itself, but what accrued from it. At least that was the stance that he felt compelled to adopt for his potential buyer.

The concerns that informed Playford's particular apology for social dancing had their tap-roots anchored in the politics of morality, especially in the relation of moral virtue to human sexuality. Even by the time Playford was writing, these issues had long been the subject of debate, one that continued throughout most of the eighteenth century, though in somewhat altered form. A pamphlet from 1603 voiced the topic in a way that not only identified sexuality as a watchword, but at the same time marked the connection between music and dance as twin components of immoral leanings which together – and through women – contrived to destroy men's virility; misogyny thus entered the equation. Dance was dangerous to the spiritual purity of men who might be (even physically) polluted by women in physical motion:

For, amongst the frivolous pleasures, which, as I may so term it, ravish men's senses with delight, not any one is more coveted than that of dancing; from which nothing proceedeth, but that which favoureth of lust, hateful to every honest man, and ought, in general, to be a disgrace to all . . . Besides, what can be more absurd, than for a man, not hearing the musician's instrument, to be leaping and skipping amongst a company of foolish women, and men worse than they? . . . Dancing is the voluntary, which is plaid before a passage is made to unlawful desires.[3]

Physical motion here is at issue; it is culturally contested. Women inflamed men through movement (beginning with Eve's *gesture* of handing Adam the apple); women should therefore be contained, immobilized (I shall discuss this in detail in a later chapter). Among such writers, women who danced moved for ill purpose, to arouse the passions of men and thereby enslave them: Samson and Delilah. For men, by contrast, dance was movement for no purpose (it accomplished nothing), hence dance was by nature unmanly, for a man's physical actions distinguished him from women. Movement was the tool of his empowerment, of enacting his will. But a man leaping and skipping among women acted only to unman himself, either through debauch or effeminacy.

Simon Eccles, the rigid Quaker convert, in 1667 repeated all this, placed blame on musicians and dance teachers, and indirectly called down Scriptual wrath on them for the ruination of God's English kingdom. At this point the personal nature of sexuality and gender identity was made tacitly political by means of its claimed threat to natural order:

O ye Fidlers and Dancing-Masters, let this President break you off from your filthy practice; Why do you dance without the Ark? Where is your

Ark? What President have you in Scripture for your Danceing? You set up the Devils Kingdom by your proud Calling: You set their Bodies in postures to enflame and take with the lustful Nature in men, and with your proud Apparrel, and Spots on their Faces.[4]

By the eighteenth century few writers condemned dancing with the virulence of those from the 1600s, and indeed most sanctioned social dancing. If this moderation reflected the fact that dancing was a firmly established general practice, it nevertheless remained true that dancing's cultural standing remained uncertain. The ideologies informing Eccles and his anonymous forebear were still operative, if more ambiguously and indirectly stated; often the grounds for criticism shifted from the issue of "morality" per se to that of the social order which presumably depended upon morality's foundations. The dialectic that characterized attitudes toward dancing during this period is evident in the oddly contrary opinions expressed within individual texts. Thus the Rev. John Bennett, writing in 1789 to a female audience, affirmed dancing's usually acknowledged benefits of graceful carriage and health through exercise, but then cautioned that dancing's popularity had grown to immoderate proportions, politely restating Eccles' position: dancing might therefore inspire "too great a fondness for dissipating pleasures, and proportionably abate the ardour for more retired virtues." He saw a passion for dancing as a distraction from domestic responsibilities and closed with a warning: "Besides dancing is not, at *certain* moments, without its temptations. An elegant, illuminated room, brilliant company, the enchanting powers of musick, admiring eyes, obsequious beaus, attitude, &c. are apt to transport the mind a little beyond the rational medium of *gentle* agitation."[5] Bennett focused on protecting female virtue. That in itself reflected considerable change over a century; yet the protection of female virtue was, after all, essentially fueled by the need to preserve male virtue – and position – as confirmed in virtually all courtesy and conduct literature of the time, except for that written by feminists. The real issue was female sexuality and its power to (re-)shape society,[6] an inherent acknowledgment that physicality in women presented a social danger. That is, female sexuality threatened the hegemony of men within the gender hierarchy upon which society was itself structured. Women's capacity for passion, enlivened by dance, might subvert the bounds of "*gentle* agitation" that Bennett recognized as necessary to women's sense of well-being. Dance offered women at least the appearance of empowerment through physical action and the emotions that physicality enlivened. (Women increasingly demanded more freedom which in itself triggered endless amounts of male-authored prose as to why men were divinely intended to dominate them.) Dance was a valve that might release the pressure women's urgings engendered. The problem was that the very presence of a release valve constituted an acknowledgment of pressure and might thereby actually contribute to the increase of that which it sought to dissipate. "*Gentle* agitation", in the metaphor of temperature, was the first sign of approaching boil.

John Locke, not favoring music for gentlemen, nevertheless found dancing acceptable on grounds of its teaching "graceful motions" and "above all things, manliness and becoming confidence." Locke perceived that dancing taught a man how better to control his body and by so doing to instill visually on the spectator of that body an impression of power and status. Yet Locke, like Bennett and others both before and after him, immediately acknowledged that this issue was more complex, for he also identified dance as a potentially destructive source of the very manliness he claimed dance promoted. His concern with the loss of virility, however, was not the sexuality of women but the pollution of a foreign culture embodied in dance-masters. Locke warned that, however necessary dancing might be to the making of a gentleman, "natural unfashionableness [was] much better than apish, affected [read 'foppish'] postures," adding "I think it much more passable to put off the hat, and make a leg, like an honest country gentleman, than an ill-fashioned dancing-master."[7] National identity was built on the preservation of cultural difference, and the purity of this difference for Locke was threatened by dance-masters, the most sought after of which in England were French, presumably the group Locke had in mind. The pollution of cultural purity for Locke was of an especially dangerous sort, because it was rendered visible, and even celebrated or paraded, via the body movements of the social elite and in public (if a public restricted to society's upper orders). All of this will need further discussion here.

John Weaver in 1712, acutely conscious of the ambiguous position of social dancing early in the century, established its pedigree in a *tour de force* of erudite citation of ancient and scriptural sources favoring the practice. He repeatedly acknowledged dancing as a social activity of high civilizations, and further pointed out that dance "fits and qualifies Men to put forth those Endowments, and Embellishments, which would else be obscure, and buried in a bashful Rusticity, and offensive Negligence, extremely prejudicial to every Man's Interest and Reputation." He later added that dancing gained a man the assurance or "*handsome Confidence*" that is "an absolutely necessary Qualification, with regard to the *Fair*."[8] He hyperbolically warned that the man who could not dance would not enjoy love. Like others before and after him, Weaver acknowledged "rusticity" as an accompaniment to Britain's insularity, a cross-class national trait both lamented as a fault and trumpeted as a virtue. As a cultural marker of Englishness rusticity was read as "lack of pretension, openness," but as a social marker it ran the danger of also being read as "oafish," hence lower class or without class distinction. Dancing, among other activities and means, could alleviate rusticity's vice easily enough; the trick was not to destroy its inherent virtue at the same time. Thus Lord Chesterfield heartily recommended dancing to his son, then abroad on the Tour, as one of the "Graces" necessary for a man of the world.[9] But to acquire the skill, Chesterfield suggested a dance-master from Leipzig. That is, Chesterfield accepted the training of a foreigner, but only on the comparatively (culturally) neutral territory of Saxony and not France, though even a Saxon dance-master almost certainly would have been trained by a Frenchman.

One learned to dance from a dance-master. London especially, but also the provinces, had many. The most sought-after were indeed French who in some cases enjoyed considerable status and also became wealthy: "At balls in great houses they [led] out high-born ladies with an air of insolent confidence; favours were heaped on them and substantial fees enabled them to live in luxury and ride in their own coaches."[10] But in England not even financially successful – hence much sought-after – French dance-masters could depend on attaining social respectability, especially because respectability itself was culturally defined by men. Male antipathy ran deep, not only on account of national difference, but also due to the potential threat that English men recognized in dance-masters' activities. Already in 1658 Richard Flecknoe in his *Enigmaticall Characters* described the French dance-master as one who "makes all dance after his *Fiddle*," by which Flecknoe seemed to mean more than the musical instrument, as he combined xenophobia with misogyny by reference to sexual liaison: "He has the *Regimen* of your Ladies Legs, (nay little *Montague* pretended higher yet) and is the sole pedagogue of the Feet, teaching them not onely the French *pace* but the French *language* too, as *Coupéz, passéz, levéz &c.*"[11] In fact, the particular foreignness taken to be most fundamental to French dance-masters was sexual license, with respect both to their own gender identity and to the virtue of English women. That is, the French were seen as characteristically effeminate, foppish, less than men. Yet their effeminacy was not equated with homosexuality; quite the opposite. Instead, they were consistently represented as womanizers and seducers – the loss of female virtue to seduction was easier for the English male to bear than the prospect of an assignation between a déclassé French steward and one's daughter or wife. In fact, the consistent representation of dance-masters as foppish may have rested largely on the fact that they chiefly attended women (upon whose support they depended for their livelihood); such attendance unmanned them in the eyes of English men. But this assessment naturally only reaffirmed that dance-masters' attentions to English women potentially unmanned English men by making them cuckolds, or so the fear ran.

In literature such fears were more easily expressed with respect to female children – a worthless daughter was less damaging than a faithless wife. For example, Thomas D'Urfey's play dating from 1691, *Love for Money*, demonstrated the lust of three male teachers in a girls' boarding school. Here children, without parental guidance or protection, are introduced to Mr. Semibrev, the music teacher, Mr. Coopee, the dancing master, and M. Le Prate, the French teacher, all of whom are sexually aggressive. Le Prate is described in the *Dramatis Personae* as "an impertinent, noisie, singing, dancing, prating, French Fop, perpetually gabling in Company, and crying up for Actions of the French King." This is interesting precisely in that the characterization is never spoken upon the stage, but appears only in the character list. So stated, the description is naturalized (how else would a Frenchman appear?) – and also politicized: a foreigner on English soil forever trumpeting the virtues of French absolutism under Louis XIV.[12]

When made to speak through English authors, French dance instructors were rarely treated sympathetically. Charles Dibdin in his *Musical Tour* introduced a Frenchman on the subject of dance:

Monsieur – Sare – look all over de varld, every ting depend pon larn to *danse. Sans cela* vidout larn to *danse* you cannot vat you call see life – you cannot know noting. De younk chentelmen *danse* away vid dere money before dey come to dere estate; de lofer *danse* away vid de laty to Scotland [that is, elope to Gretna Green]; de *marchand* clerk *danse* away vid the English bank note. Ven de housband find chentelman little too kind to his wife, he don't quarrel, make no noise, he make one very low bo – *serviture Madame.* Vat de devil you call dis but larn to *danse . . . Enfin –* in short, if you vould go vit great *eclat* troo de varld, you must do *comme en France –* vare de *pauvre danse* avay dare *misere,* de *riche danse* avay dare *conscience,* de *general danse* avay from de *enemy,* and all the rest of de varld *danse* away from dare friend, *ma foi.*[13]

Ironically in the very voice of French dance-master, Charles Dibdin thus reaffirmed every argument against dancing that English society had developed. French masters produced social disruption: gentlemen squandered their inheritance before they had it, clandestine marriages occurred, class ranks were disturbed. While clerks robbed to pay for their dance habits, thus aping activities better reserved for their social superiors, wives cheated on their husbands, husbands – emasculated – no longer cared. The poor danced to forget, the rich to forget their morals, and men deserted the field of responsibility. All of these faults Dibdin laid at the doorstep of the foreigner (whose successes he, as a native-born music teacher, deeply resented). Dance here functioned both as a barometer and as a metaphor of the nation's well-being: the grotesque chauvinism of Dibdin's broken-English discourse betrays more than vulgar comedy, for it depends implicitly on the fact that social dancing in England served, for better or for worse, as the ritual re-enactment of various fundamental components of the social and cultural order, here described in a state of advanced dissolution.

In visual representation, as in literature and on the stage, the French dance-master was ugly, thin-waisted and effeminate, a man who seldom stood straight and never still, his form and posture embodying cultural degradation conflated with cultural difference (Fig. 18). In art the very denial of bodily substantiality to French dance-masters (commonly linked to their opposites, very John Bullish natives, Fig. 19) undoubtedly also delineated, simultaneously, their inherent weakness and the irony of their ability to seduce a nation on the very basis of their physical insubstantiality. The weak can subdue the strong, just as the bear-leader can subdue the bear (Fig. 19, the picture-within-the-picture).

DANCE, CLASS AND SELF-REPRESENTATION

It is difficult to overstate the importance of dancing among the upper classes in England during the eighteenth century. Jane Austen noted that it was possible for people to do without it entirely, that some instances were recorded where young people

18 British School (late eighteenth century), *French Dance-Master.* pencil drawing, 15.2 × 10.2 cm.; Whereabouts unknown

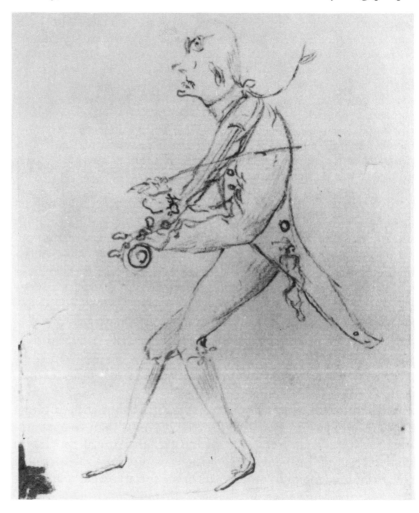

survived for many months without dancing with no apparent damage done to body or mind. But, as she put it, "when a beginning is made – when the felicities of rapid motion have once been, though slightly, felt – it must be a very heavy set that does not ask for more."[14]

Children among the upper orders were often taught dancing from an early age – according to Richard Steele's ironic comment, a

19 Thomas Rowlandson (1756/7–1827), *The Dancing Lesson* (1800), drawing; Whereabouts unknown

girl was "delivered to the Hands of her Dancing-Master" as soon as she was weaned, "before she is capable of forming one simple Notion of any thing in Life."[15] Dance instruction often took place at schools, where children were taught in groups. In 1786 Sophie von la Roche visited such an institution run by four sisters; her account documented the somewhat grim determination of dance instruction approximating military drill. The hall was an amphitheater where more than a hundred girls, aged six to sixteen, took their turns, six couples at a time, for minuets and country dances. Sophie commented that "all the parents subscribe to it and dress up their children, sit all round as spectators, and are either amused or annoyed, according to the amount of applause their children receive."[16] This is the subject of a Rowlandson drawing (Fig. 20), wherein the parents observe the performances with attention and smug satisfaction. What gives everyone pleasure, presumably, is the dancing to the tune, literally and metaphorically, of a very Frenchified instructor. It is through the medium of contrasted body types that Rowlandson ironicizes the event and critiques the participants. The dance-master, pencil-like, towers over not only the children but also their relatives, whether seated or standing. He completely dominates the scene, flitting about on thin legs and pointed toes, the extreme opposite of the thick, stationary gentleman, his foil, on the opposite side of the image. Rowlandson here retells the tale of the Pied Piper. The children, represented as miniaturized adults, to be sure are more attractive than their generally fattened, even grotesque forebears. But it is not accidental that

20 Thomas Rowlandson (1756/7–1827), *The Children's Dancing Lesson*, watercolor over pencil, 22.9 × 37.1 cm.; Boston, MA. By courtesy of Boston Public Library, Print Department

their bodies most closely approximate that of the dance-master in whose image they are being fashioned.

In 1736 a (presumably fictional) letter appeared in *Gentleman's Magazine* from a person describing himself as a man from the country, thirty years old, educated at Eton and Cambridge and now in London, who had never been taught to dance, his father thinking it folly and beneath the dignity of a man of learning. Among company going dancing he was soon asked by a beautiful lady to be her partner in a country dance, but not knowing how, he confessed his ignorance, whereafter "she left me with a Disdain which shew'd her Contempt of me." He asked the editor whether dancing was a reasonable recreation and if "it wou'd not betray my *Folly* too much to learn this Diversion in the 30th Year of my Age." (He wanted another chance with the lady.) The editor responded with citations from biblical history and the ancients favoring dancing and recommended that the man attain the skill so as not to be "either an *ill-natur'd Stoic,* or *ill-bred Pedant.* All that is [n]ecessary for a Gentleman is just so much as will give him a Kind of *Carelessness,* as if it was rather a *natural Motion* than a *laborious* and *artificial Acquisition.*"[17]

Not knowing what to do, the gentleman had the good sense to stay off the dance floor. But others more boldly plunged in. Indeed, it is clear that dance-instructors earned considerable sums from adult, rather than juvenile, pupils. The demand for instruction from adults reflected a changing cultural and social climate. In the case of the former (cultural climate), social dancing, in particular for men, became increasingly *de rigueur* rather than optional (women apparently had more consistently been given dance instruction), and this meant dancing mediated through French traditions. In the case of the latter (social climate), it reflected social climbing and the blurring of class distinction, as the middle orders aped the behaviors of the upper.

Literary and visual representations of galumphing dancers, usually men, were common throughout the century and are worth examining for more than their intended humor. Thomas Gordon, for example, described a "country entertainment" in which "the Majority made such a Rattle on the Boards, as quite drown'd the Musick. This made me call to Mind your mettlesome Horses, that dance on a Pavement to the Musick of their own Heels." Gordon described the local squire's eldest son, a bachelor and captain of the militia, who on the dance floor "not only threw down most of the Women, and with abundance of Wit hawled them round the Room, but gave us several farther Proofs of the Sprightliness of his Genius, by a great many Leaps he made about a Yard high, always remembring to fall on somebody's Toes."[18]

Both this account and that from *Gentleman's Magazine* tell tales about gentlemen, but for an audience of others. That is, the fictive anti-heroes come from the country; the readership is primarily from the city (London). The social class critiqued in these satires, was the same as that of the presumed reader. The humor was nevertheless achieved by the common technique of establishing and valorizing socio-cultural difference, in this instance that of town versus country. Dancing thus constituted a mark of urban sophistication, together with a Continental air, unavailable in its pure form to provincials. In these instances French intrusions, however else they may have been problematic, were positive forces as signifiers of subcultural difference, hence status. This phenomenon helps explain why French dance-masters succeeded in London and the other major centers. Indeed, the triumph of French dancers came apart from – even in spite of – political realities. (Thus in the season of 1780–1 two Frenchmen, father and son, named Vestris, lately come from Paris were all the rage on the London stage, despite the fact that the two countries were at war – even the King attended their performance at Covent Garden.)[19]

Nevertheless, the ambivalence of reception of French dance-masters (and what they taught) was never overcome in eighteenth-century England. And this is best borne out, significantly, by *visual* means in satirical drawings and especially prints, the latter mass-marketed cheaply. The one subject that recurred more than any other in this regard was the dancing lesson for adult learners (Figs. 19, 21–23). In some cases these prints played off the problems of men and women whose childhood education did not include dancing (provincials, parvenus). But apart from an audience of rank beginners, there were two other important reasons that French dance-masters were employed by adults: the popular social dances of the century were extraordinarily complicated, especially by comparison with almost all of the dances of our own time, and they were constantly changing. This is to say that anyone willing to put themselves on public view at a ball or assembly required constant instruction and practice simply in order to know the latest dances and to be able to execute them properly. Needless to say this fact forced adult English men and women into permanent subservience to their French instructors, compounding the problem of cultural pollution with that of a perpetual teacher–pupil relationship in which the "natural" social order was reversed.

Rowlandson's dancing lesson (Fig. 19) encapsulates the visual conventions of these satirical representations. Most notable, again, is the difference in body types of the two men in the foreground, the English gentleman depicted as overstuffed, almost furniture-like (and as difficult to move), the French master thin and taller than his student. At the back a second gentleman waits his turn, seated in misery with his feet stuck in a hollowed-out wooden device employed to stretch the leg muscles. But his pain is emotional as well. Perhaps harder to bear than his aching legs is the fact that he is being

21 John Collett
(c. 1725–80),
engraved after,
*Grown Gentlemen
Taught to Dance*
(1768), engraving,
31.4 × 24.8 cm.;
London, British
Museum. By
courtesy of the
Trustees

made to wait until his own "employee" can attend to him. This is more than role/class reversal; it is gender reversal as well. The fat, immobile man adopts the waiting aspect culturally assigned to women; as such he is entirely comic and pathetic.

"Grown Gentlemen Taught to Dance" (Fig. 21) repeats much of

this imagery, though this dance studio may be of a higher order in that the master has employed a separate fiddler for the occasion. (He plays with one broken string; he is both blind and deaf – his ear trumpet rests at his feet.) The man at the back sits with his feet in proper dance position (but without the leg board), the unnaturalness of the self-imposed constraint perfectly evident. (A sheet tacked to the wall just above his head reads: "Grown Gentlemen taught to dance, & qualify'd to appear in y^e most brilliant Assemblies, at the easy Expense of 1$^£$ 11^s 6^d. NB. those Gentlemen that chuse it May also learn to sing.") The two central characters are powerfully differentiated, and in such a way that the very tall master in every sense commands his adult ward. The English gentleman (with a copy of *The Blunderer A Comedy* in his pocket) virtually cowers to his master's gestural instructions. He bends his kness to execute a dance step, and at the same time affirms his inferiority. His face is rendered not simply as fat, but as baby-fat, a physical metaphor of his reversion. Additional commentary is provided by the little dance book at the feet of the fiddle player, *Country Dances, The Lad's a Dunce*, and by the scrapping cat and dog: a mixing of "species" that cannot produce a happy end. What the image emphasizes more than anything else is role reversal, where the real master abrogates his social position to become a servant to a foreigner, waiting like a servant to be summoned by his servant, a transposition made more damning in that the affair is entered into willingly. England surrenders to France; the elite cave in to the rabble. This episode echoes a scene in Edward Ravenscroft's *The Citizen Turn'd Gentleman*, a translation-adaptation of Molière's *Le bourgeois gentilhomme* (1670), in which Mr. Jordan calls for instruction in the minuet and his dancing master obliges with the following: "Come, Sir, begin; your hat Sir; so now your honour la, la . . . not to fast, la la . . . keep your leg straight, la la . . . don't hunch your shoulders so, la la . . . you carry your arms as if they were broken, la, la . . . hold up your head, keep your toes out . . . don't loll out your tongue, la la . . . and make such faces, as if you were on the close stool, la, la."[20]

The violation of sexual taboo (men dancing together) delineates the central paradigm of this socio-cultural perversion. The portrait of a graceful and nimble "Madame Elastique" hanging above the dancers shows that their success depends upon their replicating the gestures of a woman. Her image finalizes the scene's absurdity by the additional implication that English men degrade themselves in this fashion essentially to please their would-be female dance partners. This is subservience of the worst kind, based on the loss of gender hierarchy and as equally disruptive to cultural order as abetting the imposition of a foreigner's will.[21]

Representations of women alter this visual formula to produce quite different results (Figs. 22–23).[22] "Grown Ladies &c. Taught to Dance" (Fig. 22), the companion print to the one just discussed,

22 Rennoldson (act. 1760s), after John Collett, *Grown Ladies &c. Taught to Dance* (1768), engraving, 32.7 × 23.8 cm.; London, British Museum. By courtesy of the Trustees

addresses neither role reversal nor cultural difference. Instead, the image constitutes fairly straightforward misogyny built on the cultural cliché of female vanity. In the background two attractive girls (they embody the "&c." of the print's title) whisper of the absurdity of the old woman's youthful pretension as she accepts the flattery – and hand – of her French master, over whom she towers, a physical difference that mocks both of them, at once making him less of a man and turning her into a kind of grotesque scarecrow, accentuated of course by her wrinkled face framed by a highly inappropriate wig. The old woman is mocked both by the girls, and by the master whose flattery she both compels as part of their financial arrangement and heartily swallows, as we see by means of the girlish gestures of daintiness and modesty signified by her arm and hand gestures. That she is being led around by the nose is evident from the picture-within-the-picture on the back wall, where a monkey leads a be-gowned cat.

In another print of similar title (Fig. 23) Vanity's monkey still holds court, now holding a lady's fan. On the back wall we have the dialectic of two images, a Watteauesque couple gracefully dancing, on the right, and the bear-leader, on the left. Since gracefulness is nowhere evident in the scene below the pictures, the difference-by-analogy is clear. The same waiting seen earlier still prevails, but the level of grotesquerie is increased. The parameters of the feminine are ironically presented: tall, skinny and old (a dried-up stick), short, fat and young (a bovine creature with enormous hands and with legs that appear not to reach the floor), stupid and uncomprehending. The only intelligence evident is in the face of the French master whose business sense is astute, though his only dance success in these chambers will be with the little dog standing between the two women. Again, in both images the satire is redirected away from the overriding socio-cultural and even political issues evident in the representations of men and toward the easy and perennial target of women qua women whose supposed vanity precludes their being ideal examples of their sex.

All this relates closely to another subject for which a number of visual and textual satires exist, "Boarding School Education, or the Frenchified Young Lady" (Fig. 24). Here again misogyny and vanity make the argument, via the anecdotal metaphors of a monkey instructing a puppy, and a mirror on the back wall. (In European culture monkeys had long been held as libidinous and vain. In art the association of monkeys with vanity was often signified by giving them mirrors to hold, the identical attribute used to signal the vanity of women. The conflation of monkeys with women thereby represented women as less than human, as irrational, vain and dangerously sexual.) Two new elements also operate in this image. First, it is noteworthy that the young woman at the left is relatively attractive at least in body, though her face is unintelligent.

She is slim and moves with grace, and hence contrasts utterly with her piglike companion, profiled to exaggerate her bulk. Both are analogues to the puppy in the foreground, innocently being taught "to dance" by the French "monkey." They are fruit ready for harvest: the Frenchman's ogling of the slim one is satirically evident from his exaggerated eyebrows that seem to leap out toward her. The conquest-by-gaze is already complete, though she herself is (necessarily) totally uncomprehending of the fact. The second new feature of the print is the matter of class rank and social position-

23 P. Crochet (act. 1768), after Daniel Dodd, *Grown Ladies Taught to Dance* (1768), engraving, 26.1 × 22.4 cm.; New Haven, CT, Yale Center for British Art, Paul Mellon Collection

via-geography. The fat dancer is the daughter of a country gentleman, the thin one of a farmer; they are provincials. We are told this
via the images on the back wall, country scenes with dwellings
appropriate to each. In other words, the French dance-master plays
wittingly for a seduction and unwittingly for the crossing of class
and social boundaries (these females ought to be milking cows), the
anger over which this engenders I have discussed in a previous
chapter.

CONTRARY REPRESENTATIONS OF SOCIO-CULTURAL ORDER

At this point I want to focus more directly on the types of social
dancing practiced in England during the eighteenth century, starting with the minuet, in order to explore in greater depth contemporaneous perceptions of dancing in its relation to social order.

Though the precise origins of the minuet are somewhat obscure,
the dance was established at Versailles under Louis XIV in the 1650s
and 1660s, and fast became the predominant dance of the French
aristocracy. By the early eighteenth century it had crossed the
Channel, where it remained in vogue until c. 1750 (though it did
not entirely disappear until the nineteenth century). Two issues
concern me here: how the dance looked and, on account of its look,
how the dance functioned ideologically and hence socially.

The minuet's aristocratic bearing, enshrined by its formality,

24 British School,
*Boarding School
Education, or the
Frenchified Young
Lady* (1771),
engraving, 24.5 ×
34.9 cm.; New
Haven, CT, Yale
Center for British
Art, Paul Mellon
Collection

exaggerated grace and complexity of structure, grew from its use at Versailles as one of the means by which Louis XIV exercised control over the courtiers forced against their will to live months at a time under his roof. At Versailles the minuet (in fact, like other dances) was begun by the King and his partner, with all other couples following his lead. But once Louis had initiated the dance, he withdrew to the sidelines the more carefully to watch his semi-permanent guests perform their routines *for his benefit* as proof of their loyalty.[23] In the King's perception of dancing's function, a courtier who failed to perform well might be devoting his time to tasks impinging on the King's stately powers. To commit a *faux pas* under Louis' surveillance (literally, in the policing sense of the word) was sufficient to cause temporary banishment from Court and a cut-off of financial support. The astute courtier, in other words, stayed entirely out of state politics, devoting instead many hours a week pent up with his dance-master in order to learn and rehearse for each evening's entertainments.

The minuet was a ritualized microcosmic social order, exactly replicating a real one. It demanded an exactingly prescribed be-havior. The dance was extraordinarily complicated, not because its steps in themselves were so difficult, but because it involved precise control over the entire body, from the carriage and turn of the head to the position of the arms, wrists, hands, legs and feet. By dancing the minuet in the prescribed manner (the only way permissible), the French aristocracy nightly affirmed *visually and formally* their sub-mission to the King – and, equally important, they did so *silently*, moving without speech in time to the music and under the King's watchful eye.

The minuet began with a bow, a mutually acknowledged defer-ence to one's partner as well as to the dominance of the King who watched and waited. As such, in the Versailles minuet, the bow was not a simple (or natural) gesture. Its form, like all else, was highly articulated and self-conscious – best evidenced by the dance trea-tises of the time which devoted enormous amounts of space to describe its correct execution – two chapters in one text, sixty pages in another, and the entire book in the case of a third.[24] The dance itself reiterated submission and control at literally every step, for, as the name of the dance itself asserts, the individual steps were invariably tiny (*menu*), hence unnatural, constrained, all the more because the constraint had to be performed effortlessly, as if it were natural movement. The dance's tempo was slow to moderate, that is, deliberate, rationalized, non-spontaneous. Actual climax was prevented, for no energy was allowed to build: the individual dance-units were only two bars long. Nearly every step ended with the dancers' weight concentrated on the balls of the feet, a highly unstable stance that affirmed their weakness, especially by com-parison with that of the very stable, seated King. Similarly, the

dance ended with couples turning several circles, always in elaborate step patterns, in anticlimactic gestures of graceful stasis.

Throughout, the body's carriage was expected to be "*douce.*" Yet
this did not signal naturalness, but actually its oxymoronic opposite: naturalized control. The grace of the body in the minuet was
the signifier of total submission of the de-individualized courtly
society, the surrender of bodily power to an order imposed from
without. Submission was of course masked in beautiful gesture, in
the smooth textures of an imposed calm. In sum, the minuet
constituted the visual affirmation of French politics and state authority; it represented discipline imposed from above and outside
the self. Not necessarily danced voluntarily, the minuet was required in order to retain one's personal status and prestige. (Later in
the century, and after the death of Louis XIV, in France and
England alike the minuet was replaced by the infinitely more
energetic *contredanse*/country dance; yet balls and assemblies continued to pay it lip service by starting with a single minuet, then
abandoning it for the newer, freer forms. By preserving the minuet
for the start of balls, rather than simply dropping it, it is possible
that the dancers took pleasure in ritualistically "killing" it anew,
over and over again, thus re–celebrating liberation by temporarily
reinstituting the authority of that which was overthrown.) But, as
so far described, all this concerns issues internal to France. What of
England?

The minuet's introduction into England came not only through
dance-masters but also by way of translations of French treatises,
and also by texts first published in England. These books served a
capacity similar to self-tutors for musical instruments. In the first
part of the century the minuet received much attention. Kellom
Tomlinson's *The Art of Dancing Explained by Reading and Figures*
(London, 1735), for example, devoted nearly forty pages to the
minuet, along with sixteen plates illustrating steps and gestures.
(He devoted only three pages to country dances.) The subscribers'
list to Tomlinson's book contains nearly 170 names of men and
women from the aristocracy and gentry, as well as those of dance-
masters, including a number of names of individuals living outside
London.

However the upper-class English learned the dance, the minuet
signified to them nearly everything I have already suggested, and
something more: it represented France – a state, a political system, a
religion and a culture at once profoundly familiar and foreign, both
admired and despised. The introduction of the minuet into England
was severely complicated and compromised by these contradictions which were in fact never overcome. Yet the issues that sur-
faced were fundamentally, if not altogether exclusively, class
specific. They did not go much beyond the concerns of the upper
orders of English society. That is, the minuet engendered deep

concerns about self-definition and national identity only among those who were in social positions allowing them to define the latter and worry about the former. (What the minuet's introduction into England did *not* specifically introduce were questions of social class and class blurring, except as regards the class pretensions related to boarding school education and the like discussed earlier, an issue that would have existed without French dancing. This issue did arise with respect to country dances, as I shall discuss presently.)

English ambivalence toward the minuet can be examined through visual representations, notably in an unusual family portrait by Zoffany (Fig. 25), where the minuet itself constitutes the subject occupying the center of the picture space via embodiment in the gracefulness of the daughter's form. The girl's weightlessness achieved through dance contrasts sharply with the weighty stasis of the other family members to the right, in particular the girl's mother sitting stiffly and staring off into space (in fact, neither parent looks at the girl). To be sure, it is an odd painting, but this is not due to any lack of skill on Zoffany's part. It is because he has a socio-culturally impossible task to perform. The daughter is to be shown accomplished. We know she played the piano – Zoffany

25 Johan Zoffany (1733–1810), *A Family Party, The Minuet*, oil on canvas, 99 × 124.5 cm.; Glasgow, Glasgow Art Gallery and Museum, McLellan Bequest

includes it in silent witness to her musical skills – but that by itself apparently was not enough. She also danced (here with her little brother as temporary partner). Yet to show her off as a dancer was to distract from other family members who were, of course, more important. Here they essentially serve only to frame that which is visually much more interesting and they suffer on account of it. Zoffany compensated for this by making them uninvolved. The mother sits as though she were in another portrait where none of the distractions of the dance occur. The father adopts the usual cross-legged pose of easy assurance, his dominance somewhat pre-posterously asserted by means of the conventional baldachino-like drapery incongruously floating over his head. (The eldest son accompanies on the flute – though badly, judging from the way he holds the instrument, and takes a back-seat to his sister, in itself a profound upheaval of family hierarchy otherwise demanded by the narrative: dancers require accompaniment.) I am suggesting that the very form of the image is disrupted by allusion to the minuet – it is the minuet's gestures that the girl executes. Indeed, Zoffany painted her with the air of Watteau, whose work he admired. But what resulted was a visual dissonance, literally a French intrusion into English space, both formally (how Zoffany painted) and liter-

26–29 W. Dickenson (act. 1787), after Henry William Bunbury, *A Long Minuet as Danced at Bath* (1787), stipple engraving, 21.7 × 214.9 cm.; London, British Museum. By courtesy of the Trustees

ally (what he painted). As a result the image denied itself the easy affirmative qualities the conversation piece normally produced, and as such subverted the Englishness of the sitters. The French intrusion, centered around an event, a French dance, interrupts a visual order otherwise functioning to affirm an English socio–cultural order. (Zoffany concentrated all his attention on the sitters themselves, on their body types and gestures. This lends greater impact, hence meaning, to them than commonly occurred in his portraits, where the settings themselves were highly decorative and distracting.)

In a quite different way precisely the same is true of a satirical print called "A Long Minuet as Danced at Bath" (Figs. 26–29). Most striking is the form of the image, an extraordinarily rectangular print (actually a strip sequence of four prints, since its extreme rectilinarity could not be contained on a single plate of a standard press). The print, well known in its time, comically problematized the minuet not only by its literal content – what is represented – but also by its form. In content, Bunbury represented the minuet via a series of ten couples, each of whom executes a different gesture of the dance. Some dancers are attractive and accomplished, others are homely and graceless (the seventh man steps on the dress of the

eighth woman, not his partner, thus making his ineptitude worse). One is confused (the third man), others apprehensive (last couple) and so on. There is much to laugh at, since two essential components of the minuet are either missing altogether or are effectively made absent by their occasional presence (whereas they should be everywhere manifested), namely, decorum and, especially, grace. The minuet, in a sense, has been Englished, in a peculiar, quasi-anarchic way. But of course the minuet's adaptation into English society has not so much been de-Frenchified as its proponents have rendered themselves absurd. At this juncture the prints' form plays a crucial role, for by violating pictorial conventions via extreme rectilinearity, it powerfully articulates the cosmetic absurdity of the minuet's French formalism. These dancers simply do not get it, and make fools of themselves for pretending that they do.[25]

In order to make better sense of my analysis thus far concerning the minuet, it is necessary to consider country dances, which increasingly gained the attention of the English during the same period. The history of the country dance is lost in the obscurity of folk dancing. But by the mid seventeenth century and the publication of Playford's treatise they were already accepted by the upper strata of English society. Around the beginning of the eighteenth century they became popular on the Continent, though they could no longer be considered "folk" dances.[26] In particular, English country dances were popularized and adapted in France, where they were called *contredanses*. In altered form they were introduced back into England, the cotillion in particular, a round or square dance, as opposed to the longways form more common to English country dances.[27] In whatever form, country dances were extraordinarily popular on the Continent and in England alike, and the reasons why are directly reflected in what may be termed the politics of movement associated with them.

Country dances were, essentially, the opposite of the stately minuet. In tempo they were fast and in spirit gay. Their meters were duple and the phrase lengths four times those for the minuet, eight bars instead of two. By comparison with the minuet, country dances were social, informal and interactive – in its early form in England, prior to its reintroduction by French dance-masters, steps per se were less important than social interchange.[28] This is evident in a drawing by Rowlandson illustrating a round dance type of country dance (Fig. 30). To be sure, the apparent intent of the image is to detract from any stateliness that the participants may imagine is their social due, an ironic undercutting of which Rowlandson achieved by his characteristic juxtaposition of opposing body types – fat-thin, short-tall, as well as strong-profile caricature and the like. Yet on a political level Rowlandson undercut himself by the fact that his visual opposites interact so happily. Men and women join hands and with childlike enthusiasm move about the floor, each to her or his own highly varied skills and concerns. Indeed, as was typical of English country dances, at least in their earlier history, social interaction was more important than individual steps or gestures, so long as things kept moving. The beautiful hold hands with the ugly, the young with the old. Rowlandson created a visual community (all of one social class) – toward which he was sympathetic, given that nearly half of the dancers are represented as physically attractive (the three young women and the older man in the center at the back).

In the most common longways form of country dancing couples lined up in a row, men on one side, women on the other. Usually there were at least three couples, but very often the instructions, as in Playford's *English Dancing Master*, call for "Longwayes for as many as will." Unlike the Versailles minuet, where one couple danced at a time to public scrutiny, the country dance was, at least in spirit, all-involving: as many could join in as the room (ideally rectangular) would accommodate. The dance's pattern was shared by all, passing from one couple to another, each couple moving gradually to the head of the line. To be sure, it was a dance type of considerable order – each person having to execute the dance steps properly otherwise chaos resulted – but each person shared equal status with the others (and a different couple started each dance). This contrasts with the Versailles minuet where movement per se was everything and social interaction essentially irrelevant. Under Louis XIV the minuet was less a social dance than a test which, successfully passed, allowed one to retain membership in courtly

30 Thomas Rowlandson (1756/7–1827), *Round Dance*, watercolor, pen and ink, 19 × 31.8 cm.; Honolulu, HI, Honolulu Academy of Arts

society. But as regards the way it was danced, one couple at a time before the King, the minuet belied the nature of the society its function underwrote: the minuet inherently announced itself as a coercive device.

There was in effect a single minuet, whatever the accompanying music. There were by contrast as many country dances as there were tunes: endless variety was the most essential component. Each country dance tune required the learning of new combinations of movements (a boon to dance-masters). Thus Playford's *English Dancing Master* contains one dance per page, each consisting of one or two lines of melody beneath which are brief textual instructions for the dancers. In the first edition (1651) there were 104 dances in all (about seventy-six of which are the longways type). By the 1728 eighteenth edition, the anthology swelled to 900 dances, each with separate instructions!

What is striking about these numbers is the social politics that informed them. At Versailles the minuet's form, in its seemingly timeless unity, constituted a statement of orthodoxy, a kind of loyalty oath on the part of the dancers and an assertion of power on the part of the King. But with 900 country dances in a single collection no individual could hope to possess control. Indeed, the variety of dances was so great and the speed of change in popularity so fast that dancers employed crib sheets to help them get through an evening's entertainment. Most common were ladies' fans (Fig. 31) printed with the latest tunes and brief instructions on the movements to be used for each. In a word, the politics of the country dance, by comparison with the minuet, was democratic (within the

31 Dance Fan (1793), hand-colored stipple-engraving; London, British Museum. By courtesy of the Trustees

confines of the upper class). This is not to suggest that the English Court, even in its condition of diminished power, was incapable of exerting influence. It did, but in a way that only confirmed its political weakness. In the annual celebration of the "King's Birthnight Ball" a new dance was composed and notated by the court dance-master, then printed and distributed for sale. Individuals hoping to attend had to know the dance.[29] Yet this royal dance could not dominate the evening in the way of the minuet at Versailles. Its status was momentary – and needless to say, failure to dance it well could not result in anything worse than gossip.

The country dances' progressive movement, where each couple in turn took each position in the hierarchy of couples, where gaiety and speed overwhelmed formality, where each dance was different from the last, together expressed the fetishization of change itself. The negative dialectics inherent in this taste for change, and specifically in the semiotics of the dances themselves, however, suggested that such change might not be confined solely to the dance floor. It might spill over into the social structure. That is, within the class domains of society's upper strata the country dance, even in its French-influenced versions, activated and problematized historical memory of the dance's popular origins. This memory, constructed from the semiotics of physical movement, heralded and mirrored fundamental social restructuring. As Sachs described the phenomenon, "The advance of the *contre* is analogous with the rise of bourgeois society and the decline of the aristocratic culture."[30] Country dances in Elizabethan times presumed the mixing of the entire household, servants taking their places alongside their masters, villagers alongside local gentry.[31] Yet in this instance the dances confirmed not change but stasis, the eternity of feudal order, a secure, seamless social hierarchy. It confirmed its own correctness. In the eighteenth century by contrast, country dances were performed in class-specific groups, as was common to all social dancing, and this affirmed not stasis but change. The physical exclusion of the lower classes from upper-class balls and assemblies normally was a sign of hierarchical superiority. But the introduction into these balls and assemblies of the (rather de-rustified) music and dance of the lower classes contradicted exclusivity; the lower classes intruded in spite of themselves – without knowing it, so to speak – as present absences.

Occasionally these concerns found expression in visual form. My examples (Figs. 32–33) are nominally comic, though the comedy is recessive in favor of what can only be called pastoral "charm." Here two country dances have been moved back outdoors, in a visual embodiment of historical memory which in no sense reflected eighteenth-century practice among the upper orders (it is clear the individuals involved are people of status). In the first instance (Fig. 32) professional musicians provide accompaniment, the little band obviously having followed the revelers into the landscape. The dancers all but constitute a Maypole group, if we accept the large tree's function in that light. But more noteworthy are the physical gestures of both couples signaling an unself-conscious abandon and joy, especially in the men who have uncharacteristically, presumably temporarily, allowed emotion to take control over their conventional reserve. Most of the same applies to the second image (Fig. 33) but with three essential differences. First, the musicians are "rustics," in Watteauesque fashion playing the hurdy-gurdy and shawm. Second, the dancers now appear in the costumes of a

32 George Dance (1741–1825), *Country Dance*, pen and wash, 29.4 × 50.8 cm.; San Marino, CA, Henry E. Huntington Library and Art Gallery

33 Henry William Bunbury (1750–1811), *Ladies and Gentlemen Dancing*, watercolor, 35.4 × 58.7 cm.; Toledo, OH, Toledo Museum of Art

French *fête champêtre*, albeit anachronistically. Third, they have an audience. All present, except perhaps for the musicians, are from the upper classes. Those looking on, far in the background and off to the side, are themselves almost like shadows, de-emphasized to benefit the two couples at the frontmost picture plane. But they clearly look on, all of them at full attention, and from the positions of their heads, especially those of the women, there is a scent of melancholic nostalgia in the air.

At this point the two images sharply diverge. For in the first what is celebrated is the momentary – and fictional – freedom of a frolic outside the bounds of the assembly rooms, a semi-private revel. But in the second the image is troubling, as nostalgia always is, in its utterly false reconstruction of history, an aristocratic Arcadia: Bunbury gives us the gardens of Versailles in England, in effect, a reality that never was. Memory as lie; memory coping with a (deteriorating?) present.[32] The remainder of my comments on country dancing will consider this issue.

DANCE AND THE DIALECTIC OF ENLIGHTENMENT

At this juncture I want to consider more directly the relations between dancing's physicality and social order, as constructed around a paradigm of rationality versus irrationality. In *The Tatler* Addison wrote a comic letter describing supposed events occurring next door to his rooming house. He told of how he was awakened by a sudden shake of his building several times repeated, followed by his landlady coming to him for help. Her nextdoor neighbor had let rooms to a youngish, genteel man a few days earlier but now feared that the man was mad. Addison approached the man's door, rapier at the ready, and looked through the key-hole:

there I saw a well-made man look with great attention on a book, and on a sudden, jump into the air so high, that his head almost touched the ceiling. He came down safe on his right foot, and again flew up, alighting on his left; then looked again at his book, and holding out his right leg, put it into such a quivering motion, that I thought he would have shaken it off . . .

After this, he recovered himself with a sudden spring, and flew round the room in all the violence and disorder imaginable, till he made a full pause for want of breath.[33]

The man turned out to be a dance-master. After conversing with him a while Addison returned to his own quarters, so the story ends, "meditating on the various occupations of rational creatures."

To be sure, the letter is focused on the comic, yet the particular way Addison structured the story brings to account metaphors that represent order and disorder on a socio-cultural level. The dancer's gyrations are hyperbolically described, the effect of which is to make the man appear possessed (upon entering the dancer's room Addison is surprised to find him cogent, which he attributes to the dancer's being in a mere "lucid interval"). In other words, the dancer's extreme physicality stands in as a metaphor for irrational behavior. Further, his movements shake not only his own dwelling but also Addison's next door. Now clearly this is a literal impossibility, which the reader understands, thus shifting Addison's story into metaphorical gear: the man's actions have import beyond himself; the effects of his actions are played out in the community. The order of both the immediate community (the dancer's own building) and a surrounding one (Addison's) is disturbed. The nature of the disruption is described in terms of extreme physicality, more animal–like than human (and threatening: "I got up as fast as possible, girt on my rapier"). In closing, Addison underlined this comparison by reference to rationality and its absence. What was given in *The Tatler* as entertainment was at heart, like all satire, serious, the concerns revolving around national identity and, above all, social order.

In the first-act aria "Se vuol ballare" from Mozart's *Le Nozze di Figaro*, Figaro (a servant) expresses anger over his master the Count's designs on Susanna, to whom Figaro is engaged. Figaro pledges revenge. But as far as the text is concerned, he does so only comically, in an apparent contest of wits pretty much literary standard fare in servant–master relationships. What Figaro *says* is that if the Count wants to cut capers, Figaro will call the tune. What underscores the socio-political sentiment of these words is Mozart's music, specifically his use of two opposing metric patterns associated with dance: what is absent, or at least highly sublimated, textually, is present musically.

The "dance" to which Figaro "invites" the Count begins with a 3/4–time minuet: courtly, aristocratic. However, Mozart soon ruptures the conventional stateliness of the dance by surprising off-beat rhythmic punctuations that would cause chaos on the dance floor (all this is in an aria, not an actual dance). First he mocks the minuet, then he simply replaces it. Halfway through the aria Mozart abruptly changes both tempo and meter, as Figaro becomes more assertive, moving to an aggressive 2/4 presto *contredanse*. Now Mozart's combination of minuet–*contredanse* echoes the common practice of beginning a ball with a single minuet to be followed immediately by country dances, but with an essential difference. In *Figaro* the minuet is not simply succeeded but interrupted, overthrown. The change is sudden, unexpected. It is a musical revolution carried out beneath a tame, unthreatening text. The musical order heralds a new social order, all of librettist Da Ponte's efforts to neutralize Beaumarchais' original highly political play notwithstanding.[34] In Mozart and in Addison alike (from one end of the century to the other), dance is implicitly understood as an expression of order/

competing order, stability/instability. As the people dance, so to speak, so goes the nation.

In all their popularity, country dances, whether English or French-inspired, demanded the imposition of mechanisms to control their meaning in ways that supported the socio-cultural ideologies of the upper classes. This was notably achieved in con-temporaneous dance treatises which consistently atttempted to pre-serve in all social dancing the aristocratic air of the minuet via the careful articulation of body carriage and gesture. Kellom Tomlin-son in his *The Art of Dancing* (1735, though written in 1724) thus provided minute directions to achieve proper standing, walking and bowing (eleven pages to the last) – all prior to one's setting foot on a dance floor; and he described the body, part by intricate part, as regards the function of each in dancing, from the nose (which "points out the graceful Twists or Turns the Head makes") down to the joints of the toes.[35] Pierre Rameau's treatise devoted nearly fifty pages to the proper movements of the arms and wrists in various dances, and likewise provided an acutely detailed account of the proper manner to doff one's hat, replete with engraved illustration.[36] Only men of leisure could hope to have sufficient time available to learn such skills of self-definition as given in John Essex's amended 1710 English translation of a famous treatise by Raoul Auger Feuillet, where no less than six pages of notational signs were required to account for the requisite hand gestures and foot movements proper to social dancing.[37] Ironically, the pre-cision of decorum demanded by these treatises could hardly be maintained in a country dance, but this in fact undoubtedly only heightened concern therewith. In any event, there can be no ques-tion that dance and dance gesture, as well as body carriage not strictly part of but appropriate to the dance (standing, etc.), were self-consciously perceived as a principal means of establishing a class hierarchy of the human body. As Giovanni-Andrea Gallini, one of the most famous dance-masters of his time, put it:

When once an habit of easy dignity, with an unaffected air of portliness, has been sufficiently familiarised, it will constantly shew itself in every even the most indifferent gesture or action of the possessor . . . Does he come into a room? His air immediately strikes the company in his favor, and gives a prepossessing idea to his advantage.

Gallini was specific as to what he meant by contrast to this portrait, as when he described a young woman lacking in all such skills. Failing to execute a correct "curtesy," she "hangs her head, and makes her obeisance with her eyes fixed on the ground, or pokes out her head, sticking back her arms, *like one of the figures in Hogarth's dance* [my italics]." In a word, such a lady gave the appearance of an urban peasant.[38]

It is significant that Gallini would refer to a printed image by

which to make his point. He did so precisely because the
memorable/memory image is what his prescribed gestures were
intended to create, the failure to do so threatening instead to result
in a grotesquerie from the Hogarthian pantheon. It is important to
point out that the convention of gesture as outlined for the social
dancing carried over into imagery, in particular – for my concerns –
to portraiture, by which the same class-specific, class-defining
meanings were commonly achieved by artists and described by
artist-theoreticians.[39]

John Weaver in his *Anatomical and Mechanical Lectures upon Dancing* (1721) explicitly outlined the class distinctions delineated by
body carriage and physical motion. In his politics of motion, the
upper classes moved with seamless smoothness, at once natural-
(ized) and ordered. The lower classes by contrast moved haltingly,
without grace. Without question Weaver's paradigm is true as
regards a peasant's execution of the minuet, but it is patently false
with respect to the rhythms laboring people establish in the routines
of their work. Conversely, persons unused to working with their
hands immediately display clumsiness when required to take up an
unfamiliar tool. This says something quite obvious: as long as one
group defines the rules (in this case, ones outlining the means by
which bodily grace is measured) only they can win the game:

From the Regular or Irregular Position, and Motion of the Body, we
distinguish the handsome Presence, and Deportment of the fine Gentleman, from the awkward Behaviour of the unpolish'd Peasant; we discover
the graceful Mien of a young Lady, from the ungainly Carriage of her
Maid; and this Regulation even stamps Impressions on the Mind, which
we receive from the outward Figure of the Body; for as the Soul is
inform'd from the external Objects of Sensation, how careful ought we to
be, to give the most agreeable Impressions, which cannot be affected
without this Regularity; and how commendable, how advantageous is it,
for a Gentleman, or Lady, to be *Adroit* at every Step, and, that every
Motion, and Action of the Body, be consonant to Symmetry and Grace.[40]

It is tempting to explain these gestural intricacies to French
influences of the early eighteenth century and to the minuet in
particular: all very unEnglish. But such an explanation fails when
we examine a book by Thomas Wilson on English country dancing
published at the end of my period in 1820. What is striking about
this treatise is evident in its title, *The Complete System of English
Country Dancing*. That is, country dancing was here *rationalized*.
What this text established was an order, a scheme of classification,
one presuming its opposite, disorder. What I suggest here is not a
false accusation; to be sure, from Playford onwards country dances
were passed on through instructions, either verbally or with
choreographic notation – but in Playford, as in dance fans, these
instructions were normally very cursory. By contrast, what

Weaver had in mind was something very different. He opened his lengthy book (over 300 pages) with the following:

A COUNTRY DANCE, As it is named, is almost universally known as the national Dance of the English, and as correctly known, is constructed on mathematical and other scientific principles, clearly displayed in its operative effect, when properly and well performed.[41]

Wilson thus established at the outset two significant premises: first, that country dances were national in character, and second (in fact as corollary to the first) that they were constituted on rational grounds ("mathematical and other scientific principles"). That is to say that country dances were quintessentially English precisely because they were highly rationalized. I am suggesting that by the early years of the nineteenth century in England the *contredanse*, represented in Mozart as revolutionary, had been completely subsumed by the dominant culture (though to be sure that was a culture reformulating itself within boundaries that now also encompassed the wealthy sectors of the middle class).

Toward the end of the book Wilson appended a previously published chapter on ballroom etiquette as it related particularly to country dances, and to more recently introduced species such as quadrilles and waltzes. With respect to country dancing, Wilson outlined a code of behavior dependent on (self-)policing, all in an effort to control spontaneity:

No person during a Country Dance, should hiss, clap, or make any other noise, to interrupt the good order of the company.

No Lady or Gentleman must, during a Country Dance, attempt at Reels, or any other Figures, in the same room.

Snapping the fingers, in Country Dancing and Reels, and the sudden howl or yell too frequently practised, ought particularly to be avoided, as partaking too much of the customs of barbarous nations [in part he makes reference here to the Scots, whom the English essentially considered ungovernable].[42]

And if disputes arose they must be referred to the Master of Ceremonies "and his decision abided by." The Master of Ceremonies, playing the twin role of king and chief justice, was himself to wear a sash "or some conspicuous ensignia" to distinguish him from the rest. And in this metaphorical nation, whose citizens ideally moved only to prescribed order, there was even to be a written constitution: "To preserve greater order, and to prevent disputes, it is advisable, that the proprietors, or the conductors of Public Balls and Assemblies, should have the foregoing Etiquette, particularly so much of it as relates to the company, written and hung up in some conspicuous part of the room, during such evenings as the Balls or Assemblies may be held."[43] The resemblance to the systematized behavior at Versailles under the Sun King is not difficult to recognize.

DANCE AND THE METAPHOR OF FAMILY HIERARCHY

The rage for dancing of all kinds, especially among the young, caused other sorts of social disruptions, the most interesting of which were familial, since the family was considered the hull to society's ship. Essentially dancing raised questions about every possible combination of intra-familial relationship, that is, between spouses, and between parents and their children of both genders. The characters in Hannah More's novella, "The two wealthy farmers; or, the history of Mr. Bragwell," provided a parable formulization of these concerns. The rich Bragwells, including their two dreadful daughters, are *au courant*, frivolous, arrogant and selfish. Hannah More opposed them with a family headed by Mr. Worthy, alike in numbers and wealth, but different in every other way. Daughter Betsey Bragwell showed her true colors at a dance, at the expense of her foil, the young, good, basically simple Mr. Wilson who made the mistake of asking to be her partner. As the elder Bragwell related:

But when he asked what dance they should call, miss drew up her head, and in a strange gibberish [French], said she should dance nothing but a *Minuet de la Cour*, and ordered him to call it. Wilson stared, and honestly told her she must call it herself; for he could neither spell nor pronounce such outlandish words, nor assist in such an outlandish performance . . . Seeing her partner standing stock still, and not knowing how to get out of the scrape, the girl began by herself, and fell to swimming, and sinking, and capering, and flourishing, and posturing, for all the world just like the man on the slack rope at our fair. But seeing Wilson standing like a stuck pig, and we all laughing at her, she resolved to wreak her malice upon him; so, with a look of rage and distain, she advised him to go down country bumpkin, with a dairy maid, who would make a much fitter partner, as well as wife, for him, than she would do.[44]

In this story, told by a woman, several violations of social order ensue as a direct result of the allowance of a French minuet. Betsey Bragwell herself is displayed as a foreigner whose language the natives do not speak. As such, and because of her behavior throughout, she dishonors her father by making herself an object of ridicule to the entire assembly. Bragwell *père* has squandered money on her, given the results attained, and degraded himself into the bargain. By contrast, Mr. Wilson, the good Englishman, whose simplicity and natural unaffected goodness registers against Betsey's artificiality, is rendered impotent by Betsey's outburst. Unable to lead her in the dance, he is left to stand helplessly (or, more appropriate no doubt, slump) on the sidelines, a "stuck pig": metaphorically bleeding – and by the hand of a woman. Betsey meanwhile further violates convention by dancing alone. She becomes instantly androgynous by this act, for she subsumes the role of her male partner together with her own. Her gestures on the floor are whorelike; they also break class rank, being likened to those of a circus performer. By attempting to assert power over a man she considers stupid and beneath her she destroys herself unawares. Her final insult to Wilson, telling him to go marry a dairy maid, constitutes the last straw. Indeed, a similar challenge laid at Wilson's feet by another male would have required public retraction or retribution. Betsey Bragwell expresses an uncontrolled individuality (totally out of keeping with the ideology informing Wilson's dance treatise), particularly unacceptable on account of her gender. Her violations of social order cannot be tolerated; hence the audience derides her through laughter.

THE WALTZ AND THE BOURGEOIS ORDER

The country dance, supplanting the minuet, triumphed through most of the century, though its socio-cultural meaning (less so its form) evolved in the direction of an increasingly rationalized conservatism. But near the century's end country dances themselves gave way to a new dance, the waltz, the ascendancy of which defined the advance of a new social order, the emergent bourgeoisie, that would come fully into its own in the nineteenth century. Edward Francis Burney, c. 1800, illustrated this new dance in a way that perfectly captured the profound social changes it both engendered and mirrored (Fig. 34).[45]

In one sense his image is bitterly nostalgic, for what it recalls by a

34 Edward Francis Burney (1760–1848), *The Waltz* (c. 1800), watercolor drawing, 47.5 × 68.6 cm.; London, Victoria and Albert Museum. By courtesy of the Board of Trustees

present absence is the social–dance world of the century just past, the assembly hall of Bath's Beau Nash where decorum itself was fetishized. The floor rules for Burney's gathering, like those at Bath and in Thomas Wilson's aforementioned book, are also written out in elaborate detail (at the top center), sixteen in all, appropriately signed by "Solomon Wiseman." But each is silly, a mockery of former rules which a man at the extreme left in the background is destroying with a stick. The dancing that Burney illustrates is either ridiculous or vulgar; it degrades the upper-class people performing it – and scandalizes the morally superior lower-class witnesses standing in the balcony at the right (one lower-class mother forcibly carries her daughter away from the temptations she watches). In a related vignette a sheet affixed to this same balcony draws attention to a missing dog, in fact described as a woman: "STRAYED, A Grown Pug Bitch, answered to the name of Dreary, was missing after the WALTZ was danced last Assembly night. Anyone bringing her [here the sheet is 'torn' by Burney] good . . . no questions will be asked." At the back of the room, unobserved, hang royal portraits, including one of Elizabeth I looking on in all her stateliness; the glorious past they represent is forgotten. Just above these portraits, hence just above the dominant couple at the center of the image, is the Latin reminder of vanity: *Sic transit gloria mundi*, pointedly flanking both sides of a ticking clock.

But it is the central couple that is most important, for they are marked by Burney as the hub and key to the entire assembly. They are characters in a state of languorous collapse, self-contained, not social (no longways dance here), their twin shapes forming a sort of circle. The woman is represented well within the traditions I have elsewhere described, as a passive but most willing inducement to sex and hence the ruination of a man. The man, on whom Burney concentrates his most pointed satire, is physically womanized in every way imaginable: his hair in its abundance, gloss and curl; his body in shape, especially his hips which are distinctly female; his feet in their daintiness; and his face in its utter androgyny. This is a world come apart, the reasons for which are not of course the result of dancing but which, in Burney's hyperbolic representation, are nevertheless perfectly reflected therein and replicated thereby. It is for him a new world wholly negative, and an adjustment of the social order that will permit no happy return.

The male at music: praxis, representation and the problematic of identity

AT THE CLOSE of the seventeenth century Roger North wrote that the musical instruments appropriate to men were "the viol, violin, and the thro-base-instruments organ, harpsichord, and double base."[1] North's list was somewhat idiosyncratic, as is obvious from the lacuna of wind instruments, especially the recorder (the alto instrument in F) and transverse flute; but otherwise it reflected the typical preferences among male amateurs from England's upper classes. As the eighteenth century dawned fundamental modifications to North's list occurred. The popularity of the viola da gamba quickly waned as the violoncello replaced it; the domestic chamber organ, fairly common in the seventeenth century, was much dominated by the harpsichord and, late in the century, by the piano which itself gradually replaced the harpsichord.[2] More important, the playing of all keyboard instruments by men generally fell from favor (for reasons I shall later discuss). In fact, the instruments predominantly played by male amateurs during the eighteenth century were only two: the violin and, especially, the transverse flute, the latter after the recorder's sharp decline in popularity by the third decade of the century. The reasons why some instruments were used and others not, and why all instruments played by amateurs were used with gender exclusivity, were non-musical, socio-cultural in origin – reasons which also determined to a significant degree the functions of music in English upper-class society. In this chapter and the next I intend to trace this history by defining the relationship between musical practices among males and females and the problematic of gender identity, and to consider the ways in which the gender-uses of musical practices participated in the development of social roles and social structures.

AMATEUR MUSICIANS

Only the rare eighteenth-century English memoir preserves any account, however passing, of a parent encouraging a boy's musical interests, and most of what does exist dates from the earlier part of the century, closer in time and spirit to the last remnants of

Renaissance humanism which favored music. Thus Marcellus Laroon (1679–1774) – painter, soldier, musician and even music teacher – described an education that included music instruction and frequent home concerts: "I was then about seven or eight years of age, and was judged to have an inclination to music, by being found scraping on a fiddle in some private place. I was then put under Moret's discipline, to learn to play on the violin. [My brother, on the viol, and I] both made such progress, that in about two years we could perform *à livre ouvert*."[3] Garret Wesley (1735–81), 1st Earl of Mornington, father of the Duke of Wellington, studied the violin from age nine to fourteen – his father also played the instrument, apparently "well (for a gentleman)," as was typically the phrase. He "had always a strong inclination to the harpsichord" and fought with his sisters to get at it. He played this instrument and the organ throughout his life and composed, mainly glees.[4] The poet William Mason (1725–97) received encouragement and early instruction from his father and was devoted to music throughout his life; he played harpsichord, organ and piano (he was among the first in England to appreciate the piano, having brought one from the Continent by 1755).[5] Amateurs like these, all distinct exceptions, came to music early and with the explicit encouragement of their fathers. Indeed, that pattern (father to son, not mother to son) seems to be the operative paradigm in such cases. As adults these individuals often promoted various sorts of public or semi-public musical activity. Thus Henry Needler (1685–1760), who was also first taught the violin by his father, was active in the Academy of Ancient Music for more than thirty years. And Joah Bates (1740–99), a civil servant and amateur organist, teamed with Sir Watkin Williams Wynn and the Earl of Sandwich to establish the Concert of Ancient Music starting in 1776.[6]

Public acknowledgment of musically talented upper-class males was rare in the eighteenth century, hardly surprisingly given the ambivalences discussed in Chapter 2. One exception occurred in a listing of amateur performers printed early in 1787 in three different London papers.[7] Thirty-six people were named, nineteen of them men. Most came from the ranks of the nobility (ten men, ten women), including from the royal family – the first named is George Augustus Frederick, Prince of Wales and future George IV (1762–1830). Others were involved in banking, the military and other professions. While the list could in no sense be considered comprehensive, it may at least indicate individuals willing to be identified as devoted amateurs; as such, the list is short. Moreover, the musical assessments of individuals cannot be blindly trusted. For example, the Prince of Wales is described as "possessed by an uncommon musical genius," an opinion by no means universally held at the time. Charles Burney was complimentary about the Prince's ability to *discuss* music, but Burney was also ever in awe of royalty. Haydn said that the Prince played "quite tolerably" for an amateur (he played the violoncello and sang), but Haydn was used to deferring to patrons. John Wilson Croker, the Tory leader and Secretary to the Admiralty, remarked by contrast that the Prince's voice was "not good" and that he sang only by ear. "He is therefore as a musician very far from good."[8]

Moreover, the list's author apparently had difficulty fleshing out his assembly and felt the need of adding to it at least one individual from outside England, a "Miss Hamilton," the first wife of William Hamilton, who resided for many years in and around Naples where her husband held an ambassadorial post; they rarely returned to England. To be sure, Catherine Hamilton's musical abilities were well known. But she had in fact been dead five years when the list appeared. (Beyond that Catherine was a keyboard player, not a singer as listed – here the author may have conflated her with Hamilton's mistress, later his wife, Emma Hart, with whom he took up in 1786 after his first wife's death.)

Time and again the women named are lauded (Lady Melbourne, "A very brilliant performer on the harpsichord") – or, if their talents are limited on one instrument, they are still noteworthy on another (Miss Hudson, "A tolerable harpsichord performer; and still more accomplished as a singer"). The assessments of men are by contrast considerably more modest. In fact the most that can be said of a number of them is that while they loved music they actually played it with only modest aptitude. Lord Berkeley's instrument was the violoncello, "and though not a first-rate player, he accompanies very correctly"; Lord Balcarras "plays the flute tolerably well; which is not surprising, considering the predilection of his family for music"; Captain Tate "plays superior to most amateurs"; Lord Grey de Wilton "plays the fiddle; and though not a brilliant performer, has the credit of reading music with quickness, and stopping correctly in tune"; Lord Kinnaird "plays the fiddle and tenor . . . : – he is not in any great celebration for his performance; but a charming set of quartetts, by Shield, being inscribed to his Lordship, we thence rank him among the *cognoscenti*." In other words, this paean to male amateur musicianship is somewhat pathetic, assuming that these men constituted London's best. In fact throughout the century the nobility provided few examples of personal musical accomplishment, though a number of them loved music, and a few actively patronized musicians and, at least early in the century, even maintained private orchestras – among the best documented are Richard Boyle, 3rd Earl of Burlington, and James Brydges, 1st Duke of Chandos, both of whom played the harpsichord and were of course associated with Handel's early career in England.[9]

For the most part, well-placed (if untitled) "gentlemen" constituted the larger group of devoted amateurs, though none left an account of musical interests and practice anywhere near as detailed as that found in Samuel Pepys' diaries from the 1660s,[10] or Roger North's (c. 1651–1734) assorted manuscripts from the early years of the eighteenth century.[11] Morris Claver (1659?–1727), a physician at Wells, Somerset, kept an almost daily diary between 1718 and 1726, as well as other assorted personal records beginning in 1684. He loved music and played the full range of instruments typical of men, and more: harpsichord, organ, violin, bass, bassoon, flute, oboe; he also sang. Like Pepys, he played music with his servant, and of course with other male friends. Claver may have been the organizer of the Wells Music Club that met on Tuesdays and played the music of the major English and Continental composers of the time from Purcell, Byrd and Croft to Handel, Scarlatti and Vivaldi, among many others. His diary references indicate that evenings were often given over to music-making and that when possible he also devoted the daytime, especially afternoons, to making music with friends (he often named the composers whose works were played).[12] Charles Burney's close friend and longtime correspondent, Thomas Twining (1735–1804), besides being a clergyman, was also a classical scholar and a great music lover. He was the grandson of a man who had prospered in the tea and coffee trade, a business also followed by his father (and continuing today under the family name). He led a comfortable and quiet life in his parsonage near Colchester. He played organ, harpsichord and piano as well as the violin. And he made a number of lengthy visits to London to hear music – according to Fanny Burney his taste, like Burney's ran to "the modern and the Italian for melody, and the German for harmony."[13]

Equally serious about music, but probably more typical, was painter Thomas Gainsborough. He was devoted to music – at one point writing that he preferred it to his primary occupation ("I'm sick of Portraits and wish very much to take my Viol da Gamba and walk off to some sweet Village when I can paint Landskips and enjoy the fag End of Life in quietness and ease")[14] – and he counted among his friends a number of prominent professional musicians, including the Linleys, William Jackson, Johann Christian Bach, Johann Christian Fischer and Karl Friedrich Abel.[15] Moreover, he bought many instruments, including violin, violoncello, viola da gamba, harp, harpsichord (which he nevertheless hated), oboe and perhaps theorbo (at least he tried to buy one after having seen the outmoded instrument represented in a Van Dyck painting. Yet he seems to have played none of them well – and some not at all. William Jackson, whose assessments of Gainsborough's musical abilities were harsh, indicated that he took as much pleasure in looking at a violin as in hearing it, admiring the instrument's shape, proportion and workmanship.[16] As Jackson described it, Gainsborough moved from one instrument to another, seemingly hoping to replicate easily the beautiful sounds he had heard issue from them when played by a professional: "Many an Adagio and many a Minuet were begun, but none was compleated – this was wonderful, as it was Abel's *own* instrument, and therefore *ought* to have produced Abel's own music!"[17] It was in the context of discussing Gainsborough that Jackson made a more general assessment of male amateurs: "Should a performer of middling execution on the violin, contrive to get through his piece, the most that can be said is, that he has not failed in his attempt."[18]

The documentary evidence I have outlined here regarding actual musical practices, tastes and abilities demonstrates, if nothing else, how fragmentary is the account that exists. It is clear what instruments were played, less clear what music (except that much of it was popular and easy, though the distinctions between popular music and "art" music were still considerably blurred in England throughout the period). We can infer a good deal about amateurs' musical tastes and talents, but for the most part we must do so without benefit of the written comments of the practitioners themselves (whether male or female), and only occasionally from their auditors. Few accounts speak in more than one or two sentences about a given musical event or assess either music or musicianship.

REPRESENTATION, MUSIC AND MALE IDENTITY

Visual representations of upper-class musical activity, portrait paintings in particular, provide a primary means by which the historian can penetrate the relative silence of written records such as those I have cited here. (To be sure, art works can only haphazardly inform about given individuals' musical abilities, such as whether they could hold an instrument properly, assuming artists' abilities to render such detail accurately – visual art is an extremely problematic source for the positivistic study of performance-practice.) Visual art's value to a socio-cultural history of music develops, as I discussed in Chapter 1, from the "fact" of pictorial conventions, which are properly understood not only as ways of painting (thus described by the histories of style and technique) but also, and primarily, as ways of seeing (thus described by the histories of society and culture).

Seeing in the sense I mean it is not necessarily self-conscious or even "intentional." To the extent that such seeing was culturally "naturalized," especially through artists' ideological affinity – real or faked – with those whom they painted, the pictorial conventions implicitly became "the only way to paint." (I hasten to add that ideological affinity cannot be taken for granted but can, nevertheless, usually be assessed on the basis of evidence internal to individual images.) This suggests no more than that for any ideology to become hegemonic it must delegitimate, hence undercut, competing ideologies. Thus what *was seen* in images – what normally was expected *to be seen* – was "the way things are, or at least as we want them to be recognized." This is not to suggest that eighteenth-century patrons who ordered portraits assumed they were commissioning two-dimensional replications of themselves. Rather they assumed, and the artist understood, that what was produced would represent them well to themselves, their social equals and inferiors, and to future generations. This was accomplished via the conventionalized language of pictorial flattery, to be sure, but more important, it was built on a visual vocabulary the individual and collective elements of which constituted prestige in the society and culture. Images might lie about fact; they seldom lied about the willed "creation" of socio-culturally useful fictions which contributed to the making of "true" historical fact.

Now when this vocabulary included musical referents and, in addition, when the musical sitters were male, the inherent socio-cultural problematics presented a distinct challenge to the artist, precisely because the "visual situation" given by the sitter as the artist's subject fundamentally conflicted with pictorial convention. A circle had somehow to be squared, unless of course the image were to be presented satirically (with the foreknowledge of the sitter, which was occasionally the case as I will later show). At the simplest level, the conflict arose over the competing interests of men who may have loved music sufficiently to have its trace included in their portraits, but who were nevertheless part of a culture which increasingly and systematically marked music as improper for a man. How could an artist represent that man as both a musician and a still-proper member of upper-class English society? In responding to the challenge of the oxymoronic Musical Gentleman, artists time and again provided the historian with ample evidence of the socio-cultural importance of the task. In the remainder of this chapter I want to examine this problematic – male identity and its relation to music – in detail and from a variety of angles in order to understand more fully the place of music in eighteenth-century society.

English upper-class parents ordered portraits of their children, often posing with them in complete family groups, with increasing frequency, especially during the second half of the century. Parents' desire to preserve these likenesses reflected an increased value placed on offspring, as reflected in the prices they were willing to pay portrait artists for these commissions. For example, Sir Joshua Reynolds, admittedly better paid than most, received as much as £150 to paint children.[19] This is to suggest that parents, in spending such significant fees, took the representations very seriously. Without question, this applied to the likenesses themselves. But I am here more interested in the vocabulary of gestures selected for the children, the choice of portrait props and the paintings' background

milieu. (Obviously, children were modeled according to conventionalized patterns; a portraitist would in most instances make a
careful sketch of the sitter's face but produce the rest of the body on
the basis of standardized formulae – young children do not as a rule
sit well during modeling sessions.) Gestures, objects and settings
were the devices by which ideologically correct meanings accrued
to the facial representations. That is, in a portrait the facial features
generally provide the means by which the sitter's identity is established. But everything else surrounding the sitter's face informs the
viewer not so much as to what the sitter is like but why he or she is
important. (The exceptional portrait accomplishes much more than
sitter-identification in the representation of facial features, but this
can hardly be claimed for the vast majority of portraits by the many
dozens of very average painters to the trade.) What matters most is
that children were represented in the image of their parents' values,
in which sense they laid claim to the future by means of an eternalized present.

Now with regard to male children musical accouterments rarely
appeared as portrait props, except for one instrument, the drum;
and this instrument – a toy for toddlers[20] – was not used to reflect
parental encouragement of music, but as a device associated with
the life of action, power, statecraft and duty, the primary prerogatives of the well-born male. (Drums were employed as props
almost exclusively for the children of the nobility.) George Watson's family portrait (Fig. 35) is typical of dozens of others with
respect to these issues. Charles St. Clair, the husband-father, 13th
Lord Sinclair, presumably dressed in the uniform of a lieutentant-
colonel of the Berwickshire Militia, stands with his first wife,
Mary, who in turn supports their son James. The child, perhaps
two years of age, stands on the table vigorously beating a drum
hanging by a strap around his neck. The child mirrors the father.
Both make allusion to soldiering, both protectively encompass the
wife-mother; the child stands atop a table so as to be equalized in
height to the adults, thus making more convincing his "protective"
role. His gesture with the drum sticks is obviously masculinized by
the artist. That is, the boy beats the sticks with both a vigor and
intention (obvious in his determined face) that simultaneously pro-
duces a boy-man; he engages less in play, more in duty.

The socio-cultural expectations visually encompassed by the
drum for male children of the nobility, the first-born in particular,
were deeply held and profoundly valued. As a visual device the
drum was neither accidentally chosen nor merely decorative, as is
made clear by the striking and logically incongruous inclusion of a
pair of prominently displayed kettledrums, covered with crimson
drapery and gold tasseling, in an elegant group portrait (Fig. 36) of
Algernon, 7th Duke of Somerset, and his family. The player is
young Lord Beauchamp, son of Algernon. In a domestic setting,

the image of kettledrums leaves nothing to chance; their striking presence cannot be explained as a reflection of use, for they were not employed as toys as were child-sized infantry drums. Instead, they function only as signs that assert the elevated status of an important family and claim certainty for the continuance of the line through the male heir – the sexual implications of their shape and number requiring no explanation – who will be every ounce his father's son. Yet the painter's representation of the boy presents his viewers with a visual oxymoron, an internal problematic for which there is no easy explanation – or social solution. I do not refer simply to the sexually ambiguous dressing gown the boy wears, for that reflected custom (in fact, the kettledrums mitigate the gown's androgynous aspect somewhat, and this may have been intentional). Rather it is the fact that while Algernon holds with one hand the mallets with which to strike the kettledrums, hence establishing that it is he who is associated with them, his other hand is held by his mother, Frances, Duchess of Somerset, and it is toward her, and not his father, that he directs his body. The net effect, certainly unintended, is to belie the very assertion made by the kettledrums in

35 George Watson (1767–1837), *Charles St. Clair, 13th Lord Sinclair, with his First Wife and Son James*, oil on canvas, 233.7 × 142.2 cm.; Private Collection

36 Charles Phillips (1708–47), *Algernon, 7th Duke of Somerset, and his Family* (1732), oil on canvas, 74.9 × 91.4 cm.; Alwick Castle, Collection Duke of Northumberland

their front-and-center placement in the portrait. The drums are literally the most important item included, precisely because they visually raise the stakes of the representation. They have been rolled out in front of a boy who, judging from the way he holds the mallets, has never before laid eyes on them. Yet the intention is clear, if only in its failure to convince: in effect the kettledrums are the ideological ink for the boy's tabula rasa. (Convention demanded that the boy in some way be touched by his mother, thereby establishing her own fulfillment of familial responsibility. These contrary and competing pictorial demands define the problematic faced by the painter and only imperfectly resolved.) The same effect was undoubtedly intended for the drum hanging at the waist of five-year-old Francis Archibald Stuart, grandson of the 9th Earl of Moray (Fig. 37). But as in the previous painting, its effect is undercut by the boy's sensitive features and tentative, almost

37 Thomas Beach (1738–1806), *Francis Archibald Stuart* (1798), oil on canvas, 76.2 × 63.5 cm.; Private Scottish Collection

clumsy grip on the sticks. The face does not match what the body was made to do.

Zoffany's portrait of Prince Frederick, second son of George III and Queen Charlotte (Fig. 38), shows the boy wearing a military coat and the ribbon of Bath. At the right are a suit of seventeenth-century armour and a large infantry drum. Both objects, scaled to an adult's size, dominate the scene and overwhelm the boy. That is,

38 Johan Zoffany (1733–1810), *Frederick, Duke of York* (c. 1770), oil on canvas, 172.7 × 151.1 cm.; Whereabouts unknown. By courtesy of the Courtauld Institute of Art, London

39 Thomas Frye
(1710–62), *Jeremy
Bentham at Age
Thirteen* (c. 1761), oil
on canvas, 180.3 ×
119.4 cm.; London,
National Portrait
Gallery

on account of their size the boy's frame is made to seem even more slight, his sloping shoulders and skinniness comparing badly with the armour, and the drum obviously more than he could manage around his waist. Indeed, in the original and larger version, of which this is a replica, both these props were painted out, apparently at an early date, perhaps because of this unfortunate effect.[21] There are other anomalies as well. Prince Frederick is stationed half outdoors, half in; at the right some drapery incongruously hangs from an unseen rod, and the picture space to the right of the props appears to be a wall. These details betray the landscape to be merely a studio backdrop. This boy-soldier takes to the field only in spirit, as the image itself is at trouble to establish (whereas in actual battles young boys, commoners, were used to set the pace with infantry drums; their life expectancy was brief in these encounters). Thus everything surrounding the Prince is false, all of which helps explain why the child seems so ill-fitted to the scene. None of it belongs to him except his costume. The implications of his surroundings, which he himself would not have selected, become the definitive essence of his character. The child is less the signified than the signifier.

These images in various ways fail, only the first (Fig. 35) coming close to achieving its visual goal in the representation of the male child, a mere toddler whose spirited drumming cannot literally be taken as a rational or considered act; it *is* play. With the others by contrast the children are older, sufficiently so to have begun the acculturation typical of their class and gender. And in each instance the way chosen for them, in its visual representation, is marked for the viewer by ambiguity, or tension or lack of credibility. Yet in all these instances what is at stake is the very thing that cannot be left to chance, namely identity. When "real" musical instruments are painted the issue is further joined.

Portraits of male children at music, or in the proximity of musical instruments, are exceptionally rare (I know of only about a dozen), except when the sitters were the offspring of professional musicians. In these few images the musical props were almost invariably represented in ways that, in attempting to justify or "explain" their inclusion, mark their culturally problematic character. Thomas Frye's portrait of Jeremy Bentham at age thirteen (Fig. 39) is a case in point. The painting shows Bentham life-size; it is thus a kind of self-important presentation portrait. This is especially significant in that the sitter is a child. Bentham is presented as an intellectual prodigy (educated at Westminster, he entered Oxford's Queen's College the same year the portrait was painted). He is dressed in academic gown; a volume of Cicero rests on the table behind him. In effect, he is in a prop-created study, together with his Latin text and self-produced manuscripts as well as his music. (Bentham began his studies on the violin at age five, and he retained a passionate

interest in music all his life. By age seven his mother wrote that he
was playing Handel sonatas for dinner guests. By his twenties he
judged women primarily by their musical abilities and often played
violin to their harpsichord accompaniment.)[22] The image acknowledges Bentham's musical interests, undoubtedly in part because he
was not only devoted to music but also genuinely talented, even
precocious. Yet semiotically, music, while acknowledged, is literally given lowest rank among the boy's accomplishments: the
instrument is set on the floor. This is visually striking and not
accidental, precisely because violins are not normally, in "life," set
where they can easily be stepped on and ruined. *Practice* in other
words demands that the instrument be put on the table. *Culture*
demands otherwise, for to place the violin among the rest of the
props – Cicero and Bentham's written homework – would give the
instrument identical status. That would be an unacceptable violation of cultural convention, simultaneously producing an improper
reading of the boy's *public* values and, more important, those of his
family, and would further cloud the boy's gender identity. It is true
that the violin was almost exclusively associated with men in the
eighteenth century. (To be sure, the rare woman of the period
played the violin, but to my knowledge not a single image exists to
replicate such practice.)[23] But any male presenting himself as a
devoted, and not merely recreative, musician was suspect. It might
have been simpler to omit the violin from the portrait. But that
would in turn deny recognition of Bentham's marked accomplishment in music and, worse, advertise him as a pedantic, if youthful,
academic. In fact, Bentham's bookishness and musical interest are
both mediated by his pose, standing rather than sitting. One normally studies, and writes, seated; yet to do so here would render the
boy hopelessly Faustian. The casual stance, weight on one leg, hand
on hip, suggests the characteristic ease almost always sought by
English portrait artists of gentlemen sitters. The portrait is thus
marked by the careful balance of conflicting, even mutually negat-
ing, personal interests and cultural values. Nothing is left to chance,
though the painter was faced with considerable difficulties. A final
detail clarifies the depths of the internal dialectic. At the back of the
room Frye painted a doorway (the outside world, a conventional
vignette when painting men in interiors), yet through it we see not
the world, but glass-encased book shelves in the form of a window.
The window-bookcase must function doubly and incongruously as
a device to signal Bentham's manly worldliness and as a further
mark of his youthful erudition and intellectual seriousness. But to
accomplish these conflicting roles, the visual logic that the English
so loved had to be violated.

Arthur Devis' portrait of John Bacon and his family (Fig. 40)
represents one of the twin sons holding a flute and sheet of music as
his father gestures toward him presumably asking for a tune. A

fairly characteristic English conversation piece, the painting functions to establish the family's prestige less by what they were than
by what they had acquired. In these sorts of images, that is, the
sitters take second place (or at most only equal place) to their
surroundings. In this instance Bacon and his family are almost
overwhelmed by their London house (Bacon was the eldest son of a
large landowner in Northumberland but was residing in London
when the portrait was painted). The myriad vignettes scattered
throughout the painting – the scientific instruments in both rooms,
the Italianate paintings of the sort men acquired on the Grand Tour
and the very wealth indicated both by the architecture and the
colorful Turkish carpet – are all markers of John Bacon's prestige,
which his wife and children essentially and simply reinforce. (At
first glance Bacon's wife seems pictorially privileged, given that she
occupies the near-center of the canvas, framed by the central arch-
way at the back and sitting in the front-most picture plane. Yet she
is sufficiently off-center that our eyes shift to John Bacon – not least
because of the strong diagonal of the boy's flute pointing to him.)
The family is somewhat awkwardly arranged into component
groups, each with a role to play in visually solidifying Bacon's
position. The mother is duly maternal (and fecund); the daughter
beside her already accomplished at drawing. The children at the
right are carefree and leisured and, incidentally, playing out culturally sanctioned gender roles – the boy builds the house of cards, the
girl hands him supplies. Given that the children of the poor invariably worked, the representation of Bacon's children at play is a
powerful sign of family position. The eldest son at the left with the

40 Arthur Devis
(1712–87), *John Bacon
and his Family*
(c. 1742–3), oil on
canvas, 76.6 ×
131.1 cm.; New
Haven, CT, Yale
Center for British
Art, Paul Mellon
Collection

flute is painted standing so as to appear larger than his twin who, only moments younger, will not inherit the estate's prime wealth. Hence, this second son poses with his little sister. The older twin is in effect his father's only son, already a little man, dressed differently from his twin. Reference to music is included here but its importance is severely diminished visually, hence actually, by the accumulation of other objects and activities.[24] In addition, the flute's potentially problematic musical associations are mitigated by its obvious use value as a visual reminder of male sexuality, hence power.

If to belabor the obvious, the flute's phallic associations, no secret to the eighteenth century (or before for that matter), provide reason for its inclusion, especially in the hands of the heir. Of all musical instruments associated with males, and culturally sanctioned as such, flutes were specifically viewed as improper for women, precisely because of the visual sexual metaphor the instrument implied. In large part I believe that this explains why in portraits of upper-class males during this period it is far more common to represent them holding flutes but less so for other instruments, notably violins with which flutes competed for popularity. As John Essex put it in a conduct book from 1722:

The *Harpsichord*, *Spinnet*, *Lute* and *Base Violin*, are Instruments most agreeable to the Ladies: There are some others that really are unbecoming to the Fair Sex; as the *Flute*, *Violin* and *Hautboy*; the last of which is too Manlike, and would look indecent in a Woman's Mouth; and the *Flute* is very improper, as taking away too much of the Juices, which are otherwise more necessarily employ'd, to promote the Appetite, and assist Digestion.[25]

MUSIC AND SEXUAL AMBIVALENCE

I know of only a few portraits of upper-class males playing instruments not considered appropriate to the sex, such as keyboard instruments. There is no question that upper-class males played harpsichords, spinets and pianos during the period, though in lesser numbers than for other instruments. Yet very few chose to be painted with a keyboard instrument as a musical prop on account of its seeming effeminate. Thus an eighteenth-century father might agree to pay ten guineas for a new spinet for his teenage son but only with regret that it was nevertheless "a female instrument."[26] John Berkenhout's book of advice to his son unambiguously asserted this view in a passage concerning those instruments suitable for a gentleman. He disassociated himself from two, the oboe and harpsichord, but for very different reasons:

By all means, avoid the Hautboy, out of compassion for your neighbours; unless, at any time, you want to drive the rats and mice from your apartment. As to the Harpsichord – I once sat playing upon that instrument, in a room next [to] the square where I then lived. As two gentlemen were passing the window, I heard one of them exclaim, – "I hate to see a *man* at the Harpsichord!" I had never before annexed the idea of effeminancy to that instrument; but from that moment, I began to be of that gentleman's opinion.[27]

Thomas Hill's portrait of Garton Orme seated at a bentside spinet[28] (Fig. 41) acknowledged the visual problem created by the

41 Thomas Hill (1661–1734), *Garton Orme* (c. 1705–8), oil on canvas, 122 × 96.5 cm.; Bath, Holburne Museum. By kind permission of the Trustees

presence of such a normally unacceptable prop by means of trying to solve – or offset it. Specifically, and again by means of a visual and practical incongruency, Hill provided reassurance that, although the boy was musical, he was still "normal" – that is, a young "man" of action. Garton Orme wears a heavy coat, designed for outdoor use (hence, physical action) inappropriate for indoors, and he wears a gentleman's ceremonial sword, though young boys did not usually carry swords, especially inside the house. The weapon, like the coat, thus functions as a sign to establish that Orme's activity at the spinet is for leisure only. Music is differentiated from the responsibilities that ensue from elevated class standing, just as class standing is established by the props: the spinet itself, the drapery and the architectural pier proper to a large building.[29]

42 James McArdell (1728/9?–65) after Thomas Jenkins, *Benjamin Hallet* (c. 1749), mezzotint, 40 × 30.2 cm.; London, British Museum. By courtesy of the Trustees

The difference in treatment of Garton Orme and Benjamin Hallet (Fig. 42) is absolute but not difficult to explain. The small mezzotint shows a boy of four years, a child prodigy on both the violoncello and flute – the latter rests atop the back of the music stand. His position as a budding professional musician automatically separated him from the ranks of gentleman amateurs, which is to say that no visual assurances about masculinity like a sword as in the Orme portrait were necessary. His costume renders him sexually ambiguous to modern eyes, if not necessarily so to his contemporaries, though the foot protruding from the dress is clearly that of a boy. However, the face is utterly androgynous, and the hands and developing breasts (!) distinctly female.[30] In body as in talent the child is represented as a human oddity. (His musical feats are described in the marginal script in discourse that likewise has a slight freak-show air to it.)

The concern to establish maleness in portraits of boy musicians, like Garton Orme, is also evident in pictures of adults. Thus a portrait of James Bland Burges (Fig. 43), painted when he was twenty-two and on the Tour in Rome, depicts a man of taste and cultivation. (While on the Tour those with the financial means commonly stood for their portraits. It was a parentally sanctioned souvenir of the highest pedigree for a boy nominally entering manhood. Some left England with chosen portrait-costumes in their baggage, such as military uniforms, clothes for which there would otherwise have been very limited use.)[31] In the Burges portrait a variety of objects act as conventional signifiers. His worldliness and appetite for adventure is designated by a city map to which he points, by the guide book to Rome he holds and by the locale-setting view of the city through the window with a view on the Pantheon and Trajan's Column. A bust of Minerva, icon-like, marks him an heir to civilization. The sword at his side not only proclaims his social rank but also defines him as a man of action. His taste for music is acknowledged by his violoncello. But among all the prop-attributes music ranks the least of these. The rough compositional parallel between the musical instrument (and especially its bow) and the sword is striking and hardly coincidental. The parallel lines set up a visual relationship between two otherwise unrelated objects, thereby inviting comparison. A hierarchy is established between them by means of a logical and visual tension: swords are not normally worn in the house (they are clumsy around the furniture); violoncellos are not normally set flat on the floor (they can be stepped on or tripped over). These practical anomalies, combined with the compositional relationship they share, invite a high/low, marked/unmarked reading. That is, the sword is physically stationed above the violoncello and it is highlighted by the artist, especially by the reflections on the hilt and along the uppermost edge of the scabbard. The musical instrument by contrast is

43 Pietro Labruzzi (1739–1805), *Sir James Bland Burges* (1774), oil on canvas, 171.5 × 122.6 cm. Photo ©
Christie's

low (the lowest noteworthy object in the room, though also the one closest to the viewer) and mostly in shadow. Action and responsibility (the sword) precede taste and leisure (music). James Bland Burges was in fact a lifelong dedicated musical amateur – in later life after retirement from a career in politics he even composed some music – hence the justification for including his violoncello in the portrait. But here the twin demands of culture and portrait convention, mutually mediating one another, determine the place of music in Burges' life/image. To understand the degree to which this issue is "naturalized" (hence made a non-issue) in the painting, consider the *visual* impossibility of the artist's reversing the position of the two props, the sword and the cello. That this cannot occur is not a matter of compositional difficulty but one of cultural proscription.

In Italy the painter most in demand among English sitters was Pompeo Batoni (1708–87), a man already well known by the mid 1740s, and by 1760 and until his death the most famous painter in that country. (He painted approximately 200 portraits of British sitters, or thought to be British sitters.) Batoni's portrait of John, Lord Brudenell, later Marquis of Monthermer (Fig. 44) deviates significantly from the norm represented by the Burges portrait and from other portraits by Batoni himself. The artist posed Brudenell seated, not unknown for male sitters, though men more generally were shown standing. But the particular combination of seated male with downcast eyes not meeting the spectator, and soft, overly sensitive face (especially the pouty lips) are portrait conventions normally reserved for the portrayal of women. Beyond this, and strikingly unusual, Brudenell holds a Neapolitan mandolin under his arm and an open music book on his lap.[32] Male sitters rarely posed holding music unless they were professional musicians, by which means their profession was often signaled. By contrast, among the well-born this was a gesture again common to women. Moreover, the instrument itself is of the general sort (small plucked string, cittern type) that women played, virtually to the exclusion of men – I know of no other portrait representing a man playing a similar instrument. Now there is an explanation for the look of this portrait, in the form of yet another one of the same sitter also painted in Rome but by Anton Raphael Mengs, a full-length showing him in his "official" souvenir pose, seated in an arm chair reading, a dog at his feet, and in the presence of an inspirational bust of Cicero: exactly the kind of image to give the relatives some peace of mind. Batoni's portrait by contrast was probably painted for Brudenell himself, a kind of private image – indeed, as a half-length, it is rather small. (There is no question that he had the financial resources to order whatever he wanted; in 1758 alone he spent over £2,000 in Rome buying works of art.)

The primary evidence for this conclusion is the music book, which is not a printed score but a manuscript collection, turned to

44 Pompeo Batoni (1708–87), *John Brudenell, later Marquis of Monthermer* (1758), oil on canvas, 96.5 ×
71.1 cm.; Boughton House, Kettering, Northamptonshire, Collection The Duke of Buccleuch, K.T.

the end of Corelli's sixth violin sonata, Opus 5. The fact that the composer's name is just visible at the composition's end indicates that the works of other composers follow. This in turn implies that the anthology is a personal one, copied out and bound for Brudenell's pleasure, a treasury of favorites. The composition's identification depends on the viewer's possessing musical know-ledge, since the work is not named and the composer's identifica-tion is in tiny script difficult to decipher. The musically ignorant cannot fully understand the image, and the image itself *announces* that to the viewer: given the prominence of the score-prop, and the extreme detail with which the notation is rendered (even with a few mistakes typical to manuscript copies), the viewer is forced to confront his or her own ignorance. What he or she looks at is not just music but specific music. In short, the image resists the viewer, unlike most portraits; it ruptures the normal relationship of viewer to sitter, for in every way possible the sitter is presented in bald opposition to cultural-behavorial norms. As with all art, the por-trait can only be perceived in relation to all other portraits with which the viewer is familiar and the nature of the world that these images imprint. This image violates expectations in refusing the affirmation of expectation.

If contemporaneous accounts of Brudenell's character can be trusted, his musical interest would only have advertised his "irres-ponsible" character and, as corollary, his sexual preferences. Lady Mary Wortley Montagu wrote on both matters from Venice in 1760: "He is both singular in his manner and Sentiments, yet I am apt to beleive [*sic*] if he meets with a sensible Wife, she may be very happy with him. Whoever leaves him at his liberty will certainly meet no Contradiction from him, who is too Indolent to dispute with any body and appears indifferent to our Se[x]."[33] Robert Adam, on the other hand, disliked him from the first, referring to Brudenell in 1755 as "a stupid, meaningless creature . . . [who] has not the mein [*sic*] of a tailor nor the spirit of a louse."[34] Brudenell died at age thirty-five, having never married.

YOUTH AND REBELLIOUS AFFIRMATION

The Burges portrait (Fig. 43) may also be usefully compared to a caricature painting by the then-young Sir Joshua Reynolds (Fig. 45) from nearly the same time, also executed in Rome, representing four British sitters with the Pyramid of Cestius for a backdrop: Charles Turner on the right, Mr. John Woodyeare at the left, Woodyeare's tutor, Rev. Dr. William Drake playing flute, and Mr. Cooke on the violoncello.[35] A flute–cello duet is the painting's putative subject, though broad comedy is its real purpose. In short the music is painful to hear, as indicated by Charles Turner cover-ing his ears. (Mr. Woodyeare seems to doze.) While Woodyeare's

45 Sir Joshua Reynolds (1723–92), *Caricature Group: Sir Charles Turner, Mr. Cooke, Mr. Woodyeare and Dr. Drake* (1751), oil on canvas, 62.9 × 48.3 cm.; Providence, RI, Museum of Art, Rhode Island School of Design, Gift of Mrs. Murray S. Danforth

tutor plays the flute, competently it would seem judging from his finger position and carefully articulated embouchure, Mr. Cooke, his social better, botches the cello. His highly caricatured profile makes him appear quite stupid; his complementary musical ineptitude is equally evident from his bad hand position and the fact that he seems to be bowing simultaneously with both the stick and horse hairs of his bow. The contrast between the two musicians is complete. But in another sense, appearing not to play well (even if, in actuality, Cooke were accomplished) is the very point of the representation, as emphasized by Charles Turner's covering of his ears. That is, these English gentlemen in Italy may be playing the roles of Italians (as they chose to see Italians), pretending to be "Macaroni's," in the same spirit as a later piece of visual xenophobia by Rowlandson (Fig. 46).[36] The painting replicates and also sanctions the carefree celebration of young men away from parental eyes, if here only on a fictional lark. The setting in point of fact makes no literal sense. British gentlemen were not known to take their instruments, especially cellos, out into the woods or among the Roman ruins. The scene is as incongruous as the Tour experience itself: argued on the basis of education and good breeding, it was for many essentially a shopping spree interspersed with drinking and whoring. Lady Mary Wortley Montagu, writing in 1740 to her friend Lady Pomfret, well described the behavior of English boys turned loose on the Continent:

Their whole business abroad (as far as I can perceive) being to buy new cloaths, in which they shine in some obscure coffee-house, where they are sure of meeting only one another; and after the important conquest of

46 Samuel Alken (1756–1815), after Thomas Rowlandson, *An Italian Family* (1785), aquatint, 33 × 45 cm.; London, British Museum. By courtesy of the Trustees

some waiting gentlewoman of an opera Queen, who perhaps they remember as long as they live, return to England excellent judges of men
and manners. I find the spirit of patriotism so strong in me every time I see
them, that I look on them as the greatest blockheads in nature; and, to say
the truth, the compound of booby and petit maître makes up a very odd
sort of animal.[37]

As regards Reynolds' caricature, young men pretending to take
up music with a vengeance, never leaving one's instruments behind, even hauling them to improbable or impossible places, all
conspired at once to thumb one's nose at the parents paying for the
Tour, at the same time ironically restating in comic terms their
parents' own values as regards music. To be sure the image represents a light-hearted and essentially innocent testing of the reins of
youth. Yet the comic gestures of the central figure, Mr. Cooke,
have deep-set cultural roots reflecting specific ideological perspec-
tives. Here music served several purposes which at once challenged
and reinforced those ideologies: of xenophobia, of what it meant to
be male, of what one was to do with one's life. In fact this painting
did not indicate that these men were – exceptionably – devoted
musicians, hence cultural pariahs among their class and gender. It
confirmed precisely the opposite through deep-seated irony. Each
of the "men" was just one of the boys.[38]

THE QUALIFICATION OF MUSICAL IDENTITY

Joseph Nollekens' portrait of an unidentified cello player initially
creates an impression of an unapologetic love for music (Fig. 47).
The setting establishes the man's considerable status, the view
through the open window documenting the extent of his wealth.
(The setting may of course be a conceit, the artist's flattering of an
only modestly endowed member of the gentry. The architecture of
the room, and even more the building and grounds visible through
the window, are essentially stock details for denoting social position, rather than renditions of specific buildings or interiors.) Front
and center the cellist plays, but for good measure at the back the
artist hangs a sword and hat on the wall: music does not hinder
"business." (We are also told that his wife is accomplished, hence
reflecting well on her husband, for in the background there is a
spinet – Garton Orme notwithstanding, essentially a women's
instrument – above whose fingerboard is written "Ladyman," not
the name of an actual builder of harpsichords in the eighteenth
century, instead an indicator of the gender proper to the instrument's use.

This image contrasts sharply with one from several decades earlier (Fig. 48) of Sir John Langham as a boy playing the viola da gamba. Most obvious is the fact that Langham is painted close up, so that the picture space is tightly circumscribed around him, quite different from Nollekens' portrait or, especially, Devis' of the Bacon family (Fig. 40). There is a view onto a landscape, but little more than a village church is visible. The conventional drapery and stately column base provide the appropriate address to the boy's status. But they also force all attention onto him and to the fact that he is making music – correctly so, in that his bowing hand and finger position on the viol's neck typify a skilled player. What is significant here is that the boy's musical interests are culturally accepted; indeed, they are represented so as to leave no question that music constitutes one means by which a gentleman is distinguished

47 Joseph Francis Nollekens (1702/6–48), *Gentleman Playing a Violoncello*, oil on canvas, 44.5 × 34.6 cm. By courtesy of Sotheby's

from his inferiors. By the first decades of the eighteenth century, as I indicated in the opening chapters, this last vestige of Renaissance humanism in England vis-à-vis music had been expunged. In the eighteenth century, to be sure, comparable images existed, prints and paintings alike, but the individuals represented were professional musicians and not amateurs. Thus Gainsborough rendered his friend Karl Friedrich Abel (Fig. 49) in all the elegance of the finest gentleman, shown with his viola da gamba resting (oddly) against one of his legs.[39] However, Gainsborough showed Abel in

48 Johan Kerseboom (act. 1680–d. 1708), *Sir John Langham, 4th Baronet, as a Boy* (1683); oil on canvas, 142.9 × 106 cm.; Private Collection. By courtesy of the Courtauld Institute of Art, London

the act of composing, not playing, though Abel was equally renowned for both. For professionals, in the hierarchy of musical
activities the former had long held a rank superior to "mere"
execution. That is, Abel's representation as a composer placed him
socio-culturally above his rank as a performer. (I shall take up this
issue again at the book's end.)

This fact is immediately evident in a mezzotint of the professional

49 Thomas
Gainsborough (1727–
88), *Karl Friedrich
Abel* (1777), oil on
canvas, 238.1 ×
146.05 cm.; San
Marino, CA, Henry
E. Huntington
Library and Art
Gallery

cellist John Hebden (Fig. 50), who by contrast comes across literally as a laborer; he virtually sweats over his music, bow hand carefully poised, stopping-hand tensed, eyes intensely concentrating on the music. True gentlemen might choose to pose as musicians, but they almost never did so in any way that might suggest effort, either physical or mental. Hebden's status is further reduced by the modesty of value the image demands for itself. Further, the Hebden print denies itself status as an object, and hence limits the status that can be accorded to the sitter. This is not because it is a print, for mezzotints by nature of their reproducibility garnered prestige to those whose images were represented (spreading fame through replication, which was impossible with an oil painting to which few people had visual access, hence accounting for the fact that many

50 John Faber, Jr. (c. 1684–1756), after Philippe Mercier, *John Hebden* (1741), mezzotint, 31.8 × 26.7 cm.; London, British Museum. By courtesy of the Trustees

prints were of course based on painted originals). Rather, it is because of this particular print's very small size (mezzotints of socially important people were often large), a factor that cannot be discounted in the accumulation of meaning. Size is always a signifier. Undoubtedly this image was little more than an inexpensive souvenir for Hebden's students and others who had seen him perform (he also played the bassoon and composed).[40]

I know of one portrait representing an amateur male musician where the problematics engendered by the socio-cultural conflicts and ambiguities surrounding music are silenced (Fig. 51), but its anomalous character only proves the rule to which it is a unique exception. The painting may represent Hugh Barron, himself a portrait painter, not a very successful one though he was a student of Reynolds. The son of a Soho apothecary who apparently grew up in comfortable surroundings, he was reputed to be among the

51 Hugh Barron (c. 1745–91). *Portrait of a Man with a Violin, possibly a Self-Portrait* (c. 1768), oil on canvas, 73.7 × 62.2 cm.; New Haven, CT, Yale Center for British Art, Paul Mellon Collection

most talented amateur violinists of his day; he performed at a public concert in London as early as age thirteen.[41] He is portrayed both as a gentleman and a musician, with no other visual components employed to mitigate the gentleman-musician bond. The explanation for the portrait's "look" is, however, not difficult to fathom, presuming it is a self-portrait, as such a totally privatized image, hence less subject to the prevailing requirements of pictorial representation.

A very different but equally unusual portrait by Zoffany (Fig. 52)

can be similarly accounted for, a self-portrait of the artist, possibly with his daughter, and probably Giacobbe Cervetto, the famous and long-lived (1682–1783) cellist and his cellist son James.[42] The painting is doubly self-referential, in that Zoffany himself is not only represented as a man but also as a painter in the act of painting, the Cervettos in effect his sitters. All four individuals represented are lionized by the dignity of their handling. And music is accorded particular status, compositionally and allegorically. The sound issuing from Cervetto's cello, though silenced in paint, constitutes not only the inspirational moment for the artist himself but also the perfect metaphor for difficulty of the artist's task. His canvas is blank. He must fill it in some way that will meaningfully capture the significance of the musical act, the sounds that Cervetto brings from his instrument which decay instantly, only to exist in memory. (Beyond this, the painting is doubly allegorical in its rather poignant representation of the old topos, the Ages of "Man.")[43] The image's self-interested self-referentiality again mediates the dominant socio-cultural reality that Zoffany in so many other instances rather simply mirrored (Fig. 38). In essence this is an image that represents his own views of the world and music's place (he loved music), one that utterly conflicted with the affirmation that defined most of his portrait commissions. There he painted for others, here for himself. The rupture between the two manifests itself in stylistic difference, in turn a reflection of social, cultural (he was after all an immigrant) and ideological difference.

Finally among portraits I want to consider engraved (Fig. 53) and painted (Fig. 54) images of Willoughby Bertie, 4th Earl of Abingdon (1740–99). In the first he sits at a table composing music in the presence of his music master who holds a large theorbo. Abingdon was devoted to music and was in fact both an amateur performer, accounting for the violoncello in the print (he also played the flute), and an amateur and published composer of solo songs and duets, glees, catches, some dances and a few longer pieces. He was on warm terms with Johann Christian Bach, Karl Friedrich Abel and Giovanni Gallini, the impresario and dancer. Gallini, who operated the Hanover Square concert rooms and organized profitable balls, masquerades and suppers, married Abingdon's sister, Lady Elizabeth Bertie. Over a several-year period Abingdon himself gave the considerable sum of £1,600 to support the concerts in which Bach and Abel participated as organizers.[44]

The print, from 1800, apparently commemorates the life of Abingdon shortly after his death, though its diminutive size (27 × 19 cm.) renders the memorial considerably less effective when weighed against many other large and relatively expensive portrait mezzotints of the period. It was produced by Theobald Monzani, Abingdon's music publisher, and was included as the frontispiece to some of his compositions, including the *6 of the Last Vocal Pieces*

52 Johan Zoffany (1733–1810), *Self-Portrait of the Artist, with his Daughter Maria Theresa [?] and possibly Giacobbe and James Cervetto [?]* (c. 1779–83), oil on canvas, 193 × 164.5 cm.; New Haven, CT, Yale Center for British Art, Paul Mellon Collection

53 Michele Benedetti (1745–1810), after John Francis Rigaud, *Willoughby Bertie, 4th Earl of Abingdon* (1800), stipple engraving, 26.7 × 19 cm.; London, British Museum. By courtesy of the Trustees

Composed by the Late Willoughby, Earl of Abingdon (1800?); it is possible that the print was also marketed by itself. To his contemporaries – and especially to his class equals – Abingdon was a genuine eccentric, a man whose chief interest besides music was radical politics. The print's setting retains the clichéd conventions used to establish class rank: voluminous, non-functional drapery and a large column base, as well as the carpet and furniture – the furniture appears to be French, visually recalling his well-known political views: he wrote, unfashionably, in praise of the French Revolution as late as 1798. Abingdon's Continental sympathies are further established not only by the inclusion of a music master (extraordinarily unusual were we to view the print as a "straight-forward" portrait, which it is not): no other peers, even ones devoted to music, to my knowledge posed with anyone so déclassé as a music master. Moreover, the theorbo held by the teacher was an instrument that enjoyed considerable popularity on the Continent, but much less in England. Thus the theorbo delineates not only the master – or at least his tastes – as foreign but also Abingdon, his student.[45] Moreover, the archlute serves one other function, via its anachronism, and compositionally reinforced by its occupying the central space of the image. By the turn of the nineteenth century, when the print appeared, the lute had been in a decades-long decline. To a contemporaneous viewer its presence would have provided a key to the print, establishing at first glance that the image was, though not overtly or even intentionally satirical, at the least a documentation of the odd tastes of a human oddity, visible proof that Abingdon was a man out of time and out of place.

To illustrate Abingdon in the act of composing music was to turn a peer into a professional. In no sense was this complimentary to his reputation as a gentleman. To show him seated at his table working with such obvious earnestness was to commit a substantial visual error at the socio-cultural level. Such activity was utterly improper to a man of his station. While it was easy to argue that playing music was a leisure activity befitting a gentleman, the same could not be said of composition. That required a level of training that necessarily confirmed obsessive musical interests. In all these ways the man's musical eccentricities encompass the image, and at the same time effectively neutralize the credibility of his politics which, incidentally, found expression in some of his published music. His odd political beliefs could serve simultaneously to establish a perception of the self-marginalization evident in his musical practices. (The British Museum possesses a number of Abingdon's compositions, including two songs for solo voice. The text of the first, "The State Test or the Subversion of Parties," argues for a reconciliation between the Church of England and the Dissenters, and between the Whigs and Tories – in the House of Lords, Abingdon sided with the Americans on the issues that brought on the Revolution, and he also spoke out for reconciliation with the Irish. The second, "The Political Rationalist," deals with religion, zealotry and the need for tolerance and moderation.)

I think that Abingdon himself may have been aware of the general problem encapsulated by this print, the evidence being a group portrait with his family (Fig. 54) predating the print by

several years. In this instance no violations of either social- or gender-order occur; culturally the image is entirely affirmative. The "normal" roles have been assumed: a woman is musical, the family's adult male (Abingdon) is the hunter-provider, prepost-erously, if conventionally, shown bringing home the only-slightly-metaphorical bacon: game he has shot. Further, Abingdon is a responsible father who teaches his son the same skills of blood-sport; the boy clutches a duck in one hand and drags along a dead rabbit with the other, together with his father leaving the impress-ion that they would shoot at anything that moved. In the eighteenth century peers of the realm did not hunt because they needed to; rather, killing game was an overt sign of one's sovereign authority – about which more later. In sum, Abingdon here is the proverbial man's man, though to be sure his face betrays little interest in the posed exercise.

THE DIALECTICS OF PRESTIGE

I shall conclude with some comments about a different genre of painting, the so-called vanitas still life, produced in large numbers in seventeenth-century Holland and also in England for a brief period at the close of that century and the start of the next. Two Dutch painters were responsible for most of the pictures produced in England, Pieter Roestraeten and Edwaert Colyer (Figs. 55–56), though some vanitas paintings by Dutch artists – perhaps including some works by Roestraeten and Colyer – were actually painted in Holland and imported to England.

Vanitas paintings, which took their title from the book of Eccle-siastes 1:2 ("Vanity of vanities, saith the Preacher, vanity of vani-ties; all is vanity"), transformed textual allusions into emblems and attributes based on work by scholars from the University of Leiden. The role of the individual objects in these paintings was intentionally obscured in order to compel the reader to ponder the subject. Every object represented supposedly was intended to make the observer contemplate the brevity of life and the frailty of humankind. In short, their subject was transience: human skulls, instruments for measuring time (clocks, watches, the hourglass), candles burning or just extinguished and still smoking, flowers at their height of bloom hence about to fade, ripe fruit hence about to rot. Musical instruments fell among a second group of attributes symbolizing the tastes and pleasures, the *vita voluptuaria*, the vanity of all worldly things. Allusions to music, in the form either of musical instruments or music books, were to be read as belonging to activities that waste precious time that should otherwise be spent saving one's soul or, worse, as occasions for sin (the dancing masters' little pocket fiddle).[46]

54 John Francis Rigaud (1742–1810), *Willoughby Bertie, 4th Earl of Abingdon, and Charlotte, Countess of Abingdon, Montagu, Lord Norreys, Lady Charlotte and Lady Caroline Bertie, The Hon. Willoughby, The Hon. Peregrine and The Hon. Frederick Bertie* (1793), oil on canvas, 237.6 × 185.5 cm. Photo © Christie's

55 Edwaert Colyer
(act. 1662–d. after
1702?), *Vanitas Still
Life*, oil on canvas,
57.8 × 71.1 cm. By
courtesy of Sotheby's

56 Edwaert Colyer
(act. 1662–d. after
1702?), *Vanitas Still
Life*, oil on canvas, 97
× 123 cm. By
courtesy of Sotheby's

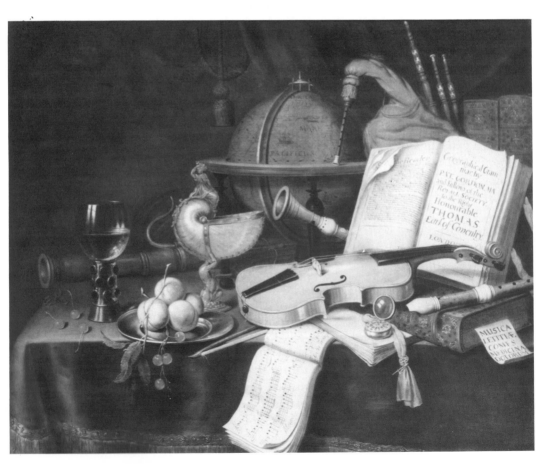

The two examples by Colyer reproduced here are entirely typical, except that in the first the pages of the music book beneath the recorder and the larger book at the back are both blank. The likely explanation is that the painting is unfinished: the texts, such as those supplied in the second example, provided the picture with a national localization appropriate to a specific market, here England (the paintings were generally not individually commissioned). That is, the subject matter of a text, in the case of books usually via title pages, coincided with a topic of importance to potential buyers. The language of the text identified the nationality of the reader (or, with Latin, his real or imagined scholarly proclivities); the book in the second example is the Rev. Patrick Gordon's *Geographical Grammar* (1693). Thus the blank pages of the first example reflect the realities of mass marketing, a ready-made painting requiring only the proper text to make it Dutch or English.

The first painting (Fig. 55) is the more typical of the genre, especially in light of the prominence given to the extinguished candle and, especially, the skull, as well as the partly obscured hourglass in the background. "*Finis coronat opus*" ("death crowns work") was a phrase commonly included, the likely place being on the blank piece of paper prominently protruding from the book just in front of the skull.

The other example (Fig. 56) is considerably more interesting. Music here is prominently represented, left to right, by inclusion of a bassoon, a lute, a violin (symbolically, with a broken string), a shawm, a bagpipe and a small recorder. Music is further celebrated by a phrase often included on Dutch virginals and harpsichords: "*Musica letitiæ comes medicina dolorum*" ("Music is the companion of joy, the healer of sadness").[47] The only direct reference to time passing is a small, highly decorative watch just in front of the violin, though ripe fruit is also present. This is a vanitas painting that essentially denies its genre; the reminders of sin are absent and the allusions to impending decay muted. What is left to rise in prominence is that which is shared by all images of this type: the celebration of material goods, rendered particularly tangible (even surreal) through the medium of oil paint.[48] The things of this world are not rendered with suspicion but with an admiration akin to fetish. They are displayed on a table in such a way that would never occur in real life: each object has been gathered from its "natural" place in the house and placed on the table so as to celebrate what these things collectively stood for – the accomplishment, wealth and prestige marked by possession. Here music occupies an important place in the economy of social and class prestige, not only by pride of compositional place, as with the violin and little music book of dance tunes, but mostly because of their number and variety. Also important, if only implicit, the image asserts that considerable time is available for the lessons on so many instruments – whether or not it was actually the case, given the painted-without-commission nature of the genre. Yet as with most of the other images considered in this chapter, what ultimately prevails is a profound ambiguity – the best that can be said about music by eighteenth-century English men. Through its consciously didactic and text-based foundation, the vanitas painting condemned music in the very terms of Locke as a waste of time. But as a visual *experience* music is paid homage for what it said about one's position. The geographical text (Fig. 56) celebrates worldly knowledge and ambitions; the musical instruments draw attention to the time available in which to enjoy that world, its microcosm also rendered visible via a terrestrial globe turned to its exotic region, distant from the North sea, the "Mare Pacificum." Pleasure and power are enjoyed in time; the difficulty is that the social, political and economic base for pleasure and power, however apparently secure, is always challenged by the clock. Music by its very nature was a reminder of that fact, in its inherent material immateriality that fades into the silent void and thereby ironically renders the void more absolute. Music for men was a reminder of the necessary failure of all they typically held dear.

7 The female at music: praxis, representation and the problematic of identity

AT THE CLOSE OF the seventeenth century Roger North wrote that the musical instruments appropriate to females were "the espinnett, or harpsichord, lute, and gittarr" as well as voice.[1] In the course of the eighteenth century the specific instruments changed somewhat – the lute fell from favor, the English guitar rose; spinets and harpsichords were gradually replaced by square and grand pianos – but what remained constant was the fact that girls and women were for the most part restricted to two types of instruments, keyboards and plucked strings.[2]

Unlike males, upper-class (and even middle-class) females as a matter of course studied music, as I have previously outlined. Yet as with males detailed personal accounts of these activities, while common enough, are almost invariably fleeting as regards private music-making, though more extended discussions occur in many novels and comic plays (the former, often written by women, often treated the subject sympathetically; the latter, usually written by men, ordinarily belittled it). It is likely that in women's writings about their own lives, through letters, diaries and memoirs, music was so "naturalized" a part of their existence that little comment about it may have seemed necessary (by contrast, women commonly wrote assessments of opera performances and public and semi-private concerts they had attended). Nevertheless, despite the limited number of relevant extant commentaries, it is clear that women essentially understood the ideological and socio-structural uses to which their own musical experiences were put in the patriarchal culture, though to be sure relatively few women either analyzed or openly critiqued this relationship in detail, apart from the feminists writing near the century's end. The music females made, and were expected to make, was either tolerated or valued largely to the degree to which it kept within the bounds of the ideology of domesticity. These are the issues I shall consider in this chapter, in the process expanding not only on the ways in which music contributed to the shaping of female identity, and hence to society in general, but also to the ultimate effects of these matters on music itself. This chapter and the preceding one will provide the foundation for an examination in Chapter 8 of the relation of music to the marriage union and to the family as a whole.

THE MUSICAL DAUGHTER IN AN ECONOMY OF PRESTIGE

In 1685 a grief-stricken John Evelyn wrote in his diary of his daughter Mary who had just died at age twenty-one. A serious musical amateur himself, Evelyn saw to it that Mary was taught music, though her studies began only about three years before her death. Evelyn's memoir of his daughter included an extended passage about her musical abilities that fundamentally encapsulated the most important issues that seem to govern the role of music among females in upper-class English society:

> She had to all this an incomparable sweete Voice, to which she play'd a through-base on the Harpsichord, in both which she ariv'd to that perfection, that of all the Schollars of those Two famous Masters, Signor *Pietro* and *Bartolomeo*: she was esteem'd the best; [for] the sweetenesse of her voice, and manegement of it, adding such an agreablenesse to her Countenance, without any constraint and concerne, that when she sung, it was as charming to the Eye, as to the Eare; this I rather note, because it was a universal remarke, & for which so many noble & judicious persons in Musique, desir'd to heare her; the last, being at my Lord Arundels of Wardours, where was a solemn Meeting of about twenty persons of quality, some of them greate judges & Masters of Musique; where she sung with the famous Mr. *Pordage*, Signor *Joh: Battist* touching the Harpsichord &c: with exceeding applause.[3]

Evelyn's panegyric to Mary, of which this passage constitutes part of a lengthy section on her education and accomplishments, was obviously heartfelt and touching. Yet to modern readers that much would generally be taken for granted and is, in any event, not what renders the account particularly interesting. Rather it is the extent to which Evelyn consciously or unconsciously viewed Mary as a positive reflection on himself and, on this account, implicitly defined in part the severity of his loss, quite aside from his genuine emotional tribulation.

In examining the entire diary entry, in fact, one finds that Mary is described not only as a perfect child/daughter, but more as the once-living embodiment of the predominant ideals of courtesy and conduct literature. She took hard to her studies; she was pious; she behaved with total correctness including within the context of class difference (her relations to house servants); she was properly scandalized by the licentiousness of modern theater; she danced "with the most grace that in my whole life I had even seene," yet she danced rarely; she charmed and she deferred; she "descend[ed] to play with little Children." In all these ways she was the perfect wife-mother in the making.[4] Yet it was by means of music, in the passage quoted, that Mary's accomplishments most clearly reflected well on her father, according to his own assessment. Evelyn established Mary's musical talents in a double hierarchy: first, like all students of the two named masters, she was accomplished; second, among this group, she was the best. When she sang her physical beauty increased; she charmed not only her beholders' eyes but also (his) ears. And those so charmed were people of discriminating taste – on two counts, one musical, the other of class ("persons of quality"). The "exceeding applause" that greeted her implicitly honored her father – the loss of which would diminish him in the eyes of others. Mary, a mark of his prestige, was now lost.[5] (There were instances where music's use value to fathers or husbands was overshadowed by genuine musical concerns on the part of men, but they were extremely rare. The example of Samuel Pepys is often cited in this regard, as with his sometimes tireless efforts to turn his unmusical wife into a musician – not to mention his music-making with his wife's servant girl, Mercer, in whom Pepys also had sexual interests.)[6]

In the eighteenth century many women merited similar accolades, for example, the famous Mary Granville Pendarves Delaney, lifelong Handelian (she first met the composer when she was ten; he played on her spinet). She was a talented harpsichordist and played throughout her long life – until she was at least eighty-four. Yet she never performed for anyone but her most intimate acquaintances.[7] As I will show, in this regard her life with music demonstrates a rule and not an exception. The implications of the privatization of women's performances are very great for the music history of England, for among the leisured elite theirs was the gender that had the time and the cultural "permission" to study music seriously, yet by and large the talents they developed could not be heard beyond their own drawing rooms.

REPRESENTATION, MUSIC AND FEMALE IDENTITY

Visual representations, especially painted portraits, of girls and women at music, are very common throughout the eighteenth century; if anything the occurrences accelerate as the period wears on. Whereas males were rarely shown with musical props, females and certain musical instruments served as mutually referential icons. To paint a portrait of a girl child, perhaps even more than of a boy, may indeed have signaled paternal affection. For unlike boys, and the heir especially, little formal debt was owed by the father to his daughter other than an emotional one. Yet such an image, even if commissioned with the "purest" affectional intention, was necessarily at the same time a representation of the father, whether or not he was included in the composition. The portrait may have preserved the likeness of a child, but in the same instance it also announced the full range of familial values to which the patriarch subscribed. More powerful than words in this respect, the painted image was frozen "action" that could be contemplated and analyzed by any beholder having access to it. The "action" encapsulated in paint spoke loudly, and on this account its semiotic values, alike with portraits of boys and girls, inherently required close attention. In this respect musical allusion played a valuable role, if one that necessitated tight compositional control. In particular, musical referents needed to reassure the ideal beholder, invariably male, that the girl was a perfect mirror of her mother.

Probably the most important values that portraits of daughters needed to transmit were obedience to their fathers and acceptance of the behavioral norms typical of their gender – the two being entirely complementary. But obedience and acceptance of duty needed to be represented as freely chosen, for by the eighteenth century it was no longer culturally acceptable among the genteel classes to coerce or subdue children openly; instead they needed to be molded to do their parents' will.[8] Parental will remained dominant, but operated through changed tactics. Accordingly, the ideal portrait of girl children would continue as previously to embody in its sitters the qualities of obedience, duty and quiet deference, but in such a way as to naturalize these character traits. Yet few such ideal portraits exist, for the challenge to artists was virtually insurmountable, it being extremely difficult to make coercion recognizable yet not seem to be coercive. That is, a father's authority still needed to be represented, for authority was his single most important attribute, but somehow the power that provided authority's foundation had to be masked.

Samuel De Wilde's picture of two girls (Fig. 57) illustrates a reasonably successful attempt at responding to the requirements for a successful portrait of daughters. The girls apply themselves to the accomplishments of female gentility, namely music,[9] art (the rolled drawing modeled from the sculpted putto) and literature (the books). As for music, it is not the performance per se that really matters, for the little flageolet one girl plays was no longer the instrument of high caste that it had been more than a century earlier, as with Pepys whose diary establishes that he was enthralled by it. During the eighteenth century it was in fact principally used by women as a device for teaching canaries and linnets to sing. The association of this instrument with birds, women's household pets, was accordingly understood, both socio-culturally and as a pictorial convention, as a marker of gender and gender roles. (I know of no image of an adult male using the instrument during the eighteenth century and only one of a very young boy.) The choice of the flageolet as a musical prop fulfilled two complementary functions. It helped establish that the child was both accomplished and dutiful – and presumably unquestioning.

Two additional components of the painting contribute to this semiotic encoding. The first is light, provided by the candle on the table, indicating that the children keep to their tasks even at night, which in turn reflects well on their upbringing: they are serious, responsible, dedicated to becoming ideal females. Just as the light softens their already delicate skin (softness to be equated with female dependency on the harder-hence-stronger sex), it also metaphorically reflects well on their family, that is, on their father. Moreover, De Wilde's particular use of light, quite striking, plays a crucial role in drawing attention to the father's symbolic presence, for the candle illuminates not so much the faces of the children (as in a La Tour) as the back wall. The halo cast around the head of the putto draws attention to the painting-within-the-painting just above the sculpture, and thereby upsets the portrait's overall re-pose. In short, this compositional device sets the beholder's eyes in motion and at the same time makes the viewer realize that the scene occurring before his or her eyes is profoundly meaningful. It under-cuts any likelihood of perceiving the event depicted as static. The beholder's eyes cannot focus on the girls. Instead, they must move back and forth between the children and the interior portrait of a man who must represent their father. This involuntary eye move-ment is the second component serving a complementary function

57 Samuel De Wilde (1747–1832), *Music* (1801), oil on canvas, 71.1 × 90.7 cm.; Manchester, City Art Galleries

to the musical event itself. The coercive power of the father, however masked within the image, is activated in the restless movement of the *beholder's* eyes, darting back and forth, down and up. Not for nothing is the father's portrait hung above his children. He enjoys a superior hierarchical position, protected by his own act of surveillance, however kind his visage. Yet it is also apparent that the man's eyes do not actually look at his children, but at the beholder. This informs the viewer that his authority is unquestioned, that force is unnecessary (as such, the interior portrait of the father represents him as an ideal man). The interior portrait acts in ideological redundancy, a visual back-up assuring an ideologically correct reading.

Among representations of girls with musical attributes the use of the tambourine roughly paralleled the use of drums by boys (Fig. 58) – and many such images exist. In one obvious and important

58 William Hoare (1706–99), *Henrietta Ann Hoare*, pastel, 57.2 × 47 cm.; Stourhead, The National Trust. By courtesy of the Courtauld Institute of Art, London

sense the parallel is striking: both are percussion instruments whose sounds regulated body movement. The infantry drums mirrored in boys' toy instruments set aggressive rhythms, literal and meta-phoric, for a life of power and the controlled use of violence for socio-political ends. And the dramatic nature of these ends was replicated in the sound-potential of the instrument itself which could be heard over large distances so as to martial the infantry into the neat – ironically rationalized – lines perfect for the mass battle-field slaughter of European eighteenth-century warfare. The tam-bourine's use was profoundly different, at least in Europe. The absence of a second drum head denied the instrument a resonating chamber; even with the addition of pellet bells, as with this paint-ing, or jingle rings the semiotics of the instrument's sound was non-aggressive, feminine. To be sure, it need not be so; the tam-bourine may be struck hard with the hand or with a stick and in such instances its sound takes on very different meaning. But that was not the way it was "played" in eighteenth-century England. In fact, I doubt if it was much played at all. Instead it seems to have served almost exclusively as an attribute in painting for female dancing. The tambourine, to the extent that it represented dance, alluded to movement, physical activity. But by employing this prop a female sitter could be literally immobilized in the portrait and her dancing still be referenced. The appeal of the tambourine in this instance was not simply as a device for solving painters' compositional prob-lems, for artists could in fact very successfully represent dance movements in portraits (Fig. 25). Rather it was a question of ideological correctness. Just as the proper boy beat his drums vigorously, the proper girl was gracefully still.

All this is effected in the painting of young Henrietta Ann Hoare (Fig. 58). The most telling confirmation is the child's right hand set on the tambourine's head. She touches it as if it were a piece of delicate lace – as differently as possible from the aggressive gestures of the boy drummer in the previous chapter (Fig. 35). Her diapha-nous gown, partly visible, flows behind her as if to anchor our reading of the girl's actions in the context of dance: graceful, soft, restrained, ethereal. (Here however the artist is confronted with a difficulty. For if the girl is to fulfill visually her gender role it is essential that she engage in the minimum of movement and physic-al assertion. Yet the representation of dance so demands movement that some allusion to it must be given. The compromise – that between socio-cultural requirements and the logic of physical real-ity – is achieved by what can only be explained as wind, a force external to the girl herself that moves across her body, fluttering out her dress, while the child herself stands impassively and stares somewhat blankly at her beholder. Were she actually to engage in a dance the tambourine would almost certainly be set aside. Hence, its presence in the portrait ironically prevents motion at the same time as it encapsulates the degree of her female perfection. She is already accomplished in a skill demanded of women, but the possession of the skill is more important than its actual practice, precisely because the practice itself is physically activating, hence ideologically dangerous, as I sketched in Chapter 5.

STATUS AND CONTROL, TIME AND PLEASURE

Keyboard instruments were not only the single most popular instruments played by girls and women – in the second half of the century only the English guitar provided serious competition – they also had the highest use value among the "female" instruments. One reason for this was economic: spinets, harpsichords and pianos were sufficiently expensive to be well outside the reach of the lower orders (not the case with many other instruments) and as such they were secure icons of social distinction. Indeed, many of the larger keyboards were affordable only by the truly wealthy. Moreover, keyboard instruments were made in a variety of sizes and degrees of decorative richness so as to indicate successive gradations of wealth from one family to another. The use value of size and decorative richness raises questions concerning the mediation of musical practices by concerns for prestige and also the relation of these practices to gender identity. These are also issues that inform the instruments' use as props in visual art, which in turn both reflects and perpetuates use value. In order for us to address these topics something must be said about the instruments themselves.

Among keyboard instruments spinets held less caste than single-manual full-size harpsichords, which in turn were less prestigious than larger double-manual models (in the later decades of the century all three types were available). Among pianos this hierarchy was repeated in the relationship of the smaller squares to the grands. Yet even within given model types considerable hierarchical variation was possible, in part because of different musical qualities and features of individual instruments: some makers were better than others; within a given type, some instruments had more stops, hence the potential for greater sound variation and so on. Yet the single greatest contributor to prestige hierarchy within any single category and size of instrument was the decoration of its case. That is, ultimate prestige for the possession of an instrument was significantly dependent on a totally non-musical factor. Thus even the relatively humble spinet could have its prestige increased through the use of multiple woods in the veneering for marquetry and stringing; brass hardware could be engraved instead of being left plain; the natural keys might be made of ivory, the accidentals of ebony and key fronts arcaded (Fig. 59).[10] None of this altered the fact that spinets were instruments of modest musical means. They had only one set of strings and one row of jacks and there was no buff stop, hence there was no possibility of varying tonal color as with harpsichords. Further, their tone was usually bad – there was insufficient sound board for the bass and the treble scale was too short.[11] In fact there were few changes made to the insides of spinets during the decades-long period of their popularity. As the instrument's caste declined, on account both of the declining social class of its user and its ultimate replacement by the square piano, there could have been little impetus to try to improve its sound, especially when altering the instrument visually probably affected sales more positively. My point here is that the musical potential of a given instrument was neither the only nor even the most important determinate of its success among English upper-class amateurs. Spinet maker Thomas Hitchcock at least once acknowledged the limitations of the actual musical interest among some of his buyers by providing the letter names of each scale degree just above each key (Fig. 60), a mnemonic device whose usefulness would normally end within a few days of the player's taking lessons but which would be of continued value to an essentially non-musical collector of musical furniture.

Late in the eighteenth century some makers of square pianos accommodated them for double functions as sewing tables, tea tables or writing tables.[12] This practice responds to dual and opposing

59 Bentside Spinet by John Crang, London (1758); London, Victoria and Albert Museum. By courtesy of the Board of Trustees

60 Bentside Spinet by Thomas Hitchcock, London (c. 1710); Washington, DC, Smithsonian Institution

pressures on the middle classes, by that time the primary buyers of square pianos. The perceived need for the piano as a marker of class distinction, on the one hand, had to be balanced with the necessity of frugality: the piano as symbol (music as a sign of leisure) and as domestic tool (work as the basis of bourgeois wealth). Ideologically, the pairing was brilliant in its self-confirmation of the association of the instrument with women and women with domesticity. The musical compromises that ensued on account of such instruments' dual functions undoubtedly assured that these experiments never caught on. But the failed attempt nevertheless is educative of the close association between musical practices, organology (a vastly unexplored history from this point of view) and the history of ideology.

In paintings of girls and women at keyboards the instrument's "look" was of the greatest importance and this mattered in art precisely because it mattered in life. Yet this is not to suggest that all representations were the same in this respect or that no changes occurred during the period. Nevertheless, the parameters were relatively narrow and can be illustrated by two portraits, one of an adult, the other of a child (Figs. 61–62). In the first Lady Strange stands beside a harpsichord while holding a song sheet. Accordingly, music provides a basis for the beholder's characterization of her. Yet the musical props possess little more than iconic status. Lady Strange is not actually performing, but posing. There is no music, but only the allusion to or the promise of music. Hence, music itself is not at issue, only what music stands for. In this respect, the painting's musical referents are complementary to the woman's elaborate costume, itself little more than an icon. (In fact, Lady Strange's costume does not seem to fit her, in part because of the ill match between her body and head, the latter disproportionately large. The costume and the body within it – her hands are too small and her arms do not seem properly attached at the elbows – function mostly as a pedestal for the head, and her head of course is what provided unique identity. All else is pictorial cliché. The painter was inept at making the transition from fancily clothed doll models he probably used for the body to the actual sitter's head.) Yet what is ultimately more significant, and probably accounts for the appropriateness of the image, is that Lady Strange is properly decorous. What is hers is the head, the rest in a sense is ideology.

As regards music Lady Strange is accomplished and domestic. She is not on a stage, the conventional drapery notwithstanding, but in her home, as that artist is at pains to represent by means of a parquet floor. She performs, if she performs at all, for her husband. Yet in fact she waits, perhaps for her accompanist but most obviously for our attention. As in nearly all portraiture of the period, the presumed beholder was male; as in nearly all portraiture of women, their cue for action came from outside themselves. Music here is time. It marks execution through action. It has spatial requirements. Yet all these components remained outside women's prerogatives. Women waited on/for men (time); their movements depended on men's authorization (performance); their actions occurred in space which itself was shaped by men (the domestic enclosure). Again, what belonged to Lady Strange was her head; even her torso seems supplied her by others. The harpsichord denoted status but status was hers on account of whom she married.

61 Edward Haytley (act. 1746–61), *Lady Strange* (1746), oil on canvas, 48.3 × 34.2 cm.; Private Collection

Mather Brown by contrast represented a girl actually playing a harpsichord,[13] rather than merely standing beside it (Fig. 62), so that by comparison with Lady Strange the instrument appears less of a standardized prop and more a reflection of her own preferences; but like Ann Hoare and the tambourine (Fig. 58) she touches the keyboard with temerity, undercutting this impression. For whom does she perform in her decorous gown, on the terrace of a Claudian estate devoid of other human form? She is dressed with nowhere to go, dressed for dancing but without a partner – she turns the page of her music book drawing attention to the piece itself, a dance tune. Yet her face is devoid of the joy that dance itself or the playing of dance music ordinarily incites. She looks out at us with a kind of tight-lipped determination that relegates her musical exercise to duty. That does not necessarily determine how she actually might have felt about music or dance. It does mean that her "look"

62 Mather Brown (1761–1831), *Girl Playing a Harpsichord*, oil on canvas, 123.2 × 99 cm.; Glasgow, Glasgow Art Gallery and Museum

was deemed appropriate to the situation. In other words, her own pleasure in her accomplishment is not an issue. Music here is not an act of self-expression but of externally imposed identity.

Paul Sandby's drawings of Mrs. Eyre (Figs. 63–64) produce entirely different effects from the two previous images, a fact explained by the medium of representation, drawing rather than painting. These are essentially private images – drawings were kept in folders or cartons, rather than put up on public display as were paintings; these two images are all the more privatized on account of their very small size. The standards of composition change in a drawing, at least one not preparatory to a painting as in these instances (the way in which Mrs. Eyre is represented is inappropriate to a formal portrait). The cultural agendas that necessarily had to be represented in portraiture are here substantially absent. As a

63 Paul Sandby (1725–1809), *Mrs. Eyre*, red chalk drawing, 14 × 19 cm.; San Marino, CA, Henry E. Huntington Library and Art Gallery

result the representation of Mrs. Eyre is radically changed and with it her revealed relation to music. Mrs. Eyre is still enveloped in domesticity but here she acts for herself. She controls her time and her space. Music serves her interests not those of others whose presence the beholder normally signifies. The harpsichord no longer functions as an icon of family prestige – though that significance is not totally lost. Instead it is her companion. For since we face her in profile she has no realization of our gaze; our surveillance is irrelevant. Indeed, we are denied the pleasure of the sound on whose making she concentrates. The image shuts us off, denies us access to her pleasure. Her existence is not free, but she is nevertheless partially empowered in the compensation and privacy (from us) her music affords. Her pleasure is not so evident in her face, except in the degree to which she ignores the beholder and through

64 Paul Sandby (1725–1809), *Mrs. Eyre*, pencil and watercolor, 16 × 12 cm.; Windsor Castle, Royal Library. © Her Majesty Queen Elizabeth II

the concentration that the artist imparts to her eyes. Instead it is embodied in the gesture of crossed legs, especially evident in the second drawing (Fig. 64). This is a mark of intimacy and comfort that could not occur in a painted portrait, not only for the reasons implicit in the arguments I have thus far advanced in this chapter, but also because it would impart onto Mrs. Eyre a personality far stronger than pictorial convention ordinarily allowed women (Lady Strange is a physical and emotional cipher by comparison).

The singularity of the Sandby drawings is particularly evident when compared with a watercolor by John Smart of the two young Binney sisters from 1806 (Fig. 65). Chronologically this image is the latest representation of them all; it is also the most politically regressive with respect both to women's identity and to the uses of music in the structuring of domestic ideology. The instrument is only partly shown, but sufficiently so to mark it as a grand pianoforte.[14] It is as up-to-date as the young women's coiffure and attire. Everything about the image contributes to an iconography

65 John Smart (1741–1811), *The Misses Binney* (1806), watercolor; London, Victoria and Albert Museum. By courtesy of the Board of Trustees

of prestige. Yet the effect of the piece is ultimately very different from the others, and the reason for this is centered on the unrelieved femininity of the composition. The very roundness of the image itself replicates the emphasis on the women's breasts whose shapes are barely disguised. The sisters are all softness; indeed, while their skin is unquestionably beautiful and flawless, their torsos seem to have no skeleton beneath the skin. The arm of the girl at the left appears utterly limp.

Their spatial enclosure is less determined than usual (though the piano nevertheless establishes it as domestic). Little distracts from their visages. But this is not thereby a feminist image, but a fetishization of the "eternal feminine." They are less domestic than decorative; they are not thereby liberated but given the most consequentially inconsequential role in socio-cultural relations. They are not empowered to be even domestics, to run the economy of a house. Drained of movement, they are "empowered" to be utterly immobile. And in this regard music once again performs a central role. Indeed, the effect of the image would be considerably weakened by the exclusion of the piano. For in that instance, the viewer's imagination could play on possibilities of (at least) sexual movement for these young women. The presence of the piano closes off that option and focuses our attention. Miss Binney's hand on the piano seems barely to have the energy to depress keys. And this in turn reinforces the semiotic use value of keyboard instruments' sound as an allusion to femininity and weakness (though what I intend to say is true of all music without regard to how it is produced): the sound once made quickly fades to nothing. It is in both literal and ideological senses inconsequential. This is how far we have come: from Castiglione through Pepys, where music functioned integrally in the lives of the educated, to the advent of the nineteenth century when its role constituted the sonic replication of the divorce from larger reality that was possible for those of economic means. The alteration in function from a music that constituted action to one of inaction both mirrored and helped formulate the profoundest of socio-cultural changes at the advent of the modern world and the ascendancy of the bourgeoisie throughout western Europe. The Misses Binney were the unwitting pictorial Eves to this history, over which, ironically, they had such limited opportunity actively to participate, except as icons of privatization, success and respectability (incidentally thus fulfilling roles identical to common usage of the concert hall in our own time).

ICONS OF DEFERENCE

In the second half of the century the English guitar as much as the harpsichord or piano served in both life and art as an icon of the domestic female, but in visual art it served this function in ways quite different from that of keyboard instruments. The essential distinction was that girls and women with English guitars were frequently depicted in the outdoors whereas with rather few exceptions keyboard instruments were represented *in situ* in family living quarters, usually a drawing room or large salon. The semiotic-iconic significance of this difference is not evident by looking at a single image, but only by setting several against each other.

In the first two examples (Figs. 66–67) English guitars are held by girls, and in the first instance the instrument is scaled down to the child's size. In the painting of children, perhaps even more than adults, the image needed somehow to root them to their family. This could be accomplished by commissioning a family portrait (Fig. 67) or by painting children by themselves but set into space identifiable as their father's estate. The latter presumably occurs with the three Walpole children (Fig. 66), probably the three daughters of Sir Edward Walpole (d. 1784), posed in a vast land-scaped park with a large house in the background commanding attention on the right side of the image, its distance from the sitters

66 George James (act. 1761–d. 1795), *The Three Miss Walpoles as Children* (1768), oil on canvas, 176.6 × 153.7 cm. By courtesy of Sotheby's

establishing the vastness of Walpole's landholdings. Indeed, the children are bunched slightly to the left in spatial deference to the house.

In the second image (Fig. 67) mother and daughter form a closed unit, each surveying the other, from which the husband-father is excluded but still dominates. His presence duplicates the function of the country house in the first example. And just as the house, even at a distance, draws our eyes away from the girls, or at least distracts us from them, so too the father in Wheatley's painting demands attention even at the expense of his more colorfully attired wife and daughter. This is accomplished by eyes, by the fact that of the three only his eyes meet ours, looking from his world into ours. The females never leave their world.

The world open to the male is encapsulated in the standard masculine props of hat and walking stick. That the world was

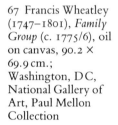

67 Francis Wheatley (1747–1801), *Family Group* (c. 1775/6), oil on canvas, 90.2 × 69.9 cm.; Washington, DC, National Gallery of Art, Paul Mellon Collection

closed to the female is signified by the English guitar which in both paintings is the dominant prop. It is an object of leisure, not responsibility, an inanimate equivalent of the kitten held by one of the Walpole girls (Fig. 66) – where the kitten itself, obviously enough, takes on the role of a surrogate infant (play being never free of cultural baggage). The adolescent girl playing the English guitar in Wheatley's portrait thereby prepares to become a reconstitution of her mother to whom she looks as if into a mirror. (In fact there is ambiguity here, for, while the girl looks toward her mother, her eyes seem unfocused. By contrast, the mother's eyes are painted to indicate total concentration on the daughter – a surveillance.) The costuming of the two females is strikingly different, though here once again the musical instrument mediates the difference into sameness. That is, the daughter's dress, by comparison with her mother's, is light, allowing freer movement. Indeed, by contrast the mother is virtually cocooned in cloth, no skin showing, every square centimeter wrapped: she is immobilized. It is the daughter's guitar, which she is learning under watchful eye, that will accomplish the same for her in due course.

Wright of Derby's portrait of Mrs. Gwillym (Fig. 68), also set outdoors, encodes the same sign. The portrait has a companion painting of Mr. Gwillym with which Mrs. Gwillym's must be discussed. She is set in relatively ambiguous space, though the presence of the village with its church tower in the background was probably intended to particularize the property as her husband's. What is more important is the fact that she is clothed in fancy dress, a Van Dyck outfit, a sort of masquerade costume, ceremonial not practical. There is a dissonance between her dress and the surroundings, just as there is dissonance between the setting and the fact that she plays an English guitar. Her open neck and low bodice displays her necklace to best advantage, but it is inappropriate in literal terms to a cool climate on a quite cloudy day. These details prevent the viewer from accepting the scene as literal. In other words, Mrs. Gwillym's costume and her English guitar together only serve to underwrite the fact that she is out of her own element in the landscape. She is an elegant lady who really lives elsewhere. Then why not simply paint her indoors where she belonged? The answer to this comes from the companion portrait. For it too is set outside, and here the outdoors is entirely appropriate and even necessary, for it shows the beholder what Mr. Gwillym is by what he has, property. His wife defers to him in the social relationship; hence it is she who in imagery must likewise be displaced.[15] Yet to place Mrs. Gwillym outdoors poses a potential problem, her competing for his space. This problem is in turn solved by the inclusion of the English guitar. She may venture from the house, so to speak, but only with her domestic, self-limiting baggage in tow.

I believe this is also the purpose of the English guitar in Arthur

Devis' portrait of an unidentified sitter (Fig. 69). Here the lady does not play the instrument (instead she holds a music book); the guitar simply rests beside her on the seat surrounding a tree. There is no specifically painterly reason that Devis needed to include the English guitar. In fact no prop at all is compositionally necessary.

68 Joseph Wright of Derby (1734–97), *Mrs. Robert Gwillym* (1766), oil on canvas, 127 × 101.6 cm.; St. Louis, MO, The Saint Louis Art Museum. Purchase: funds given by Miss Martha I. Love

Moreover, it is insufficient to explain the guitar's inclusion on the grounds that women actually played it, especially since it was an indoors instrument nevertheless shown outdoors. The fact that the English guitar was virtually never played by men underscores the fact that it fulfilled a socio-cultural function beyond the musical potential it possessed: the English guitar *was* female, within the terms of what it meant to be female. The keyboard instruments were played both privately and in public; the English guitar almost never outside the home. Given the history of its use it was an ideal emblem for the representation of the perfect woman, acquiescent and deferential. The fact that the English guitar was never an instrument of high musical caste, unlike the harpsichord or piano, reinforced female acquiescence. There was no "art" music for the instrument to speak of, even though women in many instances learned to play it well (and it was apparently not difficult to learn).

69 Arthur Devis (1712–87), *Portrait of a Lady* (1757), oil on canvas, 55.9 × 43.8 cm.; London, Tate Gallery

Men by contrast took up the violin, archetypal instrument of the "best" music from the European Courts to the opera theaters. This in itself I suspect was contributory in demarcating the violin as an instrument appropriate to men, in spite of the fact that very few amateurs ever learned to make decent sounds come out of it. There is no "natural" reason why women should not have taken up the violin; indeed, they would have had far more time available to learn how to play it well. That they did not do so was a cultural or ideological matter involving the instrument's appropriation by men, as the musical enthusiast Hester Lynch Piozzi understood perfectly and so stated in the silence of her diary: "How the Women do shine [in music] of late! . . . Madame Gautherot's wonderful Execution on the Fiddle; – but say the Critics a Violin is not an Instrument for *Ladies* to manage, very likely! I remember when they said the same Thing of a *Pen*."[16]

PLAY AND CLASS

The subject of play, intertwined cross-culturally with the topos of social class, appears in representations of both young girls and women with hurdy-gurdies. The Mason children (Fig. 70) and

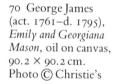

70 George James (act. 1761–d. 1795), *Emily and Georgiana Mason*, oil on canvas, 90.2 × 90.2 cm. Photo © Christie's

Miss Anne Gore (Fig. 71) alike play the role of Savoyards, that is, poor itinerant musicians from Savoy who traveled throughout France during the eighteenth century entertaining on the streets of towns and cities for meager handouts (ironically, at the same time as at Versailles the aristocratic game-players of the Arcadian *bergeries* employed hurdy-gurdies).[17] In England hurdy-gurdies were used by the lower classes as on the Continent. But there was no British Arcadian revival and the hurdy-gurdy was almost never played by members of the upper classes, except by direct reference either to Savoyards or lower-class native players. Hence, its representation in "Savoyard" portraiture relegated the instrument's function to the specifically non-musical. Its significance was as a sign that only indirectly related to music itself.

In the first image play is more "natural" on account of the sitter's age; this cannot be said of the second, though Anne Gore was only sixteen when the portrait was painted (she looks older), a year prior to her marriage.[18] Her play is more self-conscious than the Mason

71 Johan Zoffany (1733–1810), *Miss Anne Gore as a Savoyard* (1774), oil on canvas, 122 × 97.8 cm.; Firle Place, by permission of the Firle Settlement Trustees

children's; Zoffany in fact makes an issue of it, as a prerogative of her class and sex. With regard to her gender the hurdy-gurdy helped constitute an ideal image of the future and very young wife to a man twenty years her senior: a woman both simple and unspoiled, in effect a child of sorts, as faithful to her soon-to-be greybeard husband as the reassuring dog, *semper fidelis*, beside her.

Yet in another way the instrument was potentially unsettling; it was specifically an outdoors instrument, both by traditional performance practice and by necessity of its intense sound. Moreover, virtually all lower-class performers on the instrument were itinerants, belonging nowhere, moving over wide geographical areas. In other words, the associations carried by the instrument, except as modified by its aristocratic use at Versailles, were totally inappropriate to upper-class females: unprotected wanderings in a world controlled by men. Beyond that the instrument's sound was utterly alien to the sonorities sanctioned for the upper classes (Versailles notwithstanding) and for women. It was edgy, raw, assertive – appropriate to the outdoors but patently unnerving in closed quarters such as the home. And because of the drones there were no silences, no breath-taking, no rests. (Hester Lynch Piozzi wrote in her diary of Lady Hereford who "plays on the Vielle [hurdy-gurdy] to amuse her Friends, but Doctor Parker when he had listened a while, said very gravely – if your Ladyship will give me leave I'll go to the Door & hearken, for I have a Notion 'tis best at a Distance.")[19]

From this two things may be said. First, that very few such images were produced in England (there were many more in France among the Versailles-dwelling aristocracy) – I know of only one other besides these two. Second, in both these instances play was emphasized so as to mitigate unwarranted effects of the representations. That is, in the first image the instrument's use was sanctioned as child's play, in the second as part of a masquerade (adult play), for Anne Gore's costume is that of a young Savoyard. Masquerade undercut the negative associations of the Savoyard, and of a woman besides, by its self-referential confirmation that the activity was a game. As such, masquerades were expensive, often elaborate undertakings, which by this very fact brought honor to their sponsors, men. They constituted the embodiment of both leisure and pleasure, not only on account of their expense, but by the way in which they empowered the participants to cross (or "destroy") any "natural" or socio-cultural boundary in their way – people could for a moment thus become animals (via costuming and gesture) or social inferiors of whatever gradation, the lower the better so as to violate the taboo the more. The hurdy-gurdy in this instance was the perfect class prop, precisely because in actual practice it was a despised instrument – in northern Europe, before the Savoyards moved north, it was exclusively played by blind beggars.[20] And in

England it could be despised doubly, not only as an attribute of beggars but – and with irony – for its associations with the French Court (though in portraiture an English woman would never dress as a French aristocrat, even in masquerade).

THE REPRESENTATION OF REFUSAL

The portrait of the ideal woman was inherently oxymoronic, in that she should simultaneously be represented as accomplished yet as physically inactive as possible. By the latter I do not simply mean that female sitters were ordinarily shown sitting, but that they commonly showed no "promise" or potential for movement. This conflicts with the necessity to represent women as accomplished simply because the acquirement of accomplishments required repeated physical activity, if only involving small-motor movements. Since music was a principal accomplishment, visual allusions to it were necessary – all the more because of all the accomplishments, except dancing, it had no concrete "leavings" like needlework or drawing. Its results disappeared as soon as they were produced, the insubstantiality mirroring perfectly the female social and gender roles. Nevertheless, an actual musical performance was physical, sometimes dramatically so, geometrically exceeding that involved in needlework or drawing. This fact placed the portrait painter in something of a bind, one of the most typical ways out of which was simply to represent women holding a music book or sheet (Fig. 72) with no other referent to music, even though the music shown was virtually always either accompanied song or written for solo keyboard. In Devis' portrait Lady Villiers is further immobilized by her voluminous skirt from which her tiny upper torso seems to sprout as from the earth. The significance of the stasis in this image is made more evident by means of a comparison with a striking exception, a remarkable mezzotint after a painting by Allan Ramsay of Mary, Viscountess Coke (Fig. 73).

Set against the more conventional representations thus far considered, Lady Coke maintains a position of astounding assertiveness, in spite of her elegant and reserved demeanor. (Lady Coke spent much of her time at Court; she was a close friend of Princess Amelia, daughter of George II. She was also sentimentally attached to Edward, Duke of York. One contemporary described her "understanding" as "smothered under so much pride, self-conceit, prejudice, obstinacy, and violence of temper, that you knew not where to look for it.") Her face is not different from the others, nor is her costume, except that if anything its satin exudes even more luxury, in keeping with the architectural enclosure and room furnishings. What is different is created by the great theorbo she holds beside her.

The instrument was long since an anachronism by the time both

the painting and subsequent mezzotint were produced; it was in fact
a seventeenth-century instrument, one far more popular in Italy
than in England even in its heyday. The theorbo represented here,
moreover, was more than a mere studio prop. It belonged to one of
Lady Coke's talented musical friends, Lady Ancram, who also
played an ordinary lute (Ramsay painted Lady Ancram playing this
instrument). Lady Coke borrowed the theorbo, hired a master to
teach her but failed in her efforts. Lady Ancram later requested the
instrument's return, which was refused steadfastly even after
numerous written entreaties (in four different languages!).

It must have been Lady Coke herself who ordered the painting
since she was never on good terms with her husband, a profligate to

72 Arthur Devis
(1712–87) (?), *Lady
Villiers, Wife of Sir
John Villiers of
Morley, Dorset*, oil on
canvas, 46 × 34.5 cm.
By courtesy of
Sotheby's

73 James McArdell
(1728/9?–65), after
Allan Ramsay, *Mary
Viscountess Coke*,
mezzotint, 50.8 ×
36.8 cm.; New
Haven, CT, Yale
Center for British
Art, Paul Mellon
Fund

whom she brought £20,000 on their marriage (he left her at the church immediately following the ceremony!). She matched his indifference by remaining his wife in name only, though she attempted unsuccessfully to divorce him (he died only six years after the wedding and she never remarried).[21] Lady Coke's portrait

was painted five years after his death, thus indicating that the portrait was ordered and paid for by Lady Coke herself. Accordingly, it represents her to the world through *her* commission, not a man's. And it is explicitly different, not only from the paintings discussed in this chapter but from any other I know. The sitter, though not much of a musician, was responsible for choosing a musical theme for her portrait which in itself is anything but unique. Its singularity arises from what her chosen instrument, the theorbo, meant within the general context of the representation, and it is that which I want to consider in detail.

Lady Mary's choice of the theorbo as her primary prop is striking, not only because the instrument was outmoded, but also because even in its heyday few English women played it. It is a plucked string, to be sure, but one of gigantic proportion that could not be encased, womblike, in her lap like an English guitar, rather one that actually was superior to her in height. She has taken on a man's instrument, not simply by practice (which in itself no longer mattered since the instrument was essentially out of use, Lady Ancram notwithstanding), but by its size and shape. Given the prohibitions against women playing flutes on account of their phallic assertiveness, Lady Mary's theorbo violates the taboo with singular visual power, in that its shape replicates the entire male genitalia. (Thus in the sixteenth century in England prostitutes regularly carried simple lutes with them into taverns as marks of their trade. In emblematic literature of the time the bulge of the lute's back was also equated with that of the womb – these analogies were applied to the short-necked, hence less obviously phallic, instruments. In Dutch paintings from the seventeenth century, the common subject of the procuress always included a musical instrument, normally a lute.)[22]

I do not mean to suggest that Lady Coke consciously viewed her borrowed theorbo as a gigantic phallus whose tune she would play. Indeed, not only would that be absurd, it would also be irrelevant to my point. She would, however, clearly have understood (explicitly or implicitly, consciously or unconsciously) that the theorbo was outdated, and that it was not a (good) woman's instrument, with regard to her knowledge of the sexual connotations longstanding in the instrument's history. In portraits people never represented themselves with the out-of-fashion except for a purpose that overrode the negative associations with one's being thus out-of-step. What mattered here – especially since the lady actually possessed no skills on the instrument – was what the anachronistic theorbo meant to her and what she thought it would mean to the image's viewers, all the more given the wider audience of a reproduced print.

More than anything else the instrument asserted the woman's self-control and independence. This is further strengthened by the presence of two instruments, implying a duet, with Lady Mary as soloist, as such the dominant partner in the musical event. Her eyes meet ours head–on in a remarkable visual challenge: she remains very much a woman as her gender was understood in the eighteenth century, but she commands space within the image as a man. She does not defer to the setting, nor does she merely stand consonant with it. Instead, she defines the space around her – it only makes sense by her presence. There is space for only one figure, so that the harpsichord at the left, culturally feminine, must be visually co-ordinated with the huge arm chair at the right, by its size masculine, but she is without husband. These two objects stand in conflict mediated only by Lady Mary in conjunction with the theorbo. The lute established her uniqueness; only she could neutralize the inter-nal dialectics of the image. And in art, as in music, as in life such was a task rarely taken up by women in eighteenth-century England. In spite of her posed stasis, she is utterly different from the stiff, immobile Lady Villiers (Fig. 72). Lady Mary is confident she can manage on her own.

MY PURPOSE IN THIS chapter is to examine the familial functions of amateur music-making that identify themselves in group pictures of husbands, wives and children. My interest is not in the specific musical practices of the domestic scene, since I have outlined that history in preceding chapters, but in the ways that visual references to musical practices affirmed the most fundamental ideologies of social structure in eighteenth-century England among the dominant classes. In these images musical referents frequently constituted the most visually notable objects represented, thus identifying themselves as important signs whose significance could neither be left to chance nor be misread. From this two questions arise: first, why was music chosen as a visual metaphor; second, what does the employment of the musical sign say about the definition and regulation of family relationships and the larger social structuring mediated by family life? The crucial issue is how the visual representation of music related to the socio-cultural functions of music, and how music itself in turn served not only the demands of an "autonomous" visual art[1] but of ideology and the social constructions built upon ideologically dependent values. This chapter concerns the bond between music and power in a dialectical relation of domination to compensation.

Husband–wife and family portraits were among the most consistently affirmative images of the genre. They simultaneously exposed and *rationalized* relationships by visually establishing two simple hierarchies, one of biological supremacy (husband/father and male heir, followed by the wife/mother and the other children), and the other of chronology (which often compelled artists to produce a clear difference in the apparent age of the heir from that of the non-inheriting children, even in cases where little actual age difference existed). Both hierarchies encoded order in a gloss of absolute calm and via the oxymoron of posed informality. This meant that the realities of family life, always infinitely complex and changing, were smoothed over, figuratively and literally, and in effect eternalized, that is, rendered static.

The obvious lack of spontaneity in compositional arrangements was a response to the demand for the presentation of hierarchies. Few such pictures encoded affection, fewer still love, for emotional bonding per se was only indirectly relevant. As in upper-class marriages, more important issues were at stake, namely, the assertion of power. Accordingly, family portraits were highly self-conscious political statements, necessitating that every aspect of their presentation be carefully conventionalized. This is not to say that the genre never changed, from decade to decade or from painter to painter. Indeed, precisely the opposite is true. The stylistic divergence is enormous between a canvas by Arthur Devis (a premier painter of conversation pieces for about twenty years in the 1740s–1750s) and one by Sir Joshua Reynolds in the second half of the century. And the differences are not ones accountable for simply by chronology, skill and training, or by the quite different sitters for whom each worked, but by profoundly different points of view about how portraiture should accomplish its societal goals. Yet in spite of these and other differences these artists understood that the "look" and "goals" of artworks were far more than a matter encompassed or defined by the dictates of art itself or academic disputations on art carried out within a closed circle of practitioners. Every artist understood that he worked for patrons. To the extent that the demands of the patrons evolved, so did the "look" of the artworks. And of course artists themselves in both their disputations and artworks also helped mediate the ways that patrons wanted to look. Yet the complementary constants of class awareness and social position remained in the forefront of patrons' minds, however the boundaries of self-definition changed.

The common referent in language, both spoken and written, for the society that patronized artists (and musicians for that matter) was "the Quality," a denominator that naturally depended for its significance upon an unspoken opposite, the "unquality." It was the successful artist's task to know how to represent the difference. Why did so many portraitists understand that the musical sign bequeathed quality to the silent representations of the Quality? This is a question that can only gradually be addressed.

THE LANDSCAPE OF AUTHORITY

The leading painter to typical wealthy (bourgeois) landowners in the century's middle decades was Arthur Devis, who from his London studio produced numerous group portraits of Lancashire, Cheshire and Derbyshire families,[2] many prominently featuring musical props. Among all painters of this genre Devis' work most directly and obviously formulated a visual language expressive of the societal code I have outlined. His encoding became highly regularized, even repetitive, as when he repeated room interiors, landscapes or landscape elements in various paintings.[3] However these repetitions may affect our assessment of his importance as an artist, they are extremely valuable in the degree to which the formalization defined the terms of a successful response to patrons' demands. The basic features of Devis' work that interest me are evident in his well-known portrait of the Rookes-Leeds Family (Fig. 74).

Among Devis' most common compositional devices for establishing intra-familial, biological hierarchy was the treatment of spatial relationships between sitters, in particular by positioning the husband/father in such a way that he was simultaneously a sitter and a beholder of the very picture of which he was a part. The essential effect of this device was to create a world of separate spheres, one male, the other female: Edward Rookes-Leeds stands off to one side in the landscape separate from his wife and children. We look at the women as does Edward. This effect not only establishes the women's dependence on him, but also reifies them as estate property complementary to the lands Devis so attentively renders behind Edward Rookes-Leeds. His standing apart emphasizes both his separateness and importance and diminishes all other persons by comparison. The vista behind Edward is vast, open, bright; that behind the women closed and in shadow. The women

74 Arthur Devis (1712–87), *Edward Rookes-Leeds and his Family, of Royds Hall, Low Moor, Yorkshire* (c. 1763–5), oil on canvas, 91.4 × 124.5 cm.; Cottesbrooke Hall, Northampton, Collection Macdonald-Buchanan

are bunched in a slightly circular pattern that echoes their spatial arrangement in a drawing room; they are represented as displaced. Having been summoned for their portraits into the outdoors they bring with them precisely those "tasks" that are appropriate to the indoors: reading, needlecraft and music. These activities establish that the women have only a remote involvement in Edward's power – the town in the background may represent Bradford, where Rookes-Leeds financed canals, roads and coal mining ventures.[4] The women are less "sources" ("helpmeets") of his power than confirmations of it. Their lavish, light-reflective gowns are visual proof of his success as are the female accomplishments they so self-consciously "present" in characteristic conversation-piece catalogue fashion.

Devis' portrait of the Maynard family (Fig. 75) is rhetorically similar, though compositionally different. The sitters presumably include Maynard's wife and two children (the identity of the second woman is uncertain and it is not known which of the two was Maynard's spouse).[5] They are posed in the park surrounding the family's country house in Essex. Sir William himself was not painted, but his presence is both implied (by the "slot" of picture space on the left which seems strangely empty, as if held in reserve for him) and felt (by the fact that the estate is well tended, the trees trimmed, the cattle healthy). All is in order and at peace,

75 Arthur Devis (1712–87), *The Maynard Family in the Park at Waltons, Essex* (c. 1759–61), oil on canvas, 138.4 × 195.6 cm.; Washington, DC, National Gallery of Art, Paul Mellon Collection

most notably his family enjoying the easy leisure that Maynard makes possible. Sir William was a Whig Member of Parliament from 1759 to 1772 (the portrait dates from the beginning of his national service); Devis' composition "represents" him as a man of duty and greater tasks, responsible to the interests of his district which his absence itself reflects. His portrait-presence is super-fluous because his power is unquestioned; absence itself is thus a sign.

The viewer's angle of vision is somewhat above the sitters, a severely modified bird's-eye perspective often used in its high-flown form by English painters in the previous century to illustrate the parameters of large estates. By raising the beholder's angle of sight Devis subordinated his female sitters, not only placing them under surveillance but also simultaneously reifying them as estate props. He also interiorized their activities, as in the Rookes-Leeds portrait, in this instance by means of the hats that each of the four apparently wore between the house and their arrival in the protec-tive shade of the tree. The women's hats rest on the chair back atop the tree-seat. One child's still hangs on her arm. But a fourth, belonging to the other child, lies on the ground near the front picture plane between the two women. It is prominently placed; it draws attention to itself. And though an object ordinarily of little importance, its position here makes it significant. Specifically, it places the females in a metaphorical "interior" space by drawing our attention to the impermanency of – and their inadequacy to – a position in "exterior" space. The one hat draws attention to the other hats, all of which constitute "proof" of the females' domestic-ity, their delicacy and hence their need of protection. The two women's hats and the child's hat on the ground form an obvious triangle that encloses them in a separate space which the child farthest to the left enters as if from the outdoors, picked flowers in hand. The females are thus rendered safe in every sense of the word precisely because they behave – and look – as if they were not really there. The music of the English guitar in this context becomes a metaphor not only of familial calm and stability but also of domes-tic harmony. That in turn raises the question, "Harmony by whose definition?"

John Thomas Seaton, a far lesser artist than Devis, unwittingly unmasked the ideology of hierarchy that informed compositional convention in husband–wife portraits. Specifically, he mishandled perspective in a painting of Colonel Ralph Bates and his wife Anne (Fig. 76), by hustling the woman deep into the background and reducing the size of her upper body far in excess of what correct perspective required. She is literally diminished by comparison with her husband who physically dominates her as he breathes the outside air billowing out the drapery. Anne Bates, seated, with a melancholy look turns her head to look not at her husband but at the view from the open window, her cittern[6] in hand as the tangible signifier of her lack of access to that outside world.

MUSIC AND THE DIALECTICS OF "HARMONY"

Indoors husband–wife representations are particularly striking in portraits that commemorate marriages, as seems to be the case of an unidentified gentleman and lady (Fig. 77). The couple are young; the room they occupy is empty except, oddly, for a harpsichord and violin. The emptiness suggests a beginning, a bride brought home. Practicalities – like furniture – are as yet metaphorically set aside; there are few distractions to their love. Yet such a romantic reading is really not invited; the room is neither bare nor filled only by love. There are paintings on the wall, Italianate pictures, including one of ancient ruins, suggesting that the groom has made the Tour. He is a man of the world, experienced, cultivated, rich. His travel souvenirs are high-status, and he has inherited an estate within which to frame them, evident from the view through the elaborate, appropriately Venetian window. The prominent floor space, accentuated by the lines of the planking, alert the beholder to absence or emptiness. He having acquired a wife, his house is now to be filled, with furniture and children. That is the wife's role: domestic economy.

76 John Thomas Seaton (act. 1761–1806), *Col. Ralph Bates and his Wife Anne*, oil on canvas, 97.8 × 100.3 cm. Photo © Christie's

Accordingly, relationship is founded on a hierarchy that Devis carefully encodes via the metaphor of music. Devis implies a duet, for the husband's violin is atop the harpsichord. The husband, by handing her the sheet of music, in effect assigns her duties: he calls the tune. The harpsichord is her emblem; she is to accompany the solo of his life's violin. Music's emblematic function for marital harmony is, in fact, a harmony as conceived by the husband. To move from the metaphorical to the literal plane of actual musical practices, for a woman making music was a prime way of staying out of her husband's business. The man stands nearest the window to the world, the woman to the darkened corner where the painted memoirs of her husband's life in the world hang above her.

77 Arthur Devis (1712–87), *Gentleman and Lady at a Harpsichord* (1749), oil on canvas, 115.6 × 103.5 cm.; London, Victoria and Albert Museum. By courtesy of the Board of Trustees

The visual metaphor of marital fidelity and domestic bliss in this scene is music, a metaphor in use prior to the eighteenth century.[7] It was graphically employed by James Gillray in his "Harmony before Matrimony" (Fig. 78), wherein a loving couple sing to the accompaniment of a harp from a book of "Duets de l'Amour." Above them is a picture of Cupid in an oval (read ovular, ovum) frame. Cupid has dropped his quiver of arrows, taken up a blunderbuss and aimed at the two little doves cooing atop a birdhouse; they will experience love with a vengeance. Trophies of Hymen's torch and Cupid's bow and quiver flank the picture. To the left of the lovers a Chinese-style vase, containing roses of course, is decorated to show a man serenading a woman; nearby, the occupants of a fishbowl are about to kiss. Directly below is a heart-shaped vase. Between the two lovers, on the table, an open book of Ovid's poetry alerts us to passions aflame, though the satyr forming a table leg at the far right, and the two libidinously tempered cats in a brawl prior to mating, suggest that in reality there is less love here than lust.

That the union's bliss was temporary is defined by Gillray's companion print, "Matrimonial-Harmonics" (Fig. 79). As the wife screeches out her song (text: "Torture-Fury-Rage-Despair-I cannot cannot bear"), her husband blocks his ear and peruses the "Sporting Calendar." The birds, now cockatoos with three offspring in the nest, are back to back and no longer "speaking." They are no longer free, but imprisoned in a cage – metaphorically standing for marriage – ironically supported by the antlers of cuckoldom. The couple's own squawking offspring appears in the arms of its nurse at the left. The wall thermometer indicates freezing; Cupid lies asleep (or dead) on the mantelpiece, with "Requiescat in Pace" as his motto. The next musical numbers are to be "Separation a Finale for Two Voices with Accompaniment" and "The Wedding Ring – A Dirge."[8] Hymen (bust on the wall) is diseased, undoubtedly syphilitic. The husband, on the loveseat(!), eats alone. Opposite him, the chair seat intended for his wife holds an open volume, "The Art of Tormenting." (In these comedies Gillray settled blame for the marriage's failure on the woman. The man may go to fat in the second image, but the woman is metamorphosed into a hag-like monster and the producer of an equally offensive offspring.)[9]

The most striking signifier of male domination of women in eighteenth-century portraits was the emblematic caged bird. Arthur Devis' portrait of the Rev. Thomas D'Oyly and his wife Henrietta Maria (not his daughter as has sometimes been suggested) (Fig. 80) shows the husband handing his wife a letter he has read and is apparently about to respond to (he holds a quill in one hand and writing supplies are on the table). A one-manual harpsichord stands in back at the right, partly covered by drapery. Thus we know that at least one of the two is musical, almost certainly the woman. But

78 James Gillray (1757–1815), *Harmony before Matrimony* (1805), etching, 23.1 × 34.2 cm.; London, British Museum. By courtesy of the Trustees

79 James Gillray (1757–1815), *Matrimonial-Harmonics* (1805), etching, 23.4 × 34.2 cm.; London, British Museum. By courtesy of the Trustees

most interesting about the picture is the birdcage directly above the lady. Metaphorically it stands for the wife: cared for, attended to and protected by the husband, but not free. There are actually two birds here, one real and caged, the other in "free flight" serving as a decorative device on the cord suspending the cage. This second bird, free but not real, represents the antithesis of reality: the woman's cage is her home – blank wall space, closure.

By contrast, above the Rev. D'Oyly is a landscape painting, that

80 Arthur Devis (1712–87), *Rev. Thomas D'Oyly and his Wife Henrietta Maria* (c. 1743–4), oil on canvas, 73.7 × 61 cm.; British Private Collection

is, open horizon, the world outside the closed and domestic interior. The painting hangs above the fireplace, archetypal metaphor for the home hearth which in English society it was the man's duty to protect.[10] The landscape contains more than scenery, however; it contains action, specifically a hunt (both a dog and a hunting horn are visible), a culturally loaded sign of an all-male activity among the English upper classes, the sport of killing, which in the semiotics of actions ritually asserted male dominance over property of all kinds and domination of the social order.

This is evident, ironically, in a lady's fashion plate for the month of November (Fig. 81) illustrating a lady's fancy attire and at the same time defining her status in relation to that of her husband. In the background behind protective walls is the well-attended estate to which she belongs and from which she has ventured. By con-

81 Robert Dighton (c. 1752–1814), *Fashion Plate for the Month of November*, from a series, *The Twelve Months*, mezzotint, gouache and watercolor, 38.4 × 26 cm.; Minneapolis, MN, The Minneapolis Institute of Arts, The Minnich Collection

trast, in the foreground she witnesses momentarily a world she has otherwise apparently been sheltered from, but which in fact she is a victim of. To her right is a peasant cottage, mostly hidden by a wooden fence, meanly and obviously contrasted with the estate. To her left a dramatic and striking image attracts both her eyes and ours. It is a scene of death in two guises, first, that of a lifeless tree, in severe opposition to the topiaried (tended, flourishing and *regimented*) evergreens behind the walls of the great house, and, second, hunted birds hanging next to a gun: trophies of the husband's sport, ritual victims of his right to his property. The woman's eyes, focused on the birds, marks her relationship to a well-established visual metaphor. In this dangerous exteriorized space she is protected by the voluminous cocoon of fur (!) and fabric totally encasing her body. Her latest fashions provide visual assurance of her preservation from violence, to be sure, but dialectically also mirror the denial of her access to the non-domestic world. The fact that these matters are encoded onto a fashion plate reveals the extent to which the ideology of domesticity was naturalized in the culture. One might argue that such constructions in a genre as socially important as portraiture exaggerate reality by visually protesting too much. But that position cannot be maintained in light of such ephemeral imagery as the work of Robert Dighton, the function of which bears only the most indirect relation to the self-conscious presentations of value in paintings but which nevertheless reiterates the identical subjects.

The essential maleness of the "external" world is represented in the art by land, as I have shown with scenes of landscape and country houses, and by the physical action of the hunt-in-progress. A third means is evident in the fashion plate just discussed, namely, the fruits of the "labor": acquired game. Occasionally, this version of maleness spills over into a kind of visual insanity, namely, the almost shocking representation of violence, purposeless except for the ideologically important assertion of power (Fig. 82). Here are displayed the assorted trophies of death from virtually every animal type having the misfortune to occupy the sitter's woods, which by implication are vast, given the assortment of species. Yet the man at the left benefiting from the bloodsport himself enters the scene of carnage like a king making an entrance at Court, utterly at ease, even uninvolved, as if the animals were simply bowing down in his presence (for some time the image was mistakenly taken to be an eighteenth-century representation of Robert Walpole). Arthur Devis in a portrait of the Cross family made use of dead game in an equally powerful and direct way. He posed husband, wife and small child on the grounds of their estate at Shudy Camps Park, Cambridgeshire, the family home in the background separated from the sitters by an expansive lawn. Mr. Cross, just back from the hunt, hands his wife a small dead bird. Seated on a bench, book in hand, she looks up and literally visibly shrinks back from the little carcass being presented to her. On her other side, her husband's hound looks on with interest at the trophy. To choose this gesture for the husband and this response for the wife was a blatant, raw expression of hierarchical difference.[11]

The D'Oyly portrait (Fig. 80) is thought to have been painted shortly after the couple's marriage. In this context the meaning of the piece becomes clearer. Action proceeds from the husband to the wife. He reads the letter and then passes it to her; he will formulate the response (the pen is in his hand). She is passive. The actions open to the wife are those of the home, the lady's cage, so to speak. The Rev. Mr. D'Oyly's horizons were probably limited in secular society, perhaps by an older brother, archetypal cause of many priestly vocations. Yet his horizons were limitless by comparison with those of his wife. When Letitia Pilkington married her husband Matthew, a cleric like D'Oyly, "he brought her as bridal gifts a harpsichord, an owl [presumably in a cage], and a cat"[12] – in other words, two pets and an instrument, all three of which ratified his expectations of her role.

Robert Dighton's watercolor of "Winter" (Fig. 83) also contains a caged bird shown in obvious conjunction with a domestically engaged woman, the cage once again suspended directly over her head. She is seated near the hearth (surrogate signifier for her husband), so large as to force the connection. She reads a letter, but sits uncomfortably erect, not relaxed, as if reading is her duty, and as if the epistle is from her husband. She looks up from the text and turns her head in the general direction of a window providing a

82 Netherlandish School (seventeenth century), *A Hunting Party*, oil on canvas; Sherborne St. John, Hampshire, The Vyne, The National Trust

view of the world outside, an all-male world of sport, in this case, skating, where violence again occurs – the most prominent image is that of a man taking a hard fall. Her outdoors wrap, unused, is on a chair by the window.

   English women in fact often kept birds – the topos in art was not fictional – and attempted to teach them to sing. Between c. 1708 and 1730 there appeared four editions of a small tutor book called *The Bird Fancyer's Delight* designed for use with the flageolet or recorder. In a print illustrating this practice (Fig. 84) a young woman stares wistfully at a bird, momentarily uncaged, responding to the tune she has played. The sensitivity and perhaps sadness in the lady's face reflects her empathy with (and, accidentally, self-recognition in) the bird's plight. Not incidentally it also presents the woman as the vessel of emotion, the most certain sign of her gender

83 Robert Dighton (c. 1752–1814), *Fashion Plate for Winter*, from a series, *The Four Seasons*, watercolor, 34 × 26.7 cm.; Minneapolis, MN, The Minneapolis Institute of Arts, The Minnich Collection

identity and "natural" difference from men, as contrasted with the
Netherlandish painting (Fig. 82) where no emotional energy is
expended on the killed game. But this is not to say that men did not
consciously recognize the metaphorical value of caged birds. Laurence Sterne's *A Sentimental Journey* (1768) tells of a caged starling
whose cries of "I can't get out – I can't get out" so affected his hero
as to engender meditations on imprisonment and slavery – but not
of course on women's position, even though the cultural association between them and caged birds was so well established.[13]

In an anonymous satirical print from late in the century (Fig. 85),
"The Captain's so Kind as to Thrust in a Note, while Old Lady
Cuckoo is Straining her Throat," via both text and image the
association between women and birds is made explicit, alongside

84 Richard Houston
(c. 1721–75), after
Francis Hayman,
Hearing (1753),
mezzotint, 35.2 ×
24.8 cm.; New
Haven, CT, Yale
Center for British
Art, Paul Mellon
Fund

the ability of males to control and demean. The sexual connotation to "Thrust in a Note" is explicitly invited: the phallic shape of a stemmed note is clear enough, the obscene gesture of the man's bent arm, his raised leg and his leer complete the association. Music issues from the throat. Here the direction is reversed for the purposes of a sexual pun; the mans "note" is presumably to be thrust down the lady's straining "throat." The old woman performs her music unawares, though she is rendered a vain grotesque, a demeaned human version of the dancing dog and performing bear in the prints on the wall. Meanwhile the parrot on his perch looks passively on, as the Captain for the entertainment of the viewer commits sexual assault.

85 British School, *The Captain's so Kind as to Thrust in a Note, while Old Lady Cuckoo is Straining her Throat* (1777), etching, 35.2 × 24.8 cm.; Minneapolis, MN, The Minneapolis Institute of Arts, The Minnich Collection

I want to pursue the caged bird with one more example, among a larger number that exist, this time representing a young woman at her spinet (Fig. 86). Here the sense of confinement is nearly absolute: there are no windows to the outside; the girl stares at a wall, her own face averted from the viewer. She is faceless, thus anonymous. Above her an owl, age-old attribute of Minerva, goddess of wisdom, is tightly confined in a small cage around which other birds fly. The image is emblematic (it cannot be taken as literal since no rational person would allow a flock of birds in the house), according to the literature of which the cage was an attribute of hope, in the sense that the confined bird hoped for liberation. Similarly, the bird was an emblem for the element of air (possessing an obvious association with freedom). The relation between the young woman confined to her spinet within the domestic cage and the caged owl around which (lesser) birds fly is clear. The free birds

86 Lady Dorothy Savile, Countess of Burlington (1699–1758), *Girl at Spinet with an Owl in a Cage*, pen and brown wash over pencil 23.7 × 18.6 cm.; Chatsworth, Kent, Devonshire Collection. By courtesy of the Courtauld Institute of Art, London

are tormenting reminders of antithesis, of unavailable freedom.[14] It is noteworthy that this drawing was executed by a woman, Lady Dorothy Savile, Countess of Burlington (1699–1758), wife of Handel's patron Richard Boyle, 3rd Earl of Burlington,[15] clearly a woman who understood her culture.

It is safe to conclude that the caged bird in these images, save the last, was employed by the artists and seen by most viewers (certainly those who were male) as an untroubled and unproblematic statement about women, their relationships to their husbands and to their society, and the roles allowed them by the dominant culture. Thus to whatever extent this old emblem was still recognized as such (the English after all had little taste for emblematic art so much appreciated by the Dutch in the previous century), it would have been read as affirming "happiness in captivity." Yet the question is not only how the image was "read" in the eighteenth century, but how we read it. The immediate issue the emblem raises – whether considered in its use on the Continent in the seventeenth century or in England in the eighteenth – is by whose definition is the bird (and what it stands for) happy?

The fundamental point here, of course, is that the caged bird was not a visual device for making statements about animal rights. Like all emblems it was an image which metaphorically alluded to human concerns, conditions, values and aspirations. If taken to mean "happy in captivity," the caged bird was a rationalized justification for oppression which proclaimed the naturalness of its demonstrably unnatural premise. The bird raised in captivity may not have any sense that its situation falls outside the natural order. The women in Robert Dighton's fashion prints may not have questioned the premise about their lot either. But if we are to write a history that is self-conscious of our own values (here pertaining to the concern with sexual oppression) as well as those of the past we study (and it is only within this context that any history can have more than antiquarian value), the dialectical component of ideologies must be acknowledged and accounted for. This is the reason I have considered this seemingly innocent visual vignette, which in any event, once recognized, may be entirely left out and still metaphorically assert its function (Fig. 87). Devis painted Edward Parker with his wife Barbara in a way that eliminated the necessity of the caged bird, at the same time preserving its trace: Barbara Parker herself is caged behind the iron fence of their estate's grounds, her husband effectually guarding the gate open only to him. Moreover, the gate opens inward, in such a way that Parker's access to egress comes at his wife's expense, increasing the visual impact of her metaphorical incarceration by fencing her in on three sides instead of two. (One only need reverse the compositional positioning of the couple to realize the repressive force of the arrangement, here treated quite conventionally. No painter of the period could ever consider placing a gentleman in a similar position.) As was pretty much standard portrait convention, Barbara Parker registers her deference to her husband by looking at him, not us, in a gesture that replicates the spirit of Gerard de Lairesse's instructions concerning portraiture in his famous treatise on painting: "the Woman, standing on the right Side of the Man, has a sedate Motion, and set and hanging Shoulders: But the Man contrarily is in an active Motion." (Lairesse further directs that the woman's body should be turned toward her husband.)[16]

In portraiture, for women the escape – if it can be called that – from the imagery of domesticity and implicit confinement was metamorphosis into heavenly creatures. Clouds invade the terrestrial sphere of Lady Elizabeth Cromwell (Fig. 88) and young Emily de Visme (Fig. 89), painted nearly a full century apart from each

87 Arthur Devis (1712–87), *Edward Parker with his Wife Barbara* (1757), oil on canvas, 127 × 101.6 cm.; Private Collection

other, both in the role of Saint Cecilia, an old and continuing topos resurrected for use in a secular genre.[17] (To be sure, the painter of Emily de Visme wanted to have it both ways, for he arranged the girl in a distinctly unsaintly pose and clothed her in the most diaphanous of gowns.) These images must be seen not only as positive statements about the sitters' virtues or accomplishments, but also as ones inadvertently transmitting a negation of any so straightforward a reading. Both paintings imprint a deep irony: their sitters are settled into an environment which by its very abandonment of reality only recalls reality the more. It is not accidental that eighteenth-century portrait painters failed to use any

88 Sir Godfrey Kneller (1646–1723), *Lady Elizabeth Cromwell as Saint Cecilia* (1703), oil on canvas, 68.6 × 50.8 cm.; Private Collection. By courtesy of the owner

remotely comparable topos for male sitters: none was needed. The male counterpart to these well-placed women found sufficient promise in the real world. Even when a man took openly to music, as portrait convention allowed for professional musicians (Fig. 90), the etherealization by means of musical sound was not revealed in the image itself. Instead all was rooted in a reality which at every turn announced its worldliness and the sitter's comfort therein. One bowed the cello with one hand and petted the dog (not of the ladies' "lap" variety) with the other.[18]

As regards musical subject matter I know of only two conversation pieces (Figs. 91–92) that violate the pictorial order discussed in this chapter. In the first a father by himself attends his three daughters, the mother's absence so anomalous as to indicate that she was no longer alive. In this instance then the father fulfilled two roles, as necessity would dictate. But what is striking is that he willingly

89 John Russell (1745–1806), *Emily de Visme, Later Lady Murray, as Saint Cecilia* (1794), oil on canvas, 135 × 110.5 cm. By courtesy of Sotheby's

preserved the reality of these culturally opposed functions for others to see. For example, he listens with attention to his daughter play the harpsichord; he watches her, not us (even though she turns toward us, her other audience). He has entered from the outdoors (his coat is on the chair at the left) by the window that shows us his other world. The exceptional nature of the image is further strengthened by the vignette in the center foreground, the youngest child shown with a pet bird freely perched on her hand. Here the oddity is an absence: there is no cage, a prop in such representations that was very rarely omitted.

90 Sir William Beechey (1753–1839), *Robert Lindley* (c. 1805), oil on canvas, 203.2 × 144.8 cm.; Hanover, N H, Hood Museum of Art, Dartmouth College, Gift of Irving S. Manheimer

In the second example (Fig. 92) a father prepares to accompany his daughters, while his wife seemingly claps her hands setting the rhythm for the youngest child's dance. Here the harmony on every level is complete, though the father metaphorically commands attention by his gesture of tuning his violin (establishing the harmony over all).

91 John Greenwood (1729–92), *John Richard Comyns of Hylands, near Chelmsford, Essex, with his Family* (1775), oil on canvas, 90.2 × 109.2 cm.; New Haven, CT, Yale Center for British Art, Paul Mellon Collection

92 William Hogarth (1697–1764), *Richard Wesley, 1st Baron Mornington, his Wife and Daughters and their Friend Miss Donellan* (1731), oil on canvas on panel, 61.6 × 73.7 cm.; Stratfield Saye, The Duke of Wellington's Collection. By courtesy of the Courtauld Institute of Art, London

SUMMARY

Adorno pointed out that "music has something to do with classes insofar as it reflects the class relationship in toto."[19] To this statement I would add that music has something to do with the sexes, whose relationships it mirrors and is to a considerable degree mediated by. Women were the sex trained in music, yet the limitations of their social freedom ensured that their skills would seldom have influence. Men, by contrast, though largely discouraged from music, had the social freedom to take it up anyway and play in public if they so desired (without necessarily possessing the requisite skills, thereby ensuring mediocrity in eighteenth-century English concert orchestras).

John Potter wrote in 1762 that one of the reasons for English high society's contempt for music was "that it not only requires a particular genius to excel in it, but also a great deal of time to make any progress, and by this means hinders and disqualifies a person for any thing else."[20] Music's domestic function, and increasingly its public function, was to kill time. In these circumstances, as Adorno pointed out, music "parasitically clings to time and ornaments it."[21] And this function is ideological, serving at once both to confirm and hide social reality.

England's example set the stage for the place of music in Western history subsequent to the eighteenth century – not because it produced any great composers during the Industrial Revolution, indeed, because it did not. From its dominant economic and political position as an industrial nation supported by the resources and markets of a vast empire, England established the terms for cultural self-understanding and self-definition that became naturalized in the capitalist ideologies, hence social praxis, of western Europe and beyond. It is hardly surprising that the musical life of the home so mediated this history, given the dominant perception of the home as the self-perceived foundation for the values upon which bourgeois society depended.

In one fundamental way John Potter, repeating Locke, precisely defined music's problematic relation to English upper-class society, namely, music's relation to the contemporaneous conception of time. Music was established in a culture of time wherein time itself was increasingly perceived as linear and developmental, and the life led within the confines of this paradigm as segmented.[22] In other words, time was perceived not as static but as dynamic; as such it was a field of contested relations. Time was money was power. It is no historical accident that this same society produced the Industrial Revolution of the nineteenth century which so depended upon a culture of time.

The practice and function of music in the lives of English upper-class amateurs at once foreshadowed, mediated and (eventually) mirrored the practice and function of public high art music in the nineteenth century and beyond in one crucial and self-limiting way. By the late eighteenth century and among the dominant classes music, once integrated into the social fabric not self-consciously as art but as part of life-ritual, was now almost universally understood – with respect to time – in one of two ways. For men it was a misuse of time, because it was itself literally non-productive, totally abstract, hence non-developmental. Its use therefore necessitated strict control. It was a fit practice when performed by someone else (a professional, hired labor) or as a physical-spiritual relaxant from productive involvements. For women the male perception of music as a misuse of time was the very source of music's usefulness. It helped ensure that women's use of time would be non-productive (except for closely sanctioned activities), hence advantageous to men.

Ironically, of course, the pleasure that music provided both sexes – for very different reasons – threatened the very equation its use was intended to uphold. Music, as sonority, unquestionably touched the spirits of people in ways that no amount of philosophical literature or societal instruction could adequately account for, hence control. This acknowledges music's compensatory role in women's lives, and in the lives of men for that matter. The pleasures of music were indeed valuable, constituting a temporary otherness. Yet precisely because music functioned progressively essentially only as compensation from material reality it confirmed the very thing its practice served to deny. Solace after all only establishes the primacy of sorrow. For men and women alike music reminded of an alternative which, unrealized, only continued to gnaw at the hardened superstructure of dominant ideology dependent upon a developmental conception of time. Music among all forms of human expression best expresses this reminder because it is at once realized in time and, experientially, alters (even seemingly suspends) time. And when the music falls silent its memory renders the rush of "real" time all the more problematic. I believe that this accounts for the fact that so many eighteenth-century amateurs of both sexes continued to dabble at music against such striking ideological and social odds. Few attained much skill at it, for the very reasons I am addressing, but many more at some level understood its importance:

I live in the country, and sometimes entertain myself and my friends with music; and have had at different times some of the best performers come down to visit me: I find in this an ease for all anxiety, and while I join my fiddle to my wife's harpsichord, there is scarce any trouble that is not for a while forgotten.[23]

9 *Epilogue: the social and ideological relation of musics to privatized space*

JOSEPH NOLLEKENS' SMALL Watteauesque conversation piece (Fig. 93), by tradition said to represent the Earl and Countess Tylney and friends on the terrace of the Lake House at Wanstead House, defines its world not in pictorial terms congruent with the "real" world of later English conversation pictures (property and its self-conscious possessors), but as French courtly theater.[1] Nollekens painted a carefully acknowledged stage set filled with actors playing parts. His painting, extraordinarily self-reflexive, is simultaneously about space, time and artifice and the relation between all three with music as the central metaphor. My question is: what does this mean?

In typical later English conversation pictures (for example, Figs. 74–75), property per se shared equal status with the individuals who possessed it. Sitters were defined by land which established pedigree and asserted economic, class and family stability. Land marked the reality of situation, the sitters' literal rootedness in the mundane. Yet the representation of land was itself problematic in that it betrayed uneasiness, a concern that status was actually fluid, its permanence uncertain. (This may account for the English preference to paint country houses in the background, emphasizing estate parks instead. Buildings, like families, came and went; land, so to speak, remained.) The concern to represent property, in other words, was ultimately expressive not of the desire to control space but of the anxiety to control space in time. The first was totally dependent upon the second and utterly meaningless without it.

Nollekens deproblematized the space–time dimension by rendering both artificial. He painted an image, itself artifice, about artifice – an illusion about illusion, via the device of theater. He produced an outdoors painting in which land per se, in the English sense, was essentially eliminated, made a non-issue. He transferred his English sitters from their estate into an alien "geography," the exotic world of French courtly society which had long since established powerful fictive metamorphoses of space and time. To be sure Nollekens represented "land," at the far left. But it is land as painted backdrop, theatrically and literally announcing itself as unreal (the match between the bottom of the "backdrop" and the tiled terrace says as much). More to the point, this is not agricultural land but (a French) Arcadia, where only the activities of Eden transpire. There is no labor, no tending. No man hunts these lands or grazes his cows there. This is land only for the harvest of love.

Nollekens' architecture, in dramatic and foreshortened close-up, is extraordinarily stagey (whether the building represents an actual or imaginary house – traditional identifications notwithstanding – hardly matters). It is at once monumental and false, its only depth the stairs from which each sitter in turn has presumably made her or his entrance. The windows, notably the one at the extreme right, appear to have nothing behind them. What matters is not its absent depth but the pedigree of its look. The "structure" merely decorates its presumed occupants via allusion to the timeless qualities of classical form. Indeed, the sitters' bodies mirror the grace and pose of the (pseudo) classical sculptures, just as the sitters' music-making echoes the musical scene of the sculptural relief just over their heads on the stairwall. (The sculptures in fact stand in eighteenth-century aristocratic poses, thus reversing the chronology we are asked to believe in.) Nollekens finally completes his stage design via the

93 Joseph Francis Nollekens (1702/6–48), *A Musical Party* (c. 1735), oil on copper, 35.6 × 45.7 cm.; Private Collection

pavement forming the terrace, by which means he further severely limits our sense of the outdoors-ness of his sitters' outdoors experience. There is here no earth, no sky, no trees. There is in its place the order and perfection defined by the pavement's regularity and of course the activities that take place upon it.

Yet order, perfection and regularity always only have meaning when considered against their opposites. For this particularized world to have significance its difference *from* must be visually acknowledged. In this light the servant standing at the left picture edge was not an arbitrary inclusion. He *must* be there to establish an opposition. Obviously, to be at the apex of the social hierarchy meant less if what that position was superior to was not presented alongside. Yet this fails to explain the servant's blackness. Indeed, the establishment of racial difference was what really mattered, far more than the exhibition of inferior class rank per se. For as a black he represented not a Lockian inferiority by accident of birth (class not race) and environmental difference, as would be evident in the presence of a white servant, but a perceived "natural" inferiority that could never be overcome. In essence he provided the visual proof of the *moral* correctness of this illusion about reality. He is the answer to bad conscience.

The perfect activity to this setting is music, and only this kind of music. I do not mean simply that the art music connoted here represented yet another visual order, though that is important. I mean that the music is not English (no remnants of consort playing here) but French, an ensemble *visually* aristocratic rather then visually "musical." The man playing the violin, for example, is more concerned with his elegant textbook posture than with his playing, and the same can be said of the oboist at the right and the guitarist – her fingers strum the strings with an elegance of gesture that denotes only social position. In other words, the musical scene was necessary here for the ways in which it offered opportunities to represent the specifically visual constituents of rank. But to be sure, the very fact that a musical event was painted called to mind music itself and this brings me to my second point, namely, that the musical event is accomplished without effort. Arms are limp, fingers relaxed; lips barely pretend to an embouchure. The music that sounds is literally without labor; it is ethereal, perfectly harmonious, otherworldly, ironically (being music) out of time, hence unthreatened by time.

As musicians the sitters uniformly close rank – always in visual terms – with what stands (literally) outside them, the black servant off to the side holding their refreshments, toward whom the male violinist and female guitarist nearest him look in notable distraction as if he were an intruder more than a servant. These sitters' gazes thus problematize his presence; he is a necessary evil, an alien species under surveillance. Music possesses an ideological charge, not only as a visual metaphor, but also as both a physical practice and as sonority. Nollekens' sitters make music that is decorous, deritualized, necessarily unnecessary except as an expression of their achieved position, its actual disposability a proof of their importance. It is regulated activity in a world these individuals have divided up and "rationalized." It is at once the sign of their triumph and an allusion to the agency by which it was accomplished. Music here is not just sound; it is order, an imposed harmony whose very decorum has a feared and despised opposite that I will consider at the end.

Visual representations of large-ensemble music-making among the upper classes are relatively rare (Fig. 94) and for reasons not difficult to ascertain. In such settings music tended to overtake the scene, in a sense rendering the sitters – and the viewer – less significant than the event itself, since logic demands that performers attend to their business with concentration, hence ignoring everything else around them. (This performance will apparently continue for some time, judging by the servant entering at the right carrying six scores, the topmost marked "Vivaldi".) Nevertheless, the subject had use value congruent with and complementary to

94 British School, *A Musical Party* (c. 1750), oil on canvas, 99 × 124.4 cm. By courtesy of Sotheby's

more typical representations of musical activity. The most striking aspect of the painting is its crowdedness – the way the room presses in on those assembled. This closeness is of the utmost significance for it was by this means that the beholder recognized a *closed community*: as with Nollekens' painting, this is an image about space or, specifically, access to space in time.

London and other cities in England regularly enjoyed public concerts throughout the century, but the predominant non-theatrical musical experiences among upper-class audiences were so-called private concerts given in the homes of the wealthy, reg-ularly employing professional musicians as well as amateurs. It is not accurate to assess this activity simply as the remnants of the consort-playing tradition, and not only because the players them-selves were not all (or even mostly) amateurs. Rather this is because of the presence of an audience, one characteristically greatly out-numbering the performers. Audience changed everything, even though the "domestic" setting remained constant, because an audi-ence must *gain admission*; it is constituted by a group that must *be let in for a time*. Theoretically, public concerts were open to anyone interested and having the money to buy a ticket. Commerce as such was potentially leveling; nothing mattered so much as one's ability to pay, hence all classes of English society might attend the theater or even the opera, both of which were in fact highly popular forms of general entertainment. But for house concerts money itself was not sufficient, even though tickets were commonly issued for these events and a fee charged. The potential ticket purchaser had first to be issued an invitation to purchase, and the invitation of course depended upon who you were. Accordingly, admission to house concerts required entrance through two sets of gates, one commer-cial, the other social, which at once protected and delineated a highly privatized space, to which access was highly prized.

I am suggesting that the scene represented in this painting, while compositionally very different from that of Nollekens, is ideologi-cally congruent with it, despite its homey Englishness. Any single individual may be diminished by the presence of so many others, but each is in turn elevated by simply being there. (By contrast the professional musicians present, almost unquestionably the three men in front, their backs to the beholder, gain little from their presence or representation. They are but organic analogues to the rest of the physical setting.) There is reference to the outside world via the windows, but one devoid of other human figures – not by conscious ideological intention, to be sure, but for the simple fact that no one outside this room mattered.

The commanding of space in (musical) time is explored in a painting by Johan Zoffany of the Sharp family, easily the best known of all musical conversation pieces (Fig. 95) from eighteenth-century England. The painting is unique and striking in its setting, a private musical party aboard a barge on the Thames. But unlike Nollekens' painting which transformed a country house into a stage set, Zoffany's Sharp family is situated in a highly particularized and actual geography: the town (Fulham), the house on the bank with curved balconies (belonging to William Sharp, surgeon to George III), the barge itself (named "The Apollo"), even the musical instruments (most if not all of the originals still survive).[2] The landscape may be rearranged a bit, as pictorial convention allowed and compositional arrangement required, but nonetheless all the basic visual components are "true." Moreover, written records document actual musical events on one of the family's barges such as that represented in Zoffany's painting. And we know the identities of every one of the sitters, though I will not catalogue them here.[3] (The family loved music – they gathered regularly, even daily, over a period of many years to perform together. Granville Sharp, shown in the center clutching two oboes, even wrote about the teaching of music.[4] Both their barge and house concerts were

95 Johan Zoffany (1733–1810), *The Sharp Family* (1779–81), oil on canvas, 115.5 × 125.7 cm.; The Trustees of the Lloyd-Baker Settled Estates; on loan to the National Portrait Gallery, London

supplemented by professional musicians, some of them eminent. The music played prominently featured Handel.[5])

In my judgment the painting is most interesting for the way that it defines space through the dimension of sound, not in any commemorative way as regards the family's particular experiences but ideologically. The real "Apollo" was so fitted that it could be sailed, rowed and even towed from the shoreline by horses. It was fitted with bedrooms and dining rooms, and it had available on deck an awning to protect the musicians from rain.[6] It was a self-contained, highly privatized space, a floating drawing room in which music could be made in all weather. And the music was movable. But it was movable for a purpose, and this will be my main point.

The Sharps' barge concerts, which the family referred to as "water schemes," were acoustically enriched declarations of place, that is, events which took advantage of the natural enhancement of sound provided by water for the purpose of delineating their social position to a select audience. But in this instance the audience did not only come to them, the Sharps often went to the audience. The audience was in a sense geographically captive – those living along the banks of the Thames above London, which happened to include many of the country's most prestigious families, including of course its monarch: "As we passed the Prince of Wales' house they heard our Musick and all the 4 Princes and Attendance came down to the water side, and stood for near half an hour and sent to request 3 or 4 different songs."[7] In fact, they had their musical barge towed by horses through the rivers and canals of England as far as Norfolk.[8] On board the Sharps entertained foreign ambassadors, local and foreign aristocrats, politicians, high churchmen, even the King and Queen.

The Sharps' barge journeys were less musical holidays, more working vacations, their "functional" purpose to command prestige via the imposition of the sonoric order of high art "broadcast" across water and land alike, a musical prerogative otherwise exercised by few others at this time except for the King himself. A hint of the music's function as a signal is evident among Granville Sharp's papers, in a memorandum of "Things to be thought of for the Barge," which includes one prominent anomaly: "List of instruments, Violins, Horns, Kettledrums, and sticks, Boat whistle, Serpents, Harpsichord, and Stand, Flute-box, Violincello [sic], Clarinets, Hautboys. Tins. Resin."[9] Why did Sharp include a boat whistle among his list of musical instruments, if not in (un)conscious recognition that the instruments themselves served an identical function to that of the whistle, namely, to draw attention to the barge's presence? Yet at the same time as the Sharps' music called attention to them, it also created a sonic moat around their floating castle. The instruments displayed in the Sharp "orchestra" are not all held as if to be played simultaneously. Indeed, such an ensemble would make little sense. Yet the variety of instruments is important in the degree to which it defined the depth of resources available to the family in its arsenal of prestige, in the variety of means by which it could sonically command time. Their outdoors music was utterly different from the mundane, ubiquitous (popular) music (and noise) of the outdoors against whose memory it resonated in the ears of listeners. The Sharps' barge exteriorized the interior world of high art/high society, but it also simultaneously denied access to it except in the most abstract, impermanent way (musical sound), and forcibly defined the spatio-temporal quality of its otherness.

In less presentational art than oil paintings, and among individuals of lesser social importance, music operated very differently, as in a tiny drawing by John Nixon (Fig. 96) of the artist himself at the left seated with his friends Henry Angelo, center, and Samuel Maynard, right, the last a lawyer. The setting was described by Angelo himself in his memoirs: "In the year 1802 . . . I was advised by my old & estimable friend John Nixon to hire an apartment in the neighbourhood of the Mansion House . . . I had a suite of rooms on the attic . . . Henry Angelo could here return the compliment – not with soups and ragoûts, served in plate, but in the more humble shape of a skilfully cooked codshead, with a well roasted pork grisking."[10] The way in which music operates is clarified by reference to Angelo's comments on food; it was a means by which friends came together for the pleasure of the moment and as an expression of their relationship. The music here, like that in the musical parties just discussed, also involved an audience (of one) but with a fundamental difference: it was given freely in the sense that it was unselfconsciously performed, less the result of prior arrangement and more the spontaneous manifestation of mutual pleasing. It was, in short, a music without ideology. I do not mean

96 John Nixon (c. 1760–1818). *A Scene in Henry Angelo's Garret at the Pauls Head Cateaton Street* (1802), pen and gray ink and watercolor, 12.07 × 20 cm. Photo © Christie's

this in the deepest, most inclusive sense, for no human activity can escape its socio-cultural underpinnings. Rather I mean that it was a music performed explicitly for the pleasure it gave as sound and as social act, and not for the larger impressions·it might create for "outsiders" either as a sonic or visual event. Yet I cannot let this stand without acknowledging that such pleasures were not only strictly personal, they were also devalued by the very medium that here preserves their visual trace. Very few paintings, a much more "serious" medium than drawings given the "uses" of paintings, represent even remotely similar subjects.

The sense of music conveyed in musical party scenes is focused upon its significance as a regulated social activity. But there is more to this equation: underlying its importance as social activity is the growing awareness of music's function as art. Music qua art is seldom directly represented in English portraiture, but it crops up occasionally (Fig. 97), as in Gainsborough's life-size rendition of the professional musician and composer Johann Christian Fischer.[11] The entire setting, all the props, alludes to music – a Merlin piano (or harpsichord?), an oboe, a viola and music, including a stack of scores on the floor, all of which identify the instruments Fischer played. But as in some other representations of professional musicians Fischer was represented not as a player but as a composer, a far nobler coin of the cultural realm. Gainsborough, through his handling of the sitter's face, took care further to remove even the act of composition from a common terrestrial footing. While leaning comfortably and cross-legged, just as real gentlemen stood on the terra firma of their estates, Fischer waits with eyes raised, pen ready, for inspiration, much as if an angel were about to whisper in his ear. In the act of ennobling Fischer, Gainsborough, perhaps inadvertently, simultaneously established a sonic hierarchy, constructed via a separateness of musics. He marked what Fischer's music was different *from*.

A drawing by Hogarth represents this difference head-on in a poignant account that engages both professionalism and music (Fig. 98). In this instance, space once more is semi-privatized; the setting is a room, perhaps a meeting room in a tavern, where a group of reveling men and women play cards and are served drink. Their casualness is allowed by the medium (drawing); no one but Hogarth is watching. Their informality (or drunkenness) is compositionally echoed in the room itself which seems to be tipping to the right. They are entertained by background music provided by a professional cellist. And I mean "background" in more than the spatial sense. What music is played – high or low – cannot be said; but of whatever kind, it is there simply to be heard and not listened to. In one sense this apparent negative ("good" music should have our attention) is undercut in the sense that music, qua background, is specifically social, an important part of the evening's pleasure whether acknowledged overtly or not. But on another level what is more directly emphasized by the image itself is music's separateness: the musician is set spatially apart from the others. And he alone seems affected by his playing: he shares facial expressions with Gainsborough's Fischer, looking off into a distance, unaware of his surroundings, pensive (Fig. 99), though Hogarth suggests his look may be mostly the result of the amount of wine he has consumed and not the muse. In any event, it is the separateness of

97 Thomas Gainsborough (1727–88), *Johann Christian Fischer*, oil on canvas, 228.6 × 150.5 cm.; London, Buckingham Palace. © reserved to Her Majesty Queen Elizabeth II

simultaneous events, one social, one isolated and solitary, that constitute the cultural encoding of the drawing.[12]

The issues I have outlined here are perhaps best encapsulated in Hogarth's "The Enraged Musician" (Fig. 100), a dramatic representation of music as social discourse, of sound itself as class-laden, of sonority as the delimiter of separateness. And the key word here is "enraged," for the image is as violent as the invisible cultural undertow that accounts for its very form. Hogarth's engraving is not a matter of iconography but of society. It is a representation of polar oppositions, notably: inside versus outside, order versus disorder, harmony versus dissonance and so on. Here it is the exterior, public world that is spatially dominant. By the amount of picture space it occupies, the exteriorized common world characterizes itself as a tidal wave against which a literally higher order (I speak here of literal compositional arrangement) must buttress itself.

All of this is made to operate within the metaphor of sound. The exteriorized world is disharmonious, unruly, ubiquitous. It is an unmediated world in which all acts, represented by the visual tracings of their sounds, are horrid. This is a territory where every person screams to be heard and scrambles for his or her share of insufficient resources. And there is little difference between the street people in this regard and the parrot at the left or the brawling cats atop the roof at the right. They are all animals. They are physically dirty like their trades (the dustman announcing himself with basket on head and bell in hand, the chimneysweep poking his

98 William Hogarth (1697–1764), *Card Party*, pencil, pen and sepia ink and gray wash heightened with white, 23.5 × 36.8 cm. By courtesy of Sotheby's

head out at the upper right); they work in dirt (the pavior bent down to his task in the center of the crowd, his pavement rammer in action). They are vulgar without shame (a boy pisses in the street while a wide-eyed little girl watches intently). They are themselves at once violent and cruel (the knife sharpener, and the sow gelder on horseback and blowing his horn – reference to emasculation, even of animals, seldom rides easy in anyone's mind). They are smelly (the fish peddler). They are immoral (the pregnant ballad singer holding her bastard, offering for sale her song, "The Ladies Fall." They are foreign (the boy drummer as a Frenchman, bewigged and carrying Catholicism's cross in his pocket). He beats the drum for their step; they are a militant class, a mob. (In the center stands a

99 William Hogarth (1697–1764), *Card Party*, detail. By courtesy of Sotheby's

milkmaid, a ridiculously large pot on her head, crying her wares. She is different from the rest, a kind of poor madonna, perhaps the antithetical personification of the "good poor," a subject quite dear to Hogarth.)[13] This is the street version of *The Beggar's Opera*, the stage version of which is announced by the poster on the wall at the left. The scene is a garden of trouble and despair, as pathetic as the little "garden" at the lower left whose ground the boy waters. The "order" here is as humble as the little model of a brick house made by the children, as unstable as the building's propped-up roof. Everything is noise, literal or metaphorical – and added to by the pewterer's shop, hammering on metal, announced by the shop sign at the right.

The itinerant, emaciated oboist is a kind of Pied Piper, together with the drummer leading the mob onward. The crowd is at a momentary halt, as it were, beneath the window of a bewigged musician, unquestionably a professional, a man perhaps in the midst of a lesson, if not performing for himself,[14] furious and immobilized, his art interrupted, helpless except to hold his arms over his offended ears. The Apollonian strings of his violin have

100 William Hogarth (1697–1764), *The Enraged Musician* (1741), 34.6 × 39.8 cm.; London, British Museum. By courtesy of the Trustees

been silenced by the oboe's Dionysian-reed. This is the ancient dialectical opposition of order and chaos; more important it is a statement about who has the power to define and regulate the components of order. It is the representation of class structure and cultural self-definition. It is sound as ideology and visual form as social constitution. What it is *not* is things as they should be, rather what things must be opposed. Hogarth's engraving is a comedy, but like all comedy its foundation is anxiety. Here anxiety is relieved via a denial of aesthetic form to *all* inhabitants of the picture's space – even the professional musician who, after all, is himself an alien.

Above all else Hogarth's composition depends on a contemporaneous understanding of the existence and maintenance of musics of separate spheres. The music of the poor is ubiquitous, central to their lives in the sense that it seemingly accompanies their every action. It is part of what constitutes a community of class, a means of self-definition. The music of the rich (or at least the rich by comparison with the poor) is by contrast specific to time, place and occasion, equally self-defining precisely in the manner in which it is "placed" with regard to these dimensions. Music is, as Locke put it, essentially a waste of time, but if one has it at all, one pays others to make it (professionals) or else samples it carelessly. What matters is that it be channeled, that it *not* be a part of the warp and woof of existence, rather an appliqué.[15]

"The Enraged Musician" is literally silent; though it is entirely *about* sound, its sounds must be imagined. Yet Hogarth's audience (those who bought the print) knew precisely how to "hear" it, not only by the visual control exercised on their understanding by Hogarth's composition, but also because Hogarth, as always, was "telling" them what they already thought they knew (to my mind, no artist was ever more adept at preaching to the converted). There is little didacticism here, however, unlike many of his images, but there is smugness aplenty built on the privilege of separateness, in which God may be thanked for making us different, in which His Saint Cecilia patronizes only one kind of music. And in the formation of such socio-cultural discourses, both visual art and music alike at once mirror and mediate the outcome – largely, if not always, on behalf of the status quo.

Notes

1 INTRODUCTION: MUSIC VISUALIZED

1 Theodor W. Adorno, *Introduction to the Sociology of Music*, trans. E. B. Ashton (New York, 1976), p. 119.

2 Norbert Elias, *The Court Society*, trans. Edmund Jephcott (New York, 1983), p. 118.

3 Some amateurs performed in the concerts they arranged; though it falls outside my topic, such amateur musical activity is very important to the history of music in England, especially on account of the various eighteenth-century musical societies like the Academy of Vocal Music, the Academy of Ancient Music, the Philharmonica Club, the Apollo Society and the Madrigal Society, all in London.

I will only address the music that amateurs played, whether in private or public, in a tightly circumscribed way – the enormous scope of the subject requires a separate study of its own. Many thousands of musical publications, separate compositions and anthologies alike, were printed in England or imported during the century, mostly intended for an amateur audience. Much of it consisted of popular tunes and dances of the day, often adapted from popular stage hits and the opera. Toward the end of the century specialized music magazines appeared, and occasionally music was also printed in general magazines. Late in the period music lending libraries came into existence.

Among the numerous studies that touch on this subject, see Arthur Loesser, *Men, Women and Pianos* (New York, 1954), pp. 207–9, 229, 251–3, 256–8; Stanley Sadie, "British chamber music, 1720–1790" (Ph.D. diss., Cambridge Univ., 1958); Michael Tilmouth, "Chamber music in England, 1675–1720" (Ph.D. diss., Cambridge Univ., 1960); Hans Lenneberg, "Music publishing and dissemination in the early nineteenth century: some vignettes," *Journal of Musicology*, 2 (1983), pp. 174–83; Hans Lenneberg, "Early circulating libraries and the dissemination of music," *Library Quarterly*, 52 (1982), pp. 122–30, and a response, 53 (1983), p. 103; A. Hyatt King, "Music circulating libraries in Britain," *Musical Times*, 119 (1978), pp. 134–8, and response, p. 293; William Weber, "The contemporaneity of eighteenth-century musical taste," *Musical Quarterly*, 70 (1984), pp. 175–94, a particularly valuable assessment of the established taste for new music in England. Among studies of music publishing in England see A. Hyatt King, *Some British Collectors of Music, c. 1600–1960* (Cambridge, 1963); Frank Kidson, *British Music Publishers, Printers and Engravers* (London, 1900); Donald W. Krummel, *English Music Printing, 1553–1700* (London, 1975); Charles Humphries and William C. Smith, *Music Publishing in the British Isles, from the Beginning until the Middle of the Nineteenth Century*, 2nd ed. (New York, 1970); William C. Smith, *A Bibliography of the Musical Works Published by John Walsh during the Years 1695–1720* (London, 1948); William C. Smith and Charles Humphries, *A Bibliography of the Musical Works Published by the Firm of John Walsh during the Years 1721–1766* (London, 1968). Among modern editions of art music from this repertory particularly noteworthy is the ongoing series *Musica da Camera*, gen. ed. John Caldwell (London, 1973-), containing music written by composers working in England, and/or of music published in England between 1630 and 1830. The various volumes of *RISM* should also be consulted.

The bibliography on the various musical societies and of early concert life is considerable. See, for example, "London," *The New Grove Dictionary of Music and Musicians*, ed. Stanley Sadie, 20 vols. (London and Washington, DC, 1980), vol. 11, especially pp. 181-2, 192-5, 202-3; J. G. Craufurd, "The Madrigal Society," *Proceedings of the Royal Musical Association*, 82 (1955-6), pp. 33-46; Reginald Nettel, "The oldest surviving English musical club: some historical notes on the Madrigal Society of London," *Musical Quarterly*, 34 (1948), pp. 97-108; James E. Matthew, "The Antient Concerts, 1776-1848," *Proceedings of the Musical Association*, 33 (1906-7), pp. 55-79; Robert S. Elkin, *The Old Concert Rooms of London* (London, 1955). See also individual entries, by name of city, in *New Grove* concerning musical life in the various major provincial centers in eighteenth-century England – Bath, Birmingham, Manchester, Norwich, Sheffield, York, etc. For more general surveys see Stanley Sadie, "Concert life in eighteenth century England," *Proceedings of the Royal Musical Association*, 85 (1958-9), pp. 17-30; and Eric D. Mackerness, *A Social History of English Music* (London, 1964).

4 One related issue I do not consider is the domestic music room; these are only a rather late development in domestic architecture, limited essentially to the second half of the eighteenth century, and almost exclusively found in some great houses of the very rich. Music rooms were sometimes so named on account of a few ornamental trophies of musical instruments, though the rooms were by no means reserved exclusively for musical events. See further Michael I. Wilson, "Music rooms of the 18th century," *Country Life*, 134 (1963), pp. 1672-4.

5 See Pierre Francastel, ["Preface"] to François Lesure, *Music in Art and Society*, trans. Denis Stevens and Sheila Stevens (University Park, PA and London, 1968), p. xx.

6 The major formulation of the difference between seeing and perceiving is by Ernst H. Gombrich, *Art and Illusion: A Study in the Psychology of Pictorial Representation*, 2nd ed. rev. (Princeton, NJ, 1969). However, the unproblematized ahistoricism of Gombrich's argument must be read against the important account by Norman Bryson, *Vision and Painting: The Logic of the Gaze* (New Haven, CT, 1983), a sustained critique of both Gombrich and, more generally, of the dominant discursive modes of art history as a discipline (stylistics/connoisseurship and iconology). On the related issue of intentionality, considered in a broader and more useful sense than that of authorial intention, see Michael Baxandall, *Patterns of Intention: On the Historical Explanation of Pictures* (New Haven, CT, 1985), especially pp. 41-2, 105-11.

7 Cf. John Berger, "The primitive and the professional," *About Looking* (New York, 1980), p. 65: "Conventions corresponded so closely to the social experience – or anyway to the social manners – of the class he [the artist] was serving, that they were not even seen as conventions but were thought of as the only way of recording and preserving eternal truths."

8 Francastel, "Preface" to Lesure, *Music in Art and Society*, p. xiii. Frederick Antal, "Remarks on the method of art history," *Burlington Magazine*, 91 (1949), p. 74, noted that some art historians "cannot imagine that art history is a piece of history and that the art historian's task is primarily not to approve or to disapprove of a given work of art from his [*sic*] own point of view, but to try to understand and explain it in the light of its own historical premises; and that there is no contradiction between a picture as a work of art and as a document of its time, since the two are complementary."

9 Nikolaus Pevsner, *The Englishness of English Art* (Harmondsworth, 1976), p. 79.

10 Cf. Georges Duby, "Ideologies in social history," trans. David Denby, *Constructing the Past: Essays in Historical Methodology*, ed. Jacques LeGoff and Pierre Nora (Cambridge and Paris, 1985), p. 159, on the historian's task: "It must be shown how, at every moment in history, what we know of the material conditions of life in a particular society is subjected to a varying degree of falsification by that society's mental representations. The historian must therefore determine as precisely as possible – and the fact that in most documents the real and the ideal are freely juxtaposed makes the task extremely difficult – the relations of correspondence and difference existing at every point on a diachronic scale between three variables: on the one hand, between the objective situation of individuals and groups and the image which they have constructed for their comfort and justification; on the other, between that image and individual and collective behaviour."

11 Walter Benjamin, "Theses on the philosophy of history," *Illuminations*, ed. Hannah Arendt, trans. Harry Zohn (New York, 1969), p. 256.

12 Quoted from Marcia Pointon, "Portrait-painting as a business enterprise in London in the 1780s," *Art History*, 7 (1984), pp. 198–9.

13 On the conservative – even reactionary – ideology informing Reynolds' *Discourses on Art*, the single most influential statement of art theory produced in eighteenth-century England, see Robert W. Uphaus, "The ideology of Reynolds' *Discourses on Art*," *Eighteenth-Century Studies*, 12 (1978), pp. 59–73, especially for a detailed consideration of Reynolds' understanding of the constitution of "genius" and "originality." Re Reynolds on portraiture see Sir Joshua Reynolds, *Discourses on Art, with Selections from "The Idler,"* ed. Stephen O. Mitchell (1797; reprint. ed. Indianapolis, IN, 1965), from the Fourth Discourse (1771), p. 43.

14 Herbert Marcuse was very perceptive about this in an essay addressing the relation between modern arts and reality. He understood the primary part that the form of art plays in relation to time, that is, to history. See "Art as form of reality," *New Left Review*, 74 (1972), p. 52.

15 See, for example, Ralph Edwards, "Georgian conversation pictures," *Apollo*, 105 (1977), p. 253.

16 John Pye, *Patronage of British Art, an Historical Sketch* (London, 1845), pp. 97–8, reprinted a letter from the *St. James's Chronicle* (25 April 1761): "It will be urged that a few painters among us are rewarded. But what are they? Portrait-painters will succeed in every country, but don't let them imagine that they owe their encouragement to their merit, or to the general good taste of the nation. No, no; it is to the vanity and self-love of their employers that they are chiefly obliged, – to passions which must ever be gratified, and for the indulgence of these persons are ever ready to open their purses to the irresistible flattery of portrait-painting."

17 "A Portrait is the best mean devised by the ingenuity of art, to substantiate the fleeting form – to perpetuate the momentary existence. It is thine, O Painting! to preserve the form, which lies mouldering in the tomb . . . Portrait-painting subserves. It teaches beneficial lessons. It calls to mind the example of great men, when they are fled beyond the reach of observation." From John Evans, *Juvenile Pieces: Designed for the Youth of Both Sexes*, 3rd ed. (London, [1797]), from chapter "On the utility of paintings," p. 71.

18 Re the very large sums of money made by the most successful English portrait painters in the last half of the eighteenth century, see Gerald Reitlinger, *The Economics of Taste: The Rise and Fall of Picture Prices, 1760–1960*, 3 vols. (London, 1961–70), vol. 1, pp. 57–65; and Pointon, "Portrait-painting as a business enterprise," pp. 187–205. Reynolds, the richest of them all, in modern terms died the equivalent of a millionaire.

19 The definition is from Robert Raines, *Marcellus Laroon* (London, 1966), p. 64. See also on this subject Sacheverell Sitwell, *Conversation Pieces: A Survey of English Domestic Portraits and their Painters* (London, 1936); Ralph Edwards,

Early Conversation Pictures from the Middle Ages to about 1730: A Study in Origins (London, 1954), especially pp. 26–32, 52–68, 155–71; Edwards, "Georgian conversation pictures," pp. 252–61; Ellen G. D'Oench, *The Conversation Piece: Arthur Devis and his Contemporaries* (New Haven, CT, 1980) (on the use of the term "conversation" or "conversation piece" in the eighteenth century, beginning in 1706, see pp. 2–3); and Mario Praz, *Conversation Pieces: A Survey of the Informal Group Portrait in Europe and America* (University Park, PA and London, 1971).

20 On this see D'Oench, *Conversation Piece*, pp. 21–2.

21 Sitwell, *Conversation Pieces*, p. 22.

22 Ellis K. Waterhouse, *Three Decades of British Art, 1740–1770* (Philadelphia, PA, 1965), p. 65, pointed out that with Reynolds' full-length portraits the sitters, "as we watch them . . . from the early 1750's to the middle of the 1770's, seem to get more and more pleased with themselves, more filled with 'hubris.' " Cf. Praz, *Conversation Pieces*, p. 202, for an amusing quotation from Chapter 16 of Oliver Goldsmith's *The Vicar of Wakefield* concerning the vicar and his family sitting for a conversation piece, all of them dressed in allegorical costumes and in imitation of their social betters.

23 See further Elizabeth W. Gilboy, "The cost of living and real wages in eighteenth-century England," *Review of Economic Statistics*, 18 (1936), pp. 134–42. From the vast bibliography on the general subject the following are especially recommended. Some are tightly focused on the economy and social orders of England, others include such information as part of a larger overview. Thomas S. Ashton, *Economic Fluctuations in England, 1700–1800* (Oxford, 1959); Leslie A. Clarkson, *The Pre-Industrial Economy in England, 1500–1750* (London, 1971); George D. H. Cole, and Raymond Postgate, *The British People, 1746–1946* (New York, 1961), pp. 68–87; Michael W. Flinn, *An Economic and Social History of Britain, 1066–1939* (London and New York, 1961), pp. 115–222; Elizabeth W. Gilboy, *Wages in Eighteenth Century England* (Cambridge, MA, 1934); Ephraim Lipson, *The Economic History of England*, 5th ed., 3 vols., (New York and London, 1929–31, vol. 2, pp. 372–95; vol. 3, pp. 248–51, 262–78; Gordon E. Minjay, *English Landed Society in the Eighteenth Century* (London, 1963); Gordon E. Minjay, *The Gentry: The Rise and Fall of a Ruling Class* (London and New York, 1976); and Roy Porter, *English Society in the Eighteenth Century* (Harmondsworth, 1982), pp. 63–112, 201–68.

24 Quoted from Porter, *English Society*, pp. 67–8.

25 Ibid., p. 25.

26 Ibid., p. 383.

27 Ibid., pp. 70, 74, 81; and Minjay, *Gentry*, p. 11.

28 Minjay, *Gentry*, p. 59.

29 R. D. Lee and R. S. Schofield, "British population in the eighteenth century," *The Economic History of Britain since 1700*, vol. 1: *1700–1860,* ed. Roderick Floud and Donald McCloskey (Cambridge, 1981), p. 21.

30 Porter, *English Society*, pp. 96, 386–8.

31 Lipson, *Economic History of England*, vol. 2, pp. 372, 379–93, passim.

32 Porter, *English Society*, p. 100.

33 Clarkson, *Pre-Industrial Economy*, p. 225; see also Cole and Postgate, *British People*, pp. 80–5; one of the best accounts of the urban poor is by Margaret Dorothy George, *London Life in the Eighteenth Century*, rev. ed. (London, 1965).

34 Gilboy, *Wages in Eighteenth Century England*, p. 220.

35 These estimates come from the well-known, contemporaneous and generally well-regarded work of Gregory King, for which my source is Porter, *English Society*, pp. 28–9, 63.

2 MUSIC, SOCIO-POLITICS, IDEOLOGIES OF MALE SEXUALITY AND POWER

1 William Jackson, *The Four Ages: Together with Essays on Various Subjects* (London, 1798), p. 233.

2 Quoted from Eric D. Mackerness, "Fovargue and Jackson," *Music and Letters*, 31 (1950), p. 236.

3 Gwilym Beechey, "Robert Bremner and his *Thoughts on the Performance of Concert Music*," *Musical Quarterly*, 69 (1983), p. 247. Cf. remarks in an anonymous pamphlet called *Euterpe; or, Remarks on the Use and Abuse of Music, as a Part of Modern Education* (London, c. 1778): "Our young Gentlemen seldom becom[e] very *agreeable* performers, and hardly ever very *useful* ones. Their choice of easy *imperfect Instruments* occasions this complaint, in a great measure; and when they undertake the *Violin* or *Violoncello*, instead of becoming *useful Performers* in Concert, and playing real good *Music*, they are never contented without rivalling the absurd extravagancies of our modern *executioners* of Music, and imitating the *wonderful Powers* of those, who have unhappily reduced Music to the narrow limits of three inches of the *Bow*, upon two inches of the *String*" (pp. 14–15). On the authorship of this essay see Jamie Croy Kassler, *The Science of Music in Britain, 1714–1830: A Catalogue of Writings, Lectures and Inventions*, 2 vols. (New York, 1979), vol. 2, pp. 1107–9. Portions of this essay, including the passage quoted, were reprinted in *European Magazine*, 23 (1793), pp. 28–32, 103–5.

4 William Forbes Gray, "The Musical Society of Edinburgh and St. Cecilia's Hall," *The Book of the Old Edinburgh Club*, 19 (1933), p. 234.

5 Roger North, *Roger North on Music: Being a Selection from his Essays Written during the Years c. 1695–1728*, ed. John Wilson (London, 1959), p. 15.

6 James Bramston, *The Man of Taste* (London, 1733), p. 12.

7 Obadiah Walker, *Of Education, Especially of Young Gentlemen. In Two Parts*, 2nd impression with additions (Oxon, 1673), p. 197.

8 Issue no. 128, 8 July, pp. 183–9. The quotation is from pp. 184–5.

9 Mr. Humpkin's full fury is saved for the concerts his wife organized at home; see p. 186. Maria Humpkin "wrote" a response to her husband's letter in issue no. 130, 22 July 1756, pp. 197–203. Her own faults as a too-devoted admirer of music and musicians – especially Italians – are evident.

10 Ibid., p. 188.

11 Henry Fielding, *Tom Jones* (1750), ed. Sheridan Baker (New York, 1973), Book IV, Chapter 5, p. 128.

12 Thomas Southerne, *The Maid's Last Prayer; or, Any Rather than Fail* (London, 1693), Act IV, scene 2, p. 42. The passage is also cited by Stanley Sadie, "British chamber music," pp. 95–6.

13 John Berkenhout, *A Volume of Letters from Dr Berkenhout to his Son at the University* (Cambridge, 1790), p. 179. For information on Berkenhout, see Kassler, *Science of Music*, vol. 1, pp. 86–7.

14 Thomas Twining, *Recreations and Studies of a Country Clergyman of the Eighteenth Century* (London, 1882), p. 145.

15 John E. Mason, *Gentlefolk in the Making: Studies in the History of English Courtesy Literature and Related Topics from 1531 to 1774* (Philadelphia, PA, 1935), p. 291. See also Gertrude E. Noyes, *Bibliography of Courtesy and Conduct Books in Seventeenth-Century England* (New Haven, CT, 1937), and Virgil B. Heltzell, *A Check List of Courtesy Books in the Newberry Library* (Chicago, 1942).

16 Henry Peacham, *The Complete Gentleman, The Truth of our Times, and The Art of Living in London*, ed. Virgil B. Heltzell (1634; reprint. ed. Ithaca, NY, 1962), p. 109. On the lack of originality in Peacham's book, especially the chapter "Of musicke," see Susan Hankey, "The compleat gentleman's music," *Music and Letters*, 62 (1981), pp. 146–54.

17 John Locke, *Some Thoughts Concerning Education* (London, 1693), pp. 235–6, para. 185; from the first edition.

18 Philip Stubbes, *Philip Stubbes's Anatomy of Abuses in England in Shakespeare's Youth, A.D. 1583*, ed. Frederick J. Furnivall, 2 vols. (London, 1877–82), vol. 1, pp. 169–70.

19 John Brown, *An Estimate of the Manners and Principles of the Times*, 2 vols. (London, 1757–8), vol. 2, pp. 74–5. Among the best-known attacks on secular music from the period is *The Great Abuse of Music* (London, 1711) by Arthur Bedford, an English clergyman, noted authority on Jewish music and some-time chaplain to Frederick, Prince of Wales. But Bedford's primary concern was with song texts rather than music itself. He was also an enemy of the London theaters and published a tract in 1719 citing no fewer than 7,000 immoral remarks from plays of the previous four years. See "Arthur Bed-ford," *New Grove*, vol. 2, p. 345.

20 Solomon Eccles, *A Musick-Lector: or, the Art of Musick (That is So Much Vindicated in Christendome) Discoursed of, by Way of Dialogue, between Three Men of Several Judgments . . . a Musician . . . a Baptist . . . a Quaker* (London, 1667), p. 12. The pamphlet runs to 28 pp. See also the detailed biography by John Jeffreys, *The Eccles Family* (Ilford, [1951]); and Percy A. Scholes, *The Puritans and Music in England and New England* (London, 1934), pp. 52–4. This mono-graph and several more recent studies establish clearly that the sixteenth- and seventeenth-century Puritans were not generally antagonistic toward music – the Quakers, on the other hand, were strongly opposed. Regarding eighteenth-century attitudes, however, see pp. 345–60. See also H. S. K. Kent, "Puritan attitudes to music: a study in the history of ideas," *Miscellanea Musico-logia, Adelaide Studies in Musicology*, 1 (1966), pp. 191–224.

21 Anon., *The Country Gentleman's "Vade Mecum": or, his Companion for the Town* (London, 1699), p. 15.

22 David Hartley, *Observations of Man, his Frame, his Duty, and his Expectations* (1749; reprint. ed. Gainesville, FL, 1966), pp. 253–4. Second and third editions appeared in 1791 and three more up to 1834. Hartley allowed that devotional music acts as a positive force (p. 254).

23 Cf. John Dennis (poet, dramatist, political writer and critic) in his essay, "Advancement and reformation of poetry," *The Critical Works of John Dennis*, ed. Edward Niles Hooker, 2 vols. (Baltimore, MD, 1939–43), vol. 1, p. 263, and vol. 2, p. 394.

24 Jeremy Collier, *Essays upon Several Moral Subjects. In Two Parts*, 2nd ed. corr. and enlarged (London, 1697), pp. 19–21, 24–5, respectively.

25 I have traced this subject in detail; see Richard Leppert, "Imagery, musical confrontation and cultural difference in early 18th-century London," *Early Music*, 14 (1986), pp. 323–45.

26 Vicesimus Knox, *Personal Nobility: or Letter to a Young Nobleman on the Conduct of his Studies* (London, 1793), pp. 356–7.

27 Ibid., pp. 357–9. Cf. George C. Brauer, Jr., *The Education of a Gentleman: Theories of Gentlemanly Education in England, 1660–1775* (New York, 1959), p. 91.

28 James Puckle, *The Club; or, a Grey Cap for a Green Head . . . Being a Dialogue between a Father and Son* (1713; reprint. ed. London, 1900), p. 161, maxim no. 797. Cf. James Cleland, *The Scottish Academie, or, Institution of a Young Noble Man* (London, 1611), pp. 229–30. See also Jack A. Westrup, "Domestic music under the Stuarts," *Proceedings of the Musical Association*, 68 (1941–2), p. 32.

29 Philip Dormer Stanhope, *Letters to his Son by the Earl of Chesterfield on the Fine Art of Becoming a Man of the World and a Gentleman*, ed. Oliver H. G. Leigh, 2 vols. (London 1926), vol. 1, p. 170 (letter no. 68, dated 19 April O.S. 1749). In another letter (p. 186, no. 73, dated 22 June O.S. 1749) of similar vein he cites the musical proclivities of the Italians as direct proof of the country's decline.

30 Sidney L. Gulick, Jr., ed., *Some Unpublished Letters of Lord Chesterfield*

(Berkeley, CA, 1937), p. 59, dictated on 19 February 1773. The letter was not published during the eighteenth century. Cf. John Aubrey writing a century earlier, using the same images but to somewhat different purpose: "I would have as little fiddling [in my proposed education system] as may be, and that only by those who have a great and strong inclination to music, for it is a great thief of time and engages men in base company of pimps, fiddlers and barbers." J. E. Stephens, ed., *Aubrey on Education: A Hitherto Unpublished Manuscript by the Author of "Brief Lives"* (London and Boston, MA, 1972), p. 37; see also p. 114 where the remark is repeated.

31 See for example Henry Curson, *The Theory of Sciences Illustrated; or the Grounds and Principles of the Seven Liberal Arts* (London, 1702), pp. 129–31.

32 Thomas Danvers Worgan, *The Musical Reformer* (London, 1829), p. 35. The sexism expressed by his statement will be taken up as a general topic of the following chapter. Elsewhere in the book he remarked that were music taught as a science it would once again become "the manly art which it once was, instead of the effeminate gewgaw which it now is" (p. 33); by "effeminate gewgaw" he refers to applied music in the curriculum of ladies' boarding schools.

33 Anon., *Euterpe*, pp. 15–16, 19–20. John Aubrey states the association of music to mathematics as follows: "Statics, music, fencing, architecture and bits of bridges are all reducible to the laws of geometry." From Stephens, ed., *Aubrey on Education*, p. 113. Cf. the very similar views re music, order and morality expressed by John Dennis, *Critical Works*, vol. 1, p. 336. I have discussed the ideological underpinnings and socio-cultural implications of a treatise on the mathematics of sound by John Keeble, *The Theory of Harmonics: or, an Illustration of the Grecian Harmonica* (London, 1784). See Richard Leppert, "Music, domestic life and cultural chauvinism: images of British subjects at home in India," *Music and Society: The Politics of Composition, Performance and Reception*, ed. Richard Leppert and Susan McClary (Cambridge, 1987), pp. 71–5, 78.

Some who defended music as a fine art did so by piggybacking on sacred music, see John Playford. *Introduction to the Skill of Music*, 7th ed. (London, 1674), pp. [vii–viii]; and Thomas Mace, *Musick's Monument* (London, 1676), pp. 270–2. Sermons preached on St. Cecilia's day – and subsequently published as pamphlets – nearly always paid homage only to devotional music. See for example Charles Hickman, *A Sermon Preached at St. Bride's Church, on St. Cæcilia's Day, Nov. 22, 1695* (London, 1696).

34 William Darrell, *A Gentleman Instructed in the Conduct of a Virtuous and Happy Life* (London, 1704), pp. 38–9. On the author, a Jesuit active in France from 1671, see Kassler, *Science of Music*, vol. 1, p. 259. Darrell's book was also translated into Italian and Hungarian.

35 Peacham, *Complete Gentleman*, p. 111. Peacham further qualified what he meant by musical accomplishment: "I desire no more in you than to sing your part sure and at the first sight withal to play the same upon your viol or the exercise of the lute, privately, to yourself" (p. 112).

36 Jean Gailhard, *The Complete Gentleman: or Directions for the Education of Youth*, 2 vols. in 1 (London, 1678), vol. 2, p. 52. Cf. the views expressed by Rev. Gilbert Burnet, *Thoughts on Education* (London, 1741), and Chevalier Andrew Michael Ramsay, *A Plan of Education for a Young Prince* (London, 1732). On both texts see Kassler, *Science of Music*, vol. 1, pp. 124–5, and vol. 2, pp. 871–2, respectively.

37 Bernarr Rainbow, *The Land without Music: Musical Education in England 1800–1860 and its Continental Antecedents* (London, 1967), p. 25 (quoting Percy A. Scholes).

38 Thomas Bisse, *Musick the Delight of the Sons of Men* (London, 1726), p. 8.

39 Richard Mulcaster, *Mulcaster's Positions*, ed. Robert H. Quick (London, 1888), p. 39.

40 George Birkbeck Hill, ed., *Johnsonian Miscellanies*, 2 vols. (Oxford, 1897), vol.

2, p. 301. Quoted from Derek Jarrett, *England in the Age of Hogarth* (Frogmore, St. Albans, Herts., 1976), p. 159.

41 James Nelson, *An Essay on the Government of Children*, 3rd ed. (London 1763), p. 273. I will discuss in the following chapter a book by Priscilla Wakefield similar in content but addressed only to females.

42 Ibid., p. 267.

43 Ibid., pp. 277–80, 296–7, 300–1, passim. Younger sons of the gentry were to be educated according to their talents and inclinations, and of course for employment.

44 Ibid., p. 330

45 Ibid., p. 362. Nelson then warned about the neglect of more important obligations, the relation between music and bad company, and "that Torrent of Corruption, bad Songs." This position was echoed by R. Campbell in *The London Tradesman* (London, 1747), a tract providing practical information to parents and their children about entry requirements into and economic expectations from dozens of occupations: "If [a young man] is obliged to follow any Business that requires Application, this Amusement [music] certainly takes him off his Business, exposes him to Company and Temptations to which he would otherwise have been a Stranger. I believe it will agree with every Body's Observation what I have already remarked, that a Tradesman who could sing a good Song, or play upon any Instrument, seldom or never prospered in his Business: I declare it, I never found one, but in the end became Beggars" (p. 92).

46 Ibid., p. 367.

47 Quoted from Alice Anderson Hufstader, "Samuel Pepys, inquisitive amateur," *Musical Quarterly*, 54 (1968), p. 448.

48 North, *North on Music*, pp. 28–9. From an essay written c. 1695.

3 MUSIC, SEXISM AND FEMALE DOMESTICITY

1 Mary Granville, *The Autobiography and Correspondence of Mary Granville, Mrs. Delaney*, ed. Augusta (Wadington) Hall Llanover, 3 vols. (London, 1861), vol. 1, p. 435.

2 Erasmus Darwin, *A Plan for the Conduct of Female Education, in Boarding Schools, Private Families, and Public Seminaries* (Philadelphia, PA, 1798), p. 125. The book appeared in Derby and London editions in 1797. In spite of the fact that the author was male, the work is formated in a series of letters from a mother to her daughter. For more information on the author and the text, see Kassler, *Science of Music*, vol. 1, pp. 263–4.

3 John Essex, *The Young Ladies Conduct: or, Rules for Education, Under Several Heads* (London, 1722), p. 85.

4 Henry Home, Lord Kames, *Loose Hints upon Education, Chiefly Concerning the Culture of the Heart* (Edinburgh and London, 1781), p. 244.

5 Jane Austen, *Persuasion* (1814), ed. D. W. Harding (Harmondsworth, 1966), Chapter 6, p. 69.

6 John Burton, *Lectures on Female Education and Manners* (London, 1793), pp. 136–7. All but the most rigidly conservative (and misogynist) writers voiced concern that music be a rewarding activity for girls and not merely something forced on them by parents.

7 Allaston M. Burgh, *Anecdotes of Music, Historical and Biographical; in a Series of Letters from a Gentleman to his Daughter*, 3 vols. (London, 1814), vol. 1, pp. vi–vii.

8 Anna Thérèse, Marchioness de Lambert, *Advice of a Mother to her Son and Daughter*, 3rd ed. (London, 1737), p. 56.

9 Stubbes, *Anatomy of Abuses*, vol. 1, p. 171.

10 Darrell, *Gentleman Instructed*, p. 486; quoted from the 7th ed. (London, 1720).

Cf. François de Salignac de la Mothe Fénelon, *Instructions for the Education of Daughters*, trans. and rev. George Hickes (Glasgow, 1750), pp. 167–8; and Vicesimus Knox, *Winter Evenings: or, Lucubrations on Life and Letters*, 3rd ed. corr. and enlarged, 3 vols. (London, 1795), vol. I, pp. 48–9.

11 John Bennett, *Letters to a Young Lady, on a Variety of Useful and Interesting Subjects*, 2 vols. (Warrington, 1789), vol. I, pp. 234–5.

12 Knox, *Winter Evenings*, vol. I, p. 49.

13 See further Loesser, *Men, Women and Pianos*, pp. 267–79.

14 The harpsichord illustrated carries the label Thomas Kirkman. The London harpsichord makers named Kirckman were Jacob, Abraham and Joseph; there was no Thomas.

15 Lady Mary Wortley Montagu, *The Complete Letters of Lady Mary Wortley Montagu*, ed. Robert Halsband, 3 vols. (Oxford, 1965–7), vol. 3, p. 159. See further on this painting the exhibition catalogue by Edward J. Nygren and Nancy L. Pressly, *The Pursuit of Happiness: A View of Life in Georgian England* (New Haven, CT, 1977), p. 36, no. 30.

16 Anon., *Man Superior to Woman; or a Vindication of Man's Natural Right of Sovereign Authority over the Woman* (London, 1739), p. 31. This 74-page tract was written in response to a pamphlet by "Sophia," *Woman Not Inferior to Man* (London, 1739).

17 Ibid., p. 28. See further the closing remarks, pp. 73–4 ("Let [women] remember that *Man* holds his Superiority over them by a Charter from Nature in his very Production, a Charter confirm'd by Heaven," etc.).

18 George Savile, Marquis of Halifax, in his *The Lady's New-Years Gift: or, Advice to a Daughter* (London, 1700), pp. 16 and 19, respectively. Cf. Jonas Hanway, *Virtue in Humble Life*, 2nd ed., 2 vols. in I (London, 1777), vol. I, p. 282: "The greatest advocates of your sex, acknowledge that the Author of nature meant that you should be most confined to the domestic business of life." See related material on pp. 279–83.

19 Jonathan Swift, "Of the education of ladies" (a fragment), *The Prose Works of Jonathan Swift*, ed. Temple Scott, 12 vols. (London, 1900–22), vol. II, p. 62.

20 Stanhope, *Letters to his Son*, vol. I, p. 107, letter no. 49 (5 September O.S. 1748). See further Robert H. Michel, "English attitudes towards women, 1640–1700," *Canadian Journal of History*, 13 (1978), pp. 35–60.

21 See for example Sir John Fielding, *The Universal Mentor; or, Entertaining Instructor . . . Selected from the Most Approved Historians, Biographers and Moral Writers, Ancient and Modern*, new ed. (London, 1777), Chapter 96, "Women," pp. 247–251.

22 Sir William Anstruther, *Essays, Moral and Divine, in Five Discourses* (Edinburgh, 1701), p. 155. See further pp. 150–61.

23 Edward Phillips, *The Mysteries of Love and Eloquence; or, the Arts of Wooing and Complementing*, 3rd ed. with additions (London, 1685), p. 187. A new edition was issued in 1699 under the title *The Beau's Academy*.

24 Anon., *Reflections upon Matrimony, and the Women of this Country, in a Letter to a Young Gentleman* (London, 1755), p. 7.

25 Home, *Loose Hints*, pp. 228–9. Cf. the views expressed in two late eighteenth-century texts: Anon., *The New Whole Duty of Man* (London, [1788]), pp. 220–7; and [John Hill], *The Deportment of a Married Life*, 2nd ed. (London, 1798), pp. 2–3: "There is only one Path by which a married Woman can arrive at Happiness, and this is by conforming herself to the Sentiments of her Husband."

26 Home, *Loose Hints*, p. 229.

27 Robert Burton, *The Anatomy of Melancholy* (1621; reprint. ed. Amsterdam and New York, 1971), p. 704. The book reached an eighth edition by 1676. The bibliography on the status of women in the eighteenth century is growing significantly. Among recent studies see especially Lawrence Stone, *The Family,*

Sex and Marriage in England, 1500–1800, abridged ed. (New York, 1979); and an important challenge to Stone's thesis re increasingly egalitarian marriages in the eighteenth century by Susan Moller Okin, "Patriarchy and married women's property in England: questions about some current views," *Eighteenth Century Studies*, 17 (1983–4), pp. 121–38. Finally, for a more general survey see Jarrett, *England in the Age of Hogarth*, pp. 103–50, passim.

28 Jane Austen, *Mansfield Park* (1814), ed. Tony Tanner (Harmondsworth, 1966), Chapter 2, p. 55, and Chapter 29, pp. 292–3. Regarding Austen's own musical interests, based on her characters and comments in letters, see Elizabeth M. Lockwood, "Jane Austen and some drawing-room music of her time," *Music and Letters*, 15 (1934), pp. 112–19. See also Frits Noske, "Sound and sentiment: the function of music in the Gothic novel," *Music and Letters*, 62 (1981), pp. 162–6, on the use of music by females in eighteenth-century novels.

29 Jonas Hanway, *Thoughts on the Use and Advantages of Music, and Other Amusements Most in Esteem in the Polite World* (London, 1765), pp. 63–4. What Hanway intended by a husband of "true English taste" is evident by means of a comparison with the French, always the convenient foil to establish a world/ natural order gone awry. Thus Hanway in his *Virtue in Humble Life*, p. 280, remarked (in a dialogue between farmer Trueman and his daughter): "I have been told, it is not uncommon in some cities of *France*, to see the wife reading a *learned book* whilst the husband is making *lace*. Is this not reversing the rule, and departing from the true character of a good wife?"

30 Bennett, *Letters to a Young Lady*, vol. 1, p. 234.

31 Anon. female author, *The Whole Duty of a Woman, or a Guide to the Female Sex. From the Age of Sixteen to Sixty*, 3rd ed. (London, 1701), pp. 48–9.

32 Darwin, *Plan of Female Education*, p. 13. Cf. Anon., *Euterpe*, p. 18; Anon., *The Polite Lady; or, a Course of Female Education*, 2nd ed. corr. (London, 1769), p. 24; and Hester Chapone, *Letters on Improvement of the Mind, Addressed to a Young Lady*, 2 vols. in 1 (Hagerstown, MD, 1818–19), p. 193. (The book was first published in 1773, with four additional editions in Great Britain by 1783; it was published in American editions as late as 1834.)

33 Darrell, *Gentleman Instructed*, p. 129.

34 Philip Gosse, *Dr. Viper: The Querulous Life of Philip Thicknesse* (London, 1952), pp. 129–32. For a discussion of Gainsborough's portrait, see pp. 251–5, especially regarding the artist's interest in Miss Ford's viola da gamba; and Michael I. Wilson, "Gainsborough, Bath and music," *Apollo*, 105 (1977), pp. 108–9; and also the exhibition catalogue, *Gainsborough and his Musical Friends* (London, 1977), no. 16 (unpaginated). For another account of the behavior of Ann Ford's father regarding her musical career, see Aaron Crossley Seymour, ed., *The Life and Times of Selina [Hastings], Countess of Huntington*, 2 vols. (London, 1840), vol. 2, pp. 203–5. For Philip Thicknesse's own account of the portrait and of the viol, see his *A Sketch of the Life and Paintings of Thomas Gainsborough, Esq.* (London, 1788), pp. 20–7.

35 See further Deborah Cherry and Jennifer Harris, "Eighteenth-century portraiture and the seventeenth-century past: Gainsborough and Van Dyck," *Art History*, 5 (1982), p. 293.

36 Ann Ford's pose was in fact considered shocking and provocative. Mrs. Delaney, upon seeing the portrait in Gainsborough's studio, remarked that she "should be very sorry to have any one I loved set forth in such a manner." Granville, *Autobiography of Mrs. Delaney*, vol. 3, p. 605. See also Jonathan Norton Leonard, *The World of Gainsborough, 1727–1788* (New York, 1969), p. 62. Gainsborough painted another accomplished musician, Elizabeth Linley (together with her sister Mary), who was also forced by her husband, playwright Richard Brinsley Sheridan, to give up a public musical career except for private subscription concerts given in their home. See Margaret Bor and Lamond Clelland, *Still the Lark: A Biography of Elizabeth Linley* (London,

1962), pp. 70–5. Concerning Gainsborough's portraits of the Linleys – he painted family members as many as twelve times – see *Gainsborough and his Musical Friends*, nos. 4, 6 (unpaginated).

37 Anon., *The Hardships of the English Laws in Relation to Wives*, (London, 1735), p. 4.

38 [Theophilus Dorrington], *The Excellent Woman Described by her True Characters and their Opposites* (London, 1692), p. 135.

39 Daniel Defoe, *An Essay on Projects* (1697), *The Earlier Life and Chief Earlier Works of Daniel Defoe*, ed. Henry Morley (London, 1889), p. 144. Defoe favored musical education for women; see p. 148.

40 Dorrington, *Excellent Woman*, p. 135.

41 Mary Wollstonecraft, *Thoughts on the Education of Daughters, with Reflections on Female Conduct in the More Important Duties of Life* (London, 1787), pp. 25–9.

42 Hannah More, *Strictures on the Modern System of Female Education*, 2 vols. in 1 (Charlestown, MA, 1800), vol. 1, p. 49. The book was first published in 1799 and reached a seventh edition that same year; it was printed in other editions as late as 1830. According to Hannah More's biographer, 19,000 copies of the book were sold during her own lifetime. See Kassler, *Science of Music*, vol. 2, pp. 782–4. Hannah More admitted that "a well-bred young lady may lawfully learn most of the fashionable arts," though she was inclined to believe that these arts were not "the true end of education." She maintained the traditional view that the ultimate profession for women was that of mistress of the family. In this role the arts "merely embellish life" (pp. 60–1). See also Mary Cockle, *Important Studies, for the Female Sex* (London, 1809), pp. 241–2; and Maria Edgeworth and R. L. Edgeworth, *Practical Education*, 2nd ed., 3 vols. (London, 1801), vol. 3, pp. 4, 20. On the problems faced by a society which simultaneously condemned both ignorant and learned women, see Dorothy Gardiner, *English Girlhood at School: A Study of Women's Education through Twelve Centuries* (London, 1929), pp. 378–82.

43 See Mulcaster, *Mulcaster's Positions*, vol. 2, p. 177; and Robert Burton, *The Anatomy of Melancholy*, 6th ed., 3 vols. (1640; reprint. ed. New York and London, 1932), vol. 3, p. 177. (Burton added new material to each successive edition; this passage does not occur in the first. The sixth is the first posthumous edition – Burton died in 1640.)

44 Jane Austen, *Sense and Sensibility* (1811), ed. Tony Tanner (Harmondsworth, 1969), Chapter 7, pp. 67–8.

45 Jane Austen, *Emma* (1816), ed. Ronald Blythe (Harmondsworth, 1966), Chapter 32, p. 279. Cf. remarks by Edgeworth and Edgeworth, *Practical Education*, p. 8: "As soon as a young lady is married, does not she frequently discover, that 'she really has not the *leisure* to cultivate talents which take up so much time.' Does not she complain of the labour of practicing four or five hours a day to keep up her musical character? What motive has she for perseverance . . . She will then of course leave off playing, but continue very fond of music. How often is the labour of years thus lost for ever!"

46 [George Colman], *The Musical Lady* (London, 1762), p. 6. *Gentleman's Magazine*, 79/1 (1809), p. 399, printed a letter bearing on this topic.

47 Mulcaster, *Mulcaster's Positions*, vol. 2, p. 179.

48 Hanway, *Thoughts on Music*, p. 63.

49 Nelson, *Essay on Children*, pp. 282–3; see also pp. 287–8.

50 Ibid., pp. 311–15; the long quotation is from pp. 314–15.

51 Priscilla Wakefield, *Reflections on the Present Condition of the Female Sex; with Suggestions for its Improvement* (London, 1798), pp. 63, 90–1.

52 Ibid., p. 134. Portions of Wakefield's book (pertaining to the duties of women "in the superior classes of society" were reprinted in a periodical review, *Lady's Monthly Museum*, 1 (1798), pp. 34–8.

53 Ibid., pp. 58–9.

54 Jarrett, *England in the Age of Hogarth*, p. 73.

55 *Annals of Agriculture*, 17 (1792), p. 156. Quoted from Dorothy Marshall, *English People in the Eighteenth Century* (London, 1956), p. 237. Arthur Young was himself fond of music and was a friend of Charles Burney; Young's wife's sister was Burney's second wife. For additional remarks by Arthur Young and others on this matter, see Minjay, *English Landed Society*, pp. 254–6. While these views were common as the eighteenth century drew to a close, similar, if not identical, expressions of concern occasionally occurred much earlier. See, for example, an anonymous pamphlet, *The Grand Concern of England Explained* (London, 1673), reprinted in *The Harleian Miscellany; or, A Collection of Scarce, Curious, and Entertaining Pamphlets and Tracts*, 12 vols. (London, 1808–11), vol. 8, pp. 51–3.

56 Burgh, *Anecdotes of Music*, vol. 1, pp. v–vi.

57 *Gentleman's Magazine*, 71 (1801), p. 587. Quoted from Marshall, *English People*, p. 238.

58 See Mary Dorothy George, *Catalogue of Political and Personal Satires Preserved in the Department of Prints and Drawings in the British Museum* (London, 1947), vol. 8, pp. 885–6, no. 11,444.

59 Ibid., p. 978, no. 11,649.

60 Edgeworth and Edgeworth, *Practical Education*, vol. 3, pp. 17–18. See further Miss Hatfield, *Letters on the Importance of the Female Sex* (London, 1803), pp. 90–1; and P. J. Miller, "Women's education, 'self improvement' and social mobility – a late eighteenth century debate," *British Journal of Educational Studies*, 20 (1972), p. 309.

61 Anon., *The Levellers: A Dialogue between Two Young Ladies, Concerning Matrimony* (London, 1703), reprinted in *Harleian Miscellany*, vol. 12, pp. 198–9. Cf. Wakefield, *Reflections*, pp. 60–2; she tallied prostitution among the results of education beyond one's station.

4 MUSIC EDUCATION AS SOCIAL PRAXIS

1 John Lawson and Harold Silver, *A Social History of Education in England* (London, 1973), pp. 216–17. The pattern of a boy's education was subject to a number of variations within this general scheme: for example, some were educated first at home and later at public schools such as Westminster and Eton. Nicholas Hans, *New Trends in Education in the Eighteenth Century* (London, 1951), studied the educational patterns for 3,500 men born between 1685 and 1785. Of these, 967 received their first education from private tutors at home, from there generally going to the university (898), otherwise to the professions (see p. 18, table 1). In England and Wales, of a total of 160 peers, 40 were educated at home and 109 in the great public schools (principally Eton and Westminster). Of 553 baronets, squires and gentlemen of independent means, 199 were educated at home and 198 in the great public schools (see p. 26, table 3).

2 Hans, *New Trends in Education*, p. 184.

3 Brauer, *Education of a Gentleman*, pp. 74–6. Advertisements for – and by – male tutors, typically young university graduates, to serve in households as instructors for boys seldom made reference to music.

4 See further on the education of women Josephine Kamm, *Hope Deferred: Girls' Education in English History* (London, 1965), pp. 68–151; Myra Reynolds, *The Learned Lady in England, 1650–1760* (Boston, MA, and New York, 1920), pp. 258–315, and Hans, *New Trends in Education*, pp. 194–208. Hans studied 120 women born between 1685 and 1785, representing the intellectual elite of the sex. Sixty-three were educated at home, 32 at schools, 11 self-educated. No data was available for 14. He points out that "the most outstanding women of the eighteenth century belonged either to the middle or lower classes" (p. 195;

see table on same page). This is not surprising in that women from these classes would benefit to some degree from the pressures of upward mobility operative during the period. By contrast women of the uppermost classes were more restricted by modes of conservative behavior.

5 *Gazetteer and New Daily Advertiser* (London), issue no. 12,419, 21 December 1768, p. 2, col. 4. Only rarely do advertisements appear in which musical concerns are more central, as in copy from London's *Daily Advertiser* in 1771: "WANTED, A Governess in a Gentleman's Family, a Native of France, and a Protestant, who understands Musick perfectly, and to teach French grammatically." Issue no. 12,535, 27 February, p. 2, col. 2.

6 Marjorie Plant, *The Domestic Life of Scotland in the Eighteenth Century* (Edinburgh, 1952), p. 14.

7 Quoted from Rosamond Bayne-Powell, *English Country Life in the Eighteenth Century* (London, [1935]), p. 184.

8 Kamm, *Hope Deferred*, p. 69; and Gardiner, *English Girlhood at School*, pp. 211–13.

9 Kamm, *Hope Deferred*, p. 72; and "Josias Priest," *New Grove*, vol. 15, p. 226. In 1728 Daniel Defoe proposed that an academy for thirty boys be formed at Christ's Hospital, a charity school, where students would be trained to play and sing depending on their talents, all to receive composition lessons. The course of study would last seven or eight years, ultimately leading to careers as professional musicians. The plan was never realized. See Kassler, *Science of Music*, vol. 1, pp. 270–1. Charles Burney likewise proposed an academy of similar sorts, also unrealized. See Jamie Croy Kassler, "Burney's *Sketch of a plan for a public music-school*," *Musical Quarterly*, 58 (1972), pp. 210–34.

10 Thomas Shadwell, *The Scowrers*, in *The Complete Works of Thomas Shadwell*, ed. Montague Summers, 5 vols. (London, 1927), vol. 5, p. 98.

11 This method was directly criticized by the teacher Edward Miller in the preface to his *Institutes of Music, or Easy Lessons for the Harpsichord* (London, 1782?). See further Kassler, "Burney's *Sketch*," pp. 221–2; and Kassler, *Science of Music*, vol. 2, pp. 771–3.

12 See further Plant, *Domestic Life*, pp. 13–16; and *Gentleman's Magazine*, 56/1 (1786), pp. 132–3, and 85/1 (1815), pp. 346–7.

13 H. Bertram Cox and C. L. E. Cox, *Leaves from the Journals of Sir George Smart* (London, 1907), p. 6.

14 *Bath Advertiser*, issue no. 159, 28 October 1758, p. 3, col. 2. There were two common ways that a music teacher could advertise his services: either by distributing handbills at the houses of fashionable people or by advertising in the newspapers and advertisers published throughout the country.

15 See further Richard Leppert, "Music teachers of upper-class amateur musicians in eighteenth-century England," *Music in the Classic Period: Essays in Honor of Barry S. Brook*, ed. Allan W. Atlas (New York, 1985), pp. 133–58. This essay considers teachers' financial and working conditions, numbers of students taught, competition among masters for pupils and the like.

16 Charles Dibdin, *The Professional Life of Mr. Dibdin, Written by Himself*, 4 vols. (London, 1803), vol. 4, p. 192.

17 John Playford, *Musick's Delight on the Cithren* (London, 1666), from the preface, p. i. See also John Harley, "French bitches and German dogs: foreign musicians in 18th-century London," *Recorder and Music*, 4 (1974), pp. 310–12, 357–60; and Leppert, "Imagery, musical confrontation and cultural difference."

18 Quoted from Harold E. Samuel, "A German musician comes to London in 1704," *Musical Times*, 122 (1981), pp. 591–2. Cousser's commonplace book is in the Beinecke Rare Book and Manuscript Library, Yale University. See also by the same author, "John Sigismond Cousser in London and Dublin," *Music and Letters*, 61 (1980), pp. 158–71.

19 Campbell, *London Tradesman*, p. 89.

20 Roger Lonsdale, *Dr. Charles Burney: A Literary Biography* (Oxford, 1965), p. 54.

21 More, *Strictures on Education*, p. 49.

22 Darwin, *Plan of Female Education*, p. 13.

23 *Gazetteer and New Daily Advertiser* (London), issue no. 12,409, 9 December 1768.

24 Ambrose Pitman, *The Miseries of Musick-Masters: Including the Art of Fingering Key'd Instruments, and Introductory Rudiments of the Practice of Harmonicks. A Serio Comick Didactick Poem* (London, 1815), pp. 40–1, lines 456–62, 475–9. The text is partly a tutor book on the rudiments of music explained at the keyboard, and its 954 lines of rhyming couplets in iambic quatrameter often are incongruously interrupted by musical examples. For additional information on this text, its mixed critical reception and its author, see Kassler, *Science of Music*, vol. 2, pp. 843–5; and Bernarr Rainbow, "The miseries of musick masters," *Musical Times*, 127 (1986), pp. 201–3. Rainbow reproduces the book's frontispiece, a caricature by George Cruikshank showing a self-satisfied family listening with pleasure to the screeching of a boy singer, accompanied on the piano by his sister. Rainbow's chief concern is the rediscovery of *Foote's Minuet*, then a standard piece for beginners which is reproduced by Pitman, but of which no other copy is known to exist.

25 James Fordyce, *Sermons to Young Women*, 7th ed., 2 vols. (London, 1771), vol. I, p. 258.

26 Horace Walpole, *Horace Walpole's Correspondence with Sir Horace Mann*, ed. W. S. Lewis, Warren Huntington Smith and George L. Lam, The Yale Edition of Horace Walpole's Correspondence, ed. W. S. Lewis, 43 vols. (New Haven, CT, 1954–71), vol. 18/2, pp. 316–17.

27 Anon., *Euterpe*, p. 5.

28 There survive a few accounts of physical abuse of children by music masters, usually involving boys who later became professional musicians. See Jamie Croy Kassler, "Music made easy to infant capacity, 1714–1830: some facets of British music education," *Studies in Music* (Univ. of Western Australia), 10 (1976), p. 76; and John Edmund Cox, *Musical Recollections of the Last Half-Century*, 2 vols. (London, 1872), vol. 1, pp. 23–5.

29 Margaret Maria, Lady Verney, ed., *Verney Letters of the Eighteenth Century from the MSS at Claydon House*, 2 vols. (London, 1930), vol. 1, pp. 164–5, in a letter dated 27 November 1701 from Lady Gardiner to Sir John Verney.

30 Music teacher, singer, composer and author Charles Dibdin in his *The Musical Tour* (Sheffield, 1788) told the tale of a young man, a music master, charged with instructing the daughter of a gentleman. The young lady fell in love with him, declared herself and proposed elopement. The master refused, went immediately to the father and reported the incident. Dibdin describes the story as "the history of the Sabines inverted." See letter no. 24, pp. 93–4.

31 Joseph Baretti, *An Account of the Manners and Customs of Italy; with Observations on the Mistakes of Some Travellers, with Regard to that Country*, 2 vols. (London, 1769), vol. 1, pp. 288–9. The book reached a second edition the same year.

32 Samuel Sharp, *Letters from Italy, Describing the Customs and Manners of that Country, in the Years 1765, and 1766*, 2nd ed. (London, 1767).

33 Baretti, *Account of Italy*, vol. 1, pp. 291–2.

34 North, *North on Music*, p. 17.

35 [John Bicknell], *Joel Collier Redivivus, an Entirely New Edition, of that Celebrated Author's "Musical Travels"* (London, 1818), pp. 66–8. On the book's authorship, the Burney satire and the various editions, see Lonsdale, *Burney*, pp. 156–7; and Percy A. Scholes, *The Great Doctor Burney: His Life, his Travels, his Works, his Family and his Friends*, 2 vols. (London, 1948), vol. 1, pp. 272–5.

36 Thomas Baker, *Tunbridge Walks: or, the Yeoman of Kent* (London, 1703), p. 24. A century earlier, in a play by Thomas Middleton called *A Trick to Catch the Old*

One (London, 1608), reference is made to a perspective bride who "remains at London . . . to learn fashions, practice music; the voice between her lips, and the viol between her legs, she'll be fit for a consort very speedily." Quoted from Westrup, "Domestic music under the Stuarts," p. 29.

37 On Rowlandson's use of body shapes see Ronald Paulson, *Rowlandson: A New Interpretation* (New York, 1972), pp. 71–9.

38 See Samuel Pepys, *The Diary of Samuel Pepys*, ed. Robert Latham and William Matthews, 11 vols. (Berkeley, CA, and Los Angeles, 1970–83), vol. 2 (1661), pp. 127, 130, 144, 190; vol. 7 (1666), pp. 300, 347–8, 397; vol. 8 (1667), pp. 108–9, 119, 171, 209, 244, 325, 351, 411, 458.

39 Scholes, *Great Doctor Burney*, vol. 1, pp. 35–9. See also Fanny Burney d'Arblay, *Memoirs of Doctor Burney*, 3 vols. (London, 1832), vol. 1, pp. 24–35.

40 The publication records for tutor books shadow the rise and fall in popularity of individual instruments among amateur musicians, just as the contents of these books provide indications of both the accomplishment and musical tastes of their audience. However, the body of evidence is so staggering in size that a proper study of the topic demands a specialized monograph. One difficulty arises from the fact that tutor books were of a highly ephemeral character; they were usually printed cheaply, left unbound and put in soft covers. Once the instrument for which they were intended fell from favor their useful life was at an end; the same was true once the buyer either gave up on the task or superseded the instruction the text offered. Thus we know of many more titles to tutor books than tutor books themselves, through surviving publishers' catalogues and advertisements of new titles, though some of these might be ghost titles – works never actually published. In many cases more than a single edition was announced, though it is seldom possible to assemble and thus compare all editions of a single work. Piratings swell the title list further. Moreover, subsequent editions (or piratings) were often printed with no changes from previous editions, apart from a new title page. Finally, title pages do not always include publication date, and for works known only by title publication dates can be only approximately assigned.

   Besides tutors there were numerous books published during the eighteenth century for basic instruction in music theory and, especially, playing thorough bass. For the most part these were intended for serious students and not dabblers. Virtually all assumed a keyboard instrument as the basis for instruction, chiefly but not exclusively the harpsichord (some were targeted especially for women, who were of course the chief players of keyboard instruments). See further Adrienne Simpson, "A short-title list of printed English instrumental tutors up to 1800, held in British libraries," *R. M. A. Research Chronicle*, 6 (1966), pp. 24–50; and Thomas E. Warner, *An Annotated Bibliography of Woodwind Instruction Books, 1600–1830*, Detroit Studies in Music Bibliography, 11 (Detroit, 1967).

41 Tutor books were not intended for would-be professional musicians; their training came via apprenticeships. See Eric Halfpenny, "A seventeenth-century tutor for the hautboy," *Music and Letters*, 30 (1949), p. 355.

42 See further Lillian M. Ruff, "The Social significance of the 17th century English music treatises," *Consort*, 26 (1970), p. 418.

43 My comments here summarize the contents of composer-organist James Hook's *New Guida di Musica. Being a Compleat Book of Instructions for Beginners on the Piano Forte or Harpsichord* (London, c. 1796).

44 A small number of highly detailed, challenging tutors appeared during the second half of the century. Among these were: (1) the English translation by Giffard Bernard of a tract by the French theorist Anton Bemetzrieder, *Music Made Easy to Every Capacity, in a Series of Dialogues; Being Practical Lessons for the Harpsichord* (Paris, 1771; London, 1778, reprinted 1785), essentially a textbook on harmony, thorough bass and composition employing the harpsichord as the

medium through which these subjects were learned; (2) Luke Heron, *A Treatise on the German Flute* (London, 1771), a highly detailed instruction book that included a lengthy essay on the power of music and its important social role in the ancient world; (3) Francesco Geminiani, *The Art of Playing on the Violin; Containing All the Rules Necessary to Attain a Perfection on that Instrument* (London, 1751), a book intended not only for beginners but for advanced students as well and which concentrated attention on the importance of musical expression and not merely the mechanics of playing.

45 This included one edition published c. 1800 falsely ascribed to Geminiani, *The Entire New and Complete Tutor for the Violin*. More attention has been focused on violin tutors than on those for any other instrument. See in particular several studies by David D. Boyden: *A History of Violin Playing from its Origins to 1761* (London, 1965), especially pp. 244–7, 357–66; "The violin and its technique in the 18th century," *Musical Quarterly*, 36 (1950), pp. 9–38; "Geminiani and the first violin tutor," *Acta Musicologica*, 31 (1959), pp. 161–70; and "A postscript to 'Geminiani and the first violin tutor,'" *Acta Musicologica*, 32 (1960), pp. 40–7, which corrects some errors in the previous study; see also Jeffrey Pulver, "Violin methods old and new," *Proceedings of the Musical Association*, 50 (1923–4), pp. 101–27 (not restricted to English books); and Maurice W. Riley, "The teaching of bowed instruments from 1511 to 1756" (Ph.D. diss., Univ. of Michigan, 1954), pp. 144–230. (Boyden corrects and updates some of the information available to Riley.)

46 See Boyden, "Postscript," p. 44. The technical demands on average were slight; for example, many violin tutors did not take the student beyond first position.

5 MUSIC AND THE BODY: DANCE, POWER, SUBMISSION

1 Essex, *Young Ladies Conduct*, pp. 82–3. Though addressed to females his remarks are actually more typical of those intended for males.

2 John Playford, *The English Dancing Master: or, Plaine and Easie Rules for the Dancing of Country Dances* (1651; reprint. ed. London, 1933), ed. Hugh Mellor and Leslie Bridgewater, p. [i]. For information about the publishing history and contents of later editions, see "England," *New Grove*, vol. 6, pp. 188–9.

3 I. H. Æ., *The Mirrour of Worldly Fame* (London, 1603), reprinted in *Harleian Miscellany*, vol. 2, p. 525.

4 Eccles, *Musick-Lector*, p. 14.

5 Bennett, *Letters to a Young Lady*, vol. 1, pp. 235–6.

6 In this regard see George, *Catalogue of Satires*, vol. 7, pp. 508–9, no. 9299, a print entitled "Ecclesiastical Scrutiny – or the Durham Inquest on Duty" (1798) reflecting contemporaneous debates about women, dress and morals, with reference to dance thrown in.

7 Locke, *Some Thoughts Concerning Education*, pp. 190–1.

8 John Weaver, *An Essay towards an History of Dancing* (London, 1712), pp. 6, 25, respectively; see further to p. 27. This text constituted "the first apology for dancing *per se* in English," according to Richard Ralph, *The Life and Works of John Weaver: An Account of his Life, Writings and Theatrical Productions, with an Annotated Reprint of his Complete Publications* (New York, 1985), p. 101. On the *Essay towards an History of Dancing* see pp. 115–43.

9 Stanhope, *Letters to his Son*, vol. 1, pp. 114–15 (letter no. 51, dated 20 September o.s. 1748).

10 Gardiner, *English Girlhood at School*, p. 248. For example, on the wealth of the famous master Giovanni-Andrea Gallini – and of his parsimony – see Henry Angelo, *Reminiscences of Henry Angelo* (London, 1828–30), vol. 2, pp. 38–40.

11 Richard Flecknoe, *Enigmaticall Characters, All Taken to the Life, from Severall Persons, Humours and Dispositions* ([London,] 1658), p. 59.

12 Thomas D'Urfey, *Love for Money, or the Boarding School* (London, 1691).

13 Dibdin, *Musical Tour*, p. 309, from letter no. 75.

14 Austen, *Emma*, Chapter 29, p. 253.

15 *The Spectator*, ed. Donald F. Bond, 5 vols. (Oxford, 1965), vol. 1, pp. 282–3 (issue no. 66, 16 May 1711).

16 Sophie von la Roche, *Sophie in London, 1786: Being the Diary of Sophie v. la Roche*, trans. Clare Williams (London, 1933), pp. 247–50; the quotation is from pp. 249–50.

17 *Gentleman's Magazine*, 6 (1736), pp. 131–2 (the letter was reprinted from *Universal Spectator*, 6 March 1736, issue no. 387).

18 Thomas Gordon, *The Humorist: Being Essays upon Several Subjects*, 3rd ed. (London, 1724), pp. 23–4.

19 For more on the two Vestris, see George, *Catalogue of Satires*, vol. 5, pp. 532–3, no. 5903, a print by Paul Sandby, "Bass Relief Found at the Opera House" (1781).

20 Edward Ravenscroft, *The Citizen Turn'd Gentleman* (London, 1670?), Act I.

21 See further Frederic G. Stephens and Edward Hawkins, *Catalogue of Prints and Drawings in the British Museum. Division I. Political and Personal Satires* (London, 1883), vol. 4, pp. 493–4, no. 4250 (1768). The advertisements placed by dance teachers typically stressed four complementary features: ease of learning (a fabrication), the latest dances (always a necessity), teaching in the studio or in the client's home and, as a corollary to the last, privacy of instruction (to avoid public embarrassment or acknowledgment that one did not already know how to dance). The ads were common in both London and provincial papers. One example will suffice, from *The Public Advertiser* (London) (issue no. 4168, 8 August 1752, p. 2), an ad placed by N. Dukes, Dancing-Master: "Grown Gentlemen or Ladies may be taught . . . in so private, genteel and expeditious a Manner, as to render them very soon capable of performing in any polite Company or Assembly whatever. And on Monday and Wednesday Evenings there's a compleat Set of Gentlemen only, which assembles for the learning and practicing of Country Dances."

22 See further Stephens and Hawkins, *Catalogue of Satires*, vol. 4, p. 494, nos. 4251, 4252 (1768).

23 This arrangement is preserved in an engraved image in a treatise by Pierre Rameau, *The Dancing-Master: or, The Art of Dancing Explained*, trans. J. Essex (London, 1728), opposite p. 30, an oversized foldout. The extraordinarily precise regimen of the Versailles ceremonial, especially that following the King's retirement to watch each couple present themselves to him in turn, is described on pp. 28–30.

24 See Curt Sachs, *World History of the Dance*, trans. Bessie Schönberg (New York, 1937), p. 398. See also pp. 397–402 for additional information on the minuet upon which some of my comments are based, and also "Minuet," *New Grove*, vol. 12, pp. 353–4; and Frances Rust, *Dance in Society: An Analysis of the Relationship between the Social Dance and Society in England from the Middle Ages to the Present Day* (London, 1969), pp. 59–62.

25 See also the description given in George, *Catalogue of Satires*, vol. 6, pp. 444–5, no. 7229, including an explanation of the parodic citation from Horace. The original drawing upon which the print was based is in the Paul Mellon Collection, Yale Center for British Art, New Haven, no. B1975.4.1894.

26 Sachs, *World History of Dance*, p. 420.

27 See further ibid., pp. 423–5. For a comic print (1771) illustrating this dance, see *New Grove*, vol. 4, p. 829.

28 "Contredanse," *New Grove*, vol. 4, p. 704.

29 Rust, *Dance in Society*, p. 59.

30 Sachs, *World History of Dance*, p. 398.

31 Rust, *Dance in Society*, p. 58. For comments on the continuation of this practice in the eighteenth century in country houses, see p. 61.

32 See further Richard Leppert, *Arcadia at Versailles: Noble Amateur Musicians and their Musettes and Hurdy-Gurdies at the French Court (c. 1660–1789)* (Amsterdam and Lisse, 1978).

33 *The Tatler*, ed. George A. Aitken, 4 vols. (New York and London, 1899), vol. 2, pp. 273–6; the quotation is from p. 274 (issue no. 88, 1 November 1709).

34 The analysis of *"Se vuol ballare"* is in part from Wye J. Allanbrook, "Metric gesture as a topic in *Le Nozze di Figaro* and *Don Giovanni*," *Musical Quarterly*, 67 (1981), pp. 106–7; and Wye J. Allanbrook, *Rhythmic Gesture in Mozart: "Le Nozze di Figaro" and "Don Giovanni"* (Chicago and London, 1983), pp. 79–82; see also Frits Noske, "Social tensions in *Le Nozze di Figaro*," *Music and Letters*, 50 (1969), pp. 45–62.

35 Kellom Tomlinson, *The Art of Dancing Explained by Reading and Figures* (London, 1735), p. 22.

36 Rameau, *Dancing-Master*, pp. 14–15, 113–50.

37 Raoul Auger Feuillet, *For the Further Improvement of Dancing*, trans. John Essex (London, 1710), pp. 7–12.

38 Giovanni-Andrea Gallini, *Critical Observations on the Art of Dancing; to Which is Added, a Collection of Cotillons or French Dances* (London, n.d.), pp. 126, 128–9.

39 Thus see Thomas Page, *The Art of Painting in its Rudiments, Progress, and Perfection* (Norwich, 1720), passim. See also Alastair Smart, "Dramatic gesture and expression in the age of Hogarth and Reynolds," *Apollo*, 82 (1965), pp. 90–7, especially pp. 94–5; and D'Oench, *Conversation Piece*, pp. 15–18.

40 John Weaver, *Anatomical and Mechanical Lectures upon Dancing* (London, 1721), pp. viii–ix. I first came upon this passage through the dissertation by Shirley Spackman Wynne, "The charms of complaisance: the dance in England in the early eighteenth century (Ohio State Univ., 1967), p. 126.

41 Thomas Wilson, *The Complete System of English Country Dancing, Containing All the Figures Ever Used in English Country Dancing, with a Variety of New Figures and New Reels . . . Elucidated by Means of Diagrams* (London, 1820), p. 1.

42 Ibid., p. 267.

43 Ibid., pp. 268–9. In a footnote Wilson added that if the printed etiquette were put on public view, the pronouncements of the Master of Ceremonies would stand less chance of being disputed "and his authority consequently treated with contempt." On the maintenance of decorum see also Walter Besant, *London Life in the Eighteenth Century* (London and New York, 1903), p. 404. Weaver may have had "Beau" Nash, Master of Ceremonies at the Bath assemblies from c. 1703 until his death in 1761, as a model for his own ajudicator. As Goldsmith described, Nash was famous for maintaining ritual-like order at the proceedings. See Oliver Goldsmith, *The Life of "Beau" Nash* (1762; reprint. ed. San Francisco, n.d.), pp. 22–31, but especially pp. 28–9, "Rules to be observed at Bath," according to Goldsmith written by Nash himself. The rules were posted in the Pump Room and rigidly observed.

44 Hannah More, "Rural tales. The two wealthy farmers; or the history of Mr. Bragwell," *Village and Other Tales* (New York, 1851), pp. 43–5; the story was originally published by 1795.

45 The Yale Center for British Art, Paul Mellon Collection, New Haven, CT, possesses a sketch (B1975.4.1045) and a preparatory drawing (B1975.4.1046) for this print. In characteristic Burney fashion, the image is so overladen with bits of text and separate vignettes that a separate study would be required to piece them together. My interests do not justify attempting that here.

6 THE MALE AT MUSIC: PRAXIS, REPRESENTATION AND THE
PROBLEMATIC OF IDENTITY

1 North, *North on Music*, p. 16.
2 Research on the manufacture, availability and costs of instruments in the
eighteenth century remains sketchy. The best documented are keyboard instruments. Thus for the piano see the list of makers in London and its environs,
1760–1851, by no means either complete or totally reliable, in Rosamond E.
M. Harding, *The Piano-Forte: Its History Traced to the Great Exhibition of 1851*
(1933; reprint. ed. New York, 1973), pp. 385–409; the general survey by
Loesser, *Men, Women and Pianos*, pp. 216–28, 232–6; and the more focused
study by Virginia Pleasants, "The early piano in Britain (c. 1760–1800)," *Early
Music*, 13 (1985), pp. 39–44; and some valuable corrective comments to
Pleasants by Warwick Henry Cole, "The early piano in Britain reconsidered,"
Early Music, 14 (1986), pp. 563–6.
   Amateurs' favorite instruments were widely available, especially in London
where most of the makers, dealers and importers resided. Throughout the
century in all the major urban centers there was also a lively secondhand market
in instruments, commonly advertised in the daily papers as part of general
household auctions and estate sales. It was also possible to rent instruments,
especially harpsichords and pianos.
   By the 1790s London itself had about thirty-eight piano makers, about
fifty-two violin (family) makers and fifty-one makers of woodwinds, these
totals many times exceeding the numbers of makers active in the early part of
the century. See further Willibald Leo Frh. von Lütgendorff, *Die Geigen und
Lautenmacher vom Mittelalter bis zur Gegenwart*, 3rd rev. ed., 2 vols. (Frankfurt,
1922), vol. 1, passim; Lyndesay G. Langwill, *An Index of Wind-Instrument
Makers*, 6th ed. rev. and enlarged (Edinburgh, 1980), especially pp. 229–64,
passim. Little is known as to the numbers of instruments any given maker
produced in either a single year or in his total career. But the Broadwood firm,
unquestionably among the most successful and well-capitalized keyboard-
manufacturing firms, was probably making about 400 square pianos and over
100 grands a year during the 1790s, though this number far exceeded the output
of other firms. (Many English fortepianos were also exported to the Continent,
to Paris in particular.) See "Broadwood," *New Grove*, vol. 3, p. 324. David
Wainwright, "John Broadwood, the harpsichord and the piano," *Musical
Times*, 123 (1982), p. 676, states that during the 1770s Broadwood registered
about 700 transactions a year (both domestic and foreign sales), by 1784 the
number rising to almost 900. Whereas in the 1770s references to piano sales
accounted for fewer than fifty per year, by 1784 the number had risen to more
than 250.
   The costs of instruments, apart from harpsichords and pianos by the best-
known makers, are also difficult to assess except in a general way, especially
taking the century as a whole. Some instruments could be had cheaply –
between 1698 and 1715 the amateur musician Morris Claver bought two
violins for £2 and £3 5s., and a violoncello for £5, and in 1688 an oboe with
ivory fittings for £1 7s. and a bassoon for £2 10s. From Edmund Hobhouse,
ed., *The Diary of a West Country Physician A. D. 1684–1726* (London, 1934), p.
42. The most expensive instruments were harpsichords and pianos, apart from
chamber organs, for which the market was much more restricted. In the second
half of the century Shudi's harpsichords sold for 35–40 guineas for single-
manual instruments, 50 guineas for single manuals with the added "Venetian
swell" device he invented, and 80 guineas for the large double manuals with the
swell. From Frank Hubbard, *Three Centuries of Harpsichord Making* (Cambridge, MA, 1965), p. 160. At the end of the century Broadwood demanded 70
guineas for his grand pianos, and 20 guineas for his cheapest squares. From

Wainwright, "John Broadwood," p. 677. Harps, very popular by the close of the century, were approximately as expensive as grand pianos; like grands they were thus exclusively within reach of the rich.

Even the cheapest keyboard instruments were beyond the means of the lower orders, until they fell from favor among the upper classes. With the piano's ascendancy, harpsichords were sold off in the secondhand market, often cheaply. In Scotland, for example, toward the end of the century old spinets were available from auction rooms for a few shillings each. The buyers were tradesmen and farmers who, as the story goes, put them into service not only as musical instruments but also as sideboards. From Plant, *Domestic Life*, pp. 47–8; and Henry G. Graham, *The Social Life of Scotland in the Eighteenth Century*, 5th ed. (London, 1969), p. 74.

3 Raines, *Marcellus Laroon*, p. 7. Cf. North, *North on Music*, p. 22, on North's musical education.

4 Daines Barrington, *Miscellanies* (London, 1781), pp. 317–20. Mornington was born in Ireland of an Anglo-Irish father. He spent most of his life in Dublin, where in 1764 he was elected first professor of music at the university. He spent his final few years in London. See further "Garret Wesley Mornington," *New Grove*, vol. 12, p. 586. Mornington was a highly anomalous character, a gentleman-professional of sorts. Cf. my comments at the end of this chapter on Willoughby Bertie, 4th Earl of Abingdon.

5 "William Mason," *New Grove*, vol. 11, p. 753; and John W. Draper, *William Mason: A Study in Eighteenth-Century Culture* (New York, 1924), pp. 284–303.

6 Both men's biographies appear in *New Grove*; Needler is mentioned by Sir John Hawkins, *A General History of the Science and Practice of Music*, 2 vols. (1776; rev. ed. London, 1853), vol. 2, pp. 806–7, and in *DNB*. References to other amateurs occur, passim, in Hawkins. See also *New Grove* and *DNB* for brief accounts of amateurs James Sherard (1666–1738) and John Marsh (1752–1828). A "complete" listing of serious male amateurs would number no more than several dozen for the entire century. One of the best places to begin a systematic research to establish a better notion of the size and nature of such a group would be to examine subscribers' lists published in books about music, self-tutor books for musical instruments and voice (only a few of these include subscriber lists) and, of course, dedication pages to music books and published music. To be sure, the majority of these indicate many more individuals having musical interests than those who also practiced it.

7 *Gazetteer and New Daily Advertiser*, beginning in issue no. 18,125, for 12 January, and continuing on following days; *London Chronicle*, divided over two issues, no. 4703, for 11–13 January, and no. 4705, for 16–18 January; and the *Morning Herald*. I have seen *London Chronicle* only. This list was first identified and discussed by Philippe Mercier, "Quelques musiciens de la cour et 'distingués' amateurs Londoniens vers 1785," Mélanges d'archéologie et d'histoire de l'art offerts au Professeur Jacques Lavalleye. *Recueil de travaux d'histoire et de philologie*, 4/45 (Louvain, 1970), pp. 161–7.

8 See further Christopher Hibbert, *George IV*, 2 vols. (London, 1973), vol. 1, pp. 40–1, 234, 237; and *DNB*. On the other hand, the list includes Willoughby Bertie, 4th Earl of Abingdon, who was in fact a serious musician and a composer, discussed further at the end of this chapter.

9 On Lord Burlington see James Lees-Milne, *Earls of Creation: Five Great Patrons of Eighteenth-Century Art* (London, 1962), pp. 106, 114–15, 165. On the Duke of Chandos see C. H. Collins Baker and Muriel I. Baker, *The Life and Circumstances of James Brydges, First Duke of Chandos, Patron of the Liberal Arts* (Oxford, 1949); and Tilmouth, "Chamber music in England," pp. 122–3. Lord Burlington was principal sponsor of the Royal Academy of Music, established in 1719.

10 See Richard Luckett, "Music," in Pepys, *Diary*, vol. 10, pp. 258–82, for an excellent summary of Pepys' talents and limitations as a musician and the place

of music in his life; and Ivan E. Taylor, *Samuel Pepys* (New York, 1967), pp. 101–11.

11 Assorted extracts from his writings, including his autobiography, are in North, *North on Music*; see especially pp. 9–11, tracing his family's musical activities from his grandfather.

12 See Hobhouse, ed., *Diary of a Physician*, pp. 11–17, 39–43, for biographical details and remarks about Claver's musical interests. For relevant diary entries concerning music see pp. 56–134, passim.

13 D'Arblay, *Memoirs of Doctor Burney*, vol. 1, p. 262. Her account of Twining's friendship with Charles Burney is on pp. 260–5. See also Scholes, *Great Doctor Burney*, vol. 1, pp. 256–9; and John Horton, "An eighteenth-century amateur," *Monthly Musical Record*, 75 (1945), pp. 7–15. Further details of his life and some extracts from his letters appear in Twining, *Recreations and Studies*.

14 From a letter to his friend William Jackson; Mary Woodhall, ed., *The Letters of Thomas Gainsborough* (Greenwich, CT, 1963), p. 115.

15 See further *Gainsborough and his Musical Friends*, passim.

16 Jackson, *Four Ages*, p. 160.

17 Ibid., pp. 148–9.

18 Ibid., p. 158. See further Wilson, "Gainsborough, Bath and music," pp. 107–10; Angelo, *Reminiscences*, vol. 1, pp. 184–8; and D. C. Parker, "Gainsborough and music," *Monthly Musical Record*, 36 (1906), p. 200.

19 See further Rosamond Bayne-Powell, *The English Child in the Eighteenth Century* (New York, 1939), p. 3; Stone, *Family, Sex and Marriage*, p. 259; J. H. Plumb, "The new world of children in eighteenth-century England," *Past and Present*, 67 (1975), p. 67; and Praz, *Conversation Pieces*, pp. 149–59.

20 Plant, *Domestic Life*, p. 248.

21 See Mary Webster, *Johan Zoffany, 1733–1810* (London, 1976), p. 53, no. 63, re the original version (not illustrated).

22 See Charles W. Everett, *The Education of Jeremy Bentham* (New York, 1931), pp. 6, 95, 147–8; and Jeremy Bentham, *The Correspondence of Jeremy Bentham*, 5 vols., in progress (London, 1966–), vol. 3 (1783–8), ed. Ian R. Christie; *The Collected Works of Jeremy Bentham*, gen. ed. J. H. Burns (London, 1971), vol. 3, pp. 83, 99–100.

23 See for example Hobhouse, ed., *Diary of a Physician*, pp. 31–3; and below, Chapter 7, n. 2.

24 For full details of the scientific apparatus, identifications of the portrait medallions on the wall and more on the sitters, see D'Oench, *Conversation Piece*, pp. 45–6, no. 6. I am indebted to Dr. D'Oench for bringing this portrait to my attention.

25 Essex, *Young Ladies Conduct*, pp. 84–5. At the time Essex wrote, the reference to the flute indicated the recorder which like the oboe was directly inserted into the mouth.

26 Edward W. Hughes, *North Country Life in the Eighteenth Century*, 2 vols. (London, 1952–65), vol. 1, p. 384. On the continuation of this attitude in the nineteenth century see Nicholas Temperley, "Domestic music in England, 1800–1860," *Proceedings of the Royal Musical Association*, 86 (1959–60), p. 35.

27 Berkenhout, *Volume of Letters*, p. 189.

28 This painting, dating from the first years of the century, may be the earliest representation of such an instrument in England. It is typical of early spinets in that its natural keys are made from ebony and its sharp keys from ivory, though this is by no means always the case with early spinets. Its narrow compass, only four octaves, differentiates it from later instruments – for most of the century spinets usually had a full five-octave range of sixty-one keys.

29 Roland Barthes analyzed a pictorial phenomenon identical to the portrait of Garton Orme in photographs of male actors produced by Harcourt Studios.

See "The Harcourt actor," *The Eiffel Tower and Other Mythologies*, trans. Richard Howard (New York, 1979), pp. 20–1.

30 For details on Hallet's biography and documented musical performances see Philip H. Highfill, Jr., Kalman A. Burnim and Edward A. Langhans, *A Biographical Dictionary of Actors, Actresses, Musicians, Dancers, Managers and Other Stage Personnel in London, 1660–1800*, 10 vols., in progress (Carbondale, IL and Edwardsville, IL, 1973–), vol. 7, p. 51, from which some of my information was taken.

31 John Steegman, "Some English portraits by Pompeo Batoni," *Burlington Magazine*, 88 (May 1946), p. 55.

32 For additional details about the sitter and this portrait, see the exhibition catalogue *Pompeo Batoni and his British Patrons* (London, 1982), pp. 39–40, no. 13; and Anthony M. Clark, *Pompeo Batoni: A Complete Catalogue of his Works with an Introductory Text*, ed. and prepared for publication by Edgar Peters Bowron (New York, 1985), pp. 270–1, no. 202. My information about the painting and sitter comes from these sources.

33 Halsband, ed., *Complete Letters of Lady Mary Wortley Montagu*, vol. 3, p. 235.

34 John Fleming, *Robert Adam and his Circle in Edinburgh and Rome* (London, 1962), pp. 123–4. For more on Brudenell abroad see John Fleming, "Lord Brudenell and his bear-leader," *English Miscellany: A Symposium of History, Literature and the Arts*, 9 (1958), pp. 127–41.

35 See also Katherine B. Neilson, "A caricature by Sir Joshua Reynolds," *Rhode Island School of Design Bulletin* (Winter 1954), [p. 3]. Neilson suggests that Mr. Cooke may be Benjamin Cooke, the organist and composer (1734–93). But it is not apparent that he was in Italy at the time of Reynolds' painting. See the biography in *New Grove*, vol. 4, p. 709.

36 See further George, *Catalogue of Satires*, vol. 6, pp. 666–7, no. 9670.

37 Halsband, ed., *Complete Letters of Lady Mary Wortley Montagu*, vol. 2, p. 177.

38 Reynolds painted two other parodies pertinent to this discussion during his stay in Italy, one a comic version of Raphael's "School of Athens," the other a caricature group similar in composition to the painting under discussion. Both are housed in the National Gallery of Ireland, Dublin. See Denys Sutton, "The Roman caricatures of Reynolds," *Country Life Annual* (1956), pp. 113–16.

39 Among other comparable examples are Zoffany's portrait of the famous cellist Giacobbe Cervetto (English private collection), from which a mezzotint was also engraved, listed (though not illustrated) in Webster, *Johan Zoffany*, p. 45, no. 49; and Sir Nathaniel Dance-Holland's portrait of Christian Joseph Lidardi, violoncellist and composer, playing the harp, shown with painter Giovanni Battista Temesti (New Haven, CT, Yale Center for British Art, Paul Mellon Collection), illustrated in Nygren and Pressly, *Pursuit of Happiness*, pp. 46, 99, no. 73.

40 See further "John Hebden," *New Grove*, vol. 8, p. 426; and Highfill et al., *Biographical Dictionary of Actors*, vol. 7, pp. 231–2.

41 See further Nygren and Pressly, *Pursuit of Happiness*, p. 46, no. 74; and *DNB*.

42 See the biographies of these musicians in *New Grove*, vol. 4, p. 85.

43 Nygren and Pressly, *Pursuit of Happiness*, pp. 46–7, no. 75.

44 Abingdon was also on good terms with Haydn who composed an accompaniment for pianoforte or harp to Abingdon's *Twelve Sentimental Catches and Glees*. Gainsborough painted a large (but unfinished) portrait of Abingdon in the mid 1770s, reproduced in *Gainsborough and his Musical Friends* (from which my information on the sitter is chiefly drawn, no. 8, unpaginated). It shows him seated with a music book in hand and with an English guitar on a table beside him. See also the entry in *DNB*, especially regarding his political beliefs and activities; and "Abingdon," *New Grove*, vol. 1, pp. 19–20. The mezzotint was based on an oil portrait, whereabouts now unknown, reproduced in *Country Life*, 22 April 1949.

45 For no reason that I have been able to identify, reproductions of the painting that served as matrix to the print have, in their captions, named the master as a Mr. Collins. In my view it is not likely that the master was English, as the name Collins would suggest.

46 Ingvar Bergström, *Dutch Still-Life Painting in the Seventeenth Century*, trans. Christina Hedström and Gerald Taylor (London, 1957), pp. 154–6. Bergström's book is the best source in English for traditional interpretations of this genre. For an important revisionist view see Svetlana Alpers, *The Art of Describing: Dutch Art in the Seventeenth Century* (Chicago, 1983), especially pp. 90–1, 103–9, 114–15. See also M. Kirby Talley, "'Small, usuall, and vulgar things': still-life painting in England, 1635–1760," *Walpole Society*, 49 (1983), pp. 133–223. On musical subject matter in these paintings see Richard Leppert, *The Theme of Music in Flemish Paintings of the Seventeenth Century*, 2 vols. (Munich and Salzburg, 1977), vol. 1, pp. 75–84.

47 See Richard Leppert, "*Concert in a house*: musical iconography and musical thought," *Early Music*, 7 (1979), p. 4; and Thomas McGeary, "Harpsichord mottoes," *Journal of the American Musical Instrument Society*, 7 (1981), p. 27, no. 43.

48 On this point see John Berger, *Ways of Seeing* (London and Harmondsworth, 1972), pp. 83–100.

7 THE FEMALE AT MUSIC: PRAXIS, REPRESENTATION AND THE
PROBLEMATIC OF IDENTITY

1 North, *North on Music*, p. 16.

2 A few references exist to women who played the violin and the transverse flute, both instruments otherwise the exclusive domain of men. See D'Arblay, *Memoirs of Doctor Burney*, vol. 1, p. 9; William Gardiner, *Music and Friends; or, Pleasant Recollections of a Dilettante*, 2 vols. (London, 1838), vol. 1, p. 111.

3 John Evelyn, *The Diary of John Evelyn*, ed. E. S. de Beer, 6 vols. (Oxford, 1955), vol. 4, pp. 421–2; re the beginning of Mary's musical education see p. 271.

4 Ibid., pp. 420–4.

5 In the same vein see John Batchiler, *The Virgin's Pattern* (London, 1661), pp. 4–7, on the death of Susannah Perwich; see also Westrup, "Domestic music under the Stuarts," pp. 50–1; Westrup discusses both Mary Evelyn and Susannah Perwich, as well as other female performers from the seventeenth century.

6 See Roman Rolland, *A Musical Tour through the Land of the Past*, trans. Bernard Miall (New York, 1922), pp. 26–33; and Hufstader, "Samuel Pepys, inquisitive amateur," pp. 451–4.

7 Mary Delaney's life is the subject of considerable study. See in particular Granville, *Autobiography of Mrs. Delaney*; Robert Manson Myers, "Mrs. Delaney: an eighteenth-century Handelian," *Musical Quarterly*, 32 (1946), pp. 12–36; and Alice Anderson Hufstader, "Musical references in blue-stocking letters," *Musical Quarterly*, 47 (1961), pp. 82–4.

8 See Stone, *Family, Sex and Marriage*, especially pp. 254–99.

9 The instrument appears to be the so-called English flageolet, though this instrument was supposedly invented in 1803, whereas the painting is dated 1801. See further "Flageolet," *New Grove*, vol. 6, p. 624.

10 See further Raymond Russell, *Keyboard Instruments*, vol. 1, *Victoria and Albert Museum Catalogue of Musical Instruments*, 2 vols. (London, 1968), pp. 52–3, no. 22.

11 "Spinet," *New Grove*, vol. 17, pp. 833–6; and Hubbard, *Three Centuries of Harpsichord Making*, p. 152.

12 Loesser, *Men, Women and Pianos*, p. 245.

13 The instrument she plays is indistinctly rendered, though the painter probably intended a single-manual harpsichord. Yet the girl's hand and finger position on the keyboard is more appropriate to the piano.

14 The music on the rack seems to read "Ranelagh Treasury," this being a piece popularized by its performance at the pleasure gardens of that name in Chelsea. Ranelagh, however, actually closed after sixty-one years' existence in 1803, three years prior to the date of the image.

15 Benedict Nicholson, *Joseph Wright of Derby, Painter of Light*, 2 vols. (London, 1968), vol. 1, p. 33. For a reproduction of Mr. Gwillym, see vol. 2, plate 56.

16 Hester Lynch (Thrale) Piozzi, *Thraliana: The Diary of Mrs. Hester Lynch Thrale (Later Mrs. Piozzi), 1776–1809*, ed. Katherine C. Balderston, 2 vols., 2nd ed. corr. (Oxford, 1951), vol. 2, p. 748 (21? May 1789). On the English guitar see Philip Coggin, " 'This easy and agreable instrument': a history of the English guitar," *Early Music*, 15 (1987), pp. 205–18.

17 See Leppert, *Arcadia at Versailles*, especially pp. 41–104.

18 See further Webster, *Johan Zoffany*, pp. 61–3, nos. 78–9.

19 Balderston, ed., *Thraliana*, vol. 1, p. 129 (from 1777). The hurdy-gurdy's strings are set in motion by a rosined wheel turned by a crank. Melody strings are stopped by a key mechanism, visible in both portraits. The instrument also has drone strings analogous to bagpipe drones that sound whenever the wheel is turned.

20 See Leppert, *Arcadia at Versailles*, pp. 14–23. See Fanny (Burney) d'Arblay, *The Early Diary of Frances Burney, 1768–1778*, ed. Annie Raine Ellis, 2 vols. (1889; reprint. ed. Freeport, NY, 1971), vol. 1, p. 72, re a masquerade at which her sister entered playing a hurdy-gurdy, "and the company flocked about her with much pleasure" (from January 1770).

21 My sources are Lady Mary Coke, *The Letters and Journals of Lady Mary Coke*, [ed. J. A. Home], 4 vols. (1889–96; fac. reprint. ed., Bath, 1970), vol. 1, pp. lxxxi–lxxxii; David Irwin and Francina Irwin, *Scottish Painters at Home and Abroad, 1700–1900* (London, 1975), p. 59; and the exhibition catalogue *Allan Ramsay (1713–1784)* (London, 1958), no. 30.

22 See further Lesure, *Music in Art and Society*, pp. 30–1; and Leppert, *Theme of Music in Flemish Paintings*, vol. 1, pp. 85–8.

8 MUSIC IN DOMESTIC SPACE: DOMINATION, COMPENSATION AND THE FAMILY

1 On this general subject see Leppert and McClary, eds., *Music and Society*.

2 Stephen V. Sartin, with Introduction by John Hayes, *Polite Society by Arthur Devis (1712–1787): Portraits of the English Country Gentleman and his Family* (Preston, 1984), p. 30.

3 See ibid., pp. 9–10, 22, 25; and D'Oench, *Conversation Piece*, p. 20.

4 D'Oench, *Conversation Piece*, p. 66, no. 43. Wilfrid Robertshaw, "A local conversation piece," *Bradford Antiquary*, n.s. 6, part 30 (1939), p. 401, claims the town is not identifiable. Robertshaw also suggests (pp. 398, 400) that the women depicted are Rookes-Leeds' four daughters and that his wife is not included. His assessment is surely incorrect; the second woman from the left is much older than the other three. Edward Rookes-Leeds, according to Robertshaw (p. 399), was a spendthrift. In 1780, five years before his death by his own hand, he owed the staggering sum of £60,000.

5 See D'Oench, *Conversation Piece*, pp. 63–4, no. 38.

6 The instrument is rarely illustrated in paintings. For surviving examples see Anthony Baines, *Non-Keyboard Instruments*, vol. 1, *Victoria and Albert Museum Catalogue of Musical Instruments*, 2 vols. (London, 1968), pp. 53–4, no. 11/16, and fig. 75.

7   See for example Pieter Jacobus Johannes van Thiel, "Marriage symbolism in a
    musical party by Jan Miense Molenaar," *Simiolus*, 2 (1967-8), pp. 91-9.

8   See George, *Catalogue of Satires*, vol. 8, pp. 386-7, nos. 10,472-3; and Draper
    Hill, ed., *The Satirical Etchings of James Gillray* (New York, 1976), pp. 132-3.

9   For a discussion of another marriage portrait with music, a complex allegory
    by Zoffany, see Richard Leppert, "Men, women and music at home: the
    influence of cultural values on musical life in eighteenth-century England,"
    Imago Musicae, 2 (1985), pp. 100-1.

10 See also Fig. 83, below. Cf. Jarrett, *England in the Age of Hogarth*, p. 132: "The
    social unit was not the individual but the family or the household, a fact which
    gave great importance to the actual houses in which these units were contained.
    The possession of a hearth, traditionally the centre and focus not only of the
    house but also of the people who lived in it, was the thing that defined a man's
    position and gave him a place in society."

11 The painting is reproduced in Sydney H. Pavière, *The Devis Family of Painters*
    (Leigh-on-the-Sea, 1950), plate 29. See also the brief entry in D'Oench, *Con-
    versation Piece*, p. 82, no. 42.

12 Lætitia Pilkington, *Memoirs of Mrs. Letitia Pilkington, 1712-1750, Written by
    Herself*, 3 vols. in 1 (London, 1748-54), vol. 1, p. 3.

13 Laurence Sterne, *A Sentimental Journey through France and Italy by Mr. Yorick*
    (1768), ed. Garner D. Stout, Jr. (Berkeley, CA and Los Angeles, 1967), pp.
    195-206, passim. Jane Austen refers to this incident in Sterne in *Mansfield Park*,
    Chapter 10, p. 127. See Tilden A. Russell, "On 'looking over the ha-ha,'"
    Musical Quarterly, 71 (1985), pp. 27-37.

14 For additional information and variant meanings see Guy de Tervarent, *Attri-
    buts et symboles dans l'art profane, 1450-1600*, 2 vols. (Geneva, 1958-9), vol. 1,
    cols. 58-9; and Arthur Henkel and Albrecht Schöne, *Emblemata: Handbuch zur
    Sinnbildkunst des XVI. und XVII. Jahrhunderts* (Stuttgart, 1967), cols. 749-57.
    A caged bird around which other birds fly was an emblem for false friendship;
    see col. 751. Liberation from the cage could also allude to eternal freedom
    through a Christian death; see col. 754. I am reminded here of Roland Barthes'
    statement concerning drawing, to the effect that discontinuity or visual disso-
    nance (in this case birds in flight) is a signifier: "The operation of the drawing
    (the coding) immediately necessitates a certain division between the significant
    and the insignificant: the drawing does not reproduce *everything* (often it re-
    produces very little), without its ceasing, however, to be a strong message . . .
    It is certain that the coding of the literal prepares and facilitates connotation
    since it at once establishes a certain discontinuity in the image: the 'execution' of
    a drawing itself constitutes a connotation." From "Rhetoric of the image,"
    Image - Music - Text, trans. Stephen Heath (New York, 1977), p. 43.

15 She was taught drawing by William Kent. See Edward Croft-Murray, *Decora-
    tive Painting in England, 1537-1837*, 2 vols. (London, 1970), vol. 2, p. 230. For
    some biographical details see Lees-Milne, *Earls of Creation*, pp. 130-5. She
    seems to have been a strong-willed woman, and she was also a musician,
    though there is nothing to indicate that the drawing under discussion was a
    self-portrait.

16 Gerard de Lairesse, *The Art of Painting, in All its Branches*, trans. John Frederick
    Fritsch, 2 vols. (London, 1738), vol. 1, p. 360, illustrated in vol. 2, plate 57,
    figs. 7-9. See further D'Oench, *Conversation Piece*, pp. 61-2, no. 34. The
    Parkers lived at Browsholme Hall in Yorkshire. As in other Devis portraits
    Barbara Parker's gown is unlikely to be her own since it appears in several other
    Devis paintings though in different colors. Instead it is almost certainly mod-
    eled from a costume Devis possessed for a lay-figure in his London studio, that
    is, a multi-jointed doll that substituted for a sitter and that could be arranged
    into poses conveniently duplicating illustrations and descriptions in books on
    genteel behavior. Some costumes belonging to one of Devis' male lay-figures

still exist. See the exhibition catalogue, *Polite Society by Arthur Devis, 1712–1787* (Preston, 1983), pp. 16, 23, 25, 60. See further on the visual enclosure of women, Leppert, "Men, women, and music at home," pp. 114–15, figs. 48–50.

17 In 1795 the portrait of Emily de Visme was engraved by W. Bond and entitled "St. Cecilia."

18 On Robert Lindley (1776–1855) see his biography in *New Grove*, vol. 11, pp. 3–4.

19 Adorno, *Introduction to the Sociology of Music*, p. 69. Cf. p. 55: "If music really is ideology, not a phenomenon of truth – in other words, if the form in which it is experienced by a population befuddles their perception of social reality – one question that will necessarily arise concerns the relation of music to the social classes."

20 John Potter, *Observations on the Present State of Music and Musicians* (London, 1762), p. 66. See on this book Kassler, *Science of Music*, vol. 2, pp. 849–53. Cf. Thomas Robertson, *An Inquiry into the Fine Arts* (London, 1784), pp. 430–1: "The taste of England for Music is so subordinate to other greater objects, that more constantly affect it, as to be intermitting, changeable, capricious, and crude."

21 Adorno, *Introduction to the Sociology of Music*, p. 49.

22 See Donald M. Lowe, *History of Bourgeois Perception* (Chicago, 1982).

23 From a letter to the editor, *New Lady's Magazine* (1786), p. 136, quoted from Sadie, "British chamber music," p. 100.

9 EPILOGUE: THE SOCIAL AND IDEOLOGICAL RELATION OF MUSICS TO PRIVATIZED SPACE

1 Nollekens himself was a Fleming who came to England in his early thirties. His work shows the obvious influence of Watteau. Lord Tylney was Nollekens' principal patron in England. See further M. J. H. Liversidge, "An elusive minor master: J. F. Nollekens and the conversation piece," *Apollo*, 95 (1972), pp. 34–41.

2 See Eric Halfpenny, "Early English clarinets," *Galpin Society Journal*, 18 (1965), pp. 43–4.

3 See John Kerslake, "A note on Zoffany's 'Sharp Family,'" *Burlington Magazine*, 120 (1978), p. 752.

4 Granville Sharp, *A Short Introduction to Vocal Musick* (London, 1767; 2nd ed. 1777), on which see Granville Sharp, *Memoirs of Granville Sharp, Esq.*, ed. Prince Hoare (London, 1820), appendix no. 6, pp. xii–xvi. On the family in general and on their musical activities and interests see Edward Lascelles, *Granville Sharp and the Freedom of Slaves in England* (London, 1928), pp. 112–26.

5 See Sharp, *Memoirs*, appendix no. 6, p. xv. An idea of the music played at the family's concerts may be gleaned from *A Catalogue of the Manuscript and Instrumental Music in the Joint Collection of Messrs. William[,] James & Granville Sharp* (London, 1759).

6 Lascelles, *Granville Sharp*, p. 121.

7 Ibid., p. 123.

8 Ibid., p. 121.

9 Ibid.

10 Angelo, *Reminiscences*, vol. 1, p. 268.

11 See further "Johann Christian Fischer," *New Grove*, vol. 6, p. 609; and *Gainsborough and his Musical Friends*, no. 10 (unpaginated). The two, though well acquainted, were anything but close. One of Gainsborough's daughters entered into an unhappy marriage with Fischer in 1780.

12 On the active-passive, private-public in Western post-Renaissance music, see Christopher Small, *Music – Society – Education* (New York, 1977), especially pp. 7–32.

13 For a particularly convincing discussion on the representation of the "good poor" in British art later in the century, see John Barrell, "The private comedy of Thomas Rowlandson," *Art History*, 6 (1983), pp. 423–41.

14 The enraged musician may be John Festin, a prominent teacher of the flute and oboe. Concerning this identification and other possibilities, and for additional discussion of the print, see Ronald Paulson, comp., *Hogarth's Graphic Works*, 2 vols. (New Haven, CT and London, 1965), vol. 1, pp. 184–6, no. 184; Ronald Paulson, *The Art of Hogarth* (New York, 1975), discussion accompanying figs. 63–5 (unpaginated); and Stephens and Hawkins, *Catalogue of Satires*, vol. 3, p. 409, nos. 2517–18. "The Enraged Musician" is the companion to a print called "The Distressed Poet."

15 See further Jacques Attali, *Noise: The Political Economy of Music*, trans. Brian Massumi (Minneapolis, MN, 1985).

Index

Titles of books, stage plays and musical compositions referred to in the text are not indexed (with the exception of a few important anonymous works), but authors and composers of these texts are included. Only significant references to musical instruments and persons are indexed. References to illustrations are printed in italic type.